WYATT

Doc Holliday's Account of an Intimate Friendship

by

Dale Chase

erotica

A Division of Bold Strokes Books

2012

WYATT: DOC HOLLIDAY'S ACCOUNT OF AN INTIMATE FRIENDSHIP

ISBN 13: 978-1-60282-755-4

THIS TRADE PAPERBACK ORIGINAL IS PUBLISHED BY
BOLD STROKES BOOKS, INC.
P.O. BOX 249
VALLEY FALLS, NY 12185

FIRST EDITION: OCTOBER 2012

CREDITS
EDITOR: CINDY CRESAP
PRODUCTION DESIGN: STACIA SEAMAN
COVER ART BY SAM HOOKER
COVER DESIGN BY SHERI (GRAPHICARTIST2020@HOTMAIL.COM)

Acknowledgments

A big thank you to Radclyffe for taking a chance not only on the author but on a western. Likewise, her team earns my gratitude for their good-natured efficiency. Special thanks to Cindy Cresap, editor extraordinaire, who respected a story dear to the author's heart while managing to make improvements. Lastly, I thank my dear friends William Holden and Jerry L. Wheeler for making a wondrous journey even better.

This book is dedicated to Bob Steele, who made western movies in the 1930s and 40s. His films were a staple of early television, and in them he captured the author's six-year-old heart with his dark curly hair, handsome features, and small but wiry body. He became a little girl's identity in countless pretend cowboy adventures, thus providing many happy childhood hours. Steele still occupies a special place in the author's heart, although he's now had to make room for Doc Holliday.

This is a work of fiction that incorporates actual people, places, and events into a representative account. The author has adhered to historical accuracy where it suits the story and loosened the reins where it does not.

CHAPTER ONE

Much has been written about Wyatt Earp and me, Doc Holliday, but it's mostly who got shot and why. What fails to be addressed is the fact that gunplay gets a man's blood up. A fellow goes for his revolver, meaning to do me harm, and as I dispatch him, everything in me stands at attention. By the time his life runs out, my blood rushes to such extent that my dick is hard, and if circumstances did not prevent such pursuit, I would take advantage then and there. It is with this in mind that I am determined to set down a more intimate account of Wyatt and me before my lungs fail entirely and I descend to hell. I will leave instructions that the account shall remain sealed until after Wyatt's death, as he may object to public knowledge of what I reveal. If you read this, know that my good friend has gone to his reward.

I first had carnal knowledge of Wyatt Earp in Dodge City in 1878, but our initial meeting was in Fort Griffin, Texas, the year before and, as it was a meeting laced with promise, it must be told. Fort Griffin started out as a military post, but soon a town sprang up, and when the location placed it well upon the Western Cattle Trail, it further prospered. Once the Kiowas, Comanches, and southern Cheyennes had been defeated, it grew to more than a thousand residents. As such, it had the opportunity I required.

Wyatt came down in March while chasing railroad robber Dave Rudabaugh on behalf of the Santa Fe Railroad. He had followed the trail from Dodge City to Fort Griffin, where it ran cold. I'd been there about a year after finding Cheyenne, Deadwood, Denver, and other locales inhospitable due to word I'd killed a few men. Fort Griffin didn't seem to care as it had its own notorious reputation. I set to gaming at John Shannsey's Cattle Exchange Saloon, making a fine living off buffalo hunters and cattle drovers eager to lose their pay at poker or faro.

I took note of Wyatt Earp the day he walked into the saloon and struck up a conversation with Shannsey. Not initially knowing him to be the lawman of repute, I was nevertheless taken by his appearance, as he was a handsome, steely-eyed, well-bodied six-footer. When Shannsey pointed him my way, I felt a surge below that was not unwelcome.

He waited until I'd played my hand, then introduced himself and asked if we might speak. I followed him to the bar where he bought me a whiskey and had one himself. "I'm on the trail of Dave Rudabaugh, who robbed the Santa Fe train in Kansas," he began. "He headed down this way, but the trail's gone cold. Shannsey says you'd be the one to know his whereabouts."

"Not at present," I replied, "but I can try to learn where he's gone. Might take a few days, though."

Wyatt thought on this, then looked at me with those steely blue eyes. "Guess I can wait around."

I was honest with him in the time it might take to gather information on Rudabaugh and pleased it would necessitate him staying on. I also got the feeling he wasn't averse to remaining, cold trail or not. "You been here long?" he asked and I told him how I'd come down from Denver and other places. I could see he knew me by reputation as an uneasiness clung to him, although I saw it was not completely born of my exploits with a gun. Something else was afoot in Wyatt Earp, something only I was privy to. Reserved fellow that he was, expression fixed and stern and betraying not a single smile, even at the news I'd help him, he nevertheless gave off a pull of hard masculinity I found most appealing. My dick was stiff throughout our talk, and I suspect his was too.

That I carried consumption rendered me much the opposite of Wyatt Earp, though I will say I was found by most to be fine-looking. Unfortunately frail of body, I was given to coughing fits and chest pain, both of these eased with whiskey as I'd decided early on to forgo opiates until the end. When our talk was interrupted several times by my coughing, Wyatt was patient and did not ask about my malady, though if he'd heard of my gunplay, he'd likely heard me described as a "lunger," which was the common term for a consumptive.

Once we had completed our arrangement and finished our drinks, Wyatt excused himself and left. I spoke to Shannsey about him. "Knew him in Cheyenne," Shannsey said, "back before he started marshaling in Kansas. Most law-abiding man I've ever known. Good shot but not quick to kill. He's known more for buffaloing his gun barrel to a man's head rather than shooting him."

I had to chuckle. "Must rankle him to have to turn to such as me for help."

"He's a fair man, inclined to make his own judgments."

Gaining information in Fort Griffin was a matter of listening to newcomers from parts west and asking casual questions about the outlaw world. My reputation assisted me in this endeavor as men's mouths loosened when not speaking to the law. But it did take time, three days to be exact, during which I kept an eye out for Wyatt Earp.

On the second day, I found him sitting outside Shannsey's, chair kicked back, feet upon the railing. "No news yet, but I'm working on it," I said as I settled beside him. "How do you like Fort Griffin?"

"Same as most. You ever get to Dodge City?"

"Not as yet. My occupation here has proved too lucrative to entice me elsewhere."

"We have some fine gaming establishments in Dodge, and it's a bit more hospitable."

He was in his shirtsleeves as it was a hot day, and as he continued about the attributes of Dodge City, I allowed my gaze to chance over him now and then, as I found pleasure in his presence. When I stole a look at his crotch, I was pleased to find a bulge, and further, that he made no move to disguise it. He just remained laid back while I feasted on the unseen piece of meat, which, of course, got my own up. When he put his hands behind his head, it was as if to further display himself, and I began a coughing fit, at which he turned to face me but said nothing.

"Damned cough," I declared, finding my flask and taking a swig.

He continued to study me, and once I'd quieted, I locked my eyes onto him, letting him know his interest was welcome. And it was there, in that moment, that I realized we would get up to it. Maybe not then or there, but one day, because his hands drifted back down onto his body and one slid onto a thigh not two inches from his prick. His breathing became noticeable, as did the sweat on his neck, which could be attributed to the heat of the day but was more likely grown up out of his crotch. These things added to the display and led me to wonder if he had ever fucked a man. Rigid as he was, upright, unsmiling lawman, had he allowed himself what all men want even if they'll never admit it?

By way of rescue, I asked him to tell me more about Dodge City and saw his relief as he embarked on a spiel the town merchants would have appreciated. Bigger, finer, more tame. He sat up in his telling, and the promising moment was gone, but I thought this might not be for long. When he excused himself and headed for the hotel, I couldn't help but consider that he might, in the confines of his room, get out that hard cock and give it a pull.

It took one more day for me to learn that Rudabaugh and his band were holed up in Fort Davis, a post west of the Pecos River. I kept this information until Wyatt next found me at the faro table, where I told him I had news. He waited until I could free myself and we then took a walk.

We were easy alongside each other now, having found ourselves comfortable in conversation. He was obviously a well-read man as he was better spoken than many and careful with his words. A thinking man was refreshing on the frontier as most were rough, raucous, unshaven, and downright crude. When I told him Rudabaugh's location, he was most grateful. "Guess I'll head out tomorrow," he said. "I'm much obliged for your help, Doc, and would like to buy you supper."

"You are most kind."

We arranged to meet later, and I returned to my room to change clothes. I always prided myself on a good appearance, as clothes gave me the substance my body lacked. I preferred gray suits to the black most gamblers wore and leaned toward pastel shirts, although white could be contrasted with a patterned vest. I thus selected my best gray suit, sky blue shirt, and black silk tie. I added my diamond stickpin to complete the ensemble, and as I stood at my mirror, I cut a fine figure. Donning my hat, I set out to meet the lawman.

Wyatt had on his black coat and was most striking as he approached that evening. His step was sure, his gaze level, and when he saw me out front of Mackay's Restaurant, he didn't crack a smile. Me, I couldn't resist. Seeing him lit me up inside, made my dick fill. I held out my hand when he reached me. "Wyatt," I said and he took it and replied, "Doc." It was our first touch and it sent a jolt through me, never mind it was a mere formality.

Over buffalo steaks, he asked me about my exploits. "Much exaggerated," I replied. "I am said to have killed men in Denver, Leadville, Cheyenne, Dallas, and even California, where I've never been. I'll admit to the occasional need of dealing with a miscreant, but it is always when drawn upon. I do not kill for sport."

"But you've been arrested more than once."

"And always found justified at taking a life. Unfortunately, people don't always agree with legal pronouncements, and thus, I move on. My desire is simply to make a living the best way I know how."

Wyatt considered this. "But you're a dentist. Why not do that instead of cards?"

"Ah, yes, my profession. I will likely one day again hang out my shingle and attempt such practice as I do enjoy it, and in most towns a dentist is sorely needed, but the truth is, gaming pays better. People are also somewhat put off by my coughing."

He went on to ask about my origins, and I explained my Georgia roots and the diagnosis that ended a promising life in Atlanta in favor of more hospitable climes. He in turn spoke of his Midwestern start, his four brothers, and the parents in California. And then he mentioned Mattie, his wife. Though he made it plain, without actually saying so, that she had been a prostitute and there had been no formal marriage ceremony, it still set me back and I retreated to my whiskey and my food. I did note, however, that his sureness weakened when he spoke of the woman, and I ultimately saw purpose in what he said. He was warning me off him. Pure and simple, he was telling me that whatever bulge I'd noted in his pants, it was not for the taking by such as me.

"She sounds like a fine woman," I said. "You are very fortunate."

He gave but a nod, then announced his planned departure. "I'll be riding out tomorrow early. I want to thank you again, but I have to say, your willingness to help locate Rudabaugh surprised me."

"I do not discriminate between lawful or otherwise. I hope you find him."

The meal was over, drinks gone, and I saw he was going to leave. I stood and he paid the bill and we walked outside.

"Off to Shannsey's?" he asked.

"Where else?"

It was upon him then and I could see it. A man in want is most transparent, and the formidable marshal was giving off a powerful unrest. He looked off down the street, then up the other way, anywhere but to me, then said, "Nowhere. Good night and thanks again. If you ever get to Dodge, look me up." We shook hands, but it was brief and I watched him stride quickly across to the hotel, knowing that had we done the deed, he'd have slept better than he now would.

I did go on to Shannsey's and fleeced two buffalo hunters of all their money before heading to my own bed. Once there, I stroked my prick while considering that the great Wyatt Earp might be doing the same.

Some days later, Wyatt long gone, I was playing poker with some men, one of them Ed Bailey, who was losing. When he started fussing with the deadwood, I warned him against such a thing. "You know the rules, Ed. You stay out of those discards."

Ed was a ripe fellow, somewhat puffed up at being well known and popular in town. He said nothing at my warning and lost another hand, at which the other players deserted our game. When Ed's hand strayed again, I lost patience. "Keep your goddamned hand where it belongs," I snapped, at which he grew red in the face, jumped up, and sought his pistol. Unfortunately for him, he underestimated the situation. Before he could get his trigger finger working, I pulled a knife from my inside breast pocket and drove it into his gut. To ensure his not firing his weapon, I slit him well across, which laid open his innards as he fell forward onto the table. As he expired, I pocketed my bloody knife and drew my pistol in case others in the establishment were foolish enough to interfere. When all remained rooted in place, I gathered my money, all rightly earned, and called out, "Shannsey, I am sorry this man sought to cause trouble and I am sorry to have drawn his blood in stopping him. You others, you stay put while I take my leave." And with that, I fled to my horse, fled the town, and fled the state. It was four hundred miles to Dodge City, and I rode much of the way with Wyatt Earp in mind.

The place was all he had said, a thriving town offering far more substance than had Fort Griffin. I checked into the Dodge House, which appeared to be the finest hostelry in the city. Containing some fifty rooms and a bar, it also boasted a first-class laundry, which pleased me greatly as I preferred cleanliness to trail dust. Once bathed, refreshed, and fed, I set out to explore the town, hoping to run into Wyatt. When he did not appear, I stopped a deputy to introduce myself and inquire as to the marshal's whereabouts.

"He is off chasing train robbers," came the reply. "Been gone a month. No idea when he'll be back."

His absence disappointed me but not as much as learning my information on Rudabaugh's location had not panned out. The chase might go on much longer as outlaws could be elusive and lawmen were often stubborn in their refusal to give up. I did not, however, let Wyatt hinder me from enjoying all his town had to offer. The Long Branch Saloon proved a most welcome establishment and I set to gaming there, playing poker mostly with local businessmen and, when drovers brought cattle herds in to the railhead, with cowboys eager to part with their pay.

The town suffered some from these rowdy men who looked to blow off steam accumulated on the trail from Texas to Kansas, but Wyatt's deputies managed to keep most from serious damage. I noted these deputies followed Wyatt's example of hitting a man with a pistol rather than shooting him. Much of the gunfire in town was nothing more than drunks shooting into the night sky.

Being in Wyatt's town added to my pleasure, and in his honor, I made every effort to not get into trouble. More than once, I held my tongue when some cowboy with a bad hand started spouting off about cheating. All knew my reputation, and it served me well in keeping most hotheads from tempting fate. Amid this relative calm, I approached the local dentist, who was not averse to my joining his practice.

"Business is brisk," Eldred McCarty, DDS, told me when I sat across from him at his desk. "I can use another man, and you seem well qualified, Doctor." He had a good setup, office and separate treatment room boasting a fine chair he fussed over at length. This was a step up, as much frontier dentistry was accomplished in raw circumstance.

McCarty knew of the Pennsylvania dental school I had attended and was most sympathetic to my having had to close my Atlanta practice. As he seemed somewhat oblivious about my gunplay, I let him believe I'd come to Dodge from Georgia. We thus established a partnership and I became John H. Holliday, DDS, by day while still gaming by night.

Wyatt was absent another month, yet was never far from my mind. When I saw the signs that forbade guns in town, I knew them his doing. Likewise, when people spoke of the marshal, I drew to attention and encouraged the talk.

In early May, word came that Bat Masterson had arrested Dave Rudabaugh in Missouri, so I knew when Wyatt returned I would make no mention of his long and futile chase. Then one night at the faro table, somebody remarked that he was back in town. I became somewhat giddy with the news and quickly cashed out in favor of strolling around in hopes of running into him. When he had not appeared after several hours, I sought my room where I lay naked, prick in hand, thinking on us fucking. I brought myself off twice at the idea.

We caught sight of each other next day as he stepped out of the Long Branch and I the Dodge House. A moment passed with our eyes fixed before I crossed to him, hand out in welcome. "Heard you were here," he said, fingers closing on mine. "I was back through Fort Griffin, and Shannsey told me you'd had your things sent to Dodge."

"Did he also give you other details?"

"He did tell the story, but you should have allowed the law to declare you in the right."

I shook my head. "Ed Bailey was too well liked for me to ever get a fair shake. I'd venture a lynch mob would have been my fate, and I could not take such a chance."

"Trouble does seem to follow you, Doc."

"Not here. I've set up my practice and go about my business."

Our conversation thinned at this point and left us to proximity alone, which I saw pleased Wyatt as much as me. "Buy you a drink?" I asked, but he deferred.

"I have some business to attend to. Maybe later on."

I nodded and watched him walk off, wondering what it would take for him to let down his guard. I did not dwell upon this, however, as I was doing well at faro and poker. Men remained eager to lose their money, and I remained willing to take it.

What finally led Wyatt and me toward carnal knowledge of each other occurred in September of that year. We'd been around each other a good deal, but it took circumstance to put us together that fateful night.

I was, as usual, gaming in the Long Branch when I heard commotion building outside. The town was full of cowboys just in from a trail drive, but this noise seemed more than the usual behavior. The rumble of a mob became apparent, but I kept to my poker as I had a winning hand. Then disturbing words came loud enough to be heard inside the Long Branch. "By God, it's Earp!" one man shouted while another followed with, "We've got him!"

I threw down my cards, ran to where guns were checked at the bar, snatched my nickel-plated revolver, and made for the door where I heard, "If he makes a move, boys, let him have it." The situation was dire as I saw a good twenty men in the street and two up on the sidewalk, one with weapon pointed at Wyatt. When the man commanded the marshal to "Pray, you son of a bitch," I burst out the door.

"Throw 'em up!" I roared, along with a string of profanity I will spare you here. Suffice to say, Wyatt knew who had come to his aid, but the gunman made the mistake of turning my way, at which Wyatt pulled his weapon. "What shall we do with 'em, Wyatt?" I asked. Wyatt hesitated but a moment before laying his long Buntline Colt to the man's head, knocking him down.

"Throw 'em up!" he then called to the mob while to me he said of the man at his feet, "This is Ed Morrison. He caused me some trouble once in Wichita and suffered the same fate."

Morrison's fall had taken the steam out of the men, and they began to shed their six-shooters and put up their hands. There was, however, one exception as a cowboy at the mob's edge raised his pistol. "Look out, Wyatt!" I called as I fired, saving him an awful fate. It was later told in newspapers that I'd killed the fellow, but in truth he was merely winged, which disappointed me some.

Wyatt and I then marched the gang, with their hands held in the air, to jail. There they would spend the night with a deputy standing guard. Once they had been secured, Wyatt and I sauntered back through the empty streets of a town that didn't yet know it had been saved. "Thanks, Doc," Wyatt said, putting a hand to my shoulder. When he did not immediately withdraw it but rather tightened his grip, I knew we would do the deed as we were both worked up from the encounter.

How long had I wanted this man? Whether alongside him at cards or in some gunfight, he stirred a desire that persisted to such extent it at times interfered with my gaming, which was something no man or no anything had done before. Now, on a street in Dodge City, Wyatt's need came off him like some great storm. Had I reached down to his crotch, I'm certain I'd have found a hard prick. "How about a drink?" I suggested.

Wyatt, hand still upon me, thought a second, then said, "Not a saloon."

"My room, then. I have a full bottle."

I was so filled with want, it felt like an extra pistol down there. I managed to tote my swollen cock upstairs and into my room at the Dodge House, Wyatt following. He locked the door behind him and took off his coat, hat, and gun belt. I did likewise and poured our drinks.

"You turn those men loose tomorrow, they might come after you again," I said, handing Wyatt his glass.

He took a long swig, then replied, "Morrison's head is going to hurt too much for such effort, and without him driving them, the others are of no consequence."

Wyatt's unerring confidence gave him all the more appeal, which

I considered as I downed my whiskey and poured a second, enduring a coughing fit in between. Wyatt waited me out, his expression as fixed as when he faced the man looking to kill him. Finally, he said, "We gonna do it?"

"Hell, yes," I replied and I began to unbutton my pants.

Wyatt eyed me as I fished out my dick and let it stand hard. I could see him considering me like some prey and will confess I liked the idea. He then began to strip.

I didn't put a hand on myself as I was afraid, with the sight before me, I'd come at first touch, so I just stood while he tossed it all aside. He soon revealed a formidable body with dark hair across his chest and a good-sized cock below. It was already wet with anticipation, and once he was naked, he smeared his juice down the shaft to prepare himself, then said, "Let's see the rest."

My body could never do me justice as my illness robbed me of much meat, but I still bore an adequate prick. Unlike Wyatt, I was smooth bodied, and I saw him take note. When I stood bare, he came to me, turned me to the bedpost, spread my buttocks, and shoved his cock into me. "Been wanting to do that since Fort Griffin," he growled as he began to ride.

I quickly shot a load, prick firing like a repeating rifle, while Wyatt assaulted my rear. His thrust was relentless and accompanied by grunts. Soon sweat was flying and I was holding fast to the bedpost, my weakened body about at its limit. When Wyatt reached his summit, he let out a roar and slammed into me, at which my knees nearly buckled. I managed to remain upright until he finished, and when I slumped, he caught me at the waist as his cock slid out. He then laid me on the bed, where he saw to a pillow under my head.

"Pour me a drink," I said, starting to cough.

He did this and took one himself, sitting on the bed while eyeing my dick which, due solely to his own vigor, remained half-hard. It does credit to my manhood that it could keep viable while the rest of me failed. Wyatt finished his whiskey, then leaned down and took me into his mouth. When he started to suck, I began to swoon, and when the pull became great, I let go a come into his throat. This he swallowed and still kept on, as if he'd never get enough.

The second climax all but did me in, yet I wished not to be let alone. I think Wyatt saw this even though I offered no comment or outstretched arms. He likewise said nothing, but then, I didn't expect any declaration. We had done what we wanted and passed some quiet time together before I fell asleep. I woke alone the next morning, taking whiskey on rising to ease the lung pain and coughing.

I then lay back down to feast on recall of both the sight of Wyatt naked and the feel of him inside me. That I bore his come was great testament to our friendship. Stroking my cock as I considered him allowed me to bring myself off, which caused me to fall back asleep. I finally rose and dressed in the afternoon and after a meal found Wyatt at the Long Branch. Though he looked as always, I knew he bore satisfaction at having fucked me. As for me, I was puffed up with our intimacy and had a good run at faro, which I attributed to Wyatt's prowess.

I would like to say we fucked like rabbits from then on, but such was not the case, discretion being a bigger part of Wyatt than me. I would have taken him at any offer, but he became much occupied with his law enforcement and I was left to my gaming. We happened upon each other often, and I believe enjoyed a mutual pleasure in our bond, but for a while, it was left at that. Conversation passed easy between us, and at times, I even made the stern-faced lawman smile, but manly needs were not addressed, even though they remained highly present. I often thought we needed another bunch of rowdies to provoke an encounter but stopped short of stirring things. Didn't matter. I should have known my time as a peaceable man would run out.

The poker game that November night had started around noon, so those remaining at eleven o'clock were starting to wear thin in both patience and pocketbook. Three remained, Tom Roddy, Elmo Sparks, and yours truly, who had endured some losses but by evening had regained true form. Wyatt had come in not twenty minutes before Roddy lost another hand and began to spout off on my winning. "Game don't work that way," he said as he drilled me a look. I offered him no more than a glance as he rattled on. "Odds don't stay with one fellow so much," he declared. "Something ain't right."

Though guns had been checked at the bar, it was likely he carried a spare, as most men, myself included, would not go unheeled. It was not so much a matter of defying the law as protecting one's person. My second weapon was tucked into a holster inside my jacket, and my trusty knife remained in my breast pocket. Roddy wore a coat, and I figured his weapon to be concealed there. As he kept on questioning the odds of the game, I shuffled the cards and began to deal the next hand, including him as if nothing was being said.

"You ain't gonna rope me in again, Holliday," he said.

"Then hand me back those cards," I replied, "and your night will be over."

"You don't tell me what to do!"

"Indeed, I do not. I never attempt to tell a jackass which way his ass is pointing."

That did it. Roddy reached for his gun and I mine, but before I could use it, an arm of iron grabbed me from behind and the table was kicked toward Roddy, knocking him back as he attempted to draw. "That's enough, Doc," Wyatt said as he pulled me to my feet.

"Goddamn, Wyatt, the man drew on me!" I shouted.

"You both drew and you both are going to jail."

A deputy was disarming Roddy while Wyatt pushed me outside. "I did nothing wrong," I insisted, but he would not reply. He had me by the arm and all but dragged me to the jail, where I was pushed into a cell.

"Judge Andrews will see you in the morning," he said. "Get some sleep."

Tom Roddy was put into a cell down the row so we could not get at each other, but this did not stop him from spouting off. "I was cheated of my money!" he shouted until the deputy came in, pointed a pistol at him, and said he'd shoot if it didn't get quiet. Roddy let go a few more swear words, my name among them, then settled down. We lay in the dark and he began to snore while I fumed at Wyatt acting like I had caused the trouble. After a while, my thoughts on the situation gave way to thinking on the lawman's dick and I undid my pants, worked myself to a good come, and slept.

Morning came abruptly as Wyatt ran his gun along the bars. "Get up, you fellows. Time to see the judge."

Soon as I opened my eyes, I began to cough, and I spent some minutes attempting to right myself, emptying my flask in the effort. By the time Wyatt's deputy swung open the cell door, I was halfway presentable and in a foul mood. Roddy and I were ushered into the outer room where Wyatt waited, looking so grim you'd have thought I'd gone ahead and killed the man. "Let's go," he said, and he and his deputy escorted us criminals two blocks to the courthouse where the judge awaited us. As we stood before him, Wyatt spoke the charges, which were carrying a weapon in town, discharging a weapon within city limits, and disturbing the peace. As these were but misdemeanors, we were assessed fines and court costs. That I was assessed more than

Roddy got my dander up, but I held off any verbal objection for fear the sum would grow proportionately. Once we had paid, we were declared free men and allowed to leave, although Wyatt held me back, giving Roddy time to be well on his way.

"I am not a criminal," I said, pulling from his grip. He did not attempt to keep hold, as surely he could have since he had far more strength, but he did issue a sigh.

"You are trouble, Doc," he declared to which I said, "That statement is wearing thin."

Once he said I could leave, I hurried away and sought my room, where I began to wash up. I was thus half-naked when Wyatt knocked at the door. "Let me in, Doc," he called out. I enjoyed a moment's hesitation as I knew what he was up to and wanted to savor the triumph. It appeared getting him pissed off at me was as good as facing down a mob of rowdy men.

When I opened the door, he seemed surprised to find me half-undressed. "Welcome, Marshal," I said, waving him in. "Do you always make house calls on your criminals?"

"Your smart mouth is not appreciated, Doc, and one day it is going to get you into real trouble."

I chuckled. "I'm afraid that day is long past."

"You know what I mean. You stay heeled; you are breaking the law in my town."

"But it's now my town as well, and I fear it's not quite as tame as you would have it. A man who wins at cards and carries no weapon will not be long for this world."

"You would have killed Tom Roddy."

"His idea. He took exception to the outcome of the game. He sought his weapon."

"You have a mean streak, Doc."

"Among other things." Here I began to undo my pants. My prick had come up during our exchange, and I was ready to do most anything for him. He watched me push down my pants and drawers, hard cock aimed at him. "Why don't you come over here and fuck me so we can bury this disagreement?"

He was in my room for just that, of course, but he had to act the lawman, retain his dignity and authority before giving way. Such effort was almost endearing. As I waited, I began to stroke my prick and saw his breath pick up. His jaw tightened and his eyes blazed until he finally gave way, throwing his hat aside. His coat and gun belt followed while I pulled off my boots and socks and climbed onto the bed, because this time I did not want him standing.

I lay on my back, hand on my cock, while he shucked everything. He was hard as me but didn't handle himself beyond applying some spit. He then came over and got onto the bed. He ran a hand up my front and lingered but a few seconds before flipping me over, raising my bottom, and shoving in. As before, he went full out and I realized he was much pent up. The poor bed squealed something awful as he pumped in and out of my butthole, grunting with each thrust, sweat flying. He had his hands on my hips and buried himself to the root with each stroke, spearing me over and over until he started to moan. I knew then his spunk was rising and I thrilled to giving him such pleasure, and then he hit the peak, pounding me something fierce as he emptied. Once done, he pulled out and I fell over onto my back.

He sat on his haunches, cock still impressive as it slowly softened. I looked upon it and considered it had just been in my passage and left his stuff there. My gaze then traveled up to his eyes, which I found fixed not on mine but on my cock. I had not yet spent and began to writhe for him, letting him know he was welcome to devour my morsel. He came forward and I lay back against the pillow to watch him lower his mouth onto me.

Being just satisfied, he was not urgent with his meal, and for this, I was grateful. While poised near the peak, I worked to hold off a come as I wanted to savor him working me, and work me he did, his tongue licking and poking, his lips sliding up and down, pulling, playing. As he devoured me, he got a hand onto my balls and began to palm one then the other, settling then to a good suck of my cock, which sent me over. I cried out and began to buck as I spurted into his mouth while he not only took every drop, but kept on sucking until I had gone soft. Even then, he played with me some, rolling my soft prick on his tongue before finally letting me go.

I feared another quick departure and passed a moment's concern until he fell forward onto his stomach and lay beside me. "I am done in," he said as he blew out a long breath.

"Happily so, I'd reckon." I moved my arm the couple of inches between us, nudging him as I spoke. This small touch felt most good as it bore another kind of intimacy, and I found myself wanting all he had.

"Most happy," he said, turning to face me. He studied me then, and I him, and it was an interval that thrilled me. He was a man of few words, but we needed no more. What passed in silence said enough.

After this, he was more at ease in coming to my room when he got pent up, yet he still did not take advantage as much as I would have liked. That pesky wife, I'd venture, troubled him, what with him being such an upright fellow. Better if he'd been heathen like me. We could have been those rabbits, but such was not to be. Mostly, he saw to his law enforcement, slapping his gun to the head of many an unruly man while I attempted to refrain from shooting anyone.

CHAPTER TWO

Respectability is a thing of chance. After several months working together, Eldred McCarty, DDS, decided I was more liability than asset and suggested we terminate our partnership. He had begun to avoid me of late, so I knew something was up, and when he said we must talk, I saw by his unrest that the end was at hand. I sat opposite, as I had when we started, and he fussed with papers on his desk before he got down to it.

"John, I am afraid our partnership is not working out," he began, lowering his voice to add, "to my satisfaction." Here he paused to await comment, and when I offered none, he attempted to elaborate. "There is some talk around town, and a professional man must take care to maintain his respectability and not engage in pursuits that might damage his reputation. He also must not be seen to associate with certain parties who might injure his standing in the community."

McCarty was the only man in town to use my given name, which underscored his attempt to ignore the rest of my life. I had appreciated his efforts toward me and was thus somewhat disappointed at what he said. "The fact that you gamble every night puts me in a bad light," he went on. "Certainly, you can see the dilemma you present."

"I have never been a dilemma," I replied. "Many things, but never that. I do understand your position, Doctor, and hereby withdraw my services." I stood and offered my hand. "I wish you well. No hard feelings."

It took him a second to embrace his good fortune, his shoulders slumping in relief at my not shooting him. He then took my hand. "You are a good man, John," he said. "At heart, you are good."

"You are most kind, Doctor."

In the treatment room, I boxed up my instruments while he stood in the doorway, looking on. It would have been petty of me to think he guarded against theft of his own tools, so I did not dwell on such a notion. When my box was filled, I bid him good-bye and left, finding as I hit the street a certain relief. I was free of respectability and took enjoyment in this until Wyatt Earp walked up to me. "What's in the box?" he asked like some child.

"Dental instruments. Dr. McCarty and I have parted ways."

"Why is that?"

"Why do you think?" I snapped, brushing past to continue to the hotel. Once in my room, I found myself annoyed at the turn of events, swearing to forgo all efforts toward respectability and never again hang out my shingle. I had attempted to toe the line and done well, at least in my own eyes, and what had I gotten? I dropped the box of instruments into a corner and headed to the Long Branch, where I got into a poker game that went from one day to the next and landed me in my bed for two days of recovery.

"Haven't seen you around," Wyatt remarked when I finally emerged. I coughed in reply so he continued. "The boys say you won big at poker."

"Big enough," I managed, flask now in hand. I took a couple swigs to quiet my chest. "Paid a price, though. Always do."

"You ever think about taking it easier?" he asked.

"No, I do not. I am twenty-eight years old and will be fortunate to see thirty-eight. I therefore will enjoy what time I have."

"Then how about I buy you a drink?"

"I would like nothing better."

Life improved in Wyatt's company. Whatever slights or reverses I suffered from others slipped from my mind as he stood next to me at the bar. I felt pride in being his friend, and as months had passed, I had seen most people come to accept the odd pairing of lawman and killer. The marshal was highly respected, and thus his choice of friends was not questioned—at least not where we could hear. "Are you going to try tooth work again?" he asked.

"I may," I said, although at present it was the last thing I wanted to do. But I saw it gave me merit with him, as if his respectability might rub off onto me. "I suppose I could set up at the Dodge House," I added.

"Good idea."

He had not been in my bed for a while and was fidgety as a result, standing with his back to the bar to survey his realm. I thought to suggest we retire to my room, but he suddenly said he had business to attend to and was gone. I suspected conscience was at him again, the husband in him chafing against the heathen all too ready to corrupt him. I finished my drink and went out to walk about town, hoping to catch sight of him, but he had disappeared. I then sought the newspaper office and put an ad in the next edition stating my dental practice was now open at the Dodge House. Five days after it ran, Wyatt came by.

"Toothache?" I asked as he came in.

"No, I am happy to say. Just came to see your new place."

I swept my hand in a wide gesture over my meager setup, which was little more than table, shelf, chairs, and desk. I had taken a room on the hotel's ground floor and had the bed removed. In its place, a straight-backed chair accommodated customers. "A far cry from McCarty's setup, but it works. I have already seen three patients."

"I am happy for you, Doc."

I said nothing more, just fixed on him, hoping he'd pick up on what lay unspoken. It had been weeks since our last time, and I ached for him something awful, suspected he felt likewise, yet he did not make a move. "What does it take?" I finally blurted, unable to hold back the surge.

He kept his eyes on mine but said nothing for some moments, then trotted out that old saw. "I am a married man, Doc."

"That hasn't stopped you before."

I could see he wanted it as bad as me. It filled the room like cigar smoke, almost pungent. "Lock the door," I said. "Fuck me."

A shudder ran over him at hearing it outright, and when he stood motionless, I said it again. "Fuck me." I then began to undo my pants, at which he did lock the door.

He bared just the essentials to do it, dropping his pants and drawers while I pushed mine off. He bent me at my work table and I heard him spit into his hand. "You want a fuck, I'll give you a goddamn fuck," he growled and he shoved his prick into me so hard the table scooted forward. He then set to doing me like some bull broken from its pen, pounding my bottom while I got a hand on myself and stroked with a fury, as I wanted to come with him inside me. And come I did, spraying spunk as he reamed my passage until his own rise began. Panting, grunting, growling, he was fierce in his efforts, and when he hit the summit, he issued not a roar but a strangled cry. It took some time for him to empty, which I savored as it meant he had spent little elsewhere.

When he was finished, he fought for breath almost as much as did

I, although I had coughing to contend with. He pulled out and I turned around because I wanted to see him undone this way, pants down, cock still flushed and not yet soft. He stood, chest heaving, as he attempted to regain himself while I feasted on his every inch until at last he quieted. He blew out a breath, then pulled up his pants, buttoned himself, and looked at me. "That do it?" he said.

"For now," I replied. "Come by anytime."

When he slammed the door behind him, I had to laugh. He did himself a disservice, playing at loyalty to his woman when his desire clearly lay elsewhere. I was fortunate to have never ventured where he had gotten mired, but I was somewhat sorry his situation led him to such turmoil. How good it would be were he unencumbered. We might then batch together, as was common among men looking to cut costs. The idea of sharing his bed every night was so delectable that I had to push it from my mind, lest I create my own turmoil.

Wyatt and I passed the better part of a year in such a state, him succumbing now and again to his wants and the rest of the time playing husband. I watched him walk to church with Mattie and wondered what he considered God's opinion of his situation. I also wondered if she realized she shared her husband with his friend. Wyatt never invited me to his house and never introduced me to his wife, both clear attempts to separate the parts of his life. I tried to honor his effort even as it rankled me no end, for he would not be fucking me if he were the least content with her.

In early 1880, there came an evening when I sought supper at the Arden House, a fine restaurant not far from the Long Branch. As I entered, I saw Wyatt and Mattie at a small corner table. I had seen them around town on many an occasion and never intruded, but this time I reached an end and went over.

"Wyatt, good to see you," I said, removing my hat.

"Doc. I don't think you know my wife, Mattie. Mattie, this is Doc Holliday."

She was a fine-looking woman with thick blond hair piled onto her head in a most artful arrangement. She wore a green silk dress that dipped in front to entice a man, then put him off with puffed sleeves. The vibrant color enhanced her fair complexion, although she had a certain glassy-eyed quality. "Mr. Holliday, it is good to know you," she said with little enthusiasm.

"Please, call me Doc."

She nodded. "Doc."

"Your husband and I have become the best of friends."

"So I have heard," she replied, turning to her water glass.

I stood but a moment more as Wyatt gave no indication of welcome. Still, it pleased me to be acknowledged by the other party taking his dick. Before I left them, I passed him a long and knowing gaze that caused his eyes to narrow as he got my drift. You fuck us both, it said, and he, by way of a clenched jaw, acknowledged this truth. Late that night, as Dodge lulled itself into a restless sleep, Wyatt charged into my room and, in an absolute fury, fucked me raw.

"You stay away from her," he commanded when he'd pumped a load into me. He pulled out and hopped off the bed, but I saw release had not quieted him. Indeed, it seemed to rile him further. He shed the rest of his clothes, and I got out of what he hadn't torn away because his cock was still half-hard. "My private life is my own and you are not a part of it, not ever."

I lay pulling my dick. "This your public life, then?"

"You know what I mean, Doc."

"I'm afraid I do, but I don't intend to accept it. Not when you come in here like this and do what you do. Christ, Wyatt, why can't you give your preference the room it deserves?"

"You talk too much."

"Then shut me up."

This was a good spot for him to get his mouth upon mine, but a consumptive is denied such pleasure. I had kissed no one since receiving my diagnosis and accepted the fact that I never again would, even as the idea of my mouth on his, our tongues twining, persisted. As he looked me up and down, I wondered if he considered such a thing, but he climbed back onto the bed and fixed on my cock, which, with his fury, I thought he might bite off.

He scooped my soft dick into his mouth and began to suck as he pulled his prick, working himself up to get at me again. How a man who had just unloaded might accomplish such a feat was a wonder to me, but then again, if a man could ride a thousand miles chasing some train robber, he could surely get his dick up for another go. Stamina was built into Wyatt and did not fail him now.

His efforts got my own sorry cock aroused again, as his tongue was a marvel when inspired. He had me squirming beneath him when he finally pulled off, pushed my legs up around my ears, and rammed his prick into me. Once in, he issued a groan that told me this was home to him, the one and only, even if he might never acknowledge the fact. He glared at me as if he had a pistol inside me, looking to kill, and he set to fucking me as hard as before, maybe harder, the bed complaining as he went at it. My butthole, already chafed from his prior assault, hurt some, but I did not care, as this was evidence of a good go. Mostly, I reeled in pleasure at taking him deep, my entire body brought fully to life. When in such throes, my malady almost seemed to disappear, even as I coughed. For those joyous moments its painful grip weakened. Nothing in the world could get in our way, not my failed lungs, not Mattie, not a goddamned thing. We were as one, him and me, his cock and my bottom, and he knew this as well as I.

He was awash in sweat when he finally let go another load. Stamina he may have had, but it was a long haul to scale the peak. I admired his persistence in getting off another come, and when he finally reached the summit, he growled more with relief than pleasure. He rode me steadily until he lost his girth and slipped out, slumping, then he fell over onto the bed where he stretched out beside me. I lowered my legs and rolled onto my side to face him. He lay on his back, arm across his eyes as his breathing quieted.

"Don't say anything," he managed amid deep breaths. Once he'd regained himself, he got up, dressed, and left without so much as a look back. I lay wondering if he would go home to his wife or detour to walk around town.

The following month, the Santa Fe was robbed again, which set Wyatt off on another chase. He took a posse and was gone three weeks but returned with prisoners this time, much to the delight of railroad bigwigs. Word spread around town at recovery of stolen funds, and I was pleased that Wyatt shone ever brighter in people's eyes. When I encountered him on the street the next day, I joined in the praise. "Hear you brought in Marks and Soffey, along with the loot. Nice work."

"Thank you, Doc. Ran them halfway to hell, but it was worth it. I've had enough of the saddle for a while, though." He blew out a breath. "Let me buy you a drink."

"Sounds good."

I had missed him something awful. Even if he was not regularly in my bed, his presence did me well, as passing him on the street or seeing him come into the Long Branch always picked up my spirits. In honor of our friendship, I had worked at giving him room in his personal life, allowing that I would, in his mind at least, be no more than diversion. That this diversion proved most ardent helped make the arrangement tolerable and therefore missed when absent.

"I sometimes think of giving up law enforcement," he said as we enjoyed our whiskey.

I stood in shock. "You serious?" I asked.

"I surely am. A man can do far more than wear a badge. There are enterprises a fellow can pursue, opportunities where fortune might be had, something more than wages and long hours in the saddle."

"You surprise me, Wyatt. I have always thought your badge part of you."

This he considered. "I suppose it is in a way, but in truth, I sort of fell into law enforcement, just as most men don't much plan their occupations. It suited me, no doubt about that, and I have done well by it, but I still think on other lines of work. There are opportunities out west, gold and silver strikes that create boomtowns where fortunes can be made."

"You're not going to trade your badge for a gold pan."

"No, I'm no prospector. I'm talking a business of some sort. Maybe invest in some mines."

"Where would you go?"

"Arizona, I think. There's a silver strike in the southern part, and a town called Tombstone is said to be booming as a result."

"Ominous sound, Tombstone."

He chuckled. "Just a thought, but I don't mean to be a lawman forever."

The topic faded as I got him to relate details of chasing Marks and Soffey, and I noted his enthusiasm in the telling was far more than when he contemplated a life of business.

Nothing more was said of such notions, and Wyatt settled back into his marshaling, the year slipping away while Dodge City thrived. Life had become comfortable for me, the dental practice earning me some funds, but never as much as gambling. Still, I pursued both, though at times my malady asserted itself to such extent I was laid up for a day or two. Rest always saw it quiet down, and when I was in such a state, Wyatt often came by to check on me. By way of repayment, I managed not to kill a single man while in Dodge City.

Later that year, I hit a streak of luck at poker that saw me through a thirty-six-hour game. Wyatt came and went several times as I played on at the Long Branch. Men stopped to watch for a time, then went about their lives, only to come back hours later and find us still going strong. Five men stuck it out to the end, and I took a fine bundle, but when we declared the game over and stood to vacate, my malady, which had troubled me the last ten or twelve hours, flared up to such extent that I collapsed and had to be carried to my room. It was there that Wyatt found me the next day.

"Whiskey," I croaked when he came in. He poured me a glass and I took it down, but it did little to ease the cough or the pain that gripped my chest. I took more and still more to no avail.

"I'm getting the doctor," Wyatt declared. I tried to object, but my voice was lost to the cough.

The doctor said the old and familiar. "You must forgo drinking, smoking, and all nightlife. Rest is the only way ahead, complete rest."

"I understand," I said, even as I knew I would not comply. He then hit me with something unanticipated. "You also must move to a warmer climate, New Mexico or Arizona, where the air is hot and dry. If you stay here, you will surely die."

Wyatt stood over by the window, and I looked to him as soon as the sentence had been pronounced. Even with distance between us, I saw the familiar clench of his jaw.

"Thank you, Doctor," I managed. "I will consider your advice."

The good man returned his stethoscope to his bag, nodded to Wyatt, and left. Wyatt then came and sat on the bed. He did not speak, for what could he say but good-bye, one way or the other. He looked so wounded that I felt compelled to offer him comfort, even though I was the one to be robbed of a life yet again. I put a hand on his arm, held on a minute, then spoke. "Looks like I'll be the one heading toward opportunity out west."

"Damned shame," he said.

It was an awful situation, fate tracking me down again and demanding still more, but I was at least familiar with her, whereas Wyatt was not. He sat quite at a loss, and so I attempted to relieve him. "I am tired, Wyatt. You go on; let me do as the doctor says and rest."

He stood but got no further. "Go on," I urged him. At the door, he said he'd bring me some soup later on, to which I agreed. This allowed him to leave.

Alone, I could not help but call up my last failure at life, when I'd been forced to leave Georgia at age twenty-two with much the same pronouncement. I saw my family on the train platform, bidding me farewell, and while this was most wrenching, it served to keep me from thinking on leaving Wyatt, which was something I could not yet bear, even as I knew I must.

It took the better part of a week for me to gain strength enough to go about my life again. Wyatt was attentive during this period, bringing soup and other necessities, but fate now stood between us, rendering him somewhat awkward toward me. He made no attempt at sex, and I, in my reduced state, likewise sought none. My mind was most randy but had to defer to a body lacking strength to pursue relief, and so frustration piled onto the somber mood. Finally, there was nothing to do but leave.

I closed my dental office, leaving a note for patients to see Dr. McCarty. I packed my instruments, doubting I would ever again use them. I packed my other belongings, noting as I did so that my two years in Dodge had gained me a sense of home. Foolish for an itinerant gambler to attempt such a thing.

Wyatt and I crossed paths occasionally as my days in town dwindled. He would inquire as to my health and my progress in arrangements, then fall to silence, which proved most painful for us both. At last, departure was fixed. The Santa Fe would carry me west to Benson, Arizona, where I would catch a stagecoach south to my destination.

"Tombstone still has an ominous sound," I told Wyatt the night before I left. He'd found me sitting out front of the hotel, in no mood for cards.

"You'll do well," he said as he settled beside me.

"Well is a relative term. Survival seems more appropriate."

"Fair enough. I will miss you. You know that."

"I do know that, yes. And I you. It's been a fine time. You were right about Dodge City. Most hospitable."

"You saved my life," he said after a long pause. "I will always be grateful."

"I would not see you lost to me."

Just then, a bunch of drunken cowboys who had brought in a herd that afternoon began to raise hell, firing their guns into the sky and into windows of the mercantile next door. As glass shattered, Wyatt jumped up and within minutes had them disarmed and headed to jail. I sat awhile longer in my melancholy, then went to bed.

I was aboard the train for a nine fifteen departure next morning, feeling quite glum in my window seat as I looked down at my pocket watch. Suddenly, I desired a look out the window. There, across the platform, stood Wyatt. I wanted to shout or cry or some such, but the train began to move. As its wheels screeched, Wyatt raised a finger to his hat brim and I raised a hand in response. I kept my gaze upon him until distance robbed me of the sight.

CHAPTER THREE

I was not the best of travelers aboard the Santa Fe, as part of me resisted the very move I was undertaking. Those around me seemed far too eager and excitable as they ate from their picnic baskets and commented on the passing scenery. When inquiries were made as to my destination, they were put off, and I was thus left alone. My coughing and taking whiskey furthered the solitude.

Miles did not put Wyatt Earp behind me. He may have remained in Dodge, but in spirit he kept to me, for I would not let him be gone. When we crossed from Kansas to Colorado, there came a pang at leaving his state, so I called up memories of him striding about town or rounding up rowdies. Better still, I saw him naked, hard prick aimed at me. I wallowed in recollection for quite some time, losing much of Colorado to memory and whiskey.

The train stopped periodically to take on necessities and allow passengers to get a meal in town. I thus saw Trinidad and Lamar, Colorado, which were nothing special, and Las Vegas, New Mexico, which greeted me with such heat I swear my spit dried up. Never had I experienced air without a drop of moisture, and it amused me to sweat and dry at almost the same moment. Everything crackled and snapped, yet the dry heat soothed the body.

Resuming the journey, we went on to Albuquerque, where I changed to a Southern Pacific train headed south. Aboard this conveyance, I took note of the surroundings where a range of mountains gave onto endless flat. Trees occasionally sprang up alongside some river, but this was infrequent. Emptiness lay before me, which I found appropriate. From Albuquerque we went through Silver City, Deming, and a few other towns before reaching Benson, Arizona, where I was pleased to leave the train. The journey had not been conducive to my health even though I'd done little but sit, sleep, and cough.

Benson appeared to be a well-established town grown up around the railroad. I found a hotel where I inquired after the stagecoach to Tombstone. Upon learning it ran daily, I took a room for the night and enjoyed a lengthy bath, fresh clothes, and a fine meal. I then walked the town under dusky skies, finding myself oddly removed from the wanderer of old. The fact that I knew not a soul weighed on me more than anticipated and led me to consider that a certain attachment now colored my perspective.

I sought a saloon, where I joined a poker game, and while this proved a diversion, it was still wanting because Wyatt Earp would not be coming in. Such awareness could not be shaken, and at one point intruded into my game to such a degree that I misplayed the hand. I continued the game until I broke even, then headed for my room. Though far from the late hours I had known in Dodge and elsewhere, I felt most tired and thus ready for sleep.

In all my travels, I had avoided the stagecoach, as most were uncomfortable and dirtier than a ride on horseback. Both means encountered trail dust, but a horseman was continually blown halfway clean by the wind, while the stage trapped dirt until those confined gained a layer of filth. I thus pondered the situation at length, allowing my malady a place in the consideration, and finally decided to buy a horse and ride on alone. In this manner, I could travel at my own speed and spare myself confinement. The horse would also provide transportation in Tombstone. The air, though breezy, remained hot and dry, which my body continued to appreciate.

The horse, saddle, and rig that I purchased for two hundred dollars served me well. A fine bay name of Rags, the animal was energetic yet agreeable, and once on our own we got on well. The corral owner told me to follow the San Pedro River south twenty-five miles, then turn east for five more to Tombstone. As it was the stage route, the turn would be clearly visible. Before leaving Benson, I filled my flask and had my suitcases and dental instruments sent on to the Wells Fargo office in Tombstone.

Pain was losing its grip on my lungs as I found the west the doctor had prescribed. This was the sole good point in my adventure and helped make my ride south relatively comfortable. The river ambled through miles of grassland, cattle often scattered and munching. Now and then a horseman or wagon passed, but none stopped to inquire. Dusk was approaching when I finally saw Tombstone, a surprisingly large and sprawling town set on a slope above the grassy flat. I stopped to consider that this would likely be my final stop in life and I had best make it a good one.

Riding into town, I found it most lively. Every kind of establishment a person could want seemed to be at hand, and where these ran out, new buildings were under construction. People moved about conducting their business, and those not so engaged lay around as if riches were soon to come calling. The place bristled not only with the sounds of civilization, but the buzz and clack of those making more of it.

I found what seemed the main part on Allen Street where stood two hotels opposite each other: the Cosmopolitan and the Grand. The latter aimed at pretension, as it was the smaller establishment, while the former, a fine two-story brick building, was far more impressive. I stopped there and found it much to my liking, requesting a ground-floor room to spare myself stairs and also allow easy access should the need arise. It proved much to my satisfaction, boasting a good bed with furniture of black walnut. As always with travel, I bathed at length, changed into the one suit I had carried with me, and went out to secure my horse and a meal. Exploring the town would wait until I'd had a good rest.

Supper was taken at Julius Caesar's Bakery and Restaurant, which stood next door to the hotel, and by the time I emerged, full-bellied, I was presented with an entirely different view of the town. Drunken men dominated the street, intimidating citizens and poking guns at one another while laughing and generally carrying on in a loutish manner. Some fired pistols into the night sky, but shots of others went astray to such extent that many people retreated indoors. A man with a badge who looked to be about thirty soon emerged, two deputies behind him, but he did not arrest anyone. Instead he urged the men to move on which, after some antics, they did. As I returned to my hotel, eager for a good night's sleep, I considered that these men must be locals, for surely there were no trail drives coming this way. I left these thoughts behind as I slipped into my bed, but gunfire did wake me several times during the night.

Now that I had arrived at my destination, I attempted to embrace this new town, and so, next morning after breakfast, set out to explore the place. In walking the streets, I found every kind of store or entertainment a man could want: gun shop, barber, butcher, post office, telegraph, assay office, clothing stores, hardware, food market, and even a photo gallery. Two newspaper offices stood opposite each other, one the *Tombstone Daily Nugget*, the other the *Tombstone Epitaph*. Of course, saloons and gambling establishments were most prevalent. On every street and almost every corner, their noise spilled out to mingle with what seemed an ever-present wind. Dust and debris blew around in front of fine stores to prove that no matter how much civilization was attempted, man and nature would always make a mess.

Looking to find a card game, I visited several saloons and found the Oriental most appealing. It was quite grand, boasting a carved bar finished in white and gilt, a comfortable lounge, and in the back a large club room catering to sporting men. Here much activity was in progress. I wet my whistle at the bar, then took a second drink into the back where I sat in on poker with some local ranchers. A pair of brothers named McLaury and one Ike Clanton paused when they heard my name but were still most welcoming and did not object when I took a good amount of their money.

I could have been at the Long Branch in Dodge, such was my comfort at getting back to gaming. Skills I had developed from boyhood served me well to both earn a living and provide entertainment among the men. Tombstone, I was starting to see, had a teeming quality that Dodge City and other locales lacked. "A hundred people arrive every day," a miner named Harry Fisher told me when I mentioned this. "There were but five hundred when I came here. There are now over two thousand. We are destined to be the biggest town in Arizona, passing Tucson and even Prescott, as we have the riches."

"Silver," I said.

"Rich veins," he declared as he played a losing hand and laughed about it. He was no more than my age and acted like his pockets were filled beyond reason. A man who laughed when he lost was most welcome.

A few hands later, an argument broke out at the bar, and I looked over in time to see a gun drawn. Shots were fired and people ran, but apparently, the gunmen were too drunk to hit anyone, even each other. The barman got the drop on them with a shotgun and ordered them out.

"Goddamn cowboys," Fisher said. "They are roughing up the town something awful."

"Now, Harry," Ike Clanton countered, "they are good boys just blowing off steam."

Harry busied himself with his cards and said nothing more, while Ike Clanton, who looked much the ruffian himself, grinned. Something about him didn't sit well with me. He was an unwashed, curly-haired brute with a big mouth and weak intellect. He seemed close with the McLaurys, Tom and Frank, but I quickly saw they gave way to him.

The men who had caused the commotion left, but shots were still heard outside. "Lively place," I said to nobody in particular.

"Fellows like to have a good time," Ike said, and I left it at that.

After a few days observing the commerce of Tombstone, I thought to open my dental practice and went around town looking at office space. None suited me, so I tabled the matter in favor of playing faro at the Alhambra Saloon, where I had a fine time until quite late. Next morning, as I coughed my way into the day, I again considered dentistry, but, recalling my disappointment at where to set up, I set the matter aside. Instead I attended to personal matters, saw my clothes to the laundry, bought new boots, and strolled about town before landing at the Oriental, where I joined a poker game that lasted well into the following day. This excess caused my malady to take advantage, and I kept to my bed for a day before I could again partake of all Tombstone had to offer.

Law enforcement in town was in the person of City Marshal Fred White, the man I'd previously seen not arresting rowdies. He had two deputies, but the three often seemed overmatched by the raucous fellows that cut loose most nights and sometimes in the daytime. More than once, I saw one man shoot another for no apparent reason, Marshal White stepping in to haul the criminal to jail. I soon noted that one man taken away solved nothing, as another took his place, gunplay being loose in town. I kept as low a profile as possible, harking back to Wyatt's saying I was trouble. Over cards, I made friends with some ranchers and mine owners and occasionally ran into somebody I had known in my travels.

The most notable of these was Billy Leonard, who had sold me my diamond stickpin in Deadwood some years back. A friendship had grown from that purchase, but it had been left behind when I moved on due to killing a man in town and enduring jailing before being found justified. How surprised I was to catch sight of Billy one day on Allen Street, not only because it had been a while but because he looked the worse for wear. He recognized me as I had not much changed.

"Doc! How the hell are you? I thought you were in Texas."

"Hello, Billy. I was there for a while, but it didn't suit me. Been here not quite a month. You down from Deadwood?"

He deflated some at this mention, so I offered to buy him a drink. Over whiskey at the Oriental, I learned he had suffered reverses due to gambling. "I lost the store and most everything else," he admitted. "Never was much good at cards."

"I am sorry to hear you're down on your luck. Maybe you can do better here. Are you looking to open another store?"

"I'm thinking on it, but as yet have taken no action. Are you practicing your dentistry?"

"Not as yet. I'm pretty much same as you, thinking on it but taking no action. I'm earning my keep at gaming, like usual."

As we spoke, I could not help but think back on our history, and when silence fell between us, I knew Billy considered it as well. Even in his rough state, he remained an appealing fellow with unruly blond hair and a most handsome face. He was two years my elder, and we had suffered a carnal attraction in Deadwood that we had repeatedly indulged. This knowledge now played upon us both as we attempted to converse. I heard myself telling the tales of Fort Griffin and Dodge City, aware, as I spoke, that I made no mention of Wyatt. This was most telling, but then my dick was now in the lead and letting me know we would get up to something.

I got Billy to giving details of his hard time in Deadwood, but I only half listened as part of me was considering my manly needs. Absent Wyatt, I had partaken only of my own hand, and thus thoughts of a prick I had thoroughly enjoyed kept at me. I had known a good many men before Wyatt, starting up while in dental school and taking up with various fellows during my travels. With Wyatt, I had moved beyond such transience, yet now it had come to find me. As I listened to Billy's outpouring, I felt not only the manly urge but compassion for him as he was much at a loss. He had come to Tombstone with three other fellows, Harry Head, Jim Crane, and Luther King, and the four were batching in a house near the Wells, a spring where Tombstone drew much of its water.

"They are older than me," Billy said, "an unruly bunch who have had some trouble. Fine fellows, but at times I'd just as soon be elsewhere."

As he told of their exploits, I wondered if he got up to things with them. Four men in a house seemed ripe for something, yet Billy was pretty much saying that was not the case. A few more drinks and I asked him to my room. "Get a good night's sleep for a change," I said as we headed to the Cosmopolitan.

"That all?" he replied.

In my room, he was matter-of-fact, pushing down his pants to show me his stiff dick. "You need a fuck, Doc?" he asked as he wrapped a hand around it. "I sure as hell do."

I looked him up and down, the blond riot, the fine features. I knew his body well, solid and strong and dusted with golden hair that gave him an animal quality. "As do I," I said, and I began to undress.

"It has been too long," he noted when we stood naked.

"That it has."

I climbed onto the bed and he followed. In his urgency, he put me onto all fours, drove his prick into me, and set thrusting with such force the bed complained something awful. Knowing he wouldn't last, I pulled my dick and shot a load just before he let go with a roar and a come.

Billy pulled out and fell over onto his back, asleep almost before his head hit the pillow. This was not a surprise, as he had been the same in Deadwood, letting go always doing him in to such extent he could not remain awake. I was left to lie in the quiet and ponder this turn of events, which, of course, brought Wyatt to mind.

He was likely fucking his wife regular now, playing married man back in Dodge, so it served me well to move on. But as Billy Leonard lay snoring, I found myself satisfied in one way and unsatisfied in another. I liked Billy. He was a good fellow and fine fuck, but he was no Wyatt Earp. Still, he might provide a diversion and some relief, and I had best learn to settle for what lay at hand.

Over the next weeks, I visited Billy several times at the Wells. I met his cohorts, all of whom were cordial but guarded. They bore the suspicious nature of guilty men, and thus I had some concern for Billy though I did not tell him such. I simply offered what support I could along with hope he could make his way. As his friends were often in town, Billy and I would drink and fuck, though I wished he could manage more than one go. Wyatt had spoiled me with his stamina, and I found it often necessary to chase him off as I lay beside the spent and snoring Billy Leonard. Most often, I did not stay over with Billy but rode back to town.

Word soon got around about my dental occupation even though I did not hang out my shingle. Men sought me out when teeth had been knocked loose in bar fights or rotted due to poor habits. More than once, a bloodied fellow begged me to relieve him of his pain, and I took these souls to my room where I sat them in a chair and extracted the painful tooth. This proved the extent of my dentistry, as I found gaming in Tombstone suited me far better than the professional life.

My first run-in with Ike Clanton occurred after I'd been in town a couple of months and took place at the Alhambra Saloon, which was just down the street from the Oriental. Ike sat in at poker with his brothers, Billy and Fin, and two men I did not know. The Clantons were drunk, but Ike more so than the others, and therefore a concern. The McLaury brothers were at the bar, as they could usually be found around the Clantons. I had come to be cautious in their company, as they threw their guns around a bit too freely.

"That's the sixth hand you've taken," Ike charged when I took the pot. "It's not right."

I ignored the comment and dealt the next hand, knowing my failure to bite would rankle him. Caution may have been my watchword, but I still could not resist poking such a blowhard. "You hear me, Holliday?" he railed.

"Everyone can hear you, Ike, and everyone is most amused."

This punctured him to such extent he began to sputter. "You are not going to come in here and cheat me!" he declared, spitting through his scruffy beard.

"Now you are scaring the folks," I said. "They are starting to fear you will be shot here and now."

His face reddened, and I knew what came next. He jumped up, his chair going over backward, and his hand was as far as his holster when I drew my gun and took aim at his forehead. "You want to go ahead with that," I said, "it's fine with me, but I would recommend you stop where you are and either sit down for another hand or get the hell out of here."

At hearing this, Billy and Fin Clanton sprang to their feet, and Billy grabbed Ike around his middle to pull him back. Ike fought this with such force that both tumbled to the floor. As Ike attempted to right himself, he swore up a storm at both his brother and me. I rose to observe him on the floor and kept my gun pointed at him as his brothers sought to save his life by dragging him from the premises. "Don't do it, Ike," Fin counseled as he fought Ike's attempt to unholster his gun. "He'll kill you."

"He's the one needs killing," Ike shouted.

I kept my eyes and my gun on him as he got to his feet. We had room now, everyone giving us a wide circle in which to settle the matter. Just then, Marshal White rushed in, gun drawn, and ordered me to put down my weapon. "I am defending myself, Marshal," I said. "This man attempted to draw on me after making false accusations of cheating."

"That so, Ike?" White asked.

"He cheated me. He sure as hell did."

"I am not concerned with cards but with gunplay," the marshal said. "Now you get out of here, Ike. Billy, you and Fin take him home. You're drunk, Ike. Sleep it off."

Ike shook off his brothers and glared at me. "This isn't the last of it, Holliday," he declared. I nodded as he departed, then inquired of the marshal if I could holster my weapon. He agreed but told me to not provoke further unrest.

"I never provoke, Marshal. But I will, on occasion, put an end to things."

After this, I sought to make friends with Fred White, and he was receptive to my attentions, I suppose because he figured it better to be on my good side than bad. That I worked at avoiding shooting men in his town was appreciated, and he more than once commended me for good behavior. "It is not easy," I said one day as we walked along Fremont Street. I had come from the barber and was freshened and smelling fine and thus had a spring in my step. I coughed less these days, my malady having eased within two weeks of my arrival. New vigor filled me, and I could now carry on a conversation like most men.

"These men never seem to let up," I said to White as three brawled in the street.

"They grow more bold every day," he replied. "I've sent word to Charlie Shibell, the county sheriff over in Tucson, that I need help, but as yet he can't spare anyone. I'm also starting to believe these men are part of a cattle rustling operation, though I can't be sure about that. They steal them in Mexico, bring them up here, sell them cheap, then throw their money around. That steak you eat for supper is likely pilfered Mexican stock."

"Is nobody after them?"

"Jurisdictions are a question. Bringing cattle over the border makes it a federal offense, but we have no U.S. Marshal and Shibell is undermanned. That's the trouble with a town growing too fast. Law can't keep up. Guess I'd best go stop the fight before guns are drawn. See you, Doc."

I watched as he drew his weapon and ordered the men to cease their fighting. When they stopped, one fell, being too drunk to stand on his own. The others were made to haul him away, which they did after issuing threats to the law. As this took place, I noted citizens on their everyday business hurrying past as if once away from the spectacle, it need not be a concern. I too avoided things by slipping around to Allen Street, where I sought the Oriental and a game of faro.

Four months into life in Tombstone, a new fellow sat in on my poker game at the Alhambra. "Holliday, isn't it?" he said, extending a hand.

"It is," I replied, enjoying his big paw and vigorous shake. "And you?"

"Henry Hooker. I have a cattle operation north of here, the Sierra Bonita Ranch. Biggest spread around."

"Pleased to know you, Mr. Hooker."

He was a bearish older fellow, copper hair going gray, skin parched by the sun. His voice fairly boomed, as did his laugh, and I felt myself immediately drawn to his easy way.

"Dr. Holliday, I'm told," he said as I dealt him in.

"Just Doc, though I am a dentist. John Henry is the long version."

"We share a name," he noted. "I don't suppose you like it any better than I do."

"It is my father's name, and I am grateful he stuck it in the middle."

Hooker laughed. "Well, you call me Hooker, as I like to be known that way."

"That I shall."

Hooker proved to be skilled at cards, and more than once, he and I locked over a hand others had vacated. His blue eyes all but sparkled when his cards lined up well, but they also did this with the occasional bluff, rendering him a most challenging opponent. We played well into the night, and when we saw neither could best the other for long, we cashed out and went to supper.

"My foreman told me you were in town," Hooker said over a steak. "I knew Ed Bailey at one time. Worked for him on a cattle operation he had out of Houston before he gave up ranching in favor of town life."

"Small world," I noted. "I am sorry about your friend, but he brought himself to his end. And I did warn him."

Hooker studied me, now quite serious. "You really kill all those men?"

"Most."

It was to the man's credit that he neither pried for details nor fled at my honesty. He took another couple bites before offering comment. "Ed was foolish at times," he said. "I once saw him try to snooker a friend over a string of sorry ponies only to get snookered worse himself. It didn't surprise me he'd met his end in Fort Griffin."

"I appreciate your candor."

"From where do you hail, Doc? I hear a Southern cadence."

"Georgia," I said and told of the leaving, only this time the second leaving was added.

"Earp," Hooker said. "Saw him once in Wichita where I have family. He was marshal at the time. My people were much impressed."

"He is an impressive man," I said, realizing I'd gone on a bit about Wyatt. "We became good friends in Dodge City," I added. "You wouldn't think on such a pairing, but we respected each other."

"Best grounds for any bond, respect."

I could not help myself from relating still more of Wyatt, as it pleased me to talk of him. I also discovered in the telling that he had not gone far away. Though I'd thought him behind me, he was in truth lying just below the surface and now, brought out to share, took firm hold yet again.

Hooker listened with care and spoke much the same. "Widower," he said when I asked after his situation. "Two sons now grown and gone, one to New York and business, the other to sea out of Boston. Both said they'd had enough cattle, which was a disappointment, but I could not hold them back. I live in a big old house with my foreman, George McKinstry, and I've got a fine bunch of cowhands working for me. I only get down to Tombstone every couple months."

"You must look me up next time."

"That I will."

Next day, my poker game began not with Hooker but with two strangers and the McLaury brothers. Tom and Frank were so similar in appearance they could have been twins, though I'd been told two years separated them. Both dark and brooding, they kept to their cards and, unlike their friend Clanton, made no foolish moves. Still, I noted an edge to things. Hooker came in later on but did not join my game until the McLaurys had vacated. "I won't sit in with those two," he said. "Clantons either."

"Why is that?"

"Cattle rustling," he said. At this mention, the other players suddenly decided luck was not with them and deserted our game. I held off dealing in favor of hearing more from Hooker. "Stolen Mexican cattle are hurting the fair market up here, which affects my operation. I think the McLaurys and Clantons may be part of it. Both have ranches to the south and are said to serve as middlemen to the rustlers, buying cattle brought up across the border, rebranding and selling them cheap here in town."

"You're the second man to mention this to me."

"Shows people are finally taking note. I fear these rustlers are getting more bold, as nobody is making any effort to go after them. I know you can handle yourself, Doc, but you'd best take care when you sit down with those men."

"I shall be on my guard."

Hooker and I had a late supper again and, as it was his last night in town, we got drunk after. I had not cut loose in such a manner in some time, so I enjoyed getting somewhat ridiculous as such a state was most amenable with a like-minded friend. When we finally staggered to the hotel, Hooker shook my hand and slapped me on the back. "You get up my way, stop in and we'll have a drink and play some poker. Otherwise, I'll see you next time in town."

"Thanks for the invitation," I managed. "I will see you here or there."

He found this hilarious and laughed his way upstairs while I sought my own bed, into which I collapsed and had a fine sleep.

Hooker had brought Wyatt back to me, and I was most grateful. Next morning when I woke hacking and spitting, head somewhat pained from the night's excess, my first thought was Wyatt in Wichita. Didn't matter I never knew him there. Secondhand was fine, and once I'd righted myself, I wondered what he was up to that very minute. After envisioning him going around Dodge and looking in at the Long Branch, I had him stop to consider us, as I wanted to believe I remained with him as much as he did me. Such notions were fanciful, though, so after a while I pushed him from my mind and went about my day. Then, a couple months later, he pushed back.

I could scarcely believe my eyes at finding his name on a letter the postal clerk handed me. I hurried to my room to read it in private, then read it again and again.

Dear Doc,

How does Tombstone find you? I hope you thrive at both dentistry and gaming, for certainly such a booming place will welcome both. As I said a while back, I do not plan to be a lawman forever and so have given my resignation to Dodge City in favor of looking toward enterprises west. Mattie and

I will be packing up soon to come out by wagon and join you in Tombstone. I have convinced my brothers, Jim, Virgil, and Morgan, and their wives to join us. We Earp boys intend to make our mark. Look for us in a few weeks. It will be good to see you again.

Wyatt

I could not believe it. I held the letter, written in his hand, signed with his name, yet still questioned it, as life seldom dealt me a decent hand. Wyatt was coming to Tombstone. I said it aloud to get it to sink in, then said it again, as I had not considered his previous talk on the idea anything more than idle speculation. All this time, I could have been enjoying anticipation instead of heartache. I let loose a laugh and fell onto my bed to let him fill my every inch, replaying our fucking to such extent I had to get out my dick and pull it to a most glorious eruption.

The idea of Wyatt's coming to Tombstone set me to near frenzy, and from then on, I abused myself morning and night in both recall and anticipation. My improved mood was noted by several men, but I put them off by saying it was nothing more than my finally managing to acclimate to the hellish heat and eternal wind. I also put off Billy Leonard's advances by getting him so drunk he passed out.

I wrote to Wyatt, telling him my pleasure at his coming west and asking him to write again when he was to depart. I had to reel myself in, lest I begin to gush. It took over an hour to compose the letter, which I closed by stating I was at the Cosmopolitan Hotel and recommended it highly. Two weeks later, came his reply:

Dear Doc,

We depart September 4 and expect to see you a few weeks after, depending on our progress. We must go through Prescott to pick up Virgil and Allie, as he is a constable there. Jim and Bessie travel with us. Morgan and Louisa are in Montana and will come down later on. I hope you are doing well and have not shot anyone.

Wyatt

Chapter Four

That's Doc Holliday," a husky voice boomed from down the bar.

"Doctor of what?" came the response.

"Some say cards." The first laughed. "Some say teeth."

"I hear he's killed a few men."

"Quick on the draw."

Then came a scoff. "We'll see about that."

Two men standing beside me decided they should be elsewhere, one knocking back his drink before departing, the other leaving his glass half full. Their haste announced the two conversationalists who moved in next to me.

"Buy the good doctor a drink, Johnny," said the booming fellow. The bigger of the two, he bore a head of dark hair so curly his hat could barely contain it. His grin was wide, his dark eyes flashing, and he bore the stink of the unwashed.

"Have a drink on me, Doctor," said the one called Johnny. He was around my height, though heavier, as were most. In contrast to his friend, he was somewhat slick in a blue shirt, fine leather vest, and dark pants. His features were refined where his friend's were blunt, and his mustache was trimmed to a dark stripe above a wicked mouth. Had I not found his tone patronizing, he might have been appealing.

"Thank you, gentlemen, but I already have my whiskey," I said, raising my glass.

"A man should not refuse a friendly offer," Johnny replied.

"But you are not my friend."

"Then let me correct that oversight. I am Johnny Ringo and this is Curly Bill Brocius. We just got in and are looking to celebrate recent good fortune."

"Then I will leave you to it." I finished my drink, but when I attempted to pass, Brocius stepped in my way. "You gonna put up with that, Johnny? He won't let you buy him a drink and now he fixes to turn his back on you."

"I assure you, Mr. Brocius," I remarked, "I know better than to turn my back on either of you."

"You calling me out?" he said.

"I'm leaving. The air in here has turned foul."

"All right, boys, that's enough," Marshal White said, suddenly between us. His deputy hovered behind him. "Curly Bill, you go on. There is no need to stir trouble when everyone is having a fine time. You too, Johnny. I mean to keep the peace here and now."

Silence had come up around us. Men had ceased their talk, and the sounds of chairs scraping the floor had died away. The room was still, save for Marshal White's demand.

"I'm not looking for trouble," Ringo said, not to the marshal but to me. "But if I find it, I will not turn away."

"It's right here if you so desire," I said, for I would not be intimidated.

"That's enough, Doc," White snapped. "Go on, you two."

Curly Bill issued a laugh. "Come on, Johnny. He ain't worth spit."

Ringo did not laugh. His upper lip gave the slightest twitch before he turned and gave his friend a shove as they went out. Marshal White and his deputy followed, and as I watched them leave, I caught sight of a black-clad figure standing off to one side. It was Wyatt.

"I'm proud of you, Doc," he said when I reached him. "You didn't shoot him."

"Considered it."

"How the hell are you?" he asked, at which I broke into a smile and answered truthfully, "Better now."

"Buy you a drink?"

"Absolutely. When did you get in?"

"This afternoon. We put up at the Cosmopolitan like you said."

I could not get enough of him. Didn't matter the words, I filled up on his presence, six long months gone in a flash. "I can't believe you did it," I finally managed. "I thought that talk on turning in your badge was just that, talk. Your letter surprised the hell out of me, and even then, I couldn't believe it real."

"I am tired of the law, Doc, and I want to make some money. This place is as alive as I have ever seen a town. The Earp boys will do well. I mean to make it happen."

"Strange to see you without a badge."

He opened his coat to show me he wore no gun. "I travel light now," he said. "Feels good."

"Suits you."

I asked after the family and feasted on him as he told of the others, all settled at the hotel. "You'll have to meet Virgil and Allie and say hello to Jim and Bessie. Come to supper tomorrow night."

"I would like nothing better," I lied, and because I was nearly beside myself with arousal, I asked what he was up to now.

"Pretty late," he said. "I just came out to find you and let you know we'd arrived."

"That all?"

Never mind the commerce around us. That sexual storm of his swept in like a prairie conflagration. "Let's go," I said and he did not hesitate.

We strode to the hotel in silence, going in like we weren't both toting erections. He hovered behind me as I unlocked my door, and soon as it opened he pushed me inside and kicked it shut. "Strip," he commanded and we both shed our clothes. When I stood bare before him, he said only, "I cannot tell you," before pushing me onto the bed and mounting me from behind.

What surprised me was he didn't just get in and take off. Oh, he shoved it deep and I let out a welcoming "hell yes," but he remained still a couple seconds, hands on my hips. "Welcome home," I added, at which he chuckled and started to thrust.

How many times had I pulled my dick with thoughts of this? How often had I lay in this very bed dreaming of him upon me? I clenched my bottom muscle as if it could tell him this, for I wanted him to know what he meant to me, how life without him was not a true life. As I reeled with the fuck, I cared about nothing and no one, just Wyatt and me, his dick in my bottom.

"Oh, Christ, Doc," he said as he grew urgent.

"Give it to me, Wyatt, give me what I have been wanting. Choke me with come."

I kept on in this manner as he rode out his release, frenzied both from his dick work and the talk. Never before had I been so inspired, but never before had I lost and regained this man.

Finally, he finished and pulled out. "Goddamn," he said. I fell over onto my back, grateful I hadn't yet shot my stuff as I wanted his mouth to take it from me. He took but a few seconds to gain enough breath to permit just that, and I pulled a second pillow under my head to watch him descend onto me.

He was most hungry, licking my rod, then opening to take the whole of me. Closing onto my pole, he started his tongue working, sucking and pulling until I could not help but squirm. When my spunk began to rise I called out, "Wyatt!" Then I let go a load I'd built for two days, having held off self-abuse for no apparent reason beyond instinct, which must have known such restraint would come to some good.

When I had been sucked dry, my spent cock was released, but Wyatt did not right himself as expected. Instead he lay with his head on my leg, nose mere inches from my privates. He slid his legs up toward the pillow so we were in reverse, much to my amusement. I could see he meant to play awhile and I reached over to squeeze his calf.

"Is this the enterprise you seek?" I asked.

"Part of it. You were missed." He gazed quite contentedly from his place at my crotch and I coveted the sight.

"You too, as you have just seen."

"Your cough is better," he noted.

"Everything is better. The chest pain has gone and the cough is now tolerable." As if on cue, it rose up but not enough to demand whiskey. "This air will dry out your every inch," I added. "Wait and see. Sweat hasn't time to sit on your skin before it's gone."

He issued a long sigh, which I saw as comfort. How it pleased me to give him such. He appeared generally more relaxed, more at peace than I had ever seen, but I did not remark on it. I just kept my eyes on his.

When he asked about the encounter in the Oriental, he started running a finger down around my nuts. I spread my legs to accommodate and told him the men were new to me. "Johnny Ringo, the slick one, and Curly Bill Brocius, that curly head of hair. Just two more rowdies looking to make trouble."

"Is that what would have happened if the marshal hadn't stepped in?"

"Hard to say. Pair of fools like that are going to get it one day."

He palmed one of my nuts, much to my delight, but I managed to continue. "Funny thing, you not being the one to break it up. Times have certainly changed."

"I enjoyed looking on for once."

"It is somewhat a lawless place, Wyatt. Marshal White and his deputies are outmanned by rowdies and rustlers."

"That is not my problem." To close the subject, he ran a couple fingers into my butthole and after working me some, said to roll over. I did as instructed and felt him get in behind. He parted my buttocks and paused, I supposed to enjoy seeing where his dick was about to go. He then leaned in and gave my pucker a lick, which caused me to suck in a breath and cough. He offered a murmur of approval at the sight before him, then settled in to attend me at length, running his tongue up and down my crack and teasing me with pokes until I begged him to put it in. He did as asked, shoving his tongue into the filthy hole, at which I got a hand onto my cock as it began to stir.

It crossed my mind, as the former lawman ate my ass, that his wife and family were upstairs and thinking him merely out around town. This notion served to heighten my pleasure, for here he was, his first night, and instead of a hand on his wife's tit, he had his nose in my crack. I stroked my prick, savoring not only his feast but the knowledge he was working himself up to another fuck.

I knew I was going to get it good when the pig in him let loose. All men, no matter their efforts toward cleanliness, me included, are part pig, and when that porker takes over, he cannot get deep enough into the wallow. Wyatt's pig announced itself with a snorfling such as I had heard once at my uncle's pig pen. Had not a man's tongue been expertly abusing my butthole, I would have said an animal was at work back there.

At last, he was so worked up he pulled off, repositioned, and rammed his cock in to the root, and this time he did not stop to consider his whereabouts. It was a full-out, hard-riding fuck from the get-go, and I came a gusher as he got himself going. I cried out as I emptied, and in reply he slapped my bottom.

By the time he came, we reeked of sex, as did the room. A hot day had left my abode warm and stuffy and now hotter still. We swam in sweat, fucking apparently the only thing able to overpower the dry air. That I began to cough was to be expected, and when it would not relent, I got up for whiskey.

"You just about did me in, Doc," Wyatt said when he'd joined me with a drink.

"My pleasure," I replied. "It has been too long."

"Well, that's fixed."

"Most certainly." We lay next to each other, falling silent as I wondered if he would finish his drink and jump up to go home to his wife or at least speak on the entanglement to ease his guilt. He surprised me by doing neither, so I changed a subject that had not been broached.

"How was Dodge after I left?" I asked.

"I had to kill a man."

"I am sorry to hear that. What happened?"

"You remember Bert Hicks? Some fellows robbed and beat him one night when he was drunk and I happened onto the scene. I buffaloed one, but the other fired, and I had no choice."

"Is that why you left?"

"No, but it added weight to the decision I'd pretty much made."

"Well, whatever your reason, it was a good one. Opportunity abounds out here."

"It better."

I rolled onto my side, put an arm across his chest, and nuzzled his neck. "You'll do fine," I assured him. "Of that I am certain."

Lying together, we must have slipped into a doze, for Wyatt suddenly sat up. "What time is it?" he said as he hopped up to find his pocket watch. "Not here to sleep," he added as he dressed. I offered no comment. At the door he looked back. "Doc," was all he said.

Next afternoon, I saw him coming up Allen Street with a man I took to be his brother Virgil, as I knew the other one, Jim, the oldest, since he had tended bar in Dodge. Jim's wife, Bessie, had run a brothel there. Jim had been wounded in the war and thus kept a low profile. I had known him as more pliable than Wyatt and somewhat mellow. Now I wondered about Virgil, who I knew was between Jim and Wyatt in age.

"Doc," Wyatt called out. "This is my brother, Virgil. Virg, this is Doc Holliday."

"It is a pleasure to know you, Virgil," I said, extending a hand. He looked so much like Wyatt that I fixed my eyes on him in wonder.

"Your reputation precedes you," he said as we shook. His grip was iron and came with no smile.

"Virg," Wyatt said.

"Don't believe everything you hear," I cut in, to which he did not respond. "I understand you boys are going into business."

"That is our intention," he said.

"Virgil is a U.S. Marshal," Wyatt explained, and when his brother made no comment, he turned another direction. "You're still planning on supper with us tonight, aren't you, Doc?"

"That I am. I recommend Lawson's on Fremont Street. Good service, better food."

"Then Lawson's it is. See you at six."

As I watched them stride on down the sidewalk, I noted they even moved the same way, both straight-backed and determined. I wondered if Virgil cut loose in bed as Wyatt did.

After playing faro at the Alhambra the rest of the afternoon, I changed to a fresh suit, a favored yellow shirt, gray tie with diamond stickpin, and went over to Lawson's. I had waited until I knew they would all be seated in order to avoid awkwardness at arrangements. They were three on each side of a long table, each man opposite his wife, and a bottle of wine was already being consumed. An empty chair sat waiting for me at the table's end. Upon my entering, Wyatt stood.

"Jim, you and Bessie know Doc."

"Good to see you again," Jim said, remaining seated but offering his hand.

"Doc," Bessie said. For a madam, she had a surprisingly homespun air, which I knew soothed Jim.

"You met Virgil. This is his wife, Allie."

"I am pleased to meet you, Allie."

"Likewise," she said. It took but the one word to betray her Irish roots as she possessed that particular lilt one heard from those come over on a boat. She could not have been more than twenty, and thus a contrast to her husband, who I calculated to be thirty-six to Wyatt's thirty-two.

"And you remember Mattie," Wyatt said.

"Of course. Mattie, I am happy to see you did well with the journey. This husband of yours seems determined to become a businessman."

She nodded and looked elsewhere, but I did not let her lack of sociability intrude on what was to be a fine evening. It did, however, cross my mind that women were possessed of an infernal intuition and that such an aberration might have led her to suspect Wyatt had already gotten at me.

"Tells us about Tombstone," Wyatt said when we had ordered. I began to describe the nature of the place and who was prominent, who seemed in charge, and which businesses were thriving.

"Who is the Wells Fargo agent?" he asked when I'd gone on long enough.

"Marshall Williams, a fine man."

"Good. I'll stop by. I made inquiries today with a property fellow and find there are several houses for rent on Fourth Street, so we will be taking those."

It soon became obvious that Wyatt was the general of the Earp family, never mind he was the middle son. The strong and decisive nature that served him well in law enforcement did much the same in family matters. "I spoke with the owner of the Oriental Saloon today," he went on. "Milt Joyce. He says we can buy into the gaming concession."

This surprised me, as Milt Joyce was a hard man who I did not particularly like. When I said as much, Wyatt explained. "He seems just that, but when he found out who I was, he liked the idea of a man of my repute being part owner. Said it would help keep down the riffraff."

Virgil seemed amused at this, though he did not smile. "Not in town a day and already arranging things," he said of Wyatt.

"I am not a man to wait around," Wyatt countered.

"No, you are not," Virgil said. "Never have been, never will be."

Wyatt chuckled at this, and I saw brotherly affection in the exchange, the older giving way and apparently enjoying the arrangement. "We are looking to invest in water and mining claims," Wyatt went on, turning to me as our food was served. "Appears water is almost as valuable as silver." The women began to eat, as did Jim and Virgil, while Wyatt and I continued to talk of opportunity. He was afire with possibilities, which excited me as it was a side I had not seen before. Though he did not much fit the idea of businessman, he seemed bent on making prosperity work around him. I admired his gumption, as Tombstone thrived on just that.

"You said Morgan is due to join you," I noted when talk of opportunity had wound down.

"Yes. He and Louisa need to settle up where they are. Should be along soon."

"Is he in law enforcement?" I asked.

"Not at present, but he was a deputy for a while. Seems the Earps always lean that way."

"And is he the youngest?"

"No, that would be Warren, but he prefers to remain in California with the folks, so it will be just us four. Morgan is about your age, Doc. Twenty-nine."

"So he is. I enjoyed my twenty-ninth just last month."

"Well, a happy birthday to you, then," he said, raising his glass.

The others did the same, and I savored the moment of recognition from a family that was not mine.

Later, as we enjoyed a fine chocolate layer cake and coffee for dessert, I could not help but mention the resemblance between Wyatt and Virgil. This got a giggle from Allie and a roll of the eyes from Mattie. "It is uncanny," Jim said. "You look at me, you'd hardly think me an Earp, then you look at these two and think they might be twins."

Allie gazed upon her man, clearly doting on the similarity. "Same gruff manner, same hard look at life, same determination to make things better for all around them. But I will say I believe my Virgil the better looking. Mattie, you, of course, would beg to differ."

A good laugh went around the table while I kept silent. Virgil was indeed striking, the same dark blond hair and steely blue eyes, but whatever the similarity might be, Wyatt wore it better. I started to wonder if he might get away later on.

When supper ended, we saw the ladies to their rooms. Jim pleaded fatigue and joined them while Virgil, Wyatt, and I sought a poker game at the Oriental. Milt Joyce greeted Wyatt warmly as we passed the bar. We then took up a game for several hours until Virgil declared himself done in and left. Wyatt and I kept on awhile, winning mostly, then around two a.m. called it a night. Once outside, we paused to look at a clear sky whose stars sparkled down on us. He then laid a hand on my shoulder just as he had done that first time in Dodge. Leaning in close, he said into my ear, "I mean to fuck you, Doc."

"By all means," I replied and we hurried to my room.

Once alone, we stripped naked. I coughed only a little as he stood me at the bedpost, harking back to our first in Dodge. "Christ, Doc," was all he said as he shoved in and set up a fucking that was rough and quick. Before I could do much at all, he roared and pumped into me so hard my grip on the bedpost nearly failed. He grunted and growled like some bear chewing a carcass, but at last was done and slipped out.

Breathing hard, he pulled me back to him and ran a hand down to discover me still primed. Issuing a moan, he flipped me around, dropped to his knees, and sucked the cream out of me. As I unloaded, he squeezed my buttocks, sucking and slopping until he'd fairly devoured me.

My legs did not fail me and Wyatt took note as he rose back up. "You are holding up better than in Dodge," he said.

"Weather is a remarkable remedy," I replied.

He had me loosely in his arms, and while my body remained sure, my innards were in a swoon not only at what we'd done but at his hands remaining upon me. "One ain't gonna be enough," he said.

"I am at your disposal," I assured him as I reached for his cock. He sucked in a breath at this, easing his hips forward in welcome while a finger found its way into my crack. I spread my legs to admit him and he wet the finger, then put it into me, prodding while I pulled his dick.

The urge to put my mouth upon his was at me again, his proximity a wonderful agony of closeness and distance. I allowed consideration of such a thing, even as I would make no such move, thinking on how his lips and that masterful tongue would feel. I had to make myself push aside such fancy as we continued to work each other toward another go.

As a person undoubtedly headed for hell, I nevertheless knew none but heaven at this juncture, for Wyatt and I were both descending from satisfaction while ascending toward a repeat. The only better place a man could find himself would be in the throes of climax.

Soon Wyatt's prick was stiff and wet and my bottom was eager for occupation. "Goddamn, Wyatt, fuck me," I rasped.

He pushed me onto the bed, put me onto all fours, got in behind, and drove it in, which caused me to utter a squeal of sorts, man's version of stuck pig. And stick me he did, going at me so long I shot another modest load into the covers. When he finally moaned and came, my bottom was so chafed I knew I'd sit carefully next day.

"Hell, Doc," Wyatt said as he pulled out and fell beside me. "We're gonna kill each other."

"Not a bad way to go."

Chapter Five

Wyatt bought a 25 percent stake in the Oriental Saloon's gambling concession, which led him to spend many an evening there. He ran a faro game while I kept to my poker, and it pleased me to see him settle further into my life. He was a fine card player, so it was a good fit, and his air of authority meant few would challenge him when they lost. Milt Joyce even softened a little due to Wyatt's presence. Those who now sought trouble in Milt's place were soon dispatched to the street, often pulled along by an ear, as Wyatt was without fear in taming even the most unruly men.

Nights ran late for him with this arrangement and he was on occasion sufficiently wound up to want some unwinding. It would start by him giving me the eye as his players considered the cards on his table, and I would eye him back until my dick was so hard I could not stand it. I would then cash out of my game, leave the saloon, go to my room, and strip naked. He soon followed and we had a good fuck that began almost the second he was in the door. That he did not arrive home until two or three o'clock in the morning could not be questioned by his wife due to the nature of his business.

"I am taking a job with Wells Fargo," he said one night after he'd gone at me twice and we lay spent. "Shotgun messenger on the Benson stage."

"Why is that?" I drawled from near stupor. I had not a drop of energy or come left in me.

"I can't make it on my twenty-five percent at the Oriental, and the claims aren't paying anything yet. The current messenger is looking to move on, so the position has opened up."

"Smart men, Wells and Fargo. I would not want to try and get a strongbox out from under you."

"I'll ride the stage six days a week."

"So you'll be up and back in a day."

"Unless I lay over in Benson."

I rolled over to run a hand up his leg. "I won't see as much of you."

"You'll see plenty."

Two days later, he departed aboard the Benson stage. I made it a point to be nearby when he climbed up beside driver Bud Philpott, shotgun in hand. The strongbox was then handed up, a formidable-looking thing no doubt carrying silver. It was tucked under the seat while passengers got into the coach. Most were local men with business elsewhere, but one looked so ragged and worn he had to be a failed miner spending his last going home. Though riches did abound in Tombstone, failure resided alongside, as many a man, often due to bad habits, slid to the bottom.

Wyatt caught my eye and nodded and I could not help but think, as they rolled away toward Benson, how he was inching back toward his lawman role. First as enforcer in the Oriental and now much the same for Wells Fargo. How long would it be before he pinned on a badge?

The best part of Wyatt's stage work turned out to be his coming in nights impatient to get down off his perch. He kept the strongbox safe but did not care much for the work. "No different than long hours in the saddle," he said, "although I do believe a horse gives a smoother ride. Damned stagecoach hits every hole in the road."

He was always riled when he got back, and I had to wonder if his mind got working toward manly needs as he bumped along from Benson. He'd find me at the Alhambra or Oriental or wherever I'd settled for the night's gaming and he'd throw back a drink while standing near my game. Such a heat would come off him that I would cash out, even if down, which said something about his pull. On the way to my room, he'd talk about the day's trip, as there was usually some annoyance, be it a loose wheel or lame horse or just Bud Philpott, who was known to seldom stop talking.

In the first two weeks of his employment, he fucked me almost every time he returned from Benson, so I came to look most favorably on Wells and Fargo. That he came in bearing trail dirt seemed to fire him, as if he looked to get still dirtier by way of his dick. He'd do it rough and growl as he unloaded, then settle down to join me in a good wallow. Even when he'd come twice, he'd still play around with me, putting a finger or two up my butthole to prod until I squirmed. He just did not want to stop and neither did I. I petted his furry chest, nipped his tit nubs, and sometimes ran my tongue over his various parts as he became most accommodating with his body. Tombstone, I decided, was turning out to be more opportune than anticipated.

Not quite a month had passed when some fools attempted to rob the stage about halfway to Benson. News of these events came to Tombstone by wire before Wyatt returned. The local telegraph operator was prone to gossip, so word spread around town, reaching the Oriental and causing great commotion. By the time Wyatt returned, I had the details and decided to forgo cards in favor of waiting for him outside. I knew the strongbox had not been taken, nor had the mail or any valuables from the passengers. Wyatt had shot two of the four robbers, both left for dead by their fleeing cohorts. Authorities from Benson were en route to pick up the bodies.

When the stage rolled in later on, Wyatt sat up top, shotgun across his lap as if it had not moved since he left. He saw me, hopped down, and came over. "We had a holdup," he said. He was most agitated. "I shot two, but they didn't get the strongbox. I am going to Wells Fargo and make a report. Wait for me."

"I'll be right here."

Half an hour later, he came up but did not sit. "Come on, get your horse."

"Wyatt, I am not going to chase stage robbers in the middle of the night. And neither should you."

"That is not what I mean to do. It's a fine night and I don't want to be indoors just yet. You get that?"

"I surely do," I said and we walked down to the stable where we got our horses. Wyatt's had a bedroll which would serve as accommodations.

We rode over to the San Pedro River, then turned south and followed along until well away from civilization. The moon was a half, which gave us some light, things blue-gray and warm. "Here," Wyatt said, guiding his horse to a bank of trees. We dismounted, tied the horses, and without a word, he undid his bedroll and spread it on the ground.

When he looked at me, I said, "We gonna do it?" which got a sharp laugh out of him.

"Hell, yes," he said and began to strip. Soon as we were bare he came at me, prick in the lead. "Get down," he growled and I obliged, at which he wet his rod, got behind, and shoved in. "Christ, Doc," was all he managed before succumbing to a hard ride and quick come. I, meanwhile, shot a load into the bedding soon as he was into me, such was my anticipation. "Damn," Wyatt said when he regained his voice. "That was too quick."

We fell beside each other, stretched out under the stars. "No need to settle for one," I reminded him, sliding a hand onto his spent cock. He allowed a receptive moan as he gradually settled. I played around with his soft prick, then got my mouth onto him. Easing down between his legs, which he parted for me, I feasted on his morsel while my hand cupped his balls. Tempted as I was to work a finger back to his center, I thought better of it, as I doubted Wyatt Earp would allow any man his butthole. Still, the proximity of his pucker enticed me. As I played with him, his hands moved over me at times, then quieted at others. We went like this for a good while, and I felt him more receptive than usual, which I decided was due to us being outdoors, nobody down the street to be of concern.

When his prick began to stiffen and he rose up to get at me, I put him off. "Let me," I said, and he lay back down, which allowed me to wet him with spit, then climb over.

As I descended, he said, "Holy hell."

"Lie still," I said as I started to ride, first with an easy canter, then lifting myself up and down to pretty much fuck myself. It was testament to my improved condition that while I coughed some, my legs held up better than they would have back in Dodge. Another good thing in taking him astride was watching his expression, which I didn't often see, what with him usually taking me from behind. I enjoyed him there in the half light, eyes wide with pleasure, jaw set, teeth bared. Best look a man can have.

He began to eye my stiff dick after a while and grabbed hold. He pulled at me until I spurted my stuff all up his chest, which in turn fired him such that he seized me at the waist and rammed up into me, grunting as he let go. When he had emptied, I climbed off and lay beside him. He blew out a long breath, which I took as positive comment.

We lay quiet, both in need of recovery, my cough the only sound. With him so close and in such calm, feelings that begged airing churned up in me, but I knew better than to set them free. Wyatt might be able to fuck me, but I doubted he could handle what lay behind it, and I made myself accept this, satisfied there with him, just us two. No town, no woman, no cards or law or need of a living. It was perfect.

I think we dozed a bit. The warm air lulled us some, which was understandable, given our activity and his day's events. Then I felt his hand upon my chest, rubbing my tits. I issued a welcoming murmur and he leaned over and began to lick one while his fingers sought the other. I was thus groomed and pinched until he started to suck the little nub.

Though his mouth was fixed on me, his body was far from idle. He writhed and rumbled throughout until I was so worked up I had to get a hand on my dick and start to pull. When he'd had his fill of tit sucking, he reared back, wild-eyed, flipped himself around, and as he took my cock into his mouth, he dropped his own into mine. And there we lay, sucking pricks, half a moon looking on.

As we had both already come, our respective meals were lengthy, which added to the pleasure. He pulled off me once and raised up, shook himself like a wet dog, then dove back down. I attributed this to his reveling in the moment, taking time to observe where he was and what he had done, what he would continue to do. His return to my prick was most ardent, and before long I bucked and shot a remaining few drops into his throat. Not a minute later, he was pumping his cock into me and I was attempting to neither cough nor strangle as I swallowed his last.

Rolling off, he suggested we get back to town. "Why?" I asked. "A fine night like this should not be wasted indoors."

"You are the devil, Doc," he replied as he lay back down.

We did not get back to town until nearly sunrise. Though we did sleep some, much of the ensuing night was passed in exploration of each other, though I kept my hands off his bottom. He much attended mine, however, with fingers when his dick was done. And we sucked cock to excess, never mind they were spent. We wished only to be upon each other and proceeded to such extent that Wyatt, when dawn began to hint at arrival, turned me onto my stomach and raised my bottom.

"Good day starts with a fuck," he declared as he shoved in and began to go at me. I did not argue and lay happily receiving him. Climax was elusive for Wyatt this day, and sweat was flying when he finally hit the rise. He let out a roar as he rammed it home, while I didn't bother attempting much. Taking him was all I needed for my good day's start.

"Going to sit easy in my saddle," I remarked as I climbed onto my horse not half an hour later. "Though most happily," I added. Wyatt said nothing and I saw he was getting back into his authority role. Marshaling would likely never leave him, as if pinned to his skin. He rode straight in the saddle while I was pleasantly crumpled. Back in town, he said he'd tell Mattie he gambled all night. The sun was up by then, and I doubted he would get into her bed.

The attempted stage robbery prompted U.S. Marshal Crawley Dake, who was based in Prescott, to call upon Virgil and ask him to set up an office as Deputy U.S. Marshal in Tombstone. "Will he do it?" I asked Wyatt when he related this to me one night at the Oriental. He'd had a couple days off the stage run and was somewhat mellow.

"Don't know," he said. "Let's ask him." I turned to see Virgil coming in. He joined us at the bar.

"Wyatt, Doc," he said.

"Virgil," I replied. We got along no better but no worse than at our first meeting, which seemed all I was going to get from him. I had concluded he was quite different from Wyatt. Though both were stone-faced, Virgil was more granite, while Wyatt I saw as a permeable sandstone.

"You decided yet about marshaling?" Wyatt asked him.

Virgil did not hurry his reply. He was not a man to be rushed, in contrast to his brother, who was most eager in all he considered. Virgil sipped his drink, looked around, then came to it. "Suppose I will," he said. "I am in need of occupation beyond claims that may not do well."

Wyatt shook his head. "Dammit, Virg, I thought we swore off law enforcement."

"That was you. I went along, but I am not averse to getting back into it. It's what we do, Wyatt, and we have a good name at it."

"It is not a name I want," Wyatt countered.

"Fair enough, but I am going ahead. Dake is looking for office space over on Fifth Street."

"Doc Goodfellow has an office there," I noted.

"That's it. Next to him, I guess."

The two began to hash over the venture to such extent I left to play faro. Wyatt did not call on me that night, and I slept fitfully, then saw him next day beside a wagon on Allen Street. I watched as the driver hopped down and helped a woman descend. Deciding this must be brother Morgan, I went over.

"Doc," Wyatt called. "Come and meet the rest of the family. This is my brother Morgan and his wife, Louisa."

Morgan offered a wide smile as he shook my hand and said how Wyatt had spoken favorably of me.

"Your brother is most generous," I replied. "Louisa," I said as I took his wife's hand. She was delicate in appearance, small with dark hair, yet she gave off an appealing sturdiness. They made a handsome couple, though I'd have to say Morgan was the looker.

He was a six-footer, like any self-respecting Earp would not settle for less, but he did not have the ramrod stiffness of his brothers. His laugh was easy and he seemed more comfortable in his skin as he looked around.

"There is the pool hall," Wyatt said, pointing to Hatch and Campbell's place. "Morgan is an expert player," Wyatt said to me.

"We will have to have a game," I replied.

It amused me as we talked to consider that Wyatt drew me more than this stunner, so I allowed carnal thoughts of Morgan, simply to acknowledge his fine looks. Though I thought he would likely be a good one to bed, I found he did not stir me as did his brother. This pleased me by way of confirming the depth of my devotion to Wyatt. I then set aside such thoughts, knowing Morgan and I would become the friends that Virgil and I would not.

Wyatt soon got Morgan a part-time job tending bar at the Oriental while Louisa set up housekeeping in a cottage near the others. Morgan quickly settled into life with his brothers, and the three could often be seen around town together. Sometimes when Wyatt was on the Benson run, Morgan would join me at cards or I him at pool. He was indeed expert and I seldom won, but then he seldom beat me at cards, so it evened out. Mostly, he was an entertaining companion full of good stories and always ready to cut up. He also did not object to getting drunk, and more than once we two staggered down the street laughing at nothing.

"How did you come to be so different in temperament from your brothers?" I asked over pool one night.

He laughed. "The family joke is I was hatched from the egg of a doodle bird out on the prairie and Pa brought me home in a sack."

"That would explain it."

"I just enjoy life, Doc, and with Wyatt around there is no need for me to try to run things. I have a good woman and no complaints."

At this point, he went on to clear the table of all its colored balls, beating me yet again. I then sat out so Hatch, who was better at the game, could play. Joking and laughter continued, even getting Hatch to loosen up more than usual, but Morgan did that, got all in his company to have a fine time.

Some days later, four army soldiers rode into town. As the nearest fort was seventy-five miles east, heads turned. These blue-uniformed men were most impressive, sitting tall in their saddles, but in my mind they could not outdo the straight-backed Earps. Much speculation followed their arrival, especially when Virgil and Morgan rode from town with them a bit later.

"Indians," one onlooker declared as we watched them leave. "Troops only come around if Indians are on the warpath."

This served to work several people into a nervous state until another man said it was not Indians but a stage robbery and troops were needed, as the outlaws were too numerous for the usual posse. Others challenged such a notion, as the Earps were considered formidable in all circumstances. At last, Wyatt came up and set the matter straight.

"Army mules," he said. "Stolen and said to be at the McLaury ranch. Virgil was asked to assist the soldiers and he deputized Morgan to help."

"Did he ask you to go along?" I inquired.

"He knew better. I am no longer a lawman."

"No Indians?" the man still asked. "I don't believe it. The army wouldn't care about a few mules."

"They care about theft of government property," Wyatt explained. He then strode away, and I thought it better not to follow.

Virgil and Morgan got in around nine that night, minus both the army and any prisoners. As I was out front at Hafford's corner, I saw them come up Fifth Street, where they turned their horses in at the Circle Livery. When they reached the corner, I asked how it went.

"It went," Virgil snapped and he stalked off up the street.

"How about a drink?" I said to Morgan.

"Fine idea, Doc."

As we were at Hafford's, we went in there and I got the story from Morgan. "Whole thing was a waste of time. The mules were at McLaury's, being rebranded, but this lieutenant in charge allowed Tom and Frank to promise to return the mules next week over in Charleston. Virgil got hot about this arrangement, but the army fellow would not listen. Those mules will be long sold when next week comes around."

"Good thing Wyatt didn't join your posse," I observed.

Morgan laughed. "You got that. Only thing worse than a pissed-off Virgil is a pissed off Wyatt, as he is liable to crack a man's skull."

"You think Wyatt will ever get back into law enforcement?" I asked.

"I do not doubt but he will. Doesn't matter his complaints. There is too much lawlessness here to allow him the quiet he seeks, and it's in his nature to set things right. The more he says he won't wear a badge, the more likely he'll do just that."

I chuckled. "Why does it please me to hear that?"

"Because when he's not the marshal or sheriff, things are off-kilter. I don't care where we are, Wyatt is a lawman through and through. Anybody that fierce about upholding the law has to wear a badge."

I enjoyed talk of Wyatt with somebody who not only cared as much as I did but also liked to talk about him. Morgan lit up when he spoke of Wyatt, and I saw love and admiration upon him, but then Morgan was easy with his feelings, unlike the others.

"Who do you take after?" I asked later on. "Who does Wyatt?" We had decided to go to Hatch's for pool and we were walking over there.

"Pa is a no-nonsense man and had great influence over the older boys. When I came along, Ma determined to spare me and kept me close to her. She is a bighearted woman with a ready laugh who likes to sing and tell a joke. She lit up the house. Were it not for her, Pa would have had the place somber as an undertaker's."

"You Earps are an interesting bunch," I observed. "And most entertaining."

I lost to him at pool but did not care as by then I was drunk and having a high time. Morgan and I wandered home in the wee hours and I slept until noon. Later that week, word came that the stolen mules had not been returned to the army and further, that the McLaurys rode into Charleston and laughed in that lieutenant's face, telling him they'd offered to return the mules only to avoid the Earp party.

Virgil's reaction to this news became public when he and Wyatt got into an argument on Allen Street, one brother attempting to keep the other from a bad move. I had rounded Hafford's corner when I caught sight of the familiar figures across the street and, seeing them most animated, went over. Several people had paused to listen but stood well away from the display.

"You'll just make trouble," Wyatt said to Virgil as I came near. He put a hand on his brother's arm but was shaken off.

"They made fools of us all and I will not have that," Virgil declared. He was red-faced and most heated.

"You'll be the bigger fool if you go out there," Wyatt argued. "The mules are surely sold by now, so you have no evidence. You are angry, Virg, and you need to cool down. Let me buy you a drink."

"I don't want a goddamn drink. I want those McLaurys set right. They stole government property."

"And the government made a poor deal to get it back. It's over. Let it be."

"So they can laugh about it?"

"Who in hell cares what the McLaurys do?"

Just then, Virgil took note of the crowd that had gathered. "What are you looking at?" he demanded. "Go on. Go about your business. This is not your concern."

As people scattered, Wyatt began to cajole. "Come on, Virg."

"Leave me be," Virgil snarled as he walked off.

"Don't go out there," Wyatt pleaded.

"I'm not going out there," Virgil called back. "I'm going home."

"There's the mule," Wyatt said as I came up beside him. "You want a drink, Doc? I could use one."

"As could I."

Once at the Oriental's bar, I ventured an observation. "I used to think you the stubborn one. I have now changed my mind."

Wyatt threw back his drink and huffed out a sigh. "He doesn't take well to being bested even when it's the army being made the fool."

"What now?"

"Oh, he'll stew awhile, then get back to his old self, but the McLaurys had better lay low. They shit wrong, he'll bring 'em in."

I had to laugh. "Nobody killed, nobody even shot, and he's all fired up. What's he like when bullets fly?"

"Best take cover."

After this, I made more of an effort toward Virgil as I became determined to know all the men close to Wyatt. Virgil, in response, gradually warmed to me, as much as granite can warm. Tolerance was what it came to, my not killing anybody, though he did witness the occasional scrape when some fool threatened me and was dealt with. Fred White would then haul me before a judge who would find me justified in my actions but fine me for disturbing the peace. This amused me, as there was little peace to be disturbed.

Now wearing a badge, Virgil made certain his presence was known around town, sometimes on his own, and sometimes with his brothers. They were a formidable sight walking three abreast. Though Virgil was the only official lawman, Wyatt still bore an air of authority that I doubted he would ever shake. Didn't matter he carried no gun; he was sharp with his fists, and when the occasional drunk challenged him, the man was quickly dispatched. Most often, Wyatt pushed away an intruder and went on his way, but a good punch in the gut would drop those going for a gun.

The Earps also made a special effort toward Marshal White, which I saw as a telling alliance. When I noted this to Wyatt, he bristled. "It is always good to know the local law, Doc. Don't read things into it. You don't know my mind."

He soon proved I knew his mind better than he did, as next time he came in from Benson, he said he had been offered a job as deputy sheriff. He handed me a telegram from Sheriff Charlie Shibell over in Tucson. Shibell was asking Wyatt to be the local deputy, as Fred White and his men could not handle the lawlessness in Tombstone, nor could Virgil, who was authorized only for federal matters.

"I'd have authority in Tombstone and can name my own deputy. Pays better than Wells Fargo, as sheriffs get a percentage of taxes."

"Another badge."

"That it is. Hell of a proposition, though. It fixes things in a good way, but still, law enforcement was not in the plan."

"Your reputation precedes you, just as does mine," I said, "only yours works for the better. You going to take it?"

"Can't not. We've made some investments, but nothing is paying off yet, and my twenty-five percent of the Oriental is not enough to get by on. I also do not want to remain a shotgun messenger."

"Deputy U.S. Marshal Virgil Earp and now Deputy Sheriff Wyatt Earp. Plenty of lawmen," I observed.

"Add Fred White, City Marshal, and you've got three jurisdictions having to keep from stepping on each other."

"Bound to keep the riffraff in line, though."

He looked at me hard. "That gonna be you, Doc?"

"Undoubtedly."

He frowned at this, then let it go. "What say we go over to the hotel?"

"For a drink?"

"For a fuck."

Once in my room, we undressed in silence. When bare, he said, "I'll ride to Tucson tomorrow and talk to Shibell."

I approached him, reached down, and grabbed hold of his stiff dick. "I like you being the law."

"So you can play hell with it," he replied as he thrust into my palm.

"Or it with me," I said.

Here he pushed me onto the bed, got my legs up over his shoulders, and plowed his dick into my chute. "Same man under the badge," he said as he began to thrust.

"Better be."

Chapter Six

I did not dwell upon Wyatt going off to Tucson for a new badge. I had a living to earn, so I set up shop at the Oriental where I knew he would come upon his return. Billy Leonard sat in on poker, flush and in high spirits.

"You have a claim paying off?" I asked, knowing he avoided hard labor.

"Kinda," he said with a grin. When he offered nothing more, I let the matter drop, as I knew better than to inquire too much of men with questionable friends. I did take some of his money, though, while enjoying his company, as he was always a companionable fellow. Morgan Earp sat in later on that evening and was just starting to win when Wyatt came in around midnight. Billy was now drunk and at the sight of Wyatt, he vacated the game.

"Deputy sheriff?" I inquired as Wyatt took Billy's chair and was dealt into the game.

He pulled back his coat to reveal the badge. "Morg, I'd like you to be my deputy if you want it. Bob Paul can take the Wells Fargo job. He's just come to town and is looking for work."

"Hell, yes, I want it," Morgan said. "I need wages."

For somebody averse to law enforcement, Wyatt gave off a remarkable satisfaction in his new role. "I'll meet with Fred White tomorrow," he said as we played. "Let him know he's got help. Put a stop to these men running roughshod."

"You're getting right to it," I noted, unable to resist needling him.

"I am on the job now, Doc. I mean to do it well."

"And the businessman?"

He shot me a look and I had to chuckle. It was so easy to rankle him. "Leave off, Doc," he said. "I am bone tired from the long ride and will throw your sorry ass in jail."

"On what charge?"

"Disturbing my goddamn peace."

This got Morgan and me laughing. Wyatt rose. "I am going home to bed, and, Morg, I suggest you do the same. I want you on the job early."

Morgan did not argue. He scooped up his money and followed his brother out while I sat fiddling with the deck and trying to decide if I too should call it a night. Though I coughed some, I had not seriously aggravated my malady lately and thus felt relatively good as one day slipped to the next. While I pondered the situation, Johnny Ringo, Curly Bill Brocious, and Fin Clanton came over.

"The doctor appears to be in," Ringo said as he sat down.

"You gonna let him examine you?" Curly Bill laughed as he and Fin took chairs.

"Gentlemen," I said as I dealt them in, "I am but a poor dentist, but if you insist, I am certain I can find some instrument to shove up your ass." I looked at Ringo as I said this while Curly Bill began to sputter.

"You gonna let him talk to us like that, Johnny?" Curly Bill said.

"Calm down," urged Ringo. "You walked into it. It's your ass he'll prod."

Ringo studied his cards and we settled into play, though Curly Bill was too drunk to do much more than annoy me. Fin Clanton kept to his game, clearly puffed up in Ringo's company.

The remarkable thing is we managed more than an hour before things began to deteriorate. Ringo knew his cards and was as steely-eyed and determined as Wyatt, except he had a mean streak where Wyatt had a heart. Each time I coughed, he studied me, and when I had a hacking fit that held up the game, he saw opportunity. "Sounds like you are not long for this world, lunger," he said with a grin.

When I had the cough under control, I replied, "I hate to disappoint you, Ringo, but things are quite the opposite. I am very long for this world. In fact, I intend to go on breathing air long after you reside on Boot Hill."

He laughed and laid out an inside straight to take the pot. "Only way that will happen is old age," he said. "No man has challenged me and lived."

"Your circle must be rather limited," I countered, dealing a new hand.

He took up his cards, as did the rest of us, Fin Clanton wide-eyed, Curly Bill now reeling so badly he could hardly remain upright.

"Curly Bill, I do believe your night is about over," I observed.

"The hell it is," he said, downing his whiskey and attempting to hold his cards. When they fell from his hand, he began to laugh. "I am drunk, boys. Stinking drunk. I am going to go piss." He rose unsteadily but headed out front toward the street rather than out back to the privy.

"Your friend is going to pee in the street," I told Ringo. "You'd best get him pointed the right direction, as I doubt the citizens of Tombstone wish to see his dick."

Ringo shook his head. "I am playing these cards," he said. "Curly Bill can shit in the street for all I care."

"Of course," I replied. "Whatever made me think of decorum where you fellows are concerned?"

Two other men joined the game about this time and we played but one hand before gunshots were heard out front. "Curly Bill appears to be done pissing," I noted, which set Fin laughing. Ringo threw him a look and he stopped.

"Don't concern yourselves, men," I counseled as I built a full house. "Curly Bill is too drunk to do much more than shoot off his dick."

"You are awfully concerned about the man's privates," Ringo said. He was the only one at the table not amused.

"Well, now," I replied, "I suppose that comes from him having his head up his ass much of the time. You'll soon have to go help him pull it back out."

"He is not my concern while I am winning."

"Then we'll have to address that," I said as I played my hand and scooped up the pot.

"Damn," Fin said. "I am broke and going to bed."

"Not a bad idea," I added. "It's gone quiet out front, so I guess it's safe for a man to make his way home. I wonder if Curly Bill lies in the street. You should check him, Fin, seeing as Ringo cares little for his friend."

"I'll do that," Fin said and he left. Ringo then lit a cigar and I dealt another hand. I lasted half an hour more before calling it a night. Ringo gave no indication of fatigue, so I knew he would keep on until I had to be carried out, and I refused to give him that satisfaction. I thus took some of his ribbing as I stood and pocketed my money.

"The lunger can't stay out late," Ringo told the others.

"You are correct," I replied. "I need rest, whereas some creatures thrive on the night. Bats, I believe." Here I looked at him hard. "Coons too. Gentlemen, I bid you good night."

Wyatt would have been proud that I resisted temptation and did not push Ringo to draw his gun. I made my way out and sought my hotel room while thinking on the newly minted deputy sheriff of Tombstone snoring away, hand on his dick as he dreamed of me.

By noon the next day, the town was abuzz with news that Wyatt Earp was now deputy sheriff. When he appeared, heads turned, mine included, for he had truly gained in stature. The same quick enforcement he had shown in the Oriental was now applied at large, and he slapped his gun to the head of many a drunken rowdy. He and Morgan strode around town as if they had claimed it, spending time in and out of saloons, the Wells Fargo office, and those of Marshals Fred White and Virgil Earp. The two visited shops and stores, making themselves known all around town in an effort toward folks resting easier. I saw Wyatt meant to tame this place as he had Dodge City, but I also began to wonder at such ambition, as Tombstone was closer to hell than had been the Kansas railhead. The town had remained wide-open and raucous, despite attempts by citizens to create a respectable community. Miners drank up their profits, while rough men of all sorts indulged in various sins, many of which involved gunplay. The streets were thus filled with both the best and worst of man. Was it possible for the great Wyatt Earp to bite off more than he could chew?

While I was most eager to get the new deputy sheriff back into bed, he remained elusive during the first week of his new employment, and this got me wondering if Mattie might be getting his attentions out of some need toward respectability. I knew not to press, but chasing respectability in a town short on such a commodity seemed foolish, not to mention making certain deprived parties shorter tempered than usual.

I ran into Wyatt around town, as he frequented the saloons to keep an eye on things, hauling away troublemakers, slapping that pistol to keep what peace he could. Virgil and Morgan were often with him, the three formidable together but a problem for me, as I could not get close to Wyatt to say what I wanted and what he sure as hell had to know. Then one night, he was in the Oriental, standing at the bar while I played poker, my fuse shorter by the minute as his presence intruded upon my game. Around eleven o'clock, when I was starting to think mostly on fucking, Johnny Tyler, a little pissant troublemaker, began to complain about losing.

"Watch what you say, Johnny," I warned him. "This is a fair game to one and all."

"The hell it is. There is no winning with you dealing."

I stopped shuffling the cards and slammed the deck down in front of him. "You are now the dealer, Johnny, and if you start winning, we are going to know you are cheating. Now deal."

"You don't scare me, Holliday."

"All the better. A man without fear is easy pickings."

He took the deck, wisely hesitant.

"You'd best give them a shuffle," I suggested. "Mix up that winning hand I was going to deal myself."

The others at the table chuckled, which got Johnny red in the face. He shuffled and dealt, all quiet for the moment.

"Of course, if you win the hand, I'll have to shoot you for cheating," I said as I studied my cards.

Chairs scraped the floor as the other players fled. "You and me now," I said. "I hope you've given yourself a hand worth dying for."

"That's enough, Doc," Wyatt said, stepping up to the table. "Johnny, you get out of here."

"But he cheated me."

"That is not my concern. What is my concern is keeping the peace, and it is about to be disturbed if you keep on. Now hit the street."

Tyler bristled. "It's not fair!"

"Never said it was," Wyatt countered. "Now git."

I sipped my whiskey to stifle a cough while Tyler made his way out. "Thank you, Sheriff," I said to Wyatt. Just then, Milt Joyce came over and leaned into my face.

"I won't have you making a disturbance in my place," he growled. "I want your gun behind the bar to prevent any more trouble."

"But there has been no trouble," I argued.

"Your gun, Holliday, else you get out of here."

"Go ahead, Doc," Wyatt urged me. "You can have it back when you leave."

"Goddamn, Wyatt, I did nothing but defend my honor as a sporting man, and Joyce here is making like I'm ready to shoot up the place."

"Give him the gun," Wyatt said.

Anyone else making such a demand would not have been given satisfaction, but since it was my friend, I complied and handed over my revolver. This, however, was not enough for Joyce. "Now we'll get some order in here," he said, at which I let loose on him.

"You always have order with me," I replied. "It's Tyler who causes trouble and you should learn to tell us apart, you short-sighted ass."

"Out! Get out of here!"

"If I have to leave, I'll take my gun."

Silence then fell, which is rare in such an establishment, but everyone was fixed on who would back down. Determined that it not be me, I again demanded my gun and Joyce again put me off. "I won't have you shooting up the place," he said.

"If I shoot anything, it will be you," I replied.

Wyatt intervened at this point, pulling me away and shoving me outside. "Damn, Wyatt, he was in the wrong," I argued. "I did nothing but win a few hands, and you know Tyler is always looking for trouble."

"I don't deny that, Doc, but I can't have you facing off with Joyce when all you had to do was leave your gun awhile. Let things cool down. Go back for it later."

"Sometimes you are a pain," I said as I stalked off feeling way too light at not being heeled. I started toward Hafford's Saloon, then thought better of it and fetched another pistol from my room. I then went back to the Oriental where I demanded Joyce give me my gun.

"I will not arm you so you can shoot up the place," he said. "The gun remains where it is."

In response to this outrage, I pulled my weapon, at which he did likewise and shots were fired by both parties. Bartender Gus Williams even jumped in with a shot or two, and soon Wyatt was arresting me. "Damn it, Doc, you didn't have to do this."

"But I did, Wyatt. Milt Joyce dislikes me for no reason but my winning. He had no right to refuse me my gun."

"You shot him."

"Yes, but that was entirely due to his refusal to return my pistol. Had he done as he should, he would not have a hole in his hand, and you would not be in a position that requires you to arrest a friend."

"You're not going to talk your way out of this."

"Wouldn't dream of it."

I was marched to Marshal Fred White's office, where I was jailed for assault with a deadly weapon with intent to kill. When I saw that neither Milt Joyce nor Gus Williams was being charged, I protested something fierce, which set Wyatt off.

"Doc, if you don't shut that mouth of yours, I am going to slap this pistol to your head so hard you won't think straight for a week. You are in the wrong and you goddamn know it."

I held up my hands. "I concede. Justice is indeed blind."

The Tombstone jail was not unfamiliar to me, and I passed a restless night among drunks suffering the aftereffects of their liquor. Next day, I appeared before Justice James Reilly, where the prosecution's four witnesses all failed to appear. I entered a guilty plea to a lesser charge of assault and battery, paid a fine of twenty dollars as well as court costs, and was set free. Wyatt was present for the proceedings, but as soon as I was set loose, he took off and made himself scarce to me for several days. I was sure he considered my making trouble a personal affront, even though it was Tyler and Joyce who brought it on. I also considered Wyatt's perspective might be askew due to his not fucking enough. While I knew the situation needed remedy, I hesitated to approach him, so we both stewed in our juices awhile. Then one day, he and Morgan rode off chasing stage robbers, returning early next morning before the sun was up. When the knock came at my door, I was most annoyed. "Who in hell?" I called out.

"Wyatt."

I staggered to the door, hacking and coughing as I opened it, and in he came, undoing his pants. He pushed me onto the bed, cough be damned, flipped me onto all fours, and shoved in his dick. While I welcomed him back, I was little impressed with his approach, my dick stirring but not so much as to get myself off, as I was troubled by my morning cough, which always took a while to control. Thus, I coughed through a rough one and was relieved when he let out a growl and came. He then pulled out, fell over, and slept.

I lay awake considering that his posse work had riled him and hoping a snooze might settle him enough to see to my needs. I was entertaining myself with such thoughts when his eyes popped open. "Need to get home," he said, though he did not get up.

"The night's already gone," I reminded him. "Why rush off?"

He went quiet, like something weighed on him, and though I wanted to ask, I knew better. Then he got around to it. "I'm not sure what to do, Doc. Mattie says she has headaches, but she won't see a doctor. Gets laudanum, which makes her…I don't know. She says she's not sick, but when she takes that stuff, well, you know."

I did in fact know, having watched my mother take laudanum during her last months. A powerful opiate, it was in far too common use for various ailments and easily obtainable. "I am sorry to hear that," I said. "Anything I can do to help?"

"She knows about us."

"How could she?"

"She's a woman, Doc. They know things men never see. She may not have seen us do it, but she can still tell it's being done."

My heart began to race in fear of him attempting the role of good husband. Respectable deputy sheriff was bad enough. I began to cough and got up to pour a drink. "Want one?" I asked Wyatt when I'd quieted.

"Better not." He got up and started dressing. "Sorry, Doc," was all he said before he left.

After this, he continued to keep himself in check around me, and I had to admire the effort even if it left me somewhat surly at the deprivation. I drank to excess, abused my cock something fierce, and generally fit right well with the population. I kept hoping on more posse work for Wyatt, as getting worked up by a long chase seemed the only way he'd allow himself any good depravity.

The cattle rustling that I'd been hearing about came to light around this time. The *Tombstone Epitaph* gave a front page account of a gang they called the Cowboys, saying they numbered between fifty and two hundred and were based out of Charleston and Galeyville but selling their stolen cattle in Tombstone. Johnny Ringo and Curly Bill Brocious were listed as possible ringleaders, with local ranchers likely involved. The conclusion of the article was that much of Tombstone's lawlessness was due to these men throwing around their money and their guns, acting like they were more in charge than the law. The paper concluded that crime was increasing as a result of this activity.

The *Tombstone Daily Nugget*, which always opposed the *Epitaph*, ran an editorial debunking the idea of any rustling enterprise and condemning the slur on Tombstone citizens. It named the Earps as cause for the unrest, saying crime had worsened since they began enforcing the law with too heavy a hand. Honest men seeking no more than a good time after a day's hard work were bludgeoned for no reason. The editorial concluded that the Earps encouraged the false story of a gang in order to cover their own misdeeds, which were presently under scrutiny.

Knowing Wyatt had seen both pieces, as he read the papers daily, I did not rush to get his comments. I did, however, listen around town and did not like what I heard, as most seemed to be taking The *Nugget*'s slur as gospel. I finally caught Wyatt alone on Toughnut Street one day. "People are believing that rubbish in the *Nugget*," I said, "so you had best start taking public opinion seriously." He kept walking, as if he did not want to hear such a thing. "Listen to me," I said, pulling at his arm. He stopped but kept looking ahead. "You Earps are being blamed for what these Cowboys are doing. You can't walk away from it."

"I am going to do my job, as are Morgan and Virgil. I don't care what people say. The law is the law, period."

"That may be true, but you need to have the people behind you."

Here he turned to face me. "I am not going to play at being nice simply to court people who should respect the law and me with it. I do not give a damn what either paper says. This is law enforcement, and if we let up, the Cowboys will take the town for sure. Now leave me be, Doc. I have to see Judge Reilly."

He strode away, and it was not ten minutes before a bunch of men rode in whooping it up, pistols firing into the sky and a few windows. Marshal White and his deputy showed up, but the men simply rode off to some other part of town and the marshal then became occupied with a gunfight that spilled from the Alhambra Saloon. Two men were hauled to jail, a third to the undertaker as citizens fled what was now a typical afternoon.

Several nights later, Wyatt and Morgan stopped in at the Oriental, and I left a disappointing faro game to have a drink with them. I missed their company almost as much as I missed Wyatt in my bed, both men occupied too much in their work. Morgan quickly downed two whiskeys while Wyatt made do with a beer. I could see he did not want to impair his reaction time. When Fred White came in, he joined us, and I remarked that most of the town's law enforcement was supporting the bar. A laugh was enjoyed by all until Curly Bill appeared from the lounge, drunk as usual. He was a nuisance, but since he threatened nobody he was let alone and made his way outside. Minutes later, gunfire was heard out front and Fred White issued a sigh. "Curly Bill is likely at it again," he said. "I'd best go reel him in before he shoots somebody."

He left, and seconds later Wyatt said, "I'm going out there. This doesn't sit right." Morgan and I followed, reaching the street in time to see Curly Bill with pistol pointed at Marshal White.

"Give me your gun, Curly Bill," White demanded. "I have to take you to jail." As he was close to his prey, he reached out to take the pistol, seizing the barrel, at which it fired. White fell back, shot through the chest, while Curly Bill dropped to his knees still holding the gun.

Wyatt sprang into the street and grabbed Curly Bill by the collar. "Get up!" he commanded.

"What have I done?" Curly Bill slurred. "I haven't done anything to be arrested for."

Wyatt offered no comment. Morgan went over to assist, and the two dragged Curly Bill to jail while Doc Goodfellow was sent for, although it was clear Fred White was gone. I stayed on the sidewalk as White was officially pronounced dead, then saw Wyatt coming back up the street. "I fear a lynch mob is forming," he said to me.

"Not a bad idea."

This was not a prudent comment, and Wyatt let me know it. "I don't like the man either, but he deserves a trial, not a rope. Morgan is keeping guard at the jail. I want to check around town. You with me?"

"Of course."

We found Virgil and an old cohort of Wyatt's, Turkey Creek Jack Johnson, and the four of us spent several hours going around checking on the mood of both the citizens and the rowdies. The Cowboys seemed either too drunk or too loosely organized to want to spring their friend, so we ended our patrol and went over to the jail, where we found some men milling around out front. Wyatt chased them off. "No more gunplay," he shouted, "or you will suffer mine."

When these men had gone, Wyatt and I went inside. "Hell of a thing," he said of White's killing. "Good man shot for no reason. I doubt Curly Bill even knew what he was doing."

"And now no city marshal," Morgan said.

"The town fathers have to hire somebody right quick, else the Cowboys will believe they are winning."

Silence fell at this point and I asked Wyatt what he would do next.

"Tomorrow, Morgan and I will take Curly Bill to Tucson, where they will hold a hearing in the matter, decide if he is to be tried."

Wyatt instructed White's deputy to stand guard for the night as all agreed things were settling down. The rest of us went outside, and when we saw no lynch mob coming our way, decided to call it a night. Had Morgan not been there, I would have invited Wyatt to my room.

It was said a thousand people turned out for Fred White's funeral two days later, and I do not doubt this as all stores closed and all gambling stopped. It seemed the entire town saw fit to mourn the loss of a good man just thirty-two years of age who wanted no more than to keep the peace. That a drunken fool had taken such a life doubled the wrong.

The Earps, now the law in Tombstone, headed the funeral procession from the undertaker's to Boot Hill. White was not married, so there were no relatives to mourn his untimely passing. The Earp wives accompanied their men while I walked behind. From my position, I noted Mattie unsteady on her feet and Wyatt's strong grip on her elbow and, when she faltered, around her waist. Though the crowd likely thought this due to grief, I knew it was her laudanum.

A preacher said words over Fred while those of us close to the deceased stood around the grave. It was then I noted some of the Cowboys among the crowd, notably Johnny Ringo and Ike, Billy, and Fin Clanton. Cohorts of White's killer, I knew they'd come more to gloat than to honor a fallen man, and it rankled me no end to see them. When services ended and Wyatt saw them, his face darkened. It took great restraint on his part not to make a scene at their presence. Fred White would have appreciated the honor.

The women were taken home and the Earps and I made our way up Allen Street, keeping an eye out for trouble as the air was thick not only with wind and dust but the feeling something might be afoot. We reached the corner of Hafford's Saloon and took up a watch out front.

"Closing down gambling might not have been a good idea," I noted. "Men are going to be at loose ends, which Fred White would not appreciate."

"They can manage one damned day," Wyatt snapped. I didn't press further.

Nobody sat down, though chairs were available. Virgil and Wyatt stood at the ready, and Morgan and I were contemplating going inside for a drink when up the street came Ringo and Ike Clanton. When they saw us, they came over.

"Too bad about poor Fred," Ringo said. "Lawman in these parts has to be careful of whose gun he grabs hold."

When none of us bit, Ringo went on, punching Ike on the arm. "No law in Tombstone now that the marshal is dead," he told Ike. "Nobody to keep us down, and it's about damned time. Man needs room in his town, and this is our town, ain't it, Ike? Place we do our business, spend our money, place where we have a good time."

At this, Ike let out a whoop, pulled his gun, and began to fire into the air. He then shot a lamppost, which prompted Wyatt to step down into the street though he did not immediately pull his weapon. "That's enough, Ike," he said. "Put it away."

Ike began to laugh and fired his gun once more, hitting a window of the Grand Hotel. Before he got off a second shot, Wyatt drew his Buntline and slapped it to Ike's head, which dropped him like a sack of dirt. Virgil, meanwhile, took aim at Ringo, cautioning him not to draw. Ike lay moaning on the ground and Wyatt told Ringo, "Take him home and sober him up."

Ringo's hand hovered at his holster, as did mine. Seeing himself outnumbered, Ringo bent to get Ike, who staggered to his feet, blood trailing from a cut on his forehead. "This ain't over," Ringo called as he helped Ike not toward Doc Goodfellow's but over to the Grand Hotel. "We won't be set down."

When Wyatt came back to join us in front of the saloon, Virgil remarked that this wasn't going to go away. "Things are going to get worse," he predicted, not knowing how prophetic his words would be.

I noted in the ensuing days that the Cowboys made the Grand Hotel their base in town. I also learned from a hotel clerk that they had a second-floor room overlooking the street. The shutters, which always remained closed, had one slat missing. "A rifle is likely aimed at us much of the time," Virgil said as we were again outside Hafford's later in the week. "And they can look right over into the Cosmopolitan, Doc."

"My room is in the back, ground floor."

Wyatt glanced at me when he heard this, as if just speaking of the place stirred him. "Doc, I want to have a look at the Cosmopolitan," he said. "I'll see you boys later on." And without further comment, we strode toward the hotel.

Once in my room, Wyatt all but tore away my clothes. I had to stop him else he'd ruin a good suit. "See to your own duds," I said, and before I had myself stripped, he stood bare, hard dick in hand.

"Goddamn, I need a fuck, Doc," he growled as he applied spit to his cock. "Get your ass up onto the bed."

I shed the last of my clothes, set my flask on the night table, and hopped onto the bed. When I lay stroking my swollen prick, he grabbed me, flipped me over, and drove in his dick. "Only good thing about this goddamned town," he said as he began a rough fuck, the poor bed squeaking and complaining while I worked myself to a gusher of a come.

Wyatt was also quick, being so pent up with tensions inside and out. He let out a roar when he unleashed his load and he rode me hard until he was empty, then slapped my bottom and pulled out. I rolled over to see him still wild-eyed, breathing hard, sweat across his forehead. "Who told you to turn over?" he demanded. "I am not done." He all but threw me onto my stomach, pulled up my bottom, and parted my buttocks. Then his breath was in my crack, then his tongue, and it did not linger to run up and down as I would have expected. Nope. He drove it right into the hole his dick had just vacated and set to pumping me something awful, mouth plastered to my bottom as he took the worst kind of meal. He went at me for some time, working like a pig, and I reveled in such base attention, knowing only the worst of a man would satisfy him. Finally, after he had all but consumed me, he pulled off and rolled me over. I was starting to feel like some rag doll but did not mind, as I was a well-used rag doll. He now crawled up and shoved his half-hard cock into my mouth. "Suck my dick," he commanded, as if I needed instructions. I seized his big sausage and began to feast on him, which got him thrusting into my throat. All would have been well had not a coughing fit come on. He pulled out and waited as I swigged whiskey.

"Sorry about that," I said when I'd quieted.

"No matter." He then reversed himself, climbed over me, dropped his dick into my mouth while he sucked on mine. I managed to keep the cough at bay until I had swallowed more of his stuff and managed a few good spurts for him. At last, he pulled off and fell onto the bed beside me. I wondered if he'd toss the rag doll around a bit more, but he seemed finished. Still, he did not allow himself much respite. "I need to get back to work," he said, blowing out a breath.

"Fair enough. I'm glad you could stop by."

He turned to look at me. "You know how it is, Doc."

"I surely do."

And that was it. He put on his sheriff suit and left me lying naked on my bed. He may have had to get back to work, but I did not. Satisfied more than I'd been in some time, I drifted off to sleep and did not wake until suppertime, at which I had a fine meal and a good night at faro.

I began to notice the Grand Hotel more now that I knew it a sort of in-town hideout for the Cowboys. Ten or fifteen men could usually be seen hanging around the entrance, intimidating citizens, and generally acting a nuisance. Occasionally, they fought with one another, often settling their differences with fists. Wyatt did not attempt to quell this situation, as he was outnumbered. He chose to keep watch on the rest of the town, which was enough work. When the town fathers asked Virgil if he would take Fred White's job as city marshal, there was no hesitation, and so it came to pass that the Earps officially had all three levels of law enforcement in the family—city, county, and federal. You would think this would please people, but it did not. The town began to split as to the benefit of the Earps in charge, half seeing them as upholding the law and keeping the town from sinking to worse than it was, the other half spouting off that the Earps had stirred the Cowboys toward lawlessness and were themselves a bigger threat. I noted those in support of the Cowboys were mostly saloon owners and butchers, both benefiting monetarily from the cattle rustling. The two newspapers continued to spout opposing positions, the *Epitaph* unfailingly in support of the law-and-order Earps, the *Nugget* powerfully against them. More than once, Wyatt handed me a newspaper and swore as I read the latest.

Around this time, a newcomer who was to later have much impact on us all came to town. Johnny Behan was a handsome fellow and most outgoing. Word was he'd been sheriff of Yavapai County and had served in the territorial legislature, thus making him a well-connected man. Within weeks, he seemed to be everyone's friend, as he was always eager for a chat or to pass along a good story. Ever bustling, or maybe closer to hustling, he seemed to me to be working the populace, and when he soon passed along news that talk in Prescott was of a new county about to be carved from Pima, the Earps and I began to see his purpose in coming to our fair town.

"A new county means new officials getting a share of tax money," I told Wyatt. "No need to split the loot with Pima anymore, and when you take mines and railroad into account, it is quite a prize."

"Might have to try and get a piece of that," Wyatt said. "It means a new county sheriff."

Always the general, Wyatt. "Might be a nice piece," I noted.

Behan, while he glad-handed around, took work as a bartender at the Grand Hotel and soon became so well liked that he was able to influence most everyone he met. Except the Earps, of course, who remained guarded. He courted them as much as they would allow but soon came to see they would not help him toward his aspirations. I kept my distance, especially when I saw him too often with the McLaurys, Clantons, and Johnny Ringo.

"That fellow is trouble," Virgil observed one day. Wyatt, Morgan, and I did not disagree.

Chapter Seven

Wyatt spent the summer and fall chasing horse thieves, arresting lot jumpers, foiling petty criminals, hunting killers, and, of course, slapping around his Buntline Colt. He also found his way into my bed on occasion, though he remained unpredictable in this regard. More than once, he eyed me in a saloon only to disappear on some duty, real or imagined. Other times, he'd fairly break down my door to rouse me from a late sleep. He didn't seem to note any inconvenience on my part now that he was deputy sheriff. His authority had captured his dick.

It was nearly noon one fall day when he pounded on my door to wake me after my usual late night. Knowing it was him, I did not rush to answer but saw to calming my cough. When I was somewhat righted, I admitted him, expecting a pleasurable assault on my person. Instead I got fury. He charged about the room swearing about women, and it took some minutes before he got specific. He took the drink I offered, threw it back, but refused to sit.

"Damn woman," he finally said. "She took too much laudanum, and I know it was not by accident. It's her way of getting at me, but I refuse to be got at like that. My sympathies are strained to the limit, Doc. I care about her, see to her well-being, but I'll be damned to hell if I'll let her run me by way of such antics."

He continued to rail about the room, revealing that Mattie had been put to bed by Allie, who generally served as mother hen to the wives. It was she who suggested Wyatt leave, as he was not sympathetic to his woman's illness.

"Illness be damned," he roared. "She can't be without the stuff anymore, and I can hardly stand her as a result."

"Come here," I said, having shed my drawers while he paced and raged. He looked at me lying naked. Shoulders heaving, teeth bared, he was wilder than I'd ever seen him, yet he seemed stalled by the very anger that fueled him. "Fuck me," I said. "Fuck me to hell."

That did it. He opened his pants, got out his cock, which was stiff as a gun barrel, and climbed onto the bed. I kept working myself, and his tongue emerged as if he considered licking me instead of fucking, but his dick got the better of him and he rubbed spit onto it, plowed into me, and set the bed rocking with an unrelenting assault. I shot my load before him, pumping like mad while he went at my behind. When he came, he surprised me by going silent, nothing but muffled grunts as he rode to the peak. When he was done, he pulled out and I flipped around to see him still worked up, his prick the only part of him at rest.

"You need a drink," I said, hopping out of bed.

"No, I don't need a goddamn drink," he railed. "I don't need a goddamn thing." And he did up his pants and stormed out of the room the same way he'd come in. I feared if he encountered Ike Clanton or Johnny Ringo, they'd be done for.

When I saw him later, he was striding around town with his brothers, looking his old self, and I decided to take credit for his calm. A good fuck solved everything, or so I thought until he began to talk politics. Worst thing a man can suffer is ambition toward public office, especially one as upright as Wyatt Earp.

"I am going to resign," he told me over supper one evening. Until he revealed this bit of foolishness, I had been enjoying a fine meal as well as designs on his person since we had only to walk a couple doors down to the hotel.

"Why in hell would you do that?" I asked, unable to contain my annoyance.

He leaned forward. "Bob Paul is running for Pima County Sheriff against Charlie Shibell, my boss, in the November election. Well, I consider Paul the better party, as I know him to be a man of honor and courage. He's been sheriff of Calaveras County in California, so he is well qualified. He is also a friend, and I cannot in good conscience publicly support him while working for his opponent."

"Hogwash," I argued. "Nobody is going to care about that, not even Shibell."

"I am going to care," Wyatt countered. "It doesn't sit well with me."

"So you'll give up your living for political purposes?"

"If Paul wins, he'll name me his deputy, and I expect him to win."

I could see his mind was made up, but I could not hold back a shot of logic. "What about this talk of a new county? If that happens, Pima doesn't matter."

"I can't take that chance."

Shaking my head, I said nothing more by way of disagreeing and bit into a slice of apple pie, which now seemed too tart. This I ascribed more to our exchange than any failure of the cook.

"It's a gamble," I said later as we stood out front, bellies full.

"I know, Doc."

"Odds are against you."

"I'll have to chance it."

For probably the first time since I'd known him, I did not want his body. "I'll see you," I said and I went off to the Alhambra Saloon, where I played cards well into the following day. That I did not win was no surprise as I could not discard the notion that Wyatt, the most upstanding of Tombstone's citizens, was far from suited for political ambition. Such things are best left to cunning types such as me. A devious streak and a willingness to bend the law are present in every elected official, else how would they gain office? I feared my friend was sliding into deep water not only without a paddle but without a boat.

Wyatt did resign his badge. Both his brothers advised against it, but the general seldom listened to his troops. "Put me in a hell of a spot," Morgan groused one night as we worked toward getting good and drunk. "Wyatt appointed me and expects me to resign as well."

"Wyatt should keep to law enforcement," I said. "He is wading into deep water in counting on an election."

"I'll drink to that."

Charlie Shibell surprised the Earps by appointing Johnny Behan to fill the vacated deputy sheriff post until the November election. I ventured no comment to Wyatt, but Morgan did, much to my dismay. "Still think you did right to resign?" he asked Wyatt as we stood at Hafford's corner. "Isn't Shibell appointing Behan his way of letting you know he was pissed at your action?"

"I did right," Wyatt snapped. He then stalked away.

"You are fortunate to still have your head on your shoulders," I told Morgan, which made him laugh. We then went over to Hatch's to play some pool, leaving the general to his self-imposed purgatory.

The worst part of glad-handing Johnny Behan being deputy sheriff was how it pleased the citizens. In their ignorance, they thought a man who tells a good joke could do better than one proven to enforce the law. It also gradually came to light that many had seen Wyatt's stern demeanor as arrogant and they now felt well rid of him.

Ignoring this, he went back to dealing faro at the Oriental, confident he would be deputy sheriff come November and working for a man he liked. I left off any challenge, as I found that in shedding his badge, he had become more willing to shed his clothes. Playing enforcer for Milt Joyce seemed enough exercise of his authority for a while, so I determined to enjoy the two months until election time, pushing aside my notion of his foolishness in the matter. Wyatt remained in relatively good spirits and was now in my room more often.

One particular night when I'd won a bundle, I managed to entice him to bed and sucked his dick so ardently he shot his first load into my throat. I was down between his legs, glancing up at him as I fed. A man in the throes wears an expression unlike any other, I care not what his passion, and I much enjoyed gazing upon Wyatt in his throes. Coming is the Holy Grail, and I could but issue a silent amen, seeing how my mouth was full.

When I pulled off, Wyatt was panting and I slid up onto him and got my tongue into his pelt to find his tit nubs. "Christ, Doc," he said, but he did not push me off. I nipped and licked until I was beyond ready, then crawled up and put my dick to his lips. He drew a second pillow under him and opened to me, sucking briefly before I gave him my all. I coughed as I came but did not care, as my cock always won this particular battle. And Wyatt fed hungrily, like he would take more spunk if I had it to give. He even kept on as I softened, his tongue playing with me until at last my cough worsened and I climbed off to pour a drink.

"Maybe your quitting sheriffing was a good idea," I said when I'd quieted the malady. "You are less occupied, which is working in my favor."

"I am getting impatient with the waiting," he admitted as I sat on the bed's edge, whiskey in hand.

I raised my glass. "Here's to impatience."

He looked to the ceiling, which I knew meant directing us elsewhere. "Bob Paul says it's true there will soon be a new county," he said.

I had to hold back a "goddamn Bob Paul" for getting into bed with us. "That talk has been around so long I don't believe it," I said.

"You better start. He says it's in the works. Governor Fremont will be appointing officials to serve until the November eighty-two election, and I mean to make it known I am up for county sheriff. No doubt Behan will also want it."

"Well, you sure as hell can beat him, as he's done nothing to enforce the law since he took your spot. Never have I seen such grease ooze off a man, and people lap it up, the fools. He collects taxes and does nothing more."

"He's popular, I'll give him that," Wyatt conceded, "but I've proven myself at law enforcement and that's what people want."

"Don't be too sure. Sheep will feed on the sweetest grass."

"You're a pessimist, Doc."

"Pessimistic situation."

My pessimism rose considerably three days later when I came into the Oriental and saw Johnny Behan slither up to Wyatt. I did not go over for fear I would shoot the man and save both Wyatt and Tombstone an awful fate. Instead I got into a poker game in back but sat where I could keep an eye on the conversation, as I was uneasy with Behan working my friend.

Behan was about Wyatt's age and better dressed. He favored tweed suits and the round hat that had gained recent popularity, looking dapper to Wyatt's dour. I watched him work that perpetual smile on Wyatt who, after leaning in close, began to nod. This to me was not good; I don't care what was agreed upon. You do not ally yourself with a snake when he is rattling.

I did not ask Wyatt about the conversation, as it was none of my business, but I kept an eye on Behan because it had become clear to me he supported the Cowboys. While it may have appeared more of his genial glad-handing, I knew men such as the McLaurys, Clantons, and Johnny Ringo were not swayed by a slick spiel. I considered pointing this out to Wyatt but did not, as I knew it to be something he would not want to hear. Let the chips fall.

Meanwhile, as a result of Fred White's death, Virgil got an ordinance posted to prohibit carrying any deadly weapon in town. Only lawmen could be armed in Tombstone. Predictably, the town split on the matter, as did the newspapers. The law-and-order faction, voiced by the *Epitaph*, deemed the measure necessary to quell violence that had cost the town a good marshal. The *Nugget* countered that the law infringed on a man's right to protect himself while giving more power to the Earps to continue their violence.

November 1880 came, and with it, an election that solved nothing.

Tombstone got a new mayor, one John Clum, who, far as I could tell, leaned toward the law-and-order faction while keeping peace with the other side. I would have admired this had it not been simply a way to gain office. Bob Paul did not win election as Pima County Sheriff, but neither did Charlie Shibell, as the results were immediately disputed when one precinct with fifty eligible voters cast one hundred four for Shibell and one for Paul. This was to be expected since election officials for the district included Ike Clanton and Johnny Ringo.

While waiting for the election to be sorted out, the Earp boys sold some mining claims for a good profit, which helped Wyatt get by without wages. He also fell to enforcing the law even when not wearing a badge. On one occasion, tinhorn gambler Johnny Behind-the-Deuce killed a man in Charleston and a mob set out to lynch him. Charleston Constable George McKelvey got him out of town in a buckboard hell-bent for Tombstone with the mob in pursuit. Roaring into town, McKelvey spotted Wyatt as he and I stepped from the Cosmopolitan Hotel after an exceptionally rewarding session in bed.

"Wyatt, there's a mob after us," McKelvey cried. "They mean to lynch Johnny here! Help us out!"

It rightly should have been Virgil or Behan handling the matter, but Wyatt jumped right in. He ran to the Wells Fargo office, took a shotgun he kept stashed there, and hustled McKelvey and Johnny into a nearby saloon while the mob filled the street outside. Looking out at the mob, Wyatt then hatched a plan.

"Morgan, Virgil, Doc, and George," he commanded, "we are going to surround Johnny and we are going to walk him to the livery, get our horses, and escort him to Tucson, where he can be held for trial."

Without waiting for a yea or nay, he shoved Johnny, whom he had little use for, toward the door. The rest of us surrounded the accused, and with Wyatt in the lead, walked him out the door and into the street. The mob of around thirty men held its ground. When we reached them, Wyatt, gun in hand, ordered, "Stand back and make passage. I am going to take this man to jail in Tucson." When they made no move, Wyatt looked to their leader, much-respected mine operator Dick Gird. "Dick, if this mob attacks any one of us, you will die."

Gird lost his bravado at this point and indicated to his men they should back up. All gave way, allowing us to march Johnny to the stable, where we sought our horses and escorted him to Tucson. After we had deposited him with Charlie Shibell, Wyatt surprised me by saying, "They could have gotten me easily."

Never had I heard the great lawman admit any weakness. "Well, they did not," I said, "which I wish to celebrate. How about we find us a saloon and have a few whiskeys?"

He thought on this, and I saw he was up for a fuck, but as we were with others, he settled for the drinks. We then rode quick back to Tombstone, and soon as he could get loose of his brothers, he came to my room and we got at it something fierce. After he'd come once in my bottom and once by hand, spraying come all up my front, he let loose his thoughts. "You know Johnny killed that man. He'd kill a man soon as look at him, and I hate like hell that I had to step in and save his lowly life. He is what strains the law."

"You are right to make no judgments," I said as he climbed off me. I ran a hand up my chest to scoop a gob of his cream, then licked it from my fingers. Wyatt had never brought himself off in my company, preferring to engage one or more of my willing orifices, so it was much a treat to see him working that dick to a spew. I would have liked to know what prompted him toward such a turn but did not ask, as I had long decided to enjoy whatever he offered.

"I am not even the law anymore," he noted as he sat on the bed. "But I cannot leave off my support of a man's rights."

I slid a hand up his back and down his arm. "You are the most law-abiding, upright man I have ever known. And do you know, that gets my dick up?"

He chuckled. "A sneeze gets your dick up, Doc."

"If you do the sneezing, yes, it does."

He lay back across me and said, "I have to go back to Tucson next week to testify against Curly Bill in Fred White's killing. I seem to be doing just as much enforcement now as when I wore a badge."

"Is that a problem?"

"Only that I am not paid for it."

He did ride to Tucson to testify against Curly Bill, and I could tell upon his return that it had not gone well. When I saw him ride in late afternoon, I was lounging in front of Hafford's, as I had won a bundle the night before and was going to ease back into gaming later on. Wyatt rode in hell-bent, reined his horse, and hopped down. He saw me and came over, his look fierce.

"I trust the law did not see things your way?" I said.

"The goddamn law failed entirely," he ranted, refusing to sit. He looked out at the bustling town and shook his head. "Not much reason to enforce the law if it is undone by the courts," he said. "The judge found no cause to hold Curly Bill for trial, as it could not be proven he meant to shoot Fred White. It was ruled accidental because Fred grabbed the gun, and so a good man has died and justice turned her back. And Curly Bill is free to kill again, which he surely will."

"Why don't we go over to the hotel? You can take it out on me."

He glared at me like I'd suggested something deranged, but when I rose and started down the street, he followed. I knew it would be a rough one and I welcomed my ability to give him pleasure on a day of disappointment. As expected, he dropped his pants and drawers, stood me at the bedpost, shoved in, and growled like a bear until he unleashed his load. When he was done, he showed no satisfaction and scarcely looked at me before he left. I did not attempt to gain release, as I was far from aroused. Justice had failed, and nothing was going to compensate Wyatt Earp.

Word soon came that Curly Bill celebrated his freedom with a rampage that stretched across much of the county. He commandeered a Mexican saloon in Contention and made the patrons strip and dance naked at gunpoint for two hours, all for his amusement. He then invaded a church during Sunday services and, again at gunpoint, demanded the preacher dance before his congregation. He accosted people on the streets of Contention and Charleston, stealing their money and making a general nuisance of himself before heading to Tombstone. There he struck a friendship with Behan deputy Billy Breakenridge, who took him on to assist in tax collecting. Breakenridge justified this by saying the chief of the cattle rustlers knew best where cattle might be hidden, which furthered the collection of assessments due the county. Behan made no objection as it meant more money for him. A few townspeople questioned the arrangement, but most believed Johnny Behan could do no wrong.

Cochise County came into being in February 1881, which rendered Bob Paul's election as Pima County Sheriff of no consequence to Tombstone. Governor Fremont appointed Johnny Behan county sheriff, and he in turn appointed Harry Woods his undersheriff. Only when Wyatt asked me to ride with him to check a water rights claim in the nearby Huachuca Mountains did I learn what Wyatt had agreed to that time he and Behan cozied up for that talk at the Oriental. After conducting the claim business, Wyatt and I ambled along and I noted a slump in his shoulders. This caused me concern, as the man had a spine of iron. He was also quiet in the way a man is when he has much to say. Finally, he suggested we stop for water at a rocky point where a couple of trees clung to life. Once off our horses, Wyatt sipping from his canteen, me from my flask, he fidgeted something awful, which caused me to blurt, "What in hell is it, Wyatt?"

"Behan got around me," he confessed.

"How did he do that?"

Wyatt took of his hat, wiped his sleeve over his brow, and squinted out to nowhere. With his hat in hand, he finally spoke. "I should have known better than to agree to anything with that man."

"What did you agree to?"

"He told me his political friends in Prescott could all but guarantee him appointment as sheriff, but he needed me to not complicate things by actively seeking office. In return, he said he would appoint me his deputy."

"And he gave that to Harry Woods."

"I should have known better."

"It was an appealing offer," I noted. "What does Behan say about his actions?"

"He's made no effort to say anything. He's in Prescott, glad-handing, no doubt, and I don't expect a word from him. It's a hard lesson, Doc."

"That it is."

I had never seen him disheartened like that, and it caused the compassionate part of my nature to attempt escape. I wanted to tell him I was sorry for his loss and remind him of all he did have, my friendship topping the list. I wanted to tell him I would give him my all, follow him anywhere, do anything he asked, fucking or killing, didn't matter. Tears rose up in me, such was my distress, yet we simply got back onto our horses and rode back into Tombstone. There he got into a faro game at the Oriental and I left him to it because I was too full of feelings to remain near him. I went to the Alhambra for poker and played well into the following morning.

Nothing broke between us, but I saw that Wyatt needed room to right himself. If I got too close, I knew I'd attempt to assist, which would result in feelings getting loose, and those were more dangerous than all the Cowboys put together. I thus busied myself with gaming and seeing others. Well, one in particular. Billy Leonard to be exact.

It was a Tuesday in March when I decided to ride out to the Wells to visit Billy. I had seen Wyatt the night before at the Oriental, and he remained burdened with disappointment, his usual dour manner now downright glum. He had been sharp with me when I attempted conversation, so I decided to forgo gaming the next day and see my other good friend.

It was late morning when I started out, and I took my time getting to the Wells, considering as I went along, what all I would get up to with Billy. Drinking, cards, laughter, talk, and…? I was in carnal need and knew Billy was likely the same, thus by the time I arrived and found his companions absent, I was much primed. It did not take long for Billy to ask me to suck his dick. As I feasted on a good mouthful of his come, I did not think of the other dick I knew so well. I concentrated on the man I was pleasing, and when I had swallowed his stuff, I stood and bared myself, and he sucked a good load out of me. After this, we stripped down and played around on his bed for some time with him getting hard again and this time putting his prick where it belonged. When we were done, we drank a good amount, then dressed, as Billy said his friends were due back.

"What are they up to these days?" I asked as I donned my suit.

"No good." Billy laughed. "Seriously, Doc, you do not want to know."

"Then I will not know," I said.

It was around four o'clock when I started back to town. On the way, I came upon old man Fuller, who hauled water from the Wells to town and, as he was a fine and entertaining fellow, I tied my horse behind his wagon, climbed up, and rode the rest of the way while listening to his stories. Back in town, I got my supper and settled in for a long night of poker at the Alhambra saloon. I was having a fine time in spite of mostly breaking even as Henry Hooker showed up, which stepped up the game. Hooker was most welcome after events of late and we declared we would play until sunup.

"What do you think of Behan as sheriff?" Hooker asked at one point.

"I do not waste my thoughts on such a man."

"It should have been Earp," he ventured.

I could only sigh, and in response, Hooker backed off further discussion of law enforcement. We kept to the game and I scarcely noticed how late it had gotten when Wyatt strode in looking more stern than usual, which takes some doing.

"Doc, let's you and me take a walk," he said in a tone that told me I had no choice.

He waited until I played my hand, cashed out, and stood. “I am wanted elsewhere,” I said to Hooker. “I will see you tomorrow.”

I followed Wyatt outside and down the block, but he did not speak until we had turned up Fifth Street and from there into a vacant lot.

“What in hell has gotten into you?” I demanded, coughing at being run like some wayward steer.

“Word has come that Bud Philpott was killed tonight in a robbery attempt on the Benson Stage. They didn’t get the strongbox because Bob Paul ran the horses on, but a passenger was also shot.”

“I am sorry to hear that, but why pull me from my game?”

“Bob Paul says he recognized one of the men by his voice. Jim Crane. He lives with your friend Billy Leonard, who is also suspected along with Luther King and Harry Head.”

My thoughts shot back to sucking Billy’s dick that afternoon, which rendered me speechless for maybe the first time ever.

“Well?” Wyatt demanded. “Do you know about it? You were seen at the Wells today.”

“You are correct in my being out there in the afternoon, but I left around four. I saw only Billy. The others weren’t around, but he said they were due back.”

Wyatt paused to consider this, and in that moment, I felt a terrible wound as I saw he was trying to decide if I was lying. After a few seconds, he apparently swallowed his doubt, for he continued what I now realized was an interrogation.

“You sure it was four?” he asked.

“Around then, yes. If you need proof, ask old man Fuller. I rode with him coming back to town. I then had supper and went to the Alhambra and did not move until you found me.”

“You were seen back in town earlier?”

Here I began to get pissed. “How can you come at me like this?” I asked. “I am your friend and a hell of a lot more. How can you doubt me? And need I remind you, you are no longer the law?”

This got him. Few crossed the general unless they were looking to get a pistol slapped to their head. He stopped his questions and huffed out a breath. “Fair enough,” he said. “If you are confident you were seen enough to prove yourself, I’ll leave you be, but keep in mind there is already talk.”

“When it’s nothing but Bob Paul hearing a man’s voice?”

“Are you defending these men?” Wyatt asked.

“I am giving a friend due consideration.”

"Your friend's house at the Wells has already been checked on and it is empty. Behan is getting up a posse to go after them. We leave at first light."

"We?"

"Virgil, Morgan, Marsh Williams, and me, along with Behan and two of his deputies. I can't ask you to join for obvious reasons."

"That I am a suspected stage robber?"

He shook his head. "That you are friends with one."

Chapter Eight

Wyatt spent nine days with Behan's posse, and these proved very long days for me. Coupled with disappointment at his interrogating me was a growing awareness of a rumor around town that I had been involved in the robbery. Didn't matter that I had been seen at the restaurant and the Alhambra; rumors take on a life of their own, and this one quickly grew out of proportion, no doubt fueled by Johnny Behan and company. That Wyatt had signed on to posse with the man further soured my mood; thus, the nine days were a purgatory. I lost more than I won at cards, which worsened my mood. My only recourse was drinking to excess, and at this alone I excelled.

I got drunk with Henry Hooker the day after Wyatt had questioned me and was unable to hold back telling him all that had happened, leaving out only carnal events, as they were not relevant to the situation. Hooker agreed I had reason to be upset.

"He must have felt it his duty," Hooker reasoned. "Maybe he just tried to get the facts straight so he need not consider you."

"A good friend doesn't need facts to shore up consideration. A good friend sees innocence."

"Disappointment is clouding your reasoning," Hooker said.

"Disappointment has turned my sky dark," I replied.

Hooker managed to distract me some while he was in town, scoffing at the rumor circulating about me, but he left after two days, and on my own, I again descended to hell. Then on day three, Behan and a deputy rode in with Luther King, who had been captured while trying to hide at the Redfield Ranch. Word spread that Wyatt had questioned Luther until he admitted Billy Leonard and his other two friends were indeed involved. The rest of the posse thus continued the chase. Rumor was not laid to rest by this development, and I was much frowned upon as I went around town. It required a great deal of effort on my part not to shoot the flock of fools who had their minds made up and never mind the truth. As days wore on, I saw the only way to clear my name would be the capture of the outlaws, as they could be made to set things right. This idea eased my attitude toward the posse, which helped raise me from the dumps.

When Wyatt returned to Tombstone nine days after his departure, it was on foot. I was at the livery paying the bill for my horse's care when he and Bob Paul came up the street wearing so much dust I knew their walk a long one. I hurried to conclude my business and ran after them. When Paul saw me, he peeled off, but Wyatt kept on.

"Where's your horse?" I asked.

"Dead. Same with Bob Paul's."

"Where are Virgil and Morgan?"

"Kept on with the others. We've walked about eighteen miles."

"You going home?"

"Just as soon not."

He followed me to my room, where he stripped and washed while I did my best to brush his clothes. He was so quiet I feared to ask what had happened, so we attended our tasks in silence.

"I am beat to hell," he finally said as he fell onto the bed. "Those men are nowhere."

"Bad news, seeing how people are so worked up."

"Are they?" he asked, looking up at me.

I put down his coat and sat on the bed beside him. "Rumor is around that I took part in the robbery, and it won't be put down until those men are brought in and made to tell the truth."

"That may take some doing. I worked over Luther King pretty hard, but he did not know where they had gone."

"I had no idea Billy Leonard would turn to crime," I said. "He has never been in trouble that I know of. When I knew him in Deadwood, he owned a jewelry store and was a good citizen. He's fallen on hard times, but I never expected him to turn to crime. I honestly believe his difficulties allowed him to be led by his cohorts."

"I don't dispute that, Doc, but it still looks bad, you being out there that day."

"Do you know that not one goddamn soul wishes to hear the truth? And not one goddamn soul has come forward to say I was in the Alhambra, not even the men who played cards with me?"

Wyatt slid a hand onto my knee. "You will always be a notorious fellow, Doc. No matter how you attempt to toe the line, soon as suspicion rises, your past comes up."

"But you know I did not take part."

"Yes, I know that. You are too smart to stoop to crime. You make your killing by other means."

I chuckled as nine day's tension dissolved into a warm pudding. "Do you want to tell me what happened out there? Nine days is a long chase."

"Behan is useless," Wyatt began. "He took no suggestions as the best places to look, and it was only because we needed food that we stopped at Dan Redfield's, where I thought one of the hands was acting strange. When I cornered him, he said a man was hiding in a shed and it turned out to be Luther King. I took him to Behan but told the sheriff not to let King talk to Redfield or his brother Hank, as I believed them friendly with the Cowboys. I then went off to talk to Bob Paul, and when I returned, King was talking to Hank Redfield with Behan standing right there. Hank then rode away, and I went to work on King until he confessed his part in the robbery and named the others being in on it. He also told where they were camped, but with Hank Redfield on the way to warn them, this was little help."

Here Wyatt blew out a sigh and lay staring at the ceiling a bit. He then continued. "Once Behan took King back to Tombstone, the rest of us followed the robbers for six more days before reaching a place with telegraph service so we could ask him to bring fresh horses, as our mounts were worn out from the long chase. We arranged a meeting place, but when we went there, we found Behan had not delivered. That night my horse and Paul's died and we started walking back while the others pressed on."

"While Behan is here taking credit for the capture of Luther King."

"Beats all."

He looked truly worn and I suggested he sleep awhile. "I would like that, but I need some food, Doc. How about we get a meal? I then think I'd best make an appearance at home. I'll sleep there. Tomorrow I want to get in touch with Jim Hume at Wells Fargo, see what they are saying about the situation."

He rose slowly and I handed him his clothes and watched him dress. As he pulled on his pants, he made an observation. "First time I've had my pants off in here and not done you."

"Don't tempt me."

He scoffed. "I could not get it up for love nor money, Doc."

"Another time, then."

He nodded, finished dressing, and we went out for a meal. He was quiet as he ate, and I gave him the room he needed, even as I noted whispers among several people at seeing us together. After he ate, Wyatt bid me good-bye and headed home while I sought my usual occupation.

Wells Fargo Detective James Hume rode into Tombstone the next day and met with Wyatt. It was then made known that Wells Fargo had posted a three hundred dollar reward for the robbers. I wondered if Johnny Behan would collect on Luther King and voiced this to Wyatt later on. "I do not doubt it," he replied. "Behan sees only dollar signs. But there is something more troubling me. I've heard the Cowboys are looking to break King from jail, so I want to go down there and warn whoever is in charge. You can tag along if you like."

I did like tagging along, more to show the town that I was still in Wyatt's good favor than toward any warning of a jailbreak. Behan was not at the jail, which did not surprise me, as he was seldom in his office. His deputy, Harry Woods, was there.

"You need to put King in irons," Wyatt told Woods as we came in. "There are men in town said to be fixing to break him out of here."

"That so," Woods replied. "Guess I had best do that. Thank you, Wyatt. You have been most helpful."

Wyatt lingered, as this seemed too easy, but when Woods stood, we left. "Things don't feel right," Wyatt said.

"Nothing feels right anymore. You've done all you can."

Wyatt and I walked around town a bit, and I was again proud to be in his company. We stopped in the Oriental for a drink, then set out again. When we stopped at Hafford's some time later, Tom Brady ran in to say King had escaped. "Got away on a horse tied out back of the jail."

I thought Wyatt would bust a gut. He turned red, jaw clenched to likely hold back every swear word he possessed, but he did not go down there. "No reason," he said when he'd calmed enough to speak. "Woods did not do as I said. He's probably the one who put the horse out back for the getaway, either that or Behan. They were in on it. No doubt." He paused a bit, then went on. "I am thinking on Virgil and Morgan chasing down the others, but to what end? Bring them in so Behan can let them go?"

"What will people think of him now?" I ventured.

"He will shake a few hands, slap a few backs, and be seen as lawful."

Surprisingly, this was not the case. The law-and-order faction became quite vocal when it was learned about the horse in back of the jail and of the failure to put the prisoner in irons when a jailbreak was likely. It was refreshing to hear such things spoken but, unfortunately, fools have louder voices and things quickly swung back the other way. As this unfolded, the bedraggled posse returned empty-handed, Virgil in a foul temper and even the good-natured Morgan downcast. "We chased them to hell and gone," Morgan said. "I believe they are in Mexico. Either that or parts well east."

Wyatt slapped his little brother on the back. "You did a fine job, Morg. All we can ask."

Not long after their return, Wyatt found me at breakfast one day, and he was not in the best frame of mind. "We are becoming famous for all the wrong reasons," he declared, slapping *The San Francisco Examiner* onto the table. "Behan is letting the Cowboys run wild, but I still see people shaking his hand. The federal government now has an eye on us, such is our lawless state."

I read an article in which Governor Fremont voiced concern over the growing lawlessness in Cochise County, appealing to both Congress and the president for assistance. "It is an embarrassment," Wyatt said. "If we had the right parties in power, law and order could be maintained, but with Behan we have little hope."

There is not much worse than a born lawman without a badge. Wyatt's sense of right fit no other occupation, leaving his concern about safety of the townspeople with nowhere to go but out his mouth and into the wind—or my ear. I enjoyed him sitting across from me, but I did not like his frustration with things. "Behan is not going to change," I said.

"What do we do, Doc? What in hell do we do?"

"I doubt there is anything you can do without any law behind you. Virgil maybe."

Wyatt shook his head. "They're not tearing up the town, so he can't take them in as city marshal, and until he can get them for mail theft in the stage robbery, he can't touch them in his U.S. Marshal capacity. All he can do is arrest those shooting up the town, and that is not the criminal element that needs containment. It is up to Behan, as these men are terrorizing the county. I hear the Mexican government is now up in arms over the rustling."

"Good. Stop it at the border and the Cowboys cannot turn a profit."

Wyatt considered this but did not look to believe it would ever happen. Then he leaned over and said, "Behan didn't pay us for our posse work."

"What? Doesn't the county pay for that?"

"And they did. He billed them more than seven hundred dollars for our services, but he put it all into his personal account. He does not wish the Earps to have any gain."

"Are you going to call him on it?"

"Nope. He's got such sway with county officials that there is no sense trying."

A couple days later, I was accused of taking part in the stage robbery in nothing less than the *Arizona Weekly Star*. After the *Nugget* ran an account of King's escape that stressed outsiders planned the getaway, the *Star* ran a story in sympathy with the account and told how three robbers were headed to Mexico. "The fourth, Doc Holliday, is in Tombstone and has been shadowed since his return." When I saw the story, I cornered Mayor John Clum.

"I will make a sieve out of the next lowdown who repeats the gossip," I declared and he, knowing my reputation, did not attempt to defer the notion. "You know Behan is behind it," I continued. "The Earps see it too. It's a tactic to divert attention from his association with the very Cowboys who committed this crime and a host of others."

"Doc, I don't disagree with you, but what can we do? Newspapers are a world of their own, free speech and all."

"And never mind the man who let King escape is the man saying I'm the criminal?"

"News story doesn't have to be accurate, sorry to say," Clum said. "Just news."

"I do not goddamn know what to do," I railed, my protest getting louder. "Without capture of the men who can clear me, I am seen as a stage robber."

He shook his head, slapped me on the back, and moved on as, like most, he was eager to get away from the truth.

That same night, Milt Joyce lit into me soon as I entered his establishment. "I do not like a stage robber going free," he said loud enough for all to hear, "let alone see him coming in here."

"You throwing me out?" I asked. Though I respected the law against carrying a gun in town, I refused to go unheeled and thus had my pistol concealed inside my coat. As always, my knife resided in my inside breast pocket, both weapons at the ready in case Joyce kept on.

"I am telling one and all," Joyce continued, "a criminal is in our midst and the law has yet to take proper action."

"I am about to take action against you if you don't stop spouting falsehoods."

"You'd best not threaten me, Holliday."

"You are right. Best I shoot you so one and all are spared your foul accusations."

Though I made no move toward my weapon, I was at this point seized from behind and wrestled to the floor, where I was disarmed by none other than Virgil Earp.

"I didn't draw," I complained as he pulled me to my feet.

"That keeps the charge short of murder," Virgil said. "I am arresting you for threats against life and carrying a gun in town."

"What about Joyce's threats?" I demanded as I was shoved outside.

"He was shooting nothing more than his mouth, which so far is legal. You know better than this, Doc."

I settled down enough to not be manhandled and we walked to the jail. "I am being called a stage robber when I was here in town when it happened," I told Virgil.

"I understand and that is unfortunate, but you have to start taking care with that mouth of yours."

He left me in a cell where I was too angry to sleep, so I faced Judge Reilly the next morning in poor shape, my cough intruding on the proceedings. Reilly knew me and was the first man other than an Earp sympathetic to my plight. He dismissed the charges when I agreed to pay court costs and I walked out a free man, much to Virgil's dismay. It felt the first fair shake I'd had in a while.

As Tombstone continued to enjoy a fine spring, weather-wise, with summer fast approaching, I found myself hemmed in by rumor and accusations that, by way of repetition, were now seen as truth. Only my reputation as short-tempered and quick-triggered kept merchants from refusing to deal with me, and yet when the Cowboys rode in they enjoyed full welcome. Compounding the situation was Wyatt starting to distance himself from me. Though we often passed long nights at our respective gaming tables in the Oriental, he seldom came to my room. This, coupled with Milt Joyce's blatant dislike of me, led me to take my gaming business elsewhere.

I could not condemn Wyatt for the distance even though it plainly did not serve his cause. He obviously thought it did, however, never mind the Earps were still seen as trouble. Then one night in late April, Wyatt gave way. I do not know if need simply got the better of him, but he found me playing pool with Morgan and said he wished to speak with me privately. As Morgan was winning, we called the game in his favor, I paid up, and left with Wyatt, not knowing if he was still on his law-and-order high horse.

"What's up?" I asked as we reached the sidewalk.

"My dick," he growled.

I could not help but laugh, which annoyed him, but I did not care. I was tired of the law, tired of politics and rumor and accusations, tired of being hauled to jail for no reason. And I did not, by way of him depriving me so long, give a good goddamn if his dick was up.

"You think that's funny?" he asked.

"It surprised me is all. You've been scarce lately."

"Well, I am here now, and you have about two more seconds to decide on taking me."

"I would be honored," I said, letting all else fall away. I was getting blissfully hard in the presence of the man I craved. It was not time to get him pissed.

"Come on," I said and we walked briskly to my hotel room.

He did not tear at my clothes nor get rough with me. We undressed, and when we stood naked, I saw he was pent up not just with sex need but with life itself, events piling onto him until he now sought the only release possible. I went to him and pressed myself into his arms, our hard dicks up against each other, and he held me tightly for a minute or two before starting to grind his lower region against mine.

"You do that, I'll come right now," I warned him, but he kept on and I could not contain the urge, frantic against his body until I came a gusher. As I spurted between us, I cried out since the relief was more than what churned up out of my balls. The whole of me let go in those moments, my feelings for him now absent the trappings and hardship of the times. I kept at him until my cough got in the way and I sought a drink. Wyatt remained standing, hard prick aimed at me.

"You are some sight," I said when I'd quieted.

His stern expression did not change, yet I saw something behind the mask give way. He cocked his head slightly to one side, and in that small gesture, my heart leaped. He then came to me, led me to the bed, put me on my back, legs up, and put his cock into me.

He was not urgent, as if he sought the coupling as much as the payload. He pumped in and out and a couple times popped clear out and ran his dick up between my balls so he could see it mid-fuck. I saw then he wanted this to last because communing with me in this most intimate manner was all he had anymore.

His juice was wetting his efforts, so I knew it wouldn't be long, and sure enough, he let out a soft moan and picked up the pace. He then pushed my legs up around my ears and began to drive into me with great force, rampant as he took on the familiar grimace and grunted out a come. As I took his stuff, I thought it a fitting reward for my troubles of late.

Once Wyatt was done, he pulled off and lay beside me. I rolled onto my side and slid a hand up onto his chest. "This is the best I have felt in days," I said.

"Likewise," he replied.

Though my cough intruded some, I still managed a sense of floating, as if life had eased some. I thought how we were as we belonged and that Wyatt knew this, even if he might not admit it. "We are a good fit," I remarked, unable to contain my joy.

"Sure as hell are," he said, but I could tell he was slipping away, his thoughts already elsewhere.

"You've run off on me," I noted.

"Don't mean to."

I reached down to play around with his soft piece of meat and he chuckled. "Doc, you are the devil."

"Is that such a bad thing?"

He thrust up at me, grinding his hips. "No, it is not. With things as they are, I might as well enjoy the descent to hell. Why don't you get down there and suck me?"

He pulled an extra pillow under his head and watched as I crawled down between his legs so I could look up at him while I fed. And I made a show with my tongue, poking and licking, rolling his soft thing around awhile, then sucking it into my mouth where I fed until it began to stir. When I glanced up at him and saw his eyes fixed on me, I enjoyed the visual contact nearly as much as the sexual one, the two of us enraptured above and below. Once I had him stiff, I pulled off and said, "I am getting back in the saddle," and I climbed over him and squatted down to take his prick up my passage. "You ready for a long ride?" I asked as I began an easy canter.

His eyes closed in a contentment I rarely saw. "So long as I've got it in you, Doc, you can ride to hell and gone."

"Then we are off."

I had a good time atop his dick, fucking myself on it but also settling to simply work my muscle. I also squirmed and leaned both forward and back, enjoying the way it made his cock rub me inside. At one point, I even worked in a circular motion. As this went on for a good amount of time, my own cock came up and Wyatt took hold as I kept astride him. When he set to working me, I increased my canter and his breath grew short and loud, a moan mixed in, and he pulled my dick until I began to spurt up his front. He then let out a cry and bucked up into me as he let go. He fixed his eyes to mine as we emptied together, and in that moment I saw us complete, safely away from Tombstone's assaults.

I had held my cough in check throughout the fuck, but now, likely due to such exertion, it asserted itself to such extent I had to dismount my stallion for a whiskey. I brought one to Wyatt, who took it down in one swallow and asked for another. When I had myself somewhat quieted, I sat on the bed beside him.

"Now, that was a fuck," I observed.

"Two, I believe," he replied. "And from what is left of me, it feels like my last. I am done in, Doc. You have sucked out every drop of my juice."

"Life's elixir."

He chuckled. "Whiskey and spunk. Some diet."

"I would live on it if you'd allow."

"I do not doubt you," he said, eyes closed. He was relaxed, the iron back fluid with contentment. "If only life did not exist outside this room."

"We could lock the door and be done with it," I suggested. "I'll venture we could last a long time on fucking alone."

"Tempting."

I doubted he realized I was talking specifics by way of avoiding them. I wanted to challenge his distance of late and saw his comment on life outside this room as an opening. Of course, my dick objected to such direction, but as it had been more than satisfied, it had little weight in the matter. So I jumped in. "I have to ask, Wyatt. Has your scarcity of late been due to the accusations against me?"

"Doc, I am in a hell of a spot where you are concerned, and you have to know it."

"The law-and-order Earps can't be seen supporting a stage robber?"

He did not offer comment, which hit me hard. I stood, poured another drink, but remained at the dresser. "What we need is to get those men and make them tell the truth," he said. "And I think I may have a way to do that. Wells Fargo has increased the reward to twelve hundred dollars each for their capture, and I am thinking we need to make that work for us."

"How?"

"Leave that to me. Just know that I want to fix this as much as you."

I studied him some, then returned to the bed. I crawled in beside him, and we lay quiet for some time and did not talk of the larger world. Two days later, Johnny Behan arrested me for murder.

Sheriff Behan grinned as he served a warrant he had no doubt engineered. He had deputy Billy Breakenridge with him, both with guns drawn as if armed resistance was expected.

"Two counts," Behan said. "The passenger died yesterday."

"And you got right on it," I replied.

"Now, Doc."

As I was hauled from Hafford's Saloon, I caught sight of Morgan Earp. "Tell Wyatt," I called to him, "and tell Earl Brimmer."

"Will do," he called back. I was then marched to jail with such a lack of haste that I saw Behan was making a show of my arrest. This rankled me more than the arrest itself since I knew Earl Brimmer, my attorney, would make hash of the charges. It might even work to my favor, I decided, in getting the matter before a judge with evidence presented on my behalf, especially since Behan had none. I thus began to feel more confident.

I knew Behan had timed my arrest so I would spend a night in jail before seeing Judge Reilly, but I determined to give him no satisfaction by way of rancor. Thus when he stood outside my cell in a suit boasting at least four colors thrown together in an awkward plaid, I did no more than ask where he bought his clothes.

He offered that greasy smile and ran his walking stick along the bars. "You are done for, Holliday," he said.

"I beg to differ," I replied. "Never have I felt more robust or more certain that your latest effort will prove little more than an inconvenience."

He shook his head. "Evidence has come to light putting you at the scene of the crime. It has also been learned that the stolen silver has been funneled off by the Earps, so warrants for their arrest will be along soon."

"Amusing, since Wells Fargo confirmed the strongbox and all contents arrived intact at Benson."

"You are dreaming, Doc."

"Then I suggest you depart and leave me to it. I need some sleep before I am exonerated."

He tapped the bars, tipped his hat, and left. I saw neither Wyatt nor Earl that night but knew they would show with morning.

Before court next day, Earl Brimmer got the whole story from me. He was an honest man who supported the Earps and detested Behan, but he still was not able to quash the warrant. Bail was posted, a trial date set two weeks hence, and I was released. As I turned to leave, I saw Wyatt and Virgil in the back, both looking grave. Outside, Earl said his plan was to stall for the moment. "I'll ask for a continuance when we next appear, and after that, another."

"Why not face them down?" I asked. "They have no evidence."

"You don't know what they have, Doc. Even if they're lies, enough of those have been believed to get a warrant issued, so we'd best move with caution."

"Am I never going to be allowed to state the truth?"

"Possibly not. I know that goes against your grain, but this is Tombstone, Doc, not St. Louis or some other civilized place."

"He's right," Virgil chimed in. "Much as I hate saying it, seeing as I represent the law, there is little justice here."

I looked to Wyatt. "I agree," he said.

None of this sat well with me, as I wanted to speak in court and call witnesses who saw me in town that night. "Gentlemen," I said, "based on your learned conclusions, I am going to go get drunk. I bid you good morning."

There was not enough whiskey, but I tried. Sometime in the afternoon, Wyatt pulled me from whatever saloon I'd landed in and pushed me to the Cosmopolitan. I swore as he manhandled me, but he ignored this, as a good friend would do. In my room, I repeated what Behan had said. "He is going after you too. Funneling off silver that was not even stolen."

"So I've heard."

"Doesn't it concern you?"

"Well, since Wells Fargo confirms nothing was stolen, no, it does not."

Here I set to laughing because he didn't make the connection. "You don't see it?" I said. "Then you are a damn fool."

"See what?"

"If I can be charged with murder when I was not there, then you can be charged with larceny of silver not stolen. Such is the law in Tombstone."

"You are drunk, Doc."

"That I am," I said, catching my boot on the bedpost and lurching against the dresser.

"Come on," Wyatt urged me. "Get undressed and into bed."

"Are you planning to fuck me?"

He blew out a sigh and turned back the covers. "Stay here and sleep it off. You're too drunk to be outside. You'll just get into trouble, and you already have enough of that."

I reeled some and fell onto the bed. "Wyatt," I said as he reached the door.

"What?"

"I am sorry my lack of involvement in robbing the stage has caused you problems. Since I did no wrong, I have little else to offer."

"I know, Doc. I know."

While I did as recommended, I found an inhospitable town the next day. Now branded the murderer of two local men, I was given a wide berth by both upstanding citizens and those of lesser repute. Behan continued striding around like a peacock, and when my trial date arrived, Brimmer got his continuance. "They don't want this case in court," he told me afterward. "It will disappear if you'll be patient."

"And I forever remain an accused murder?"

"You say that like it is something new to you," Earl replied.

"It is, goddammit. I have been charged many times and always found justified, as I do not kill unless drawn upon. This is not the same. And I was not there."

"All right, Doc. I am sorry for what I said, but this is the only way. If we get into court, I fear Behan will put some of the Cowboys on the stand to lie and say you were at the scene."

I threw up my hands in defeat, causing Earl to pat my shoulder and depart. Wyatt then came up and offered to buy me a drink.

"It will take more than one," I said.

CHAPTER NINE

As summer slipped past, Earl Brimmer got two more continuances and became even more certain the court would eventually drop the charges against me. "We are making progress," he insisted, and I had learned not to dispute his wisdom. Sure enough, after one more continuance, the matter was set aside without the court's comment. I bought Earl Brimmer several drinks to celebrate his brilliance.

During this period, businessmen supporting the Earps formed a vigilance committee due to Sheriff Behan's failure at law enforcement. These men met with Wyatt and his brothers, expressing full support should any show of force be needed to maintain the peace. At last, the citizens were standing up for themselves. Though Wyatt spoke little about the committee, I knew he had to be pleased to have someone visibly for us.

Good news came in August when Wyatt found me leaving the barbershop one day. "I've learned Crane's whereabouts," he said. "He's been seen at old man Clanton's ranch near Cloverdale."

"Where'd you get that?" I asked.

Though it was a question he surely could have expected, it made him pause as if he had to think up a good answer. "Ike Clanton," he finally said.

I didn't believe it. Such a thing made no sense, as Wyatt would surely never believe one of the Cowboys and especially not one so stupid as Ike. Likewise, Ike would never draw Wyatt to his old man's place, but still, I played along. "What about Leonard and Head?" I asked.

"Word is they're dead over in New Mexico. Bit off more than they could chew. Virgil has deputized me and is getting up a posse to go get Crane. Are you in?"

"Of course."

It was the first time in over a month that I felt the weight of accusation lift off me. A Deputy U.S. Marshal allowing me into his posse was most encouraging, and I was eager toward both the show of faith as well as the idea of getting Crane.

The plan was to take Crane alive so he could tell the truth about the holdup and thus clear both the Earps and me. Virgil, Wyatt, Morgan, and I, all well armed with shotguns and pistols, made up the posse and rode determinedly toward Clanton's place near the Mexican border. I did not ask Wyatt anything more about relying on Ike Clanton for his information, but it still made me uneasy. Something was afoot between them, and any dealing with a Clanton could only come to no good. Still, I rode with enthusiasm, all of us in shirtsleeves due to the summer heat. Wyatt looked his old stern and upright self, and as we rode along side by side, I saw how much I'd missed that.

We were not far from the Clanton ranch when night fell upon us. We kept on through Devil's Canyon where we spotted a campfire up ahead. Thinking it might be Crane, we tied the horses in a clump of trees some distance away, and Virgil and Wyatt crept up for a look. I was not asked to go, as my cough could not be trusted. When the boys came back, they said Crane was there with a herd of cattle.

"He's not alone," Wyatt added. "There's five or six others, and one is old man Clanton."

"How do you want to do it?" I asked.

"Surprise them at daybreak. We can be in position, guns drawn, and get a good drop."

Everyone agreed and Virgil suggested we go back to a little out-of-the-way spot for the night. "I doubt they'll make a move until dawn," he added.

"You and Morg go on," Wyatt said. "I want to keep watch. Doc, you stay with me."

"All right, Wyatt."

When we were alone, I said to him, "What about my cough? I can't go up there."

"We're not going up there, Doc. Crane and his party are tucked in for the night. Get down."

Holy hell, I thought. We're gonna fuck.

With little moon and no fire, we did it mostly by feel, but that was enough. We tied the horses and stood between them, baring just enough to do it. We had to be quiet because of the others, good and bad, but managed. Wyatt got his dick into me and rode out a quick come while I stood leaned against his horse. The only sounds were the slap of his flesh upon mine and the horses nickering at the smell of sex. When Wyatt finished, he reached down to find me hard and he flipped me around, dropped to his knees, and sucked the juice out of me. It felt like a month of come—which I guess maybe it was. When we were done, I started to pull up my pants.

"Leave 'em down," Wyatt commanded. "I am not done."

"Then how about we spread a bedroll?"

He thought on this, which amused me as I knew him well enough to see his caution on the prospect of getting caught unawares by either his brothers or Crane, never mind he presently stood with pants open. He could, I suppose, grab his dick if approached and start to piss. He relented finally and allowed one bedroll onto the ground.

We proceeded to pass the night playing around with each other, which was heightened by the fact that criminals were nearby and arrests ahead at morning. Wyatt got my pants down far enough to give my butt a good long lick before putting his cock in again. Throughout our night, I hardly consulted my flask, as I felt quite drunk with the pleasure of his attentions.

His second fuck was lengthy and again quiet, though this time we disturbed some nocturnal creature who scuttled away as we went at it. While Wyatt worked toward another come, I started palming my rod and let go just as he grew urgent and started to grunt. How I enjoyed coming while his cock fired inside me. Once spent, Wyatt lay atop my back and nuzzled my neck. "You do it for me, Doc," was all he said.

"Likewise," I replied. "Likewise."

After a while, he crawled off and said we should button up. "I'll go check on Crane." When he came back, he announced the fire low, the men asleep.

"We should too," I said.

"You go on. I want to keep awake."

I stretched out on my side so I could enjoy what little of him I could see. He was no more than a dark outline but still remained impressive, standing tall and straight. As I gazed upon him, I wondered if maybe once we had Crane locked up, he might come to my room to celebrate our good fortune.

As planned, we were in place at dawn, shotguns at the ready. We'd taken positions close to the campsite, and when the first head raised up to greet the day, Virgil called out, "Throw up your hands," and showed himself. I saw the man was Bill Ayers, a known rustler, and he did as told, raised his hands, but just then another man jumped up, gun in each hand, and started to shoot. It was Jim Crane, and Morgan nailed him with a blast to his middle. The rest of the party began to fire, and we fired back until the air was heavy with smoke and five men were dead, two gotten away. Cattle scattered when the shooting started, and by the time the dust had settled, were some distance away.

The four of us stood silent until Wyatt uttered a loud "Goddamn to hell."

"Amen," Virgil said.

"I am shot in the foot," I said as pain pulled me down. The others gathered round as I removed my boot, which bore a bullet hole on top. Absent the boot, blood gushed from the foot.

"The leather slowed it down," Virgil declared, "else it would have done real damage."

Wyatt tried to wrap his kerchief around the wound, but I stopped him while I sought my flask, took a swig, then poured some over the wound before allowing Wyatt to continue. Once bandaged, I sat while the others examined the dead men: old man Clanton, Dixie Gray, Bud Snow, Harry Ernshaw—all part of the Cowboys gang, the cattle likely rustled out of Mexico. And Jim Crane, of course, who in death took away our opportunity for vindication.

Coming back to me, Wyatt said we'd best get me back to town. I was helped onto my horse and rode with one leg across the saddle in an attempt to keep the foot elevated. This may have kept me from bleeding to death, but it also furthered my discomfort, not to mention shot to hell any chance of getting Wyatt into my bed.

By the time we reached Tombstone, I was in great pain. Doc Goodfellow removed the bullet, declaring me fortunate it did not do more damage. "Bones look mostly good. I removed a couple of chips, but your boot saved you worse. You'll need to stay off it as much as possible, keep it elevated. Get yourself a walking stick to help ease the weight when you must be upright."

I paid the doctor and thanked him while working at keeping my temper in check because things certainly had not gone as planned. Crane was dead, and with him the hopes of exoneration, plus I'd come away half-crippled. Morgan, who had stayed with me at the doc's office, helped me to my hotel room. "I'll go buy the walking stick," he said, and I saw he got a kick out of that, me hobbling on a stick since I was younger than him.

"Make it something fine," I replied. "I will not be seen with some branch."

He brought me a fine silver-tipped stick and two bottles of whiskey and we sat drinking much of one. "Tomorrow is my thirtieth birthday," I announced to him. "Hell of a way to celebrate."

"You're finally catching me," he noted, which amused me, him being four months older.

I kept to my bed the rest of that day but, as the next, August 14, was mine, I ventured out with my stick. The foot hurt like hell, but I managed to get to the Alhambra for a meal at the lunch counter and then to a poker game where I played for some time with the foot propped on an empty chair. Word spread of how my wound had been acquired and the faction determined to slander my name furthered their rumors by stating I had killed all three stage robbers to keep them from telling of my involvement. Never mind Head and Leonard had been killed in another state the week before; they were now included in the gang we had dispatched. Johnny Behan did his best to have us arrested for the killings, but as Virgil was a Deputy U.S. Marshal and Wyatt his deputy, Behan could not, for once, jail us.

Wyatt proved most attentive during my convalescence, though he laid off fucking in deference to my wound. I tolerated his caution even though it rankled me, but I could not bring myself to tell him he was being somewhat an old woman. His actions were too endearing to dispute, and so I let him bring me whiskey and sit at my bedside when the foot kept me down. When he saw me playing cards, he sometimes frowned like a damned mother hen.

Though he still spoke of running for sheriff in eighty-two, it did not consume him as had the earlier fiasco. He worked at speaking more to people, attended musicals and dances, while still being occasionally drawn into enforcing the law. Though he wore no badge, many still considered him in authority, and, of course, he was just that inside the Oriental. The Cowboys continued to terrorize the county, wreaking havoc with the Mexicans along the border and tearing up Charleston and Galeyville, but their presence in Tombstone was not as a force. Ike Clanton and Johnny Ringo got drunk now and then and were arrested for carrying weapons in town, but they always paid their fines and were released. Curly Bill continued to collect taxes for Behan. Wyatt remarked on the relative quiet when he came to my room one evening.

"No cards tonight?" he asked as he filled my glass and poured himself one.

"Damned foot's giving me hell," I said. "Been six weeks and I still hobble worse than old man Fuller."

Wyatt took the chair beside my bed. "You'll mend in time," he said, then sipped his whiskey before going on. "Quiet out there tonight. Feels downright respectable."

"Don't let it fool you."

"Always the pessimist, Doc." He looked around the room. "You need anything?"

"What do you have in mind?"

He set aside his drink and stood to unbutton his pants. When he pulled out his dick, I saw it hard. He wrapped a hand around it. "Speaks for itself," he said, which brought a smile to my lips. He crawled onto the bed, careful not to disturb my elevated foot, and on his knees, got his dripping cock to my mouth. I opened up like some baby bird and began to feed. Apparently, a quiet night got him as riled as one filled with gunplay.

He allowed me to suck and pull while he squirmed with pleasure. As I feasted on him, I got my underdrawers down and my own cock free, hand upon it, working myself as I fed on him. I thought I would receive his spunk in my throat, but he pulled back, breathing hard, and said, "Not in your mouth."

He then began to peel away my drawers, careful when he took them over the foot. Once naked from the waist down, I raised my legs high to show him my butthole, which he looked upon as if he hadn't made use of it before. He issued a sound much like a man about to dig into the sweetest pudding, slathered spit on himself, then got into position and shoved in. I grabbed my prick and set to pulling as he set to pumping, and holy God, it was some fuck.

I soon spurted all up my belly at which he began to call my name, "Doc, oh hell, Doc," as he grunted and thrust. I kept my eyes to his as he unloaded. He carried on through a good long come after which he pulled out and sat back on his haunches. "I'll be damned," he said when he had regained his breath.

He cleaned up at the basin, then lay down beside me. "How's the foot?" he asked.

"What foot?"

This got a laugh out of him, which was a rarity, and I took the opportunity to squeeze his upper arm. I did not let go, however, and he tolerated this, which pleased me greatly. "I must stay in more often," I observed. "Maybe there is some good to being shot."

"Long as it's just your foot," he replied.

I think that was the most at ease I'd ever seen Wyatt. He'd managed to put much behind him and maybe looking ahead to the eighty-two election was good for him in that it gave him new purpose. He was surely not a man to be content dealing faro.

"We're doing pretty good these days," I said.

"Except for your foot."

"Well, yes, but as you said, I am mending and soon it will be nothing but an ugly scar. How are the claims going? Anything more come of them?"

He was happy to tell me about buying and selling of such. Water claims were as valuable as silver claims, and he and his brothers were most active in both, investing here and there, selling at a profit. Collectively, they managed a good deal of business, and I saw how Wyatt thrived among his family. Sometimes it made me think back to Georgia and my cousins there, Robert especially, who had planned to go into dental practice with me. We had been best friends as boys, much like the Earps were now. I was not unaware that the Earps served to fill my empty spot.

I should have known better than to think things would stay calm in Tombstone. The place might have been taking on the look of respectability, adding theaters and banks and all manner of commerce, but the bad element called the Cowboys was gradually coming together as a reckoning force. As summer slipped into fall, a cauldron bubbled underneath us, but nobody much realized until it boiled over in late October.

My foot was healing well by then, so I rode to Tucson for a couple of reasons. The four-day San Agustin Fiesta was a good place to cut loose on my own, which I'll confess I did, not to mention winning a good amount at faro. A festival draws suckers from near and far, and the more they drink, the more they lose. I thus had a full pocket when, on the third day, I was found by none other than Morgan Earp.

"Doc, we want you in Tombstone tomorrow," he said. "Better come up this evening."

I could see from his look that trouble was brewing. "All right," I said and I cashed out and headed home. We arrived in Tombstone around ten o'clock on the night of October 25 and went immediately to join Wyatt at the Alhambra saloon. "Morg, I need to talk to Doc alone," Wyatt said and Morgan nodded and left us. Wyatt took me to a corner table where we could sit undisturbed. I parked my walking stick and waited.

"I'm having some trouble with Ike Clanton and fear you are drawn into it through no fault of your own."

"How's that?"

"Ike and I had a secret business arrangement and he's got it into his head that I told you about it. We had strong words earlier and he refused to listen to reason, so if he comes around, keep that in mind. He's got himself pretty worked up."

"I'll tell him I don't know anything, and maybe that will settle him down."

"Maybe."

"Do you want to tell me what the business arrangement was?"

"Not particularly. I've kept my part of the bargain and mean to still."

"Fair enough."

Wyatt then left and I gave our talk no more thought as I settled in at faro. Around one o'clock in the morning I found myself hungry and went to the lunch counter located in the front of the Alhambra, opposite the bar. There I came upon Ike Clanton, who began to berate me for having knowledge of his business with Wyatt. "I have no such knowledge," I said. "This is the first I've known of you doing any business with him, and it surprises me as he's not the kind of man to agree to anything with the likes of you."

"Don't try to get around me," Ike said in his shrill, high-pitched voice. For a big man, he sounded more like a small one or maybe a boy whose voice has yet to mature. "You two are thick as thieves, and I know he told you, which puts my life in danger. You are lying to me and I don't appreciate it."

Well, that did it. "You are the goddamned liar and a fool to boot," I snapped. "If you think Wyatt Earp would break a confidence, then you haven't the brains of a gnat, but then I always knew that. You're nothing but a son of a bitch of a Cowboy."

Clanton evidently saw the error of pursuing his accusations and began to backtrack. "I only told where Jim Crane could be found so as to get you and the Earps out of town so we could fill you full of lead."

"Didn't see you boys out there," I returned. "Think better of it, did you? Your old man should have. He's dead along with Crane, in case you haven't heard, and the county is better for it."

Ike's anger flared to such extent he began to sputter. "You ain't fit to live, Holliday," he managed.

"You son of a bitch!" I said. "If you ain't heeled, go and heel yourself!"

About this time, Virgil Earp stepped between us. "Knock it off, boys, or I'll arrest you both. Ike, you sit yourself down over there and shut your mouth. Doc, you get the hell out of here."

I hadn't noticed Wyatt come in. He came up, laid a hand on my arm, and gave me a pull. "Son of a bitch," I said as I turned to go.

"That's enough, Doc," Wyatt said.

We walked up Allen Street toward the Cosmopolitan. "I'm sorry about that," Wyatt said. "Ike has it all wrong but won't see it."

"Are you going to tell me what he's got wrong or just leave me dangling out here?"

He went quiet, no doubt wrestling with the idea of breaking a confidence, so I pushed some. "Wyatt, whatever confidence you shared with Ike is pretty well broken down, based on his actions tonight. I doubt my knowing it now will harm anything beyond your sense of propriety, which for one goddamned time I wish you'd let go."

"Shit," was all he said. We walked a bit more, then he blew out a sigh and began. "Back when Marsh Williams told me Wells Fargo had increased the reward for Leonard, Head, and Crane to twelve hundred each, I got an idea to offer it to Ike if he'd get me information on their whereabouts. He agreed if I'd swear to keep it secret, as the other Cowboys would kill him if they knew he had aligned himself with me. He then wanted to know if the reward was dead or alive, so I asked Marsh and he wired Wells Fargo about that. When he got the reply that it was dead or alive, I borrowed the wire and showed it to Ike. At the time, it pleased him and we shook hands on our agreement."

Here he paused, likely thinking I would tell him it was a bad idea all around, but I said nothing, knowing he'd stew himself far worse by way of having had to tell me what he'd done.

"You'd think now that the men are dead he would calm down," Wyatt went on, "but he's gone off the rails entirely as he is certain you know about the agreement and Marsh Williams does too, all because of that wire. He's decided I showed it to you, told you the whole story. He says I told Marsh Williams, and never mind he's wrong on both counts. What I didn't know is all these months he's been living in fear the McLaurys and Ringo and Curly Bill would find out and he'd be done for. Now he's starting to come apart from that fear, as you saw tonight. And I don't know what to do. I almost wish he'd try to shoot me so I could put an end to him."

"Hell of a fix," I said as we reached the Cosmopolitan. "Nothing more to be done tonight and he's pretty liquored up, so maybe he'll sleep it off and wake up tomorrow thinking better of things."

"Now who's being the optimist?"

"Get some sleep, Wyatt. Look at things fresh tomorrow."

At two o'clock the following afternoon, I was awakened from a good sleep by Morgan Earp, who said trouble was brewing and Virgil wanted me at Hafford's saloon. I did not ask what was afoot, as events of the previous night remained fresh. I said I would be along soon as I got my clothes on and my coughing under control. Taking some whiskey, I was then able to begin the day. As always, I took care with dressing, choosing a black suit and pale gold shirt. Since there was talk of trouble, I strapped on my gun and holster, laws against it be damned. The weather had turned cold lately, so I added my long gray coat. I also carried my walking stick. Breakfast would have to wait even though my stomach grumbled.

Tombstone held an air of apprehension as I walked to Allen and Fourth streets. Fewer people were about, and those in the street took note of my passage with a look of concern, if not downright fear. Word had obviously gone around that something was up, and I seemed the only one not in the know.

At Hafford's, I found the three Earps out front and fully armed. "What in hell is going on?" I asked as I came up beside them.

Virgil shook his head. "Wyatt and I had to disarm Ike Clanton this morning," he began. "He was waving his gun around, saying he would kill us all, but he was too drunk to do much and I buffaloed him and arrested him for gun possession. Took him, bloody head and all, to Judge Wallace, who fined him and then set him loose. I said he could pick his guns up at the Grand Hotel when he left town. Things were fine until Wyatt jumped in."

"I was not about to stand by while he went over and picked up his guns and came to kill us."

"You just made it worse."

"What did you say?" I asked.

"Said I was tired of his threats and if he wanted a fight, I would go anywhere on earth to make that fight with him."

"Sounds fair to me."

"But then he got into it with Tom McLaury, who said he'd had enough of us Earps and would fight us anytime," Virgil went on. "Got heated, then Wyatt here buffaloes McLaury and walks away saying he could kill the son of a bitch which, of course, McLaury heard."

"And I slept through it all."

"Better you weren't there, Doc," Virgil said. "You'd likely have killed 'em all."

"Needs doing."

I saw that people were watching us, some taking spots on upstairs balconies, others in doorways. A few brave souls remained on the street, and I thought how we were becoming an awful entertainment.

"Clanton got into my card game at the Oriental last night after I sent you home," Virgil told me. "Behan and Tom McLaury sat in and we went until after sunup when I got up to leave. Clanton stopped me and asked me to take a message to you. When I asked what it was he said, 'The damned son of a bitch has got to fight.' I replied that as an officer of the law I could not deliver the message, as I did not want any trouble. He then said, 'You won't carry the message, you may have to fight before you know it.' Judging from his appearance this morning, I'm guessing he did not sleep and is stewing his juices because word is that since his release, he's been in and out of several places, drinking and talking how he's going to kill us all. It was Ned Boyle who heard him and came to wake me. He was also spouting off in Kelly's Wine Room and the Oriental Saloon, so he's got a fresh snoot full."

"Are his guns at the Grand?"

"Yep. I took them there before I went home to bed. He can pick them up so long as he leaves town."

I looked at Wyatt, who bore a most determined expression. He clearly meant to put an end to things one way or another and saw from my look that I was in agreement. If Clanton and McLaury wanted a fight, they would get one.

"I saw Billy Clanton and the McLaurys at Spangenberg's buying ammunition this morning," Morgan said. "You tell me they don't mean to fight us. And Bob Richards said he saw Ike in the telegraph office, which means he's probably sent for Ringo and the others. We've got to stop this before it gets worse."

Just then, Reuben Coleman, a local miner, ran up to us. "I was just down by the OK Corral and ran into Ike and Billy Clanton. They're with the McLaurys, who are armed. I told Sheriff Behan he should go and disarm them before anybody got shot, but he took no action, so I am coming to you, Marshal Earp, asking you to do it."

"We'll take care of it," Virgil said and Coleman hurried inside Hafford's. "I think we have to go down there," Virgil said to us. "If they are just getting their horses at the corral and fixing to leave, we'll let them go, but if they are staying put, then we'll disarm them."

Wyatt then turned to me. "Doc, you don't have to do this. It's our fight."

"That's a hell of a thing to say to me," I replied and he saw he'd wounded me. He nodded and I let it pass as I knew he was well intentioned.

Virgil held a shotgun, but Wyatt suggested he take my walking stick while I put the shotgun under my coat. This was done and I saw how Wyatt was trying to defuse things with the stick being shown rather than a gun. I knew the Earps would try to solve things without gunplay, as none of them was easy on the trigger. I was the one who had little hesitation toward killing a deserving man.

Though I wore no badge, I was considered part of a marshal's posse that day, while Wyatt and Morgan had been duly deputized. Thus, we were going up Fourth Street toward Fremont Street when Johnny Behan accosted us. "I have disarmed them," he declared. "You don't need to go down there."

Now, Johnny Behan may have been sheriff, but he had never once put himself in harm's way, and it was foolish to think he would do so now. We brushed him aside and continued ahead, turning onto Fremont, where we saw the two Clantons and the two McLaurys in the vacant lot west of Fly's Photography Studio and behind the OK Corral. When we reached them, they spread out abreast and we did the same. Then Virgil raised my walking stick and called out, "Boys, throw up your hands. I want your guns."

Billy Clanton and Frank McLaury reached for their holsters, and when Virgil heard the click of hammers being cocked, he called out, "Hold on! I don't want this!" There passed maybe one second before Billy Clanton raised his gun and two shots were fired, one from him and one from Wyatt, which set everybody to shooting. Wyatt caught Frank McLaury in the gut, which caused Frank to lurch forward but keep firing. Virgil tossed the stick and took up his pistol while I hit Tom McLaury with the shotgun as he tried to hide behind a horse. This sent him staggering into the street full of buckshot. Ike Clanton rushed forward and grabbed Wyatt by the arm.

"I got no gun!" he cried.

Wyatt shoved him aside, saying, "The fight has commenced. Go to fighting or get away." Ike ran off through the Fly house.

Virgil took a bullet in the calf, likely from the wounded Frank McLaury, who refused to give up. Morgan's bullets hit Billy Clanton in the chest, wrist, and stomach, which caused him to fall but not to stop firing as he now had his pistol balanced on his knee. "I am hit!" Morgan cried out, clutching his shoulder as I tossed aside my shotgun to take up my pistol.

Frank McLaury tried to get away using a horse for cover and got out into Fremont Street, but the horse bolted, leaving him for me. He lifted his pistol at me, saying, "I've got you now," to which I replied, "Blaze away. You're a daisy if you have." I fired then, as did Morgan, and at last he was done, but not before he managed to shoot me in the hip, which caught mostly my holster.

Tom McLaury had reached the corner of Third and Fremont and lay dying beside a telegraph pole. Billy Clanton was trying to reload his pistol when photographer Fly ran from his rooming house and took away the pistol. The shooting then stopped, the fight ended.

Billy Clanton was taken to a nearby house, where he soon died. Frank McLaury died in the street, while his brother Tom managed a few hours, then died in the house beside Clanton. The coroner called to the scene noted no weapon upon Tom McLaury.

The air was heavy with blue smoke from the gunfire. People looked on from a distance as quiet descended. Then Johnny Behan came over. "I have to arrest you," he told us.

Wyatt looked hard at him for a couple seconds, then spoke. "Any decent officer of the law may come and arrest me, but you or any of your kind had best not try it. You deceived me, Johnny. You told me they were not armed. I will answer for what I have done, and I will not leave town, but you will not arrest me."

Mr. Comstock, a town official, then jumped in to say, "There is no hurry arresting this man. He done right in killing them and the people will uphold them."

"You bet we did right," Wyatt said. And to Behan he added, "We had to do it. And you threw us, Johnny. You told us they were disarmed."

Wyatt and I, assisted by others, then saw to getting Morgan and Virgil to their homes, where they were given medical treatment. Fortunately, neither wound was too serious. Once they were seen to, we walked back up Allen Street and that was it. The town was rid of the McLaurys and there was one less Clanton to trouble us, yet it gave little satisfaction. Things may have been quiet on the street, but we were far from settled. You don't kill a man, justified or otherwise, without consequence. It sets the heart to pounding, the nerves to twitching, the body toward unrest. Anger that has built for weeks was not discharged with bullets, no matter how many we fired. The fight had lasted less than a minute, yet clung to us as if we'd been bloodied. "Christ, Doc," Wyatt said as we neared the Cosmopolitan. "I should go sit with my brothers, but right now, I don't think I can do that. Come on." And he led me to my room.

Once behind a locked door, he threw off his coat and tossed aside his gun belt. He was shaking with a rage that started to seep out of him, and I poured us drinks, which we downed quickly, then took another. Nothing helped, of course. I thought he would speak or swear, but he did not vent his anger. He paced the room while I quietly undressed. "Wyatt," I said when I was naked.

He looked at me like he was some hawk who's just spotted a juicy rodent, except this rodent was not running for cover. Then he looked toward my hip. "You're grazed," he said and I glanced down at a two-inch slash of red.

"Nothing but a scrape," I replied. "Not a concern." I began to tug my cock, which responded with enthusiasm. "Fuck me," I said. "I can tend my hip and you can tend to everyone else later on. Right now, you're the one needs tending."

He downed the last of his drink. "Ah, hell, Doc," he said and he began to undress. He threw off everything and was stiff by the time he was bare. "Goddamn fuck is all we've got," he growled and I readily agreed. I climbed onto the bed, happy my foot had improved enough to no longer interfere with pleasure. I rolled onto my stomach and raised my butt. "Fuck me," I said again and he got in behind and stuck it to me.

He swore as he went at it and he was relentless, driving into me with such force it caused me to shoot a load into the bedding. How the man could drive the come out of me. He wasn't as quick as usual, which I attributed to recent events. Wyatt did not consider himself a killer, always going to great lengths to avoid it; thus it weighed on him even when he was in the right and he was exterminating vermin. His fucking may have been a steady pounding, but his juice did not readily boil.

Sweat began to fly off him after a while and his fingers dug into my hips. His grunts and groans were mighty, but at last came the rise. He began to utter a sound like that of a horse at full gallop, the deep panting that makes you think it might be the creature's last. When the climax finally hit, Wyatt let out a roar, at which a responding hallelujah would have served well, had I been of a religious bent. As it was, I gloried in receiving his spunk, which he drove home to great length. When he at last was empty and pulled out, he collapsed beside me, eyes closed. I rolled onto my side facing him, listening to his breathing gradually settle.

"There's going to be hell to pay," he said after a while.

"For this?" I replied, attempting to lighten the situation. This did not land and I saw he would not be deterred from the position we had been forced into.

"For the goddamned killing," he snapped.

"I know. I just thought to ease your concern. Should have known better."

"No, Doc, you're right. I'm sorry, but it weighs on me. You know Behan is out there right this minute stirring up the wrong of what we did; I don't care how justified we were."

I slid a hand onto his chest. "It is going to be the same tomorrow as it is right now."

He looked at me. "What are you after?"

"I'm after all I can get," I said, fingering his tit.

"I should check on Virg and Morg."

"They are being seen to. How about I see to you?" And before he could argue further, I slid down and took his soft dick into my mouth.

He did not object to me sucking him. For a while, he lay with arms stretched out to his sides, like some beautiful manly cross. Then he raised up to look at what I was doing, his prick now filling, and he tugged my butt around toward him and got me to crawl over and drop my cock into his mouth. As we fed on each other, I thought how we managed some good on a truly awful day.

Neither of us worked up a good come, despite a great period of sucking, licking, and such. We finally pulled off and I crawled up beside him. "First one was too good," I noted.

"Tired," was all he said, but I knew what he meant. A cumulative tired, the killing, the need for the killing, the situation we would face in the aftermath, his brothers wounded, and other things we likely had not considered that would drop onto us in days ahead.

I blew out a sigh and agreed. "Tired as hell."

We lay quiet awhile, then he got up and dressed. "I'm going to see to the boys," he said. "And I need to find Ike. He shouldn't get away since he started the whole damned thing."

I got up and into my pants. "I am going to get some supper," I said. "See you later."

He passed me a long look, nodded, then left. I dressed and set out for supper. I would have liked to go by and see Virgil and Morgan but thought against it. When I was in the room, the women tended to see me as part of the trouble, thus I had a meal and ventured to the Alhambra where I played poker among men more cautious than usual. Nobody mentioned the gunfight, likely in fear I'd shoot those offering comment.

Quiet then settled onto the town, and for much of the next forty-eight hours, the Earps were seen as heroes. The *Epitaph* editorialized in our favor:

> *The feeling among the best class of our citizens is that the marshal was entirely justified in his efforts to disarm these men, and that being fired upon, they had to defend themselves, which they did most bravely. So long as our peace officers make effort to preserve the peace and put down highway robbery—which the Earp brothers have done—they will have the support of all good citizens. If the present lesson is not sufficient to teach the Cowboy element that they cannot come into the streets of Tombstone, in broad daylight, armed with six-shooters to hunt down their victims, then the citizens will most assuredly take steps to preserve the peace as will be forever a bar to further raids.*

Newspapers all along the Pacific Coast offered much the same comment, the Earps being congratulated on their fine law enforcement. That I was not praised was of little consequence, as I remained a suspicious character and praise of me at such a time would have worked against the Earps. I was pleased for them to be seen in a good light, but on the second day after the gunfight, I happened past Ritter & Ream Undertakers where in the front window hung a large sign, MURDERED IN THE STREETS OF TOMBSTONE. Under this were propped the coffins of the three departed men, each with glass at the top so the upper bodies were visible. At that moment, I considered the praiseworthy period ended.

Next day came a most imposing funeral. I stood with Wyatt at Hafford's corner as the procession passed by, both of us stunned at what we saw. The town's brass band led things, followed by two hearses, one with Billy Clanton, another the two McLaurys. Ike and his brother Fin rode in a wagon following the hearses, and after them came about three hundred people on foot, at least twenty carriages, one four-horse stage, and too many on horseback to count. People lined both sides of the street to watch, and it looked like everyone not marching in the procession had come out to view its passage.

"It's more than a block long," I said as I looked up what seemed a never-ending line of men on horseback.

"Not good," Wyatt added.

I was flummoxed by the outpouring and said as much to Wyatt. "I understand respect for the dead, but these men were criminal. Good people are out there marching behind the worst kind."

"I don't want to imagine the words that will be said over them."

"And against us."

Ten days later, Wyatt and I were jailed for murder.

Chapter Ten

A coroner's inquest, held the day after the McLaury-Clanton funeral, gave us our first sight of how court proceedings would be played. Sheriff Behan and Cowboys Ike Clanton and Billy Claiborne testified that the deceased parties were all unarmed and we had approached them with guns already drawn. Five so-called neutral witnesses gave accounts conflicting with one another, which added up to a verdict that did no more than confirm the men had died by gunshot. This accomplished so little that the next day Ike Clanton filed first-degree murder charges against us, alleging we killed with malice aforethought—the maximum possible charge and a capital offense. On the strength not of the inquest verdict but of the testimony given, the town council suspended Virgil as city marshal.

"Why wouldn't Behan have filed the charges?" I asked Wyatt once warrants had been served. He and I were to appear on Monday, October 31, in Judge Wells Spicer's court for a hearing to decide if we should be held for trial for murder. Virgil and Morgan, though charged, would be excused from appearing due to their wounds.

"My guess is he doesn't want to be seen as too allied with the Cowboys," Wyatt replied, "so he had Ike do the dirty work and Ike is too dumb to see it."

"Doesn't much matter," I reasoned. "Hell of a thing, though."

Wyatt hired Tom Fitch to defend us. Fitch, known as the Silver Tongued Orator of the Pacific, was a formidable presence and his first order of business in Spicer's court was to apply for bail. After lengthy objections by the two prosecutors, it was granted. Spicer then issued an order that no public or press would be allowed in the courtroom, in compliance with Arizona law allowing defendants the right to a closed courtroom. Testimony began the next day.

Newspapers soon began to pick up on what had been said at the inquest and ran stories about unarmed men gunned down at the OK

Corral. People eager to gather into a flock for easy herding took these stories as fact, so by the time the hearing commenced, we were much on the downside.

Wyatt spent time with his brothers most evenings, which was to be expected. Virgil and Morgan might not have been required in court, but they were still very much involved, and discussion of the situation was likely long and thorough. I, meanwhile, continued sporting at various establishments and was treated no differently than previously, save for increased caution by those venturing to my table. The Cowboy element laid low during this period, apparently confident we would be done in by the legal system.

Testimony began with the coroner reviewing the details of wounds and again confirming the men died by gunshot. Billy Allen, friend of the victims, then testified that Wyatt had struck Tom McLaury with his gun that morning. Allen, who had seen the gunfight, said Tom McLaury had thrown open his coat, shouting, "I ain't got no arms," while Billy Clanton had cried, "I do not want to fight." He then insisted I had fired first, which was incorrect, as was the rest of what he said. Fitch objected on several points and was overruled.

Next day, Johnny Behan took the stand, saying how he went to great efforts to disarm not only the Clantons and McLaurys, but to disarm the other parties as well. He told of attempts to stop us from getting to the men and how we brushed him away. He said Wyatt issued threats as Virgil told the men to throw up their hands. "You sons of bitches, you have been looking for a fight and now you have it," were the words he said Wyatt spoke. He said he saw my nickel-plated revolver in hand from the first and he repeated the statements from Tom and Billy about not being armed and not wanting to fight. Outside of his comment at us brushing past him, not a word of truth came from his mouth.

Fitch, in cross-examination, went after Behan for his bias against Wyatt, his lack of enforcing the law, and his association with the Cowboy element. Fitch even asked him to define the term Cowboy, as known in the town, and Behan had to pause at length before coming up with "stockman."

On Friday, neutral witnesses were heard with each giving a varying account of events. Two had been inside a butcher shop as our party passed en route to the corral. One told how Morgan had said, as we walked along, "Let them have it," and I had supposedly replied, "All right." Such bits and pieces were knitted together to portray us as aggressors looking for a fight rather than men trying to control a lawless element bent on killing us. Fitch cross-examined all who spoke but gained little.

That night, a new player entered the scene. William McLaury, brother to the two dead men, was an attorney in Texas who, when he got word of the killings, closed up shop and headed for Tombstone. Arriving in town, he immediately contacted the prosecutors and got himself added to their team. Word came to us that when court resumed on Monday, after a weekend adjournment, we would face a new unknown.

I felt like blowing off a head of steam that Friday night, as it had been a grueling week in the courtroom, so I drank to a bit of excess in the Alhambra. Wyatt came in late, undoubtedly after spending the evening with his brothers. He took up at the end of the bar where he could look back into the sporting room and to me in particular. His look was downright fierce, which fired me to such extent I lost the next hand and exited the game.

"Wyatt," I said as I joined him at the bar. "How are the boys?"

"Faring well."

"And you?"

This threw him. God forbid he speak on how he felt. Just once, I would have liked to have him spill at least a drop, but that would not be Wyatt Earp. Closed-mouth son of a bitch, until he got a dick into it. "You want to get out of here?" he finally asked.

"Hell, yes."

I thought he meant my room, but when I started toward the hotel, he stopped me. "Out of town," he said. "Ride for a bit."

"As you wish."

We sought our horses and were soon on an easy canter out toward the river, going past the place where we'd been before. I wasn't sure if Wyatt sought more privacy or just wanted to get further away, but no matter; I went along, slightly sloshed and quite happy. Maybe getting out of Tombstone was the only way to get past our troubles.

When Wyatt finally pulled up, I noted we were under a full moon. Leaning back, I saw a sky filled with stars. "Look at that," I said and Wyatt looked up.

"You're drunk, Doc."

"I beg to differ. I am comfortably sozzled but not so far gone as to make a fool of myself, as might a drunk. In any case, I am alert enough to appreciate nature's handiwork and thank her for providing us a full moon."

"Get down," he said, failing to appreciate the grandeur.

"Where are we?" I asked.

"Doesn't matter." He began to spread his bedroll and I sought mine, laid it out beside his, thus making our bed. When I began to cough, he grew impatient. "Haven't you about pickled that?"

"Now, now, Wyatt. The whiskey helps suppress the cough but can't finish it. Nothing can, short of death. As for pickling, that remains solely for the rest of me."

He threw off his hat and coat, then undid his gun belt and let it drop. "Can you get your pants off?" he asked in a sharp tone.

"I believe I can manage." He was starting to annoy me with his condescension, but I pressed on, removing boots, pants, drawers, never mind it was November and chilly. I doubted he took note of the weather any more than he had nature's bounty.

He undid his pants, got out a stiff dick, and told me to get down. I took a moment to feast on the sight of him rubbing spit onto himself, then crawled onto all fours and felt him get in behind. When he stuck it in, there was no pause, no happy-to-be-home moment. He was thrusting from the first, issuing not a sound as he fucked like a madman, and when he quickly came, all I heard were strangled grunts, like he held back the worst of cries.

He pulled out soon as he finished, and I heard his breathing was not the usual heave of satisfaction but rather the panting of need. He'd satisfied nothing. I flipped over and lay back so he could see my hard cock. He looked at it like he wanted to chew up and swallow the thing, but he descended with care, sucking urgently while palming his own, and I saw then he wanted to keep coming and coming because there was nothing else for him now.

I flailed about with my hands as I wanted to reach for him, grab hold, but dared not. He pulled my cock into his throat and when I let go my load, he swallowed it all, then kept at me, getting a hand under to squeeze my balls and run a finger up my crack. Christ, there was no letting up.

The cold night air was soon forgotten as Wyatt proved himself inexhaustible. I was roughly fucked three times, licked thoroughly, tongue-fucked, finger-fucked, cock-sucked, ball-sucked, and generally handled to excess while spurting come now and then. Wyatt's juice seemed to boil up anew each time he spent a batch. I had never been so thoroughly used in my life, yet when he finally relented, after I don't know how many hours, he still did not rest. I, meanwhile, had all but dissolved. My butthole felt raw, my every fiber frayed, my head spinning, my mouth beyond dry. I lay trying not to cough, which was hopeless, and I had to retrieve my flask and take a couple of swigs to quiet myself.

Wyatt lay silent, looking up at stars I doubt he noticed. "There is not enough," he said at last, voice as raspy as that of an orator gone on too long.

"Good try, though," I said. "I doubt I can walk."

"I can't…"

"Can't what?"

"I am not some goddamned criminal," he said. "Sitting in that courtroom as a defendant against a pack of lies is more than a man should have to bear."

"Agreed. It is a travesty through and through, but you yourself know how badly justice works in these parts."

"This isn't justice, Doc. We will not have the opportunity for justice. They mean to see us hang."

Ah, death. Welcome to my world. I said nothing toward this, however, as I had to allow that Wyatt, and everyone else I knew, did not have a sentence already laid down. I must work at sympathy for those facing an untimely end for the first time. My own first facing up was so long removed that it was far from mind. Not much would be gained in hanging me, but hanging Wyatt, well, that would be something.

"It won't get that far," I assured him. "Tom Fitch will put an end to the lies when he presents our case."

"But now we've got a McLaury in there, and he is highly motivated. What were the odds of those two buzzards having a lawyer for a brother, and a damned good one from what I hear?"

"Fitch can handle him."

"Can he?"

I rolled over and got my hand down between Wyatt's legs. He was more than spent, but a man will always enjoy another's pull. "Let's talk about something else," I said. "Or maybe stop talking."

As I started down to get my mouth on him, he ran his hand through my hair, which was a most intimate gesture, not made before. It touched me greatly, and when I began to suck his cock, I savored a warming to my heart along with pleasure upon my tongue.

We stayed outside all night, finally pulling coats over us but refusing to do up our pants, as our important parts were in use much of the time. The long slits in my greatcoat allowed me to pull aside enough to get at him while keeping us warm. Men who wish carnal knowledge of each other become highly resourceful.

At dawn, Wyatt got up to piss and only after this did up his pants. "I had best get home," he said. When I did not reply, he continued. "Mattie's having difficulty with my arrest. She says her headaches are worse and is at the laudanum, and I don't know what to do but try to comfort her best I can. Staying away all night does not help things, but on the other hand, she may not even notice."

I never wanted to know what went on in that house, but he needed, on occasion, to tell me. I knew it an assurance of a sort, his way of showing me my importance, and I clung to that view even as I hated hearing what he said. I got up slowly, coughing some, and began to dress. Wyatt was saddling his horse when he said he'd come by later on. "Will you be at the Alhambra?" he asked.

"After I get some sleep," I replied. "Night like the one just passed, I need to recuperate. Don't you?"

"I don't know. Maybe."

It meant him crawling into bed with Mattie, and I saw he was reluctant about that. Dared I invite him to the hotel? Could the two of us manage a rest together? "You are welcome to rest in my room," I said as I saddled my horse.

"Let me think on that."

We rode back to town under a clear sky, the air warming slightly. I felt bone tired yet invigorated, truly spent and happier for it. Never had I felt Wyatt more mine than I did on that ride to Tombstone. And we did not hurry. We rode mostly in silence, just going along. Once in town, we put our horses up at the livery and walked to the Cosmopolitan. There Wyatt said he'd best get on home and I nodded and we parted. But later that afternoon, I was awakened to him at my door.

"McLaury is down at the Grand talking up how he's going to hang us and he's drawing a crowd," Wyatt said, charging in. He looked like hell.

"Have you been to bed?" I asked, which he ignored.

"He's going to be trouble," Wyatt went on. "Big-mouthed, loud, and people will listen to that sort. Behan's there too, riding coattails like always."

"Best not to dwell on that which we cannot control," I said.

"I know that, Doc, but goddamn, it's not right. We are condemned before we are heard."

"We'll have opportunity," I reminded him. "Or at least you will.

Fitch won't damage things with the likes of me on the stand, but he will surely put you on in our defense."

He looked at me. I was sitting on the bed in just drawers. When I started coughing, Wyatt poured me a drink but took none himself. He wouldn't sit either but kept looking out my window, which gave him a view on nothing but a side passage between buildings.

"You'd better save your energy for Monday," I said. "That's when you'll need it. Let McLaury run off at the mouth. Long as Judge Spicer is not over at the Grand slapping him on the back, he doesn't mean a thing."

"I wish I had your confidence. Opinion has a way of bending things around here."

"Is that what you came in here for?" I asked as I peeled off my drawers. "There's a better way to occupy the day than dwelling on something you need not consider." Here I tugged my prick, which began to stiffen soon as let loose. Wyatt looked down at it like he honestly might prefer to keep talking. "Christ, Wyatt, what do I have to do? Stick my ass up in the air? Get on with it or go back to the Grand and torture yourself."

"Son of a bitch," he said as he started to undress.

The bed was most welcome after our Friday-night encounter on open ground. We soon set it to rocking as Wyatt mounted me from behind and rode out a quick come. The way he growled as he unloaded made me think he was angry at even his own need, but at that moment, I did not much care about such details. And when I rolled over afterward, he dove onto my primed dick and sucked me off in a near frenzy, working himself as he fed. It was as if we had not spent any time together the night before.

"Goddammit, Doc," he said when he finally pulled off and fell back onto the bed. "Fucking is all the good we have anymore."

"Amen to that," I said, reaching down to his spent cock. He issued a low moan at this but did not discourage my attention. "Whole damn world can go to hell so long as I've got this," I said, giving him a squeeze.

"Come around here," he urged me, tugging at my hip. I scooted around so he could get a finger into me and we lay skewed together, playing and prodding while I refrained from pointing out this was far superior to listening to gasbag McLaury at the Grand Hotel.

There was not a drop of come left in either of us when Wyatt departed around dusk. "Going to see the boys," he said as he slowly dressed. He had on just his pants when he sat back on the bed. "Best part about this, Doc, is right now I don't care a shit about McLaury or any of them."

"Best part?"

"Oh, hell, you know what I mean."

I ran a hand up onto his back. "I surely do, Wyatt, I surely do."

Before he left he stood at the door looking at my naked and well-used body. "Damn," he said and then he left. I lay resting and dozing until hunger drew me to dress and seek my supper, after which I strolled over to the Grand Hotel.

It was indeed far more crowded than usual. I did not go in but could hear talk out front, the words "hang 'em" all too frequent. When one such speaker caught my eye, his words died away and he rushed into the hotel, likely to attend a commode.

This entertainment soon wore thin, so I moved on to the Alhambra, where I sat in on poker for several hours. Piano music accompanied, and when several of the Cowboys came in, they milled about the card room, noting my presence.

Johnny Ringo and Curly Bill were among them and soon sat in on my game. As they played, they began to discuss McLaury's presence. "Says he's going to hang some disreputable killers," Ringo announced, at which Bill began to elaborate on aspects of a hanging death. In compliance with town law, I carried no gun, but I did have a knife tucked into my breast pocket, as I refused to go completely unheeled. As the two ran on, I considered Bill's fleshy gut the better target since Ringo was stringy in build and likely gristle, but for once, I did not act. I kept to my cards and managed not to kill a deserving man.

Other players began to desert the game as the night wore on, fearing my wrath would ultimately be provoked. By one a.m., it got down to just the three of us. I think Ringo and Bill were disappointed I held my temper, but I knew any move by me would damage our court case. Thus I endured their nonsense until I'd won their money and they wore out their mouths and left. I had not seen Wyatt come in until he sat down in a vacated chair.

"Have to hand it to you, Doc. You held off on them."

I tossed back the last of my whiskey and stood. "It was not easy," I declared. "There will be a reckoning. It is simply postponed."

He walked outside with me. "How are the boys tonight?" I asked.

"Virgil is having trouble with his leg. Just doesn't want to heal and he's crabby as hell. Morg is doing better, up and around a little bit."

"Takes a long time to mend—says my foot."

"You headed home?" Wyatt asked.

"I suppose."

He stood silent so long I asked if he had something in mind. "Yes, but I am going home instead."

"Tomorrow?"

"I promised to spend my Sunday with Mattie. We'll all gather at Virgil's for one of Allie's Sunday dinners."

"Fair enough. Then I'll see you Monday in court."

"You think we'll come off okay, Doc?"

"Have to," I replied.

CHAPTER ELEVEN

Will McLaury made his courtroom debut on Monday and was impressive in reducing the two prosecutors to mere spectators. His first move was a demand to revoke our bail, saying those accused of murder were too dangerous to be free. This was entirely unexpected, and I felt Wyatt bristle. Had either of us been heeled, I don't doubt we'd have shot the man then and there, never mind it would have proved his point.

Judge Spicer was a study in retreat as he listened to McLaury run us down, then Fitch object, then McLaury again portray us as cold-blooded killers. This ran on for much of the morning and set the judge to fidgeting and clearing his throat. He appeared uneasy where before had shown confidence, and by the time arguments ended, he seemed truly worn. In this state, he revoked our bail and remanded us into Sheriff Behan's custody.

It was not an easy turn to take quietly, but we did just that, making not a motion save my coughing. After a noon recess, during which Fitch offered his apologies to us and said we still could prove ourselves innocent of murder, court resumed with testimony of Billy Claiborne, one of the Cowboys, who had been near the OK Corral that fateful day. He repeated much of what had already been said about unarmed men and declarations of no intention to fight. He said we all had our six-shooters in our hands when we reached the corner. Virgil was then said to have called out, "You sons of bitches, you've been looking for a fight," which was a different sequence from earlier accounts. He also insisted I fired the first shot and had not been carrying a shotgun.

When Claiborne declared that Morgan had shot Billy Clanton point-blank, I knew Fitch had an opening, as that would have left gunpowder on the body and sure enough, after picking at much of the testimony, he asked if Claiborne had seen any power marks on

Clanton's body after his death. This was a winning proposition either way, as saying he saw no powder marks would undermine Billy's earlier testimony about point-blank range, but if he said they were there—and they were not, as we well knew—he would show himself a liar. He gave no straight answer to the question, saying he couldn't remember any powder marks.

Claiborne's testimony was not done when the day ended and we went to Behan's jail. As we entered the place, we saw the vigilance committee had surrounded it, which we much appreciated since being without weapons while in the care of a known Cowboy cohort did not bode well. The Cowboys could easily come as a mob and kill us, thus the men supporting law and order saw fit to secure our safety. As we entered the jail, both Wyatt and I nodded to these men to indicate our appreciation.

"Mr. Earp and Mr. Holliday are to have the best accommodations," Behan told his deputies as we were ushered into adjoining cells. Deputies Billy Breakenridge and Dave Neagle, both as friendly to the Cowboys as was their boss, nodded and smiled at such patronizing drivel while Wyatt and I let it slide. We were patted down for weapons, at which my flask was found.

"No alcohol in jail, Doc," Behan said.

"It is medicinal," I replied. "I am consumptive and without it cannot sleep or much function when awake, due to my coughing."

Behan considered the plea, spreading his toothy smile and finally giving way. "Very well," he said. "Just don't abuse it to excess."

"I abuse nothing," I replied, putting an end to the encounter.

There were four cells in the red brick one-story building on Sixth Street. These were separated from the front office by a single door, while a back door stood at one end of the cell block, the same door through which Luther King had been allowed to escape. The other two cells happened to be unoccupied the night Wyatt and I took up residence. I was pleased we would at least have the place to ourselves. That Behan put us into adjoining cells surprised me, but I did not question that particular bit of good fortune. It gave me Wyatt's nights, and the iron bars, in that context, were less a barrier than Mattie.

Once into a cell, Wyatt said more by way of silence than he could have with the most violent outburst. He had uttered not a word when our bail was revoked and was likewise quiet when put behind bars, and yet he raged.

It came off him like that sexual storm I'd grown fond of, only now it was as ominous as a blackened sky ready to drop down a funnel and tear away the town. He leaned forward on the edge of his bunk, elbows on knees, head down, and when not in such pose, he stood below the high iron-barred window, leaning against the brick wall as if taking the air. He said not a word the whole first night, and I left him to it. We were in serious trouble and I wouldn't speculate on it, much less attempt to lighten the mood.

I don't know that he even slept, as when I awoke he was still standing at the window. I coughed and hacked my way to consciousness, addressed the toilet pail, then set about dressing in clothes from the day before, which annoyed me no end. Clean shirts were in my room, clean drawers and socks. I would not be reduced to slovenliness by Johnny Behan and meant to address such soon as he made himself known. Wyatt didn't seem to care how he looked.

I could not begin to imagine what a lawman felt to be inside a cell, let alone accused of murder. For the likes of me, there was familiarity. I knew to adapt to my surroundings but doubted, even if Wyatt gave way, he'd ever manage well. It was a terrible come down, and having Behan in charge made it worse.

Claiborne testified all of the Tuesday session, and I will admit threads of worry began to wind around me, as there were too many people repeating lies, and everybody knows if you tell a lie enough times, it becomes a blackened truth. I was thus uneasy and would have liked to talk about our situation, but Wyatt remained unapproachable. He did, however, speak to his brother Jim, who was allowed to bring us fresh clothes, shaving implements, and such. Jim even saw to getting my flask refilled. I did not ask why Mattie hadn't come. Neither did Wyatt.

Next day, clad in fresh clothes, we settled in to hear the prosecution call Ike Clanton, who said his occupation was cattle dealer, at which I could not hold back a loud guffaw. We then spent the full day listening to him portray his brother and the McLaurys as innocents put upon by men determined to make a fight while hiding behind badges. He repeated the unarmed men statement and insisted they were trying to leave town when accosted. He had Morgan and me firing the first shots and described Billy Clanton with hands up when bullets hit. He said he saw Morgan's pistol several feet from Clanton, which helped undo Claiborne's statement.

By late afternoon, testimony focused on events leading up to the shooting, including his exchange with me the night before. Describing the incident in terms favorable to himself, he said we had been separated and that as he walked off, he asked us not to shoot him in the back. This ended his testimony for the prosecution and the day, leaving us once again mired in untruth.

Once back in our cells, Wyatt and I were advised by Tom Fitch that Ike's testimony had been suspended while he sought medical treatment for neuralgia of the head, which he attributed to Virgil's pistol slap some two weeks before.

"Did you notice the prosecution did not ask Ike to explain why you were so keen to murder him?" Fitch asked us. "He's a weak link in their case and McLaury has to be careful with what he says. Ike is the kind of man who'll try to vindicate himself as much as put you away, and this makes him vulnerable. I think we have a good chance to undo much of what he says on cross-examination."

"Why do you think he wants time off?" I asked.

"McLaury undoubtedly wants to coach him further before I cross-examine."

Late that night, when Deputy Neagle had looked in on us for the last time and lights were out, Wyatt started to talk. "I'd rather posse a thousand miles than walk back into that courtroom. I don't care how Fitch sees things."

"Elsewhere," I replied, somewhat wistfully. We both lay in the dark and, though we were separated, it felt most intimate. "Elsewhere does have great appeal."

"Have you considered what happens if Spicer finds against us?" he asked.

"I know that we will face a trial by jury, but I choose not to consider such a thing before being condemned. They are all lying, Wyatt. You and I know it and Spicer surely has to see it."

"He doesn't look too sure of himself."

"That he does not."

"You getting any sleep these nights?" Wyatt then asked.

"Not much. Makes for long hours, and I get up feeling like hell."

"Me too."

Talking to Wyatt had gotten my dick stiff and, unknown to him, I had it in hand, my drawers comfortably down. Such activity will drive a man to get up to things, and I began to consider what might be done to relieve our tension and bring on sleep. Knowing vigilance men stood guard outside and might hear our talk, I kept my voice low. "You know what helps a man toward sleep," I ventured, which got silence from the other cell. "I can accomplish it on my own," I went on, stroking myself, "but together we might do better."

"Take a horse cock to get through these bars," Wyatt said.

"Not talking about a fuck. You want to stand and poke through, I can suck it."

I heard him get off the bunk. "Over here," he said, as we had almost no light. I found my way to him, groping along until, between the bars, there stood a stiff prick.

"Praise be," I said as I dropped to my knees and got my mouth onto him.

"Oh, hell," he said as he started to push into my throat. I had but to receive him, which I did most admirably, and he shot a formidable load while his hands clutched my hair. I sucked and swallowed with face pressed against the bars and when he was done, I sat back.

"Best meal yet," I said. "Want some?"

"Get it through here," he replied and I did as he had, stood with dick poked through the bars while he sucked out my come. I lasted no longer than he had, balls too full to hold off. It was the first good thing either of us had known in days.

Afterward, we collapsed onto our respective bunks. "There now," I said.

"Mmm-hmm," Wyatt murmured and I soon heard his soft snore. I too dozed off and had my first good night's sleep in jail.

Fitch could not get Judge Spicer to release us during the two-day suspension of testimony. McLaury was determined on that account, so everyone else got to go back to their business while Wyatt and I remained in our cells. We were allowed visitors, however. Mattie managed to arrive, and Wyatt made every effort toward her, but she was most agitated, broke into tears, and had to be taken home. This annoyed me no end, as she was more burden than blessing to a man who tried to do right by all.

On the second day of the suspension, we had a long discussion with Tom Fitch about what lay ahead. "You must not let the prosecution's case get you down," he told us. "We shall present a strong defense and the truth will win out. Of this I am certain."

"Nice you're so certain, Tom," Wyatt said with a touch of sarcasm. "You're not the one locked up in here."

"True, and I don't mean to make light of your situation or the weight of the case presented thus far, but we will have our day next week. The truth will come as a refreshing blast to blow away all the falsehoods, and it will come from a man known for truth. Testimony resumes tomorrow," he added. "More of Ike. Let's hope he puts his foot in it."

"If anyone can step in shit," I said, "it's Ike Clanton."

That night in the dark, Wyatt surprised me. "Doc, you up for some diversion?"

"I suppose."

"Then divert your dick over here and I'll suck hell out of it."

I took off my drawers and presented my prick to him. As he sucked it in, his hand reached around to my backside and prodded my crack. I spread my legs to admit him and he found my center, pushed in, and gave me a good finger fuck while he sucked. I could hardly keep quiet, such was my arousal, and when I unloaded into his throat, I had to clamp my jaw to keep from crying out with pleasure.

"Holy hell, Wyatt," I said when I'd sunk to the floor in a heap. "That was most powerful."

"Crawl over here," he replied and I got onto my knees and found him poked between the bars. I took him in hand and pulled some, which got a moan from him, then a couple swear words before I started at him. He squirmed as I treated him like a sweet, licking and smacking until he reached through and grabbed a handful of my hair. "Suck the goddamn thing," he demanded.

I did just that, tongue going at him until he began to thrust and shot his load. When he was empty, he pulled back and dropped to his knees. "First thing when we're set free, I am going to get you into a bed and fuck the shit out of you."

"Let's hope the hearing does not last too much longer," I said as I reached through the bars and found his arm. Gripping tightly, I fought off a torrent of feelings and satisfied myself with a few seconds of him in hand, which I know spoke just as well.

Ike Clanton looked none the worse when he resumed testimony the following morning. After assuring Judge Spicer that his medical treatment had been successful, he was sworn in and Fitch set to work. He began with Ike's threats the morning before the shooting, challenging Ike's claim that he'd never threatened us. Fitch cited Ned Boyle, bartender at the Oriental, as willing to testify to Ike's rant toward killing Earps and Holliday. Ike said he could not recall speaking with Boyle. Fitch then asked if Ike had been in Kelly's that morning brandishing a rifle and, when asked what was the matter, saying, "the Earp crowd insulted me the night before when I was unarmed, but I have heeled myself now and they have got a fight on sight." Ike, realizing this could be proven by Kelly himself, said there was near that conversation in the saloon. Fitch went on to question Ike about more threats during the previous months, but McLaury objected with favorable results. Fitch continued with questions about Ike's cattle rustling and his cowardice during the gunfight, then at least came to the heart of his cross-examination, which was his agreement with Wyatt about Leonard, Head, and Crane.

With the agreement laid out before him, Ike acknowledged he had been approached but said he never made any deal. Instead, he claimed Wyatt wanted the three men killed to cover up the Earps' involvement in diverting stolen loot from the stage robbery. This was as far-fetched as things could get, considering Wells Fargo had confirmed nothing had been stolen, as Bob Paul's actions had gotten the strongbox to Benson intact.

Ike's unexpected testimony caught Fitch off guard and he changed the subject as quickly as possible, but the accusation was out there now, Wyatt Earp now charged with robbery, conspiracy to commit murder, attempted murder, and murder itself. Regaining his composure, Fitch returned to the agreement, laying out the truth and even showing Ike the Wells Fargo wire that had confirmed the reward would be paid dead or alive. Ike continued to deny all of it. McLaury then stood for redirect examination and where he had before shied away from Ike's supposed agreement, he now embraced the situation. He asked Ike to tell what I had said on the subject and what the Earps had said as well.

Ike then created an amazing story about how we had all taken him into our confidence about involvement in the robbery. In addition, he said I had confessed to killing Bud Philpott and that Morgan had given $14,000 of the loot to me. He also said Virgil had helped the three men escape by leading Behan's posse astray. As he kept on with his imaginary version of events, a funny thing started to happen and Fitch caught it. He went so far in his fabricating that he lost track of what he'd said and began to stumble, catching himself in the truth at one point and quickly backtracking. While he did a good job at showing premeditation for murder, he muddled it terribly. Fitch, on re-cross-examination, decided to make a point of Ike's lack of credibility.

"Did not Marshal Williams, the agent of Wells Fargo Express in Tombstone, state to you that he was personally involved in the attempted stage robbery and the murder of Philpott? Did not James Earp, a brother of Virgil, Morgan, and Wyatt, also confess to you that he was a murderer and stage robber?" Prosecution quickly objected to such statements, as they were outlandish, yet the point was made. Nothing Ike Clanton said could be trusted. His testimony thus ended.

McLaury then set about to undermine us with statements by witnesses to Wyatt buffaloing Tom McLaury. This made Wyatt look quite aggressive and unruly in light of what later took place. Other witnesses to the gunfight and aftermath testified that no weapons were found on Tom McLaury. He was thus portrayed as an innocent at the hands of murderers, and on this, the prosecution rested.

Tom Fitch met with us that night to explain his strategy for our defense. "In spite of what you've heard, the prosecution has no coherent theory on what happened, as they are unable to prove whether you acted in sudden anger or as part of a plan, nor can they seem to decide if these murders were to cover up other crimes or just swaggering lawmen gone too far. Ike's testimony served well to muddle things."

"What's next, then?" Wyatt asked.

"Remember that Spicer's only job is to decide whether there is sufficient evidence to send the case to a jury trial. He does not have to resolve conflicts in testimony or decide your intent. He need only decide if there is sufficient evidence against you.

"As defendants, we are not required to put on a case at this time. Normally, such things are left for a trial, but I believe we need to conclude things in this hearing. Your lives are already in danger. If you are bound over for trial, things will only get worse. I also fear witnesses at a trial would be put in more danger then than now. We will therefore begin with you, Wyatt, but I am not going to question you in the usual manner. Arizona law allows a defendant in a preliminary hearing to make a narrative statement without facing cross-examination. We will invoke this right. You and I are going to sit here tonight and go over the events in great detail. I will then write it up and you will read the statement in court and not divert one word from what is on the page."

"Why do it that way?" Wyatt asked.

"It will have far more impact for you to tell the entire story uninterrupted and to not have McLaury picking it apart in cross-examination. You're an imposing and respected figure, Wyatt. We are going to use that to our advantage. Now, I know everything that happened, but I want you to go back to the start of the difficulties and take me through it all with as much detail as you can remember."

They went late that night and I listened to it all, trying to control my coughing so as not to interfere. I gained great respect for Tom Fitch, and while I realized he would use Wyatt's words, I did not doubt some of the language would not be that of my friend. Wyatt spoke well, but Tom Fitch knew and appreciated language far more than any of us, even me.

Next morning, when Fitch announced to the court that Wyatt would make a narrative statement without facing cross-examination, as allowed by Arizona law, the prosecutors were momentarily caught off guard. They sat in silence as Wyatt was asked to state name, age, place of birth, residence, and profession as required by the statute. The judge then asked Wyatt to "give any explanations you may think proper of the circumstances appearing in the testimony against you, and state any facts which you think will tend to your exculpation."

Wyatt then began to read from his many pages but hardly got through the first sentence before objections began. McLaury said the defendant might have a right to avoid cross-examination but that right did not allow him to use a manuscript. The fine points of the law were then hotly debated until Judge Spicer finally gained his backbone and ruled that the statute was very broad and the defendant could make any statement he pleased, whether prepared or not. Thus, Wyatt began to read.

Fitch's intention was clear from the first sentence. "The difficulty which resulted in the death of William Clanton and Frank and Tom McLaury originated last spring." Wyatt's testimony would be broad rather than narrow and would not center on the single gunfight but rather on a long history of threats and criminality that led to an unavoidable encounter. Objections were immediately raised as to relevance of such testimony but were overruled. Wyatt then laid out the time he pursued the stolen mules found at the McLaury ranch, which drew another overruled objection. On and on things went, with Wyatt laying out how the McLaurys seemed determined to pick a fight with him. He drew his brothers in as having been repeatedly threatened by not only the McLaurys but also the Clantons and others of the Cowboy element, naming several others. He also portrayed the ranches of the dead men as gathering places for the Cowboy gang of rustlers. When Wyatt came to the deal he made with Ike Clanton, he was most humble.

"I had an ambition to be sheriff of this county at the next election, and I thought it would be a great help to me with the people and businessmen if I could capture the men who killed Philpott. There were rewards offered of about twelve hundred dollars each for the capture of the robbers. I thought this sum might tempt Ike Clanton to give away

Leonard, Head, and Crane when they came to town. I had an interview with him in the backyard of the Oriental Saloon. I said if he would put me on the track of the men, I would give him all the reward and would never let anyone know where I got the information."

Wyatt then elaborated on several subsequent meetings, the "wanted dead or alive" issue, the telegram from Wells Fargo. He then denied any involvement in the stage robbery or Philpott murder. "The testimony of Isaac Clanton that I ever said to him I had anything to do with any stage robbery is a tissue of lies from the beginning." He then began on incidents leading up to the gunfight and told his efforts to reassure Ike about keeping the bargain a secret. At last, he got to the day of the fight and told of his belief that all were armed. Because of earlier testimony on Tom McLaury being unarmed, he said if Tom was unarmed, he did not know it. "I believe he was armed and fired two shots at our party before Holliday, who had the shotgun, fired and killed him."

As the court at last heard truth, I began to feel we had a good chance at being rid of the awful murder charge. Wyatt, even when reading the statement, remained a powerful man. Judge Spicer sat at full attention, displaying none of his earlier discomfort at the hands of McLaury. I almost wished the public had been allowed to view the proceedings, as Wyatt's account would surely turn a few from against to support. The best of it all, though, was Wyatt's statement on our justification for shooting the men.

"I believed then, and believe now, from the acts I have stated and the threats I have related and the other threats communicated to me by other persons, as having been made by Tom McLaury, Frank McLaury, and Ike Clanton, that these men last named had formed a conspiracy to murder my brothers, Morgan and Virgil, Doc Holliday, and myself. I believe I would have been legally and morally justified in shooting any of them on sight, but I did not do so, nor attempt to do so. I sought no advantage when I went as deputy marshal to help to disarm and arrest them. I went as a part of my duty and under the direction of my brother, the marshal. I did not intend to fight unless it became necessary in self-defense and in the performance of official duty. When Billy Clanton and Frank McLaury drew their pistols, I knew it was a fight for life, and I drew in defense of my own life and the lives of my brothers and Doc Holliday."

How I welcomed such testimony. Fitch had taken Wyatt's words and crafted them into a powerful statement of justification, which was at this point sorely needed. Wyatt then embarked on details of the shootout, saying how he did not draw his pistol until Billy and Frank had drawn theirs, saying how he had fired, and bringing to life once again those awful seconds. As he went on, I realized how brilliant a move had been Fitch's no-cross setup for Wyatt. There were dozens of places the prosecution could have torn apart. As it was, the testimony stood fast and appeared the first solid account yet given.

When Wyatt finished reading his statement, Fitch called corroborating witnesses, and after these, two days later, called Virgil Earp. As Virgil was still bedridden, court was convened at his bedside. He remained in obvious pain and at times he seemed to get lost in his facts, but he managed to get forward much in our support. And unlike Wyatt's going back much of a year, Fitch had Virgil focus only on the gunfight itself. Once again, the facts were laid out, but this time they were subject to cross-examination.

Fitch saw it necessary to clarify my lawful position in the matter since I had not been deputized. Virgil managed to state that a territorial statute allowed him to enlist the aid of other persons without the formality of a badge. Such persons were not official deputies but still were authorized to assist in enforcing the law.

Virgil then told of a witness who had seen him on the corner of Fourth and Allen Streets that afternoon of the shooting and said he'd just passed the OK Corral and said he saw the men armed and one said, "Be sure to get Earp, the marshal," and another said, "We will kill them all." The man then asked Virgil if he was an Earp and when told yes, he asked if Virgil was the marshal. Virgil said he did not know the man at the time but had later learned his name was Sills.

This appeared to stifle the prosecution's objections, as it was a powerful statement. The cross-examination of Virgil weakened from that point on, and soon he was left to his recuperation. That night, Fitch met with us and said he was going to again apply for bail, thinking the upcoming four-day Thanksgiving recess would make it a more hospitable request.

"I can't afford more bail money," I said.

"Not to worry. I've contacted the mine owners, who are ready to post any amount for you both. There are law-and-order supporters in this town, no matter the picture the prosecution attempts to paint. I've also notified your family that we expect your release after Wednesday's testimony."

"Optimistic," Wyatt noted.

"Confident," Fitch countered. I hoped he was right.

Next day, we returned to the courtroom where Fitch produced several lesser witnesses to the gunfight and on the Wednesday before the Thanksgiving holiday, produced one H. F. Sills to tell firsthand what he had seen.

Sills was a furloughed locomotive engineer with the Santa Fe Railroad who was visiting Tombstone and was merely passing by the OK Corral when he heard the men talking of trouble they had with Virgil Earp. "They made threats at the time and said on meeting him they would kill him on sight." He confirmed his action to warn Virgil and when we headed to the corral, he followed. He testified that he saw Billy Clanton and Frank McLaury draw first and he went on to corroborate our truthful version of events. As if this wasn't good enough, Sills did remarkably well under cross-examination, likely because he told the truth.

At the close of the day's proceedings, Fitch requested Wyatt and I be released on bail for the remainder of the hearing. It was granted in the sum of $20,000 each, which was quickly posted by the mine owners. We were thus set free in time for the four-day Thanksgiving recess. We were much relieved to be out of Behan's jail, and yet I found a thread of regret as I would no longer have Wyatt's nights.

CHAPTER TWELVE

A day of Thanksgiving did not sit particularly well with me, nor did Wyatt's familial devotion to it. As we left the courtroom, his brother, Jim, and sister-in-law, Bessie, were waiting to sweep him into the fold, as was his wife, Mattie. He slid his arm around her waist while Jim slapped him on the back. Other well-wishers shook his hand, assured him their support had never wavered, and I watched him then start down the street toward home. The fact that Wyatt, while incarcerated, had said the first thing he would do upon being set free was get me into bed and fuck the shit out of me was not lost, although at that moment I rather wished it was.

I set out to chase him off the best way I knew, and after some supper, settled in at the Alhambra for poker. Henry Hooker was in town with two friends and was happy to lighten my mood with some fine card play. Best of all, he made no mention of my legal plight and instead told stories of life on his ranch. As he was expert at spinning a good yarn, it became a pleasurable evening. Our gaming was fierce, as always, wins and losses about even, which resulted in us going at it some thirty hours. Though I did not win especially big, I had a good time and, as a result, Wyatt found me in my room, much indisposed, on Friday afternoon.

"I hear they carried you out of the Alhambra," he said as he came in.

"That is entirely possible," I managed, "though I do not recall the details." This brief exchange set off a coughing fit that brought up some putrid stuff from my lungs. Handkerchief at my mouth, I hacked and heaved for a good minute before attempting whiskey.

"Your bottle is about empty," Wyatt noted. "I'll bring you some."

"Much obliged."

I settled back but did not pull up the covers. No matter how sick, I still felt the urge and wanted myself displayed even if in drawers.

"How was your holiday?" I asked, not wanting to know but making an effort toward the life he chose to live.

"Fine, Doc. Family meal, good talk."

"And the boys?"

"Virgil's leg is starting to improve, so he managed to get to the table for dinner, and Morgan is doing really well."

"That is good news. Soon all will be as before."

He sat on the bed. "Anything I can do?"

"No. Rest is all I need."

"You need to start living clean."

"That, my friend, is not living."

He shook his head. "You look like hell."

"As I feel."

"All right, I'm going to go. I'll call back later, bring the whiskey."

"Sunday will be soon enough," I said through a cough. "I have another bottle in the dresser, so you need not worry on that. By Sunday I should be ambulatory."

He considered this and I wondered if he got my drift since his desire seemed to have been smothered by his family time. Either that or my invalid appearance put him off. "All right," he said. "Sunday." He then left and I slept on and off until Sunday morning.

While the pious sat in church, I bathed and dressed, as my malady had by then relented. How well I knew its awful habits. It preyed upon me whenever I weakened, a monster rising up to chew at my ruined lungs. Then, when my body had sufficiently rested, it gave way to the whiskey, content to suckle the bottle while allowing me a semblance of life. Though I was not fully recovered, I was well enough to anticipate a good fuck, and so I set out to have a hearty breakfast and walk around town in hopes of running into Wyatt. It was early afternoon as I exited the Eagle Brewery after wetting my whistle that I saw him crossing the street. When he caught my eye, he paused out in the middle, letting wagons and horses go around him. We may have been thirty feet apart, but it didn't matter. Cocks were on the rise and what passed between us was as powerful as anything any God could have sent down, wrath or otherwise.

"Doc," he said when he reached me. "You look a damn sight better."

"My old self," I said. "Rest, a good breakfast, and the day is mine. Or yours, if you wish."

I could see his breathing increase. He set his jaw as that storm of need swept over him. "The hotel," he rasped and I nodded and started toward the Cosmopolitan.

How good that walk felt. My step lightened, my heart raced, and I toted a swollen prick toward fulfillment, all of it my reward for enduring his absence those few days. In my room, he slammed the door, locked it, and began to strip. When I stood enjoying the sight, he barked, "Get 'em off," and I undressed but still kept an eye on his emerging body. As anticipated, his cock was stiff and wet. He grabbed hold of it as I hung up my suit, and when I was finally ready for him, he charged forward, stood me at the bedpost, and drove it in. I came almost instantly.

Spewing spunk, I felt, among other things, home again. Wyatt's cock was all I needed. He didn't last much longer than I had, grunting loudly and pounding me unmercifully until he unleashed his load. That my knees didn't buckle said much for my recovery effort.

When finished, he pulled out, but instead of backing off or falling onto the bed, he wrapped his arms around me and pressed his body to mine. He said nothing, but the gesture was more telling than any words he could have offered. I slid a hand onto his arm and clutched him tightly, and there we stood, communing in an entirely new way. He then laid his forehead on my shoulder and I realized feelings were stirring inside him and he had no idea what to do. Wyatt Earp may have been fearless when confronting a gun-waving Cowboy, able to grab a loaded weapon and slap it to the man's head, but what he felt within was essentially orphaned. And when that inside part grew to such proportion that it demanded acknowledgment, he was at a loss. Just as the lawman lived by action, the lover did as well. I therefore enjoyed a silent intimacy until he finally let go and said we should drink to our return to freedom.

"I missed you," I boldly stated as he filled our glasses. Our return to my bed and his embrace had emboldened me. He might not have words, but I did.

He threw back his whiskey and poured a second. "Likewise," he managed as he handed me my drink. We then stood naked together, sipping, the air around us all but crackling with our combustion, for that is surely what we conjured, fire stoked to dangerous level. Set outside us, it would burn the town. Contain it within, and we would fuck like rabbits.

Wyatt polished off his drink and set the glass aside, then fell to his knees and began to lick my spent dick. I thrilled to the unexpected turn, as he was usually more forthright in sucking me off. Now he played with me, and I began to squirm, delighted at this new attention. I soon began to stiffen, at which he fixed on my knob and began to suck while his hand went under to cup my balls.

He played with me for some time while I finished my drink and tossed the glass toward a chair. As he continued below, I couldn't help but thrust, and soon he had his hands on my buttocks, kneading and squeezing, until at last my juice rose up and spurted into his mouth. He grew noisy as he received it, slopping and slurping like it was far more gusher than I gave. Then he sat back and turned me around.

"Wouldn't this be better in bed?" I asked.

"Time for that," he said before he pulled open my cheeks and began to run his tongue up my crack. He teased me for some seconds before finding my pucker and starting to poke. This set me squirming again, spreading my legs, pushing back at him. He issued a wicked chuckle before he ran his tongue into my hole.

How the lawman could tongue-fuck. I doubted he did such depraved things with his woman, and that is the better part of men upon men. We know no limits. Wyatt was truly himself with me, the animal who lived within allowed free rein.

The feel of his mouth plastered against my bottom fired me to near my limit. Sunday go-to-hell tongue fuck but, hot as it was, I knew it mere prelude. His dick had to be on the rise again, and he was going to get himself good and worked up before he put it to me. We'd get on the bed then, me ass high, him mounting like some stallion, and oh Lord in Heaven, it was going to be some good fuck.

How well I knew my man. Just then, he withdrew, pulled me to my feet, and pushed me to the bed. I got onto all fours and he crawled in behind. "Fuck me, Wyatt," I said. "Fuck the shit out of me." Whether or not he recalled his jailhouse declaration made no matter. It felt good to quote him back to himself, and I liked to think it might stir the memory. He rammed his hard prick into me and set the bed to rocking, and I was again home, fucking at last. The weeks without it had been too long, but now fell away, as did all concerns on law and order.

"Oh, Christ, fuck me," I said, "fuck me to hell and back. Fuck me to where I can't walk. Fuck me, Wyatt. Fuck me."

The talk riled him. Already sweating and pumping into me at a good clip, he began to rasp and growl at hearing the filth. "Give me that dick," I kept on. "I want a load of come that will drown my ass. Fuck me to hell and back. Fuck me. Fuck me."

He shuddered and carried on as I kept begging the fuck, and when he began to come, he issued not only his spunk but a cry not unlike that of a mountain lion claiming his hill. Had he shredded me with claws, I could not have been more thoroughly taken. As it was, the come was a long one and he kept pumping in and out, going at me as if he could call up more spunk and more and still more on determination alone. This amused me. If anyone could will more juice, it was Wyatt Earp.

At last, he was spent. He pulled out and fell beside me, mouth open, breath labored. I lay on my side facing him, venturing my fingers onto his upper arm. I had no idea if these small touches meant as much to him as they did me, but I didn't dwell on this. I simply enjoyed letting him know there was more to us than fucking.

"You recovered well," he said after a while.

"Highly motivated," I replied, squeezing his arm. "I needed you."

"Needed you too."

"We are most compatible," I ventured, and when he did not reply, I slid a hand down to his prick. "A six-shooter should fire so well."

He shut his eyes and blew out a long breath, as if he had at last truly settled, and I contented myself for a while with fingering not only his cock but much of his body, tracing into his hairy patch, then up onto his stomach and chest, circling his tits, tweaking them, then working back down onto his thighs, rubbing, squeezing. It was like a feeding. I was gaining knowledge of him that filled me as nothing else could. He made me, by way of himself, more substantial than I was. He erased my malady and almost did away with the death sentence.

After a while, when my hand had come to rest on his chest and nothing passed between us but our respective breathing and some of my coughing, Wyatt began to consider things I would rather, at that moment, he not have approached.

"Even if we win this thing," he said, "how much will be gained?"

"Well, you're not in law enforcement any longer, so you can get back to your business ventures, start making money again, manage your claims and such. The life you'd planned, fully exonerated."

"Seems out of reach anymore."

"Why is that?"

"I do not know." Here he got up and poured himself a drink, knocked it back, then turned to me. "We've gone down a road we hadn't planned and I fear there is no return."

"You're starting to sound like the pessimist."

"Well, don't you start playing the optimist because I won't believe it." He poured another drink and one for me, then came back to bed and sat, clinking his glass to mine. "To justice," he said. "Fuck her." And we drank to that poor bedraggled lady, after which he rolled over on top of me and began a slow grind, his dick stiffening against my own. I wrapped my arms around him and gained his rhythm as we lay working ourselves toward another round.

When we were slippery with anticipation, Wyatt sat back and raised my legs, then looked down at my butthole like he wanted to crawl into it. He then eased forward and shoved in and, holy hell, he took it deep. Bending me some gave him leverage, which he used to the fullest. When he began to go at me, I got a hand onto myself because he was going to drive the come out of me. As he fucked, he watched me handle myself and he began a low growl of satisfaction. That we'd already come worked in our favor, as this one went on for some time, Wyatt again displaying a remarkable stamina. His prick was indeed like his pistol, gun barrel stiff but not about to fire until ready. I stroked my cock in time with him as I did not want to precede him but rather shoot when he did. By the time he worked himself to coming, he had my legs back around my ears and his cock well into my gut.

I didn't manage to last until he shot his load. His spearing me so deep set me on that path of no return, and I began to frantically pump my cock, juice rising then spurting while he drilled ever deeper. Soon as he saw my spunk, he issued a series of grunts and started coming, sweat flying, bed squeaking, and I swear fireworks exploding. It was the wildest come we'd ever shared, a downright good Sunday-afternoon fuck.

"I am done for," Wyatt rasped when we'd separated and lay sprawled on our backs. The room reeked of sweat and spunk, the bed was a tangle, and I could barely breathe for my coughing. I staggered to the whiskey bottle, poured and drank a quick one, then fell back onto the bed. "Can a man fuck to death?" Wyatt asked.

"Don't know, but worth a try," I managed. When my cough quieted, sleep rushed in, and there was no holding back. Wyatt slept as well because when I woke the room was dark and he was still beside me. I got up to piss, then crept back to bed. He awakened as I crawled in.

"What in hell time is it?" he asked.

"No idea," I said because I did not want to know.

He got up, lit the lamp, and began to dress. "Sunday supper," was all he said. Once presentable, he sat on the bed and looked at me. "You know I wouldn't leave if I didn't have to."

"I know."

"Tomorrow at the courthouse, then."

I nodded. "We'll face it better now."

"That we will."

Incarceration had forced me into good bedtime and early rising habits, but free of such restraints, I enjoyed a long night of faro that then made my Monday rising difficult. Coughing and hacking, I endured an awful start and thus was somewhat shaky when I saw Wyatt out front of Spicer's courtroom. He extended his hand as I met him, the common greeting amusing. We gripped tightly and held on an extra second or two.

"Doc, you look tired," he said.

"Early hours are an abomination," I replied. "Shall we go in?"

We settled in with Fitch, who called a Dr. Gardiner, who testified he saw Tom McLaury the morning of the gunfight enter the butcher shop unarmed and leave it five minutes later with his right pocket bulged as if it carried a pistol. When his statement went unchallenged by the prosecution, Fitch called Albert Bellicke, hotel owner, who had been with Gardiner and said much the same thing. "Right pocket protruding when he left the shop."

Had there been spectators in the courtroom, I'm certain they would have snickered at such testimony, and I had to smile. Will McLaury, failing to see the suggestive quality of things, asked how it happened that Bellicke watched the right pocket so closely. Bellicke paused, but I saw he was confident, as many a man took note of bulges in the front pocket area though few would admit it. But Bellicke was most proper. "Every good citizen of this city was watching all those Cowboys very closely on the day the affray occurred, and as he was walking down the street my attention was drawn to McLaury by a friend, and so it happened that I watched him very closely."

This was a wonderful statement in that it cited "every good citizen" and thus portrayed the townsfolk in our support. When McLaury asked Bellicke if he knew every good citizen, the reply was, "I know not all of them, but a great many." What worked in our favor was McLaury being an outsider. He had little knowledge of who was in our support and how confident those men were. I nudged Wyatt and he allowed himself a nod.

Fitch then called Addie Bourland, a dressmaker who lived near the OK Corral and saw the fight from her window. She related the fight much as we had, but her strongest point was that at no time did she see the McLaurys or Clanton throw up their hands. She said they only fired their guns. The prosecution tried to tear her down on this point, but the brave little woman would not be swayed. Lastly, Judge Lucas of the Probate Court, whose office was not two hundred feet from the gunfight, testified but added little of consequence. Fitch put him on the stand, he told us later, only to show that the Tombstone establishment supported the Earps. This completed the case for the defense.

McLaury called a few rebuttal witnesses, but none added much of anything beyond what had already been said. Judge Spicer then announced he would retire to consider the matter and reconvene when a decision had been made. We were dismissed shortly before noon and Wyatt, in a show of good spirit, bought me lunch at the Alhambra. Over the meal, he said he had a claim he needed to inspect and asked me to ride along, which I did.

"Whereabouts is the claim?" I asked after we were well out of town.

"No claim."

"I see."

"I don't think you do."

"How's that?"

He blew out a sigh and looked in every direction but to me. "You're starting to undo me, Doc."

This didn't sound like a bad prospect, so I said nothing, knowing he could not drop something like that without explanation. "Mattie is asking why I don't touch her anymore," he went on, "and there is no answer I can give. She was unpleasant at Sunday supper and worse later on at home."

"I am sorry you are having such difficulty," I said, "but you must know I am not sorry at the cause."

"Me either. It's just hell to live one way and crave another."

"Pleased to hear of your craving."

We rode a bit more in silence, then he spoke again. "There's a place a couple miles ahead that I found a while back, rock formation all around a nice open space. Private."

"Well, how about we get into it and you undo me?"

He chuckled. "Out here like this, no wife or court or law. All I want anymore."

"Likewise."

"There it is," he said, pointing to boulders clustered at the foot of a hill, a few trees nearby. "You'd never know what's in there. I only found it when I stopped to piss."

We tied our horses to the trees and took our bedrolls through a narrow passage between boulders taller than a man. Inside was indeed a small patch of flat ground that rendered the place a rustic sort of room. "Amazing," I said as Wyatt unrolled his bedding and I saw he had an extra blanket and a bottle of whiskey. The air was quite cool, but this did not matter as we'd soon heat things up, whiskey and otherwise.

"Whiskey or fuck?" Wyatt said, which made me laugh.

"What in hell do you think?"

When I started to slip off my coat, he took my arm. "I want to do it," he said and he held the coat as I shucked it off. He then undid my tie and my shirt, eased them off, undershirt as well. He was calm and methodical in undressing me, like this was not even a prelude to a fuck, and I enjoyed this new aspect. He was becoming comfortable with the fact of us and starting to enjoy things associated with coupling. He seemed to savor undoing my pants and pulling them down. He got hold of my drawers and they went down with the pants, but he hadn't addressed my boots and chuckled at the oversight. He then bent to attend my footwear and socks before peeling off the rest. Looking me up and down, he eased forward and ran a hand up under my balls and to my cock. "I'm hungry for you all the time now, Doc. All the goddamned time."

"Then why don't you get undressed and make a meal of me."

He stripped in a flash, then pulled me to him, grinding his hard dick against mine while biting my neck. "I can hardly sit still in that courtroom," he rasped into my neck. "A man's dick should not be stiff in a legal hearing deciding his fate."

"I don't know about that," I ventured. "Sounds like a good diversion from a bad play."

"You are so good for me, Doc. And so bad for me."

"Ideal combination. Now fuck me before I come all over you."

He pulled me down onto our makeshift bed, flipped me over, parted my buttocks, but instead of shoving in like usual, he paused. "Beautiful sight, that butthole," he remarked. Then he speared me. "Hell, yes," he said as he began to thrust. "Hell, yes."

You would never know we had worn each other out the day before. Wyatt was as rampant as a bull, and I came without touching my dick, shooting a good load into the bedding, at which I began to cough. I appreciated that this did not deter Wyatt from his efforts. He knew the hacking was of no consequence, thus he kept on pounding my ass until at last he let out a roar that rattled around those boulders. Again, I savored the taking of his juice.

Once emptied and still, he pulled out and opened the whiskey, handed me the bottle. As I knew it unwise to share anything by mouth, I found my flask, filled it from the bottle, then handed the bottle back to Wyatt. "Best not to drink from the same," I said. We then enjoyed our refreshment, which calmed my lungs.

No matter we were secure in our private outdoor room, it was late November and thus cold. We lay down on our bedding and pulled the extra blanket over us to lie drinking and exploring each other as if we'd never before laid on hands. I basked in such attention, always aware my body lacked the substance of most, and happy Wyatt seemed not to notice. But maybe he appreciated my whole self as I likewise did him. It wasn't just where he put his dick. It was the friendship and the caring that rides along when two men take up regular with each other.

We did nothing new that afternoon, but we did everything with new freedom because we could not be discovered in the little grotto. All the fucking and sucking and poking and licking was done to serious extent, and by the time the whiskey was gone and dusk was upon us, we were both well used and happy. I thought to ask Wyatt about happiness but held back as that might be pushing things. We were still charged with murder. He still had a wife at home. Maybe another time we could look at happiness, but I still felt giddy. Drained of every drop of come and wondering how I would ever make any more, I lay in a blissful stupor until Wyatt said we had to go. "Going to be dark by the time we get back."

I had my hand on his soft cock and gave it a tug. "I don't want to let go," I said.

"Neither do I, but we can't stay out here. Have to get back and get ready for Spicer's decision."

"I hate that man intruding on us," I declared, giving him another pull.

"Enough, Doc. Come on." And he eased my hand off him and stood up. As I got to my feet, I picked up my blanket, which was awash in come. "Look at this. Going to be stiff in a couple hours. Folks at the laundry are going to think somebody is randy as hell."

"Get dressed," Wyatt said, trying not to laugh.

When we'd exited our grotto and were at the horses, I embraced him from behind. "I don't care what happens in court," I declared. "You are all that matters to me."

"They'll have to hang us together."

I let go of him. "All right, back to town."

At the Cosmopolitan, he tipped his hat, which I found so absurd that I grabbed his arm and got up close. "Soon as it's all over, I want a good goddamn fuck." And with that, I turned and left him.

Next day, Wyatt found me at the Hafford's and said Spicer was ready with his decision. I cashed out and we hurried to the courtroom where Fitch waited on us. McLaury and the two prosecutors were already at their table and looking most grim. We settled in and Spicer took up pages to read.

He opened by reminding us this was not a trial but a hearing and as such the only question he was to address was if there was sufficient cause to believe the defendants guilty of a crime. He then laid out a review of the case, describing the Clantons and McLaurys as "armed and defiant men, accepting their wager of battle and succumbing only in death." When he detailed the specifics, laying out Ike's rampage of the night and morning, he noted how the threats were then communicated to the Earps and me. While this worked to our favor, he then came down hard for Virgil adding Wyatt and me to his party that day.

"I am of the opinion that defendant Virgil Earp, as chief of police, calling upon Wyatt Earp and J. H. Holliday to assist him in arresting and disarming the Clantons and McLaurys, committed an injudicious and censurable act." This, he explained, was due to the prior history among us all and most particular the events of the night before. But as soon as this had been stated, he seemed to turn back in our favor.

"Although in this he acted incautiously and without due circumspection, when we consider the conditions of affairs incident to a frontier country; the lawlessness and disregard for human life; the existence of a law-defying element in our midst; the fear and feeling of insecurity that has existed; the supposed prevalence of bad, desperate, and reckless men who have been a terror to the country and kept away capital and enterprise; and consider the many threats that have been made against the Earps, I can attach no criminality to his unwise act. In fact, as the result plainly proves, he needed the assistance and support of staunch and true friends, upon whose courage, coolness, and fidelity he could depend, in case of an emergency."

I glanced over at McLaury just then and his jaw had dropped open because he knew right then, as did the rest of us, how Spicer would rule.

Though there was much more to the judge's statement, it was apparent he was behind us. At last, he got to what mattered most.

"When, therefore, the defendants, regularly or specially appointed officers, marched down Fremont Street to the scene of the subsequent homicide, they were going where it was their right and duty to go, and they were doing what it was their right and duty to do, and they were armed, as it was their right and duty to be armed when approaching men whom they believed to be armed and contemplating resistance."

I nudged Wyatt who blew out a long breath. Spicer then added, "There being no sufficient cause to believe the within named Wyatt S. Earp and John H. Holliday guilty of the offense mentioned, I order them to be released."

CHAPTER THIRTEEN

Johnny Ringo, Ike Clanton, and Curly Bill Brocius stood across the street from the courthouse as we exited, reducing our well-wishers to a cautious Jim Earp and three of the more stalwart vigilance committee members. When I started over to let the Cowboys know we would not be intimidated, Wyatt stopped me. "We have no authority, Doc. Anything you do now will land us back in jail."

This irritated me, as I refused to let the criminal element gain the upper hand. We had just been exonerated in killing three of them, we had justice on our side, yet they acted like they had won.

"They're looking for a fight," Wyatt continued, hand still on my arm. "Don't play into it."

"Goddamn, Wyatt, they are calling us out and you don't walk away from that."

"This time you do. You can't play into it. That's what they want, to get you back in jail almost before you're out. Now come on."

He urged me up the street and I went with great reluctance, walking up Fifth toward Allen, boiling inside because all we'd been through for the last month seemed to have been tossed aside.

"People are afraid," Jim said as we went along. "Word is that the Cowboys are going to take revenge on the whole town, so don't be surprised if you take the blame for it."

Jim was right. A veritable shunning occurred as we walked through town. Backs turned. People hurried inside and slammed doors or rushed to cross the street while the few standing fast glared at those they saw responsible for a new threat.

"You were right, Wyatt," I noted after the gravity of our predicament sank in. "What you said before. We've gone down a road we hadn't planned and there is no return."

"Wish I'd been wrong," he replied.

We were on Allen Street when he said he was going home. "I'm tired," he added and I saw this disappointment as much as fatigue. The lawman in him couldn't help but believe in justice, however often she failed him. I found myself feeling much the same, having expected tolerance rather than blame.

"Maybe see you later," Wyatt said before moving on.

Worked up from the Cowboys' blatant challenge, I sought a few drinks at the Alhambra and then a game of poker. While I found this profitable, there remained a standoffish mood. Such things were not new to me, being somewhat notorious, so I ignored the efforts and kept to my game. It was around ten that night when Wyatt came in and said trouble was brewing. I immediately cashed out and followed him outside.

"The Oriental is filling up with Cowboys, and Grady Lowe just told me there are about thirty at the edge of town. We may have a situation."

As we hurried along, I wondered who would represent the law. Jim Flynn had been appointed city marshal in Virgil's place, and I asked Wyatt if he was about.

"Haven't seen him."

"Figures. What about Behan?"

"He's at the Oriental, knee-deep with the Cowboys and acting like nothing is afoot."

"What do you want to do?" I asked.

"Don't know yet. We are in a terrible position, no authority, unarmed."

"Speak for yourself."

"Well, then, no authority," he amended. "One shot and we're in jail with people saying they were right about us being the problem."

"Then why go down there?"

"I cannot stomach the idea of not facing it down."

The piano at the Oriental tinkled its tune like always and men played cards in the back while the bar held a line of Cowboys. I'd never seen the place so full. "Well, looka here," Milt Joyce said when we entered. "Jailbirds flew the coop."

Wyatt continued on to the gaming room and I followed. Two men quickly exited their poker to give us room and we settled in, playing cards as if nothing had changed. Soon we noticed men were cashing out and leaving, which allowed Cowboys to take their places. When

Johnny Ringo entered, two men all but flew from our game. Ringo then sat down and placed a wad of cash before him. "Feel lucky tonight," he announced. "Things are about to turn."

"Are they now?" I said. The knife in my breast pocket and the gun in my belt both begged attention, but I kept to the game, mindful of Wyatt's words toward our unfortunate position. Still, the temptation was great to blow a hole in the arrogant son of a bitch or at least slice him open and let stink run.

"Spicer ain't the law around here," Ringo said while looking at his cards. "Everybody knows he's as corrupt as they come. Grand jury meets in a couple weeks, and they'll be looking to set things as they should be."

"And how should they be?" I asked, at which Wyatt shifted in his chair.

"Cards?" rasped the dealer, who I swear was about to drop the deck from his shaking hand.

"Two," Ringo said.

"One," Wyatt said.

"I'll stand," I announced, eyes fast on Ringo. His blazed as he returned the look, refusing to defer. Money was put down, called, raised, and it was down to the three of us, Wyatt, Ringo, and me, when somebody called, "Fire!" We turned to see Seth Richards rushing to the bar in a most agitated state, shouting there was a fire down the street. "Need everybody! Come on!"

Just then, the horn at the mine began to call the town to an emergency. This method served to notify us of mining accidents, fire, and also to call the vigilance committee into action. Card players gathered their money and ran outside. People were streaming out of every restaurant and saloon, all headed up Allen toward the plume of smoke. Wyatt walked with me while most ran ahead.

"You shouldn't go," he said.

"I can handle a bucket."

"But not the smoke. Bad for anyone, worse for you."

I kept with him until we reached the fire where a bucket brigade was already forming. A newly constructed saloon was in flames, and as we reached the scene, fire leaped to the clothing store next door, a fancy dress in the window quickly consumed. Beyond this were new grocery and hardware stores, both now threatened, as was the butcher shop on the saloon's other side. Fires were not uncommon in Tombstone, and we had, as yet, no engine to assist in putting them out, thus pieces of town were lost every few months, then quickly rebuilt.

Wyatt ran to where men pulled water from the storage tank and handed it down to the line. Second and third lines manning buckets were forming and Wyatt took command of one. As our ever-present wind pushed smoke about, I was quickly set to coughing and forced to retreat, which I did most reluctantly. As I moved against the crowd, I could not help but consider they saw me a turncoat, which added to the harsh judgment already formed by way of our court battle. Still coughing, I returned to the deserted Oriental where Milt Joyce remained. He did not question my presence as I hacked my way through purchase of a bottle of whiskey, which I then took to my room. It was near midnight, but there would be no sleep, never mind the hotel was far enough from the fire to be quiet. Quiet was not what I wanted just then.

Alone, I paced and swore while downing several drinks, then fell onto the bed feeling beyond useless. I thought of Wyatt helping the others and how he might redeem himself in their eyes, working shoulder to shoulder to save the town while I, notorious Doc Holliday, fled the scene. It didn't matter that many knew me a lunger. Many others surely did not, and as the worst of a man seemed to carry more weight than the best of him, I would likely now be seen as a coward. I therefore attempted to drown myself but found one bottle not up to the task.

Wyatt woke me around eight in the morning. Soon as the door closed, he stripped off his filthy shirt and began to wash.

"You smell like you've been roasted," I said.

"I have."

"Fire out?"

"Close enough. Smoldering."

"How bad did it get?"

"Four buildings gone and two badly damaged. No lives lost."

"Awful." I was sitting on the bed, morning cough at me. As the bottle was empty, I retrieved my flask from my pants pocket and took a quieting swig.

"Hell of a thing, though," Wyatt said. "Whatever the Cowboys had planned last night got sidetracked. They were manning the buckets, even Ike."

"And Ringo?"

"Don't know. Too much going on to see. Ike happened to be in my line."

Wyatt had himself cleaned up then and looked at me. "You sleep in your clothes?"

"Too pissed off to strip."

"I know you wanted to help, Doc."

"That's one of you."

"You'd have folded up with the smoke."

"Might have been better than people watching me turn back," I said.

"You have a point, but it's over now. Fire's out."

"That fire." I let that sit, then added, "We're in a real fix, aren't we."

"That we are."

"What do you want to do about it?" I asked.

He began to undo his pants. "I want to fuck."

It would solve everything while solving nothing, and as such, became a most welcome diversion. I threw off my clothes and lay back onto the bed where Wyatt crawled on top of me, dick already hard. He still smelled of smoke. His hands slipped around to clutch my bottom as he humped against me, and soon we were awash in anticipatory juice. I had my arms around him, holding on until he had himself worked to such heights that he hopped off, raised my legs, drove in, and in about three strokes started to come.

He held nothing back, growling and swearing as he pumped me full of hot lead. I did no more than allow myself to be used, the unfortunate events of late finally asunder. As I took Wyatt's spunk, I felt myself warmed in both heart and body. Life itself might be on the path to hell, but Wyatt Earp was a man forceful enough to deter even fate.

"Christ, Doc," he said when done. "I kept thinking on this last night while slinging buckets down the line, hours of it, and you back here naked, even if you weren't. I kept thinking we'll put out this fire and I'll go start one."

"There is a sizzle in the room," I said as I lowered my legs. He looked at my hard cock. "How about some breakfast?" I said, wagging my dick at him.

He looked down to it, then back up, and I caught in his eyes the look of a smitten man, which caused both my heart and my gut to pleasurably seize. We passed a long moment in such communion before he got his mouth onto me.

While I expected a voracious suck, he surprised me with a playful tongue that set me squirming and finally begging. He poked at my piss slit, licked my knob, then descended the shaft to lick until I raised up and grabbed him by the hair. "Suck me!" I demanded and he did as asked, which resulted in me bucking as I shot a veritable stream into his throat.

When he'd swallowed it all, he sat back and said, "Reminds me, I'm hungry."

My stomach was already weighing in on the matter, rumbling several times during our antics, but my nether region was in command. "Rather fuck than eat," I said.

He chuckled. "Me too, but there are things I have to get to," he said as he climbed off the bed and started to wash. "Buy you breakfast,"

I lay stroking my cock. "Trying to buy me off?" I asked.

"I suppose. Come on, Doc, you know I'd keep on if I could."

"I have no doubt you could."

"That's not what I mean. There are important things waiting on me. Now, do you want breakfast or not?"

"All right," I conceded.

Over steaks and eggs at the restaurant next door, Wyatt explained what he had to get to. "I'm moving Virgil and Morgan and their wives to the hotel. It's not safe for them at the houses, especially with what was brewing last night."

"What about Jim and Bessie? And you?"

"Jim wants to stay put since he says he's not in the line of fire, and he's got a point, not being a lawman. I asked Mattie to move, but she refuses. She's close to Bessie, so I didn't fight it."

"Where will you be?"

"Same as always, I suppose, but I'll be at the hotel more."

"I like the sound of that. When are you doing the moving?"

"Today," he said. "December first, the rents are due, so it has to be today."

"Need any help?"

"No, thanks. Jim is going to pitch in. We'll do fine."

I saw not to press, so we ate awhile in silence. As we finished, he said he was also going over to register to vote. "Need to do it in Cochise County so I can run in eighty-two."

"Sheriff."

"Damn right. Somebody has to clean up after Behan."

Later on, I sat outside the Cosmopolitan while Wyatt moved in

Virgil, Morgan, and their wives. I was greeted by all and Morgan, always genial, asked me to come up later for a drink. "Haven't seen enough of you, Doc," he added.

"I'll come by," I said, noting his high spirits. Though his arm was still in a sling, he seemed much his old self while Virgil hobbled in as grumpy as an old fart. Allie was a miracle of patience with that man.

From my spot, I soon took note of activity across the street at the Grand Hotel. Pete Spence and Frank Stilwell, both on bail for mail theft charges, went in and a while later, as the Earps busied themselves inside, there came Ike Clanton, Curly Bill, and Johnny Ringo. I made note to discuss this development with Wyatt as it seemed the two sides in a deadly conflict were taking fortifications opposite each other, which surely could not bode well.

After a while, I stretched my legs with a walk down to Hafford's, where I bought the two town newspapers and the *San Francisco Examiner*. Since all contributed to the town's attitudes toward the Earps and me, I thought it best to keep abreast of what was being said.

The *Nugget*, always against us, came down hard on Spicer for his decision to free us and insisted the wrong would be set right by the grand jury, which would surely bind us over for trial for murder. The *Epitaph*, always for us, lauded Spicer for serving justice and repeated his statement of us acting right and proper. These articles did not surprise me, but the *Examiner* sure as hell did:

> *Doc Holliday is responsible for all the killing, etc., in connection with what is known as the Earp-Clanton imbroglio in Arizona. He kicked up the fight, and Wyatt Earp and his brothers stood in with him, on the score of gratitude. Everyone in Tombstone conversant with the circumstances deprecates the killing of the McLaurys and Clanton.*

I don't know which angered me more, being "responsible for all the killing" or that "everyone in Tombstone." The Earps and I had supporters. The mine owners and many businessmen backed us, as well as the vigilance committee, but they were outnumbered by the vast flock of sheep that fed on lies presented as inside information. The court had unintentionally given credibility to falsehoods, and the newspapers, printing them as truths, fed them back to the people to add still more credence. If this kept up, we hadn't a chance.

Leaving Hafford's, I started toward the Cosmopolitan but turned off partway, as I decided it unwise to intrude on the Earps too soon. So I detoured to the Alhambra, where a young sharp joined my poker game. He couldn't have been more than twenty, was darkly handsome and well turned out. He would have mirrored me had he not been ill-mannered and somewhat foolish. When he began to lose, he attempted to examine the deadwood, at which I issued a warning. "A man in Texas died doing that," I said. "You had best keep your hand fixed on the cards you hold."

He grinned with youthful confidence. "Why?" he asked. "Did you shoot him?"

"As a matter of fact, I did not. Before he could fire the pistol he had drawn, I gutted him, which made a mess with his innards spilling onto the table."

"Weapons aren't allowed in town," said the sharp.

"No, they are not."

"Then you are not armed."

I looked him hard in the eye. "I suggest you do not try to find out. Now, let us continue our game."

His hand moved from the discard pile to the cards he'd been dealt, and I was grateful further action was not required. He would, however, run up against it one day if he did not change his ways. When he'd been cleaned out some hours later, he again grew foolish.

"No man can win like that honestly," he declared.

"Watch what you say, son," I replied.

Fred Bradley, a mining engineer sitting to the sharp's right, laid a hand on his arm and suggested it was time for him to leave. "This is Doc Holliday," he told the kid. "Don't bite off more than you can chew."

"Don't bite at all," injected Axel Cutler with a laugh. He was seated on the kid's other side and most amused. "Come on, kid. Save your life. Get out of here and be happy you only lost your money."

The sharp suddenly became downcast, his bravado slipping to reveal the boy inside the man, which gained him an inch of sympathy since we have all, early on, made mistakes. And I likely would not have gutted him in any case, mindful of Wyatt's words on not causing trouble, even though the urge to act in such a way remained upon me. Once the boy had gone, the urge quieted down, and I played a few more hands.

It was after supper when I called on Morgan. His room was on the second floor front, and Louisa, his pretty wife, let me in. While I was happy to see Morgan, I was delighted to find Wyatt standing at the window. Morgan, mellow from a few drinks, offered me one, which I took as I joined Wyatt. "Good view?" I asked.

"See the whole street."

"And the Grand."

He nodded. "Look over there, that room all closed up. See the missing slat in the middle shutter?"

"The Cowboys. So now you're directly opposite each other. Is that such a good idea?"

"I doubt they'll commence firing upon us like some fort," Wyatt said. "Our presence will more likely make them think twice before shooting anyone from that window."

"Why would it?" I countered. "They know we're not the law, and I have yet to see Jim Flynn."

"Maybe so, but I won't be in the back. That would make us more vulnerable."

Morgan looked out the other window. "I'm not going to stay cooped up all the time," he announced.

"Fine," Wyatt said, "but if you go out, you go with me."

"I think you're making too much of things," Morgan argued.

"I am trying to keep you alive, Morg. This isn't some effort to keep you from billiards."

Morgan raised his good hand. "All right, sorry, you know best. You always know best."

Louisa sat in a corner sewing while we men dominated the room. If Morgan felt confined, I could not imagine how it was for the women who could not simply traipse down to the saloon and blow off steam. What little domesticity they had enjoyed was now all but lost. Wyatt had given orders none were allowed out without escort. It was more a fort than Wyatt would admit.

After a while, I brought out the *Examiner*. Each read it, even Louisa. "Ah, hell, Doc," Wyatt said. "This is such a shit pile of words. I had no idea it had gone this far."

"Me either. Bad enough to be looked down upon here in town, but to be accused in San Francisco is beyond me. How do you stand up against such a thing?"

Here Wyatt went quiet. He turned to the window as if fixed on something below, but I suspected he just had no answer. Finally, he came back to me. "Doc, we have worse things to fear than bad press. Mayor Clum says the Cowboys now have a death list."

"Death list?"

"Those they plan to assassinate. He says he's on it along with all of us, Spicer, Tom Fitch, and even Marsh Williams."

"Assassinate."

"Their word, not mine."

CHAPTER FOURTEEN

How marked is a marked man? I had already been singled out and vilified in the press, falsely accused of crimes committed by others, and turned criminal in the eyes of the populace. Could a target on my back be much worse?

"I will not be cowed by threats," I told Wyatt when he found me outside the hotel.

"Just keep your back to the wall."

"Can we get away for a while?" I asked. "Ride out to that place in the rocks?"

"No, I wouldn't feel comfortable leaving the family. It's too risky."

"Not if they stay inside."

"Well, Morgan won't stay put, and besides, I'm just not in that frame of mind."

"Your mind is not what I am after."

"I'm sorry, Doc. Until I can figure out a way to handle this…" He trailed off, leaving me to finish the thought on my own.

"Goddamn, Wyatt," I snapped.

"I know, I know."

I stewed a minute, then went on. "I can't just leave off you," I said.

"Well, you're going to have to leave off me some." And with that, he stalked away.

"Goddamn," I said again.

True to his word, Wyatt did not come to my room, nor did he ask me to ride out and inspect any claim. When I did spend time with him, it was with one or both of his brothers, as Virgil was now able to get around with a walking stick. Old man grumpiness had been overcome by lawman vigilance, thus he and Wyatt went on at length about the death list and how to avoid its fulfillment while not compromising their lives.

"I am still a Deputy U.S. Marshal," I heard Virgil say one day. "I still stand for law and order, and as such, cannot be viewed as cowering in my room. And besides, I doubt they'll gun us down in broad daylight."

Wyatt had no response, and who was to say the death list wasn't more rumor than fact? Rumors thrived in Tombstone, as we well knew. When I pointed this out, Virgil agreed while Wyatt remained skeptical. "Only takes one bullet to make it a fact," he said.

I had to work at maintaining composure while in their company as I quietly seethed over the Cowboys coming between Wyatt and me. While Wyatt practiced his own brand of restraint, I was forced into it by default, which I did not appreciate. Sometimes I caught his eyes upon me and saw in them the battle being waged. Unfortunately, he was a man compelled to put needs of others ahead of his own, me excepted, of course. I knew he was badly in need, but I waited, knowing I could not turn him from his righteous path. He grew quick-tempered and even began to snap at Morgan over his naturally playful nature. When Morgan chafed at Wyatt's confinement, the two had words so harsh Virgil had to step between them, which caused Wyatt to turn on his older brother. As I was witness, I followed Wyatt when he stormed out.

"Talk some sense into him, Doc," Morgan called as I left.

I caught Wyatt on the stairs. "They are both inside," I said. "They are safe."

"Get away from me."

"No." I put a hand to his arm and gripped tightly. "No."

Heat and sweat came off him, never mind it being December. He blazed with anger at the situation and fueled it further with his ridiculous restraint. His breathing was labored, and I knew if I reached down, I'd find him hard.

He shook off my grip and kept on down the stairs, me behind him. When he got to the bottom, he stopped to look up at me, then headed toward the back. I quickly followed.

Inside my room, he was a madman. "You want a goddamn fuck, I'll give you one," he said, yanking down my pants and shoving me onto the bed. He got out his dick, got on, got in, and began to give me what I wanted, thrusting like a bull. He grunted with each push, but as pent up as he was, he did not immediately hit the peak. Instead, he rode me long and hard, which was probably best as he needed to run himself to lather. Finally, after it felt like he'd worn me a new butthole, I heard his strangled cry and he slammed into me as he unloaded. It was the most violent come I'd known from him, and as it went on I pumped my own cock to get off around the same time.

Of course it did him no good. He pulled out, climbed off the bed, and did up his pants. "There," he said. "Happy now?"

I said nothing, hoping he'd hear himself, but this did not work in my favor.

"I am not going to let you pull me in, Doc," he said as he made ready to leave. "I need my edge sharp. I can't lie around getting my dick sucked when men are out to kill us."

When he was gone, I entertained myself with thoughts of who to shoot first—Ringo, Clanton, or Curly Bill. Any would do, but rather than proceed, I took myself to Hafford's and played faro until late the next evening.

A couple days later, Wyatt told me Mayor Clum had telegraphed our new Governor Gosper asking for guns to arm the vigilance committee and that a message had been forwarded to President Arthur saying release of the Earps had enraged the Cowboys and new dangers were feared. "Give us the use of the military, and we will give you peace at the borders," Clum urged him.

"What does it say of our town that we have to ask for military help?" Wyatt fumed.

I tried to envision soldiers riding into Tombstone, men in fine blue uniforms shotgunned from the Grand Hotel by the Cowboys, but still it seemed a viable alternative. "Wonder what the president will have to say," I ventured.

"Wonder if he'll give a good goddamn," Wyatt railed.

Two days later, word came of an attack on Mayor Clum while aboard the Benson stage. Milt Joyce began to pontificate on this development from behind the Oriental bar while I stood nearby. "Wire in from the Grand Central Mill says the Benson stage was attacked, but Clum escaped and walked twenty miles to safety," Joyce bellowed. "He insists he was targeted, which is a horse load if you ask me. Who cares about him? He's got three weeks left in his term."

Anything from Milt Joyce was suspect due to his growing alliance with Behan and the Cowboys. If there indeed had been an attack, it was most likely due to the death list, so I had to hand it to Wyatt. Maybe he was right about our chances. I knew Clum had been going to Washington to seek appointment as Indian agent at the San Carlos Reservation, and

I had, in fact, seen him depart on the stage. We would not know the full story until his return, but I could already see, by Joyce's telling, that opinion would be as divided on this as it was on everything else.

The next night, Virgil struck up a conversation with Joyce at the Oriental. I happened to be nearby, wetting my whistle prior to engaging in my favored pastime, and heard their exchange. After relaying yet again the attack on Clum, Joyce began to laugh. "Been expecting something like this ever since you Earps and Holliday got liberated from jail."

At this, Virgil hauled off and slapped Joyce across the face. "You goddamn son of a bitch," he railed as others jumped in to restrain them both. Joyce, as he was hurried away, issued a parting dig. "Your favorite method is to shoot a man in the back, but if you murder me, you will be compelled to shoot me in the front."

Next day's *Nugget* replayed the incident and commended Joyce. "His coolness and good judgment undoubtedly saved Tombstone from the disgrace of another bloody tragedy, all who are cognizant of the peculiar characteristics of the Earp party will readily admit."

There was just no winning, and to make matters worse, Will McLaury remained in town. He continued to aggravate the situation, as he had gained much respect, and thus always found an audience for his running mouth. I have never seen more wind come from a man—and more people suck it down. He berated us no end, and the *Nugget* saw fit to quote his every utterance. He portrayed those killed at the OK Corral as a young nineteen-year-old boy and two respected ranchers, conveniently leaving out their links to rustlers. He also talked up our supposed involvement in the Philpott murder and the stage robbery, fanning the flames about us making off with loot. The fact that no loot had been taken was now entirely lost.

"Damned McLaury should be shot," I told Wyatt one night in mid-December. "Either that or his tongue sliced off. I've got my knife handy and it is a tempting prospect."

"The *Nugget* is no better," Wyatt added. "The bigger the lies, the more weight they carry, and there seems nothing we can do. The *Epitaph* tells the truth, but I'd venture it has a smaller readership since people seem to prefer bad news. They want villains and we are convenient."

"Do you know when Clum is coming back?"

"A month at least, and now Tom Fitch has gone to Tucson."

"Business?"

"No, he's moved there. Closed his practice and gone."

"Because of what happened to Clum?"

"He won't say. I caught him just before he boarded the stage and asked him point-blank if the death list was the reason. He denied it and said that was nothing but rumor, then he hopped aboard before I could call him on it. Damned coward."

"So two are effectively gone."

"That they are."

Just then Virgil came along. We were outside the Oriental and he was on his way inside. "Don't worry, Wyatt," he said as he passed by. "I'll keep my back to the wall."

I could feel Wyatt bristle at the indulgence. Morgan was already inside, laughing it up and having a fine time. His recovery was complete, arm back in use for lifting a glass and holding his cards. Virgil bore a limp but was without his stick and standing straight as his upright brother.

"The grand jury meets in two days," Wyatt said when Virgil had gone in. "They are going to decide if Spicer's decision needs review, and if it does, we'll go to trial."

"Fitch said that might not be a bad thing, as we could set the facts out in more detail and make things right."

Wyatt was shaking his head before I finished my argument. "Impossible. There's too much weight against us to get anywhere near a fair shake, and with Tom gone, I don't know who could represent us. Better hope they leave things alone."

I pondered this and realized there was another turn. "If they don't take it up, it might make things worse."

"I have considered that."

"We cannot win."

"No, we cannot. Best we have is holding our own."

Wyatt started to walk up Allen Street, and I fell in beside him. "Do you ever think of leaving?" I asked. "Why stay if the situation here is hopeless?"

"Because we've set down roots, Doc, and will not be driven out by criminals. We're in business, we're making money for the first time ever, and doing well. It's what we've always wanted. I don't expect you to understand since you can set up shop at any table, but we have families and want to be settled."

"Do you honestly think you can ever get that around here now?"

"Honestly, I do not know, but I am not going to give up. That is not my way."

On December 16, the grand jury decided against reviewing Spicer's controversial decision. Along with this, of course, came the *Nugget* trumpeting a lack of justice for innocent men murdered in the street in broad daylight by the ruthless Earp party. When I saw Wyatt playing poker at the Oriental that night, he was lacking his usual determination. I sat in just to be near, which I found both comforting and pitiful. I wanted the man badly, and in such need had been reduced to getting next to him while in company of others. We passed several hands before Johnny Ringo came in and sauntered to our table.

"Wyatt, I think the wind has shifted," I noted. "A stink just blew in."

"Doc," he said, but I ignored his exasperation.

"Cow shit," I continued. "Yes, that fine Mexican excrement those boys keep dragging across the border."

Two men jumped up and departed our game, one leaving his money behind. Ringo sat down and picked up the vacated hand. "I'll play these," he said, shoving the other man's money into the pot.

"I'm afraid we can't accept this money now," I said. "Got that Mexican cow shit all over it. You'd best go for a wash, Johnny, although now that I think on it, the stuff is likely permanent."

"You are looking to get drilled, lunger," he shot back.

"And you will be dead before you crook your trigger finger, and I do not mean some clean bullet hole. I am known to slice open those who annoy me and you, Johnny, are stinking up my game."

The entire room had gone quiet and two nearby tables had been vacated when Milt Joyce shouted, "I'll blow your head off, Holliday," which caused Wyatt to turn but not me. I had set down my cards and had my hand poised near my breast pocket.

"That's enough, Doc," Wyatt said. "Let's cash out."

"But I am winning, Wyatt. I wish to continue our game as soon as the stink is dispatched."

I heard the cock of the shotgun Milt Joyce had pointed at me but kept my eyes on Ringo, who now bore beads of sweat on his upper lip. I waited, as did he. It was Wyatt who broke. "Come on, Doc. He's not worth it." And he pulled me to my feet. Trying to shake him off was futile since I was outweighed, so I let him push me outside.

"Goddamn, Wyatt, why'd you get in the way?" I demanded.

"Because Milt Joyce was going to shoot you soon as you drew, and I don't care how fast you are, you can't beat a gun already cocked. And anyway, it was foolish what you were doing."

"I want him dead," I cried as I walked away. "I want them all dead and buried!"

Wyatt caught up with me. "You go shooting off your mouth in this tinderbox, you'll get yourself killed and maybe me too."

"I will not tolerate his thinking he can intrude on me like that. And you would have felt the same a while back."

"This ain't a while back, Doc. You know the fix we're in."

I stopped and turned to him. "You know as well as I do there is only one way out of it and it is to kill them all."

This struck him badly, as I knew it would. "I won't go gunning for anyone without authority," he said.

"There is no authority and never will be."

Another low blow, as he still planned to run for sheriff in January even though he knew the turn against us had finished his chances.

"You won't kill them, I will," I said. "I am done tolerating such an element."

"Simmer down, Doc. I understand, but you're going to get yourself killed if you go after them like that."

"I'll take them with me and we can all descend to hell and keep on shooting among the flames."

"There is no talking to you sometimes," he said. "What in hell does it take to make you see?"

I paused to frame my reply. "Wyatt, I am so boiled over I am ready to kill the next man that happens along. You damn well know what it takes."

"Are you playing with me?" he asked.

"No. I would not do such a thing. Circumstance is upon us now and you have the power to avert a tragic end."

"I should shoot you myself."

"Whatever your pleasure," I replied and I started toward the Cosmopolitan. He huffed but followed.

In my room I poured us drinks, but he remained standoffish. "I do not like being manipulated," he said as he took the glass.

"No man does, not even Johnny Ringo," I replied. I then downed my drink and began to undress. "Shall we attempt to set things right?"

Naked, I stroked my stiff prick. "I need to come in the worst way," I said, inching forward. He threw back his drink and dropped to his knees. When he got me into his mouth, he had only to briefly suck before I shot him a throat full.

He slurped and swallowed, and when he'd gotten it all, he flipped me around and drove his tongue up my butthole, ramming it like a mean little prick, which got him so worked up he nearly tore off his clothes. He then stood me at the bedpost and shoved his dick into me and went at it so hard that I swear the bed attempted to run for cover.

When he came it was in silence, like he felt compelled to hold something back. Once empty, he pulled out and fell onto the bed sprawled crosswise and facedown. I eased in next to him, onto my side, and ran a hand onto his back. As his breathing quieted, I rubbed him gently, for if there ever was a man needing soothing, it was Wyatt Earp.

"It doesn't help," he finally said, face turned away.

"It would if you'd let it," I countered.

"I'm not you, Doc. I can't just let go of things."

"You don't have to hold on for every breathing hour. A man needs to tend himself on occasion."

"This the occasion?"

"Can be."

He rolled over to face me. "You're good for me when you're not bad for me."

"No shots fired."

"Few more gray hairs, though."

"I will try to minimize those in future."

"Somehow I doubt that," he said. "It seems your nature to piss people off."

"Among other things," I said, reaching for his dick. When this caused him to issue a welcoming sigh, I added, "Let them go for a while."

"Let who go?"

"Virgil and Morgan. They can take care of themselves."

He shut his eyes because he didn't like me getting inside him, but what he didn't see was how this was on the outside now, wrapping him up like some coat he couldn't shed no matter how hot. I gave him a few seconds, then crawled down to suck his cock. He rolled onto his back, which allowed me to straddle him and drop my dick into his waiting mouth.

Best thing about sucking a man is how quietly it can be done. Serene almost. Calming. The juices stir, but the demand need not be urgent. It was in this state that I remained atop Wyatt, feeding on him slowly, savoring the weight of his dick on my tongue and the feel of his knob in my throat. He was likewise easy with me, addressing my morsel with lips and tongue until it filled to his liking and he began to seriously feed. We then swam in a mutual wallow, away from circumstance at last. After what seemed a glorious age, Wyatt began to squirm and moan and started a furious suck of me, which caused me to thrust and spurt just as he did the same. For a brief moment, we shared the best of meals.

Not a word passed between us for a while after. I climbed off and lay next to him until a coughing jag passed, then rolled to throw an arm across his chest. Lying together in the quiet, I enjoyed that elusive warming of the heart, hoping he did too, but then he said he needed to get upstairs. "Check on the boys."

"Are they even up there?"

"Don't know."

"So you'd rather leave off this just to check?"

"I am trying to keep them from getting killed," he snapped.

"Why not leave that to them? You can't guard them every minute, and I doubt they want you to."

"It's what I want."

I paused to gather courage. "Is that all you want?" I asked.

"Don't corner me, Doc."

"I am not asking you to choose," I explained. "You have room for us all."

"It's not a time for indulgence."

"Says the naked man in my bed. Wyatt, I am simply trying to get you to allow yourself some pleasure and some leisure, both of which you deserve."

Even as I said this, I saw it was too late. He'd finished his pleasure and was already upstairs in his mind. "Go," I said and he hopped from the bed and dressed. At the door, he stopped and looked at me. I tried to maintain some dignity even though I suffered disappointment.

"I'm sorry, Doc," he said.

"I know."

Then he was gone. It was one thirty in the morning, but I got dressed and went to the Alhambra, where I again played cards until I had to be carried out.

Chapter Fifteen

Amid Tombstone's continued expansion came the Bird Cage Variety Theatre, which opened just before Christmas. This fine establishment boasted an ornate bar, stage and dance hall, upper boxes where any and all sorts of personal play might be accommodated, and a gaming area in the basement. Musicals, dancing girls, dramas, and comics entertained with a risqué flavor that appealed to most everyone, including Morgan, me, and, on occasion, Virgil and Wyatt. Laughter and nonsense at this point were most welcome, and in a town such as Tombstone, both were sorely needed.

The Earps sometimes attended the Bird Cage as a group, their wives pleased to be free of confinement and able to enjoy a bit of levity. Such entertainment was welcome amid continuing assaults from the press, such as a December editorial in the *Nugget*:

> *The Earps and Holliday place no value on their own lives, have no conscience for law or respect for public opinion, and are therefore reckless of and dangerous to the lives of others. Their supporters are foolish in their eagerness to suppress imaginary assassins...*

I left off reading Wyatt the rest of this as he hadn't wanted me to begin in the first place, but I was fuming at the latest slander. "Things will never settle so long as the papers are spouting this shit," I groused.

"No point in getting ourselves more worked up, Doc," he said. "It does mention assassination which, even in denial, serves to acknowledge."

"Good point, but it is a weak sort of good."

"I hear Jim Flynn is taking out an ad saying he is independent of any town faction," Wyatt said. "Trying to distance himself from us so he can win election."

"Well, that is a slap in the face. Does Virgil know?"

"Not yet. He'll be pissed."

"Rightly so."

Flynn had been Virgil's deputy when he was city marshal and had always been in our support. Now he was running for the marshal's job, which meant loyalty had run out.

"Anything to get elected," Wyatt mused, which was ironic given he was running for sheriff against Behan. But he did not stoop to compromise, as he was determined to gather votes solely as a law-and-order man, whether or not people supported such a concept.

The newspapers continued to rail at each other at our expense on through Christmas, keeping the town on edge as it tried to make a celebration. Sporting saw me through, as I was always pleased to get past such days. Henry Hooker was in town for a while and we squared off at poker, which meant a fine time. A calm almost descended. Almost.

Three days after Christmas, we were at the Oriental. I did not often play poker with all three Earps, and it was good to see them recovered from wounds and enjoying the evening. Around eleven thirty, Virgil said he was tired and going home. "Broke about even," he noted before he left. Not ten minutes later, he staggered back in, blood gushing from buckshot in his back and left arm.

"Virg!" Wyatt cried as he and Morgan sprang to their feet. Others parted to allow them to ease him to the floor, though it was quickly decided Virgil should be taken to the hotel as it was in the next block. Wyatt, ever the general, took charge, and Virgil was soon in his room, wife and Doc Goodfellow at his side. The vigilance committee showed up and stationed themselves out front, in the lobby, upon the stairs, and outside Virgil's door. Being a lightweight, I did not assist in Virgil's carrying but followed along and remained in the hall near the room. Wyatt, as he carried his brother inside, looked most grim with Virgil's blood all up his front.

More than an hour later, Wyatt stepped out appearing absolutely stricken. As the hallway was full of people, I took him down to my room and gave him a drink. "How is he?" I asked.

"Likely to lose the arm if he lives, which is doubtful. It's torn up bad and they're trying to decide if he can keep it. His back is also a mess. Doc Goodfellow said I had to leave, as I was getting in the way. Christ, Doc, he's my brother."

"You have to place him in the doctor's hands now."

"They can't take his arm."

He wouldn't sit down, and I knew better than to try to corral him. "Any idea who shot him?" I asked.

"He says just as he came out of the Oriental he saw Frank Stilwell duck into that burned-out building across the street."

"Stillwell. That means Spence was likely there too and probably Ike."

Wyatt went quiet then and I saw it come over him that he had failed to protect Virgil. His face went blank, which made him appear, for the first time since I'd known him, defeated. "You couldn't have prevented it," I said.

He considered this. "Man says good night, starts home to bed, and is shot for no reason beyond who he is. It did not seem dangerous to let him go alone, but it was. I should have gone with him."

"Then you'd both be full of buckshot."

He started for the door and I grabbed his arm. He was generous on not shaking me off, as he surely could have. "You're not needed up there right now," I reminded him. "Give the doctor time to help Virgil."

"If they take his arm, I want to be there."

"I doubt they'll do that tonight. The priority right now is saving his life. Why don't you sit down? You're going to run yourself into the ground and be of no use to anyone if you keep on like this. You need to sit still for a few minutes, have some whiskey, and gather your wits. Then go up and be of some good."

He allowed me to settle him on the bed beside me and took another drink, as did I. "I can't face him dying," Wyatt said after a bit.

"He's strong, a fighter. He's an Earp, and you boys never give way."

"Thanks, Doc. You're a good friend." He gripped my knee, and as much as I wanted an arm around him, I held back.

"I can't sit here," he then said. "I have to go back up to him."

"Keep out of the doctor's way," I counseled him. "Your presence is enough."

When he reached the door, I said I wasn't going to bed. "Come by later and tell me how he is. I'd be up there too, but it's already too crowded."

"I'll see you," he said and left.

I was dozing fully clothed when he came back next morning. He sank onto the bed. "They don't know if he'll make it," he said, tears spilling down his cheeks. "They are hellish wounds. He won't let them take the arm, but Doc Goodfellow says if they don't they'll have to remove about five inches of shot-up bone, which will make it useless."

"Wyatt, I am so sorry." I didn't hesitate this time. As we sat side by side, I put an arm around him, and while he wouldn't allow himself the cry he needed, he shuddered with the containment. We sat thusly for some time.

It didn't take long for the lawman to step back in, however. Wyatt gradually righted himself and when he announced, "I'm going down there," I knew he meant to view the crime scene.

"You're all bloody," I said.

"Good. Let people see what they've wrought!"

We walked down to the Oriental and heads turned as we passed. The bloody shirt drew attention, as intended, but I suspected it was seen by far too many as deserving. At the burned-out building Virgil said he'd seen Stilwell enter, it took less than a minute for Wyatt to find a hat near the back door. "Look at this," he said, holding it so I could see inside. There on the band was a name: Ike Clanton.

"Son of a bitch."

"That's two of them," Wyatt noted, "Clanton and Stilwell for sure, and I'd guess at least two more as they are nothing without their cohorts. You notice anything else, Doc?"

I looked around and shook my head.

"No lawmen. No sheriff or city marshal at the scene of a crime, no effort toward finding out who shot Virgil. I'd venture Behan is electioneering somewhere and Flynn is scarce because to attend to his duty would put him in our favor."

"What are you going to do?"

He looked at the hat, then walked outside and glanced over at the view Stilwell had. "Easy shot, the coward," he said and he started up the street, Ike's hat in hand. At the telegraph office, he wrote out a message and showed it to me.

> TO: U. S. MARSHAL CRAWLEY DAKE, PHOENIX, ARIZONA
> Virgil was shot by concealed assassins last night. His wound is likely fatal. Telegraph me appointment as Deputy U.S.

Marshal with power to appoint deputies. Local authorities are doing nothing. The lives of other citizens are threatened.
WYATT EARP

The wire was sent, and before the day was out a reply came with the appointment. Wyatt found me in front of the hotel and handed it to me. "Now we're talking," I said. "Get warrants issued, arrest them all."

Wyatt sat down beside me. "Soon enough. I won't leave Virgil until I know he's going to make it, and Doc Goodfellow says it may be a week or more before we know for sure."

"Well, Stilwell and Clanton won't go far. Probably back to Charleston or Galeyville. We can get them when you're ready."

Ten days went by before Virgil beat back the grim reaper, ten days with Wyatt both attentive brother and bear ready to kill. Though a round in my bed would have taken the edge off, I knew it unthinkable with Virgil near death. I thus became reacquainted with my hand while thinking on better times.

The January third election came and went with hardly any notice by the Earps. Behan was reelected sheriff, while John Carr, a Cowboy supporter, became mayor. Dave Neagle, Behan's deputy, beat Jim Flynn for city marshal, so Flynn's attempt to distance himself from the Earps had failed. The anti-Earp faction, as the opposition had come to be known, won it all. What they didn't realize was Wyatt now had federal authority.

Around this time, I encountered several well-dressed entrepreneurs from New York who had come to Tombstone seeking riches and had managed to gain enough to lose. A most jovial band, they were more refined than the usual fare and thus appreciated my manners, even as I fleeced them. It took me a day, a night, and much of another day to strip them clean, after which I had a meal and sought my bed, priding myself that this time I had not been carried from the saloon.

I did suffer, though, as my malady always opposed my extended gaming efforts. My cough took hold with such authority that whiskey did little, reducing me to lying prone yet failing to rest. In this sorry state I did not particularly welcome Wyatt's visit.

"I hear those New York boys now travel light," he said as he brought me a drink. I noted he took none.

"And once I recover, I shall enjoy their bounty," I managed.

"I am putting together a posse to go after some men who robbed the Benson stage Sunday," he told me, "but I'll not ask you to join."

"Maybe next time. How much did they get?"

"There was no strongbox on board, but they took fifteen hundred dollars from passengers. Wells Fargo is offering a three hundred dollar reward."

"Why?" I knew it not Wells Fargo's habit to offer rewards when no strongbox had been taken or nobody had been killed.

"Remember their special agent, Jim Hume? Well, he was aboard and they took his two fancy pistols and seventy-five dollars off him, which is causing embarrassment, what with him being a company man. He came to me with descriptions of the men, and we think they may be over at the Ayers place in Charleston."

I had to laugh—and cough—at the idea of a Wells Fargo man robbed on his own stage. "Who's good for it?" I asked.

"Pony Deal, maybe, or Ringo, the Clantons. They had masks, but Hume says he kept them talking and would recognize their voices."

"Who'll posse with you?"

"Morgan, Fred Dodge, Sherm McMasters, along with Hume. Doc Goodfellow says Virgil is improving, so I figure we can leave him awhile. There was another stage holdup Saturday on the Bisbee line, got six thousand five hundred dollars. Wells Fargo is so pissed they are threatening to shut down the Tombstone operation."

This was terrible news, as the stagecoach was the sole transport for the mines' bullion and cash. It would affect all commerce in the southern state. "Holy hell," I declared. "Why do you think we've suddenly got more stage robberies?"

"I believe the Mexicans are putting soldiers on the border to stop the rustling, which shuts down the Cowboy operation."

"So they are looking elsewhere."

Wyatt nodded. "Henry Hooker reported rustlers at his place, so they are turning local."

"And law enforcement?"

"Not Behan, even though it's a county matter. I can chase stage robbers but not local rustlers. Too many goddamn jurisdictions to get anything done. At least I can go after Clanton for shooting Virgil since Virg is still technically a Deputy U.S. Marshal."

It was all bad news, and yet, as he spoke I saw some good as he was much his old lawman self. Gone were the guilt and grief and uncertainty, and in their place the man who took charge and got things done. I wished I could saddle up and go along, but I'd be more burden than help in my present condition. When he stood to leave, I asked him to call again. "When you've arrested them all." He tipped his hat and I was left to recuperate.

Three days later, I was coming out of Hafford's when Wyatt and his posse rode in. I noted they had no prisoners. I strolled down to the Cosmopolitan and caught him as he started inside. "Buy you a drink?" I asked. He hadn't seen me come up and he started like I'd demanded he throw up his hands. "You look mighty dusty," I added before sauntering toward my room.

"I need to talk to Doc," I heard him tell Morgan. "Be up after a while."

Footsteps sounded behind me, and when I opened my door he stepped inside, shaking trail dust off himself. He was sweaty and dirty and angry, which had me hard.

"Goddamn Hume was useless," he began. "Couldn't identify a one, even when they stood right there, so I had no cause for arrest."

"Who was it?"

"Fin Clanton and Pony Deal, maybe Jim Arnold. Hume just folded up and I considered arresting him for wasting my time."

"Wells Fargo won't be too happy."

"Damn right, but Hume will throw it off on me."

I poured us drinks and he downed his in a gulp, then took another. "I won't ask how things are here," he said.

"Quiet for some, not so others." I unbuttoned my pants and pushed them down, my hard cock springing forward.

"Doc, I'm filthy."

"Filthy is my preference."

He began to strip with marginal enthusiasm, but as his naked body emerged, he got into the notion. When he was bare, he took another whiskey, gave one to me, and we drank them down with hard pricks facing off.

"One good thing about today," he said as he set aside our glasses.

"What's that?"

He shoved me onto the bed, pulled my ass high, and rammed his prick into me. "This," he said as he began a spirited ride.

"Welcome home," I said as I took him.

He reeked from his lawman work, and I sucked in that reek, the smell of fucking mixing in. He went a good distance before he came, likely due to fatigue from long hours in the saddle, but when he did give me his load, he let out a cry of satisfaction it pleased me to provide.

When he pulled out, he sat back on his haunches and I rolled onto my back. He glistened with sweat and I reached out a hand to partake, at which he succumbed and crawled onto me. As my arms went around him, he began humping my hard dick until I spurted between us. I couldn't keep quiet in my ecstasy, and held the embrace as I delivered a good measure of noise and cream. It seemed fitting to add my stuff to the filth he'd brought in.

When I quieted, he nuzzled my neck and I basked in such small intimacy. It was the equivalent of a kiss, as we both knew. He murmured some, then went quiet a minute or two before startling himself. "Damn, I'll fall asleep if I don't watch out."

"Fine by me if you do."

"Always fine by you, Doc," he said and he bit my neck before getting up off the bed. "Christ, we're a mess," he added, heading to the basin to wash. "I need a bath," he then declared, to which I gave no comment, as that meant home. "I'd stay if I could," he said as he dressed.

"I know."

"Tomorrow I'm going to move the rest of the family to the hotel," he added. "It's not safe anymore all spread out."

"That might have other benefits," I noted. I was still stretched out in bed. He studied me up and down.

"Never know," he replied, and then he was gone.

I made a point of sitting out front the next day, and sure enough, there came the wagon with Jim, Bessie, Wyatt, and Mattie, and all their belongings. Jim offered greetings to me, as did Bessie, but Mattie, when I said hello and tipped my hat, passed me a frosty look. Wyatt scarcely noticed me, which led me to wonder how much thought he had given to our personal proximity up against his efforts toward his family.

When the Earps had all gone inside, people began to discuss them, and it was not good. The recent stage robberies were seen as evidence the OK Corral shootout had done nothing but make things worse. "I hear they're involved in these latest stage holdups, just like before, piping off the proceeds," said one man.

"Something has to be done," declared another. "People are afraid to walk the streets."

It took great restraint not to challenge these misinformed dolts, but

I managed, as any such display would be seen to validate our supposed lawless nature. It truly rankled me, though, that new stage robberies had been tacked on to us along with the old.

I had not realized Wyatt living upstairs would undo me. Whatever hour I fell into my bed, my thoughts always climbed to the second floor, where I envisioned him alone in bed, stroking a hard dick. The mind is such a convenient organ, tossing a wife away without a care. And when I awoke, be it night or day, subject to my sporting hours, I would picture Wyatt with that erection that arrives unbidden with sleep. I'd see him rise and tote it to the commode or possibly lie and indulge himself much as did I. We thus had a fine time, even if he didn't know it.

When he next called at my room, I was preparing to depart for an afternoon at the Alhambra. Those momentarily flush had congregated there of late and were giving me a fine living. Happy to see him, I asked Wyatt in, but he said he wanted me to come upstairs. "I want to show you something."

I stopped myself from making some witty remark on what I'd like to see as he was all business and so I followed him up. "We've got four rooms at the front," he said, entering one. I was surprised to find not Mattie but Morgan and a veritable arsenal. As I looked around, Wyatt explained.

"We will not be taken unawares again. A store of weapons guarantees we'll always be well armed, here or on the street. As lawmen, we have that right."

There were shotguns, rifles, pistols, and boxes of ammunition. Could Spangenberg's Gun Shop have anything left? "A fine arsenal," I said. "I suppose there is much the same thing across the street."

"I don't care what the Cowboys have," Wyatt snapped. "We mean to be fully armed."

"Well, you have certainly accomplished that."

"The other thing I mean to do, Doc, is make a show of it around town. I did that with some success in Kansas, going out accompanied by several armed men. It says to one and all that we are prepared to fight if necessary, and if we must fight, we will win. Can I count on you as part of that effort?"

"Of course. You always have my full support."

"Won't be all the time," he explained. "The vigilance committee will rotate as needed and some others want to help. The Earps are to be guarded from here on out, and the town is to know we stand for law and order."

His confidence filled the room as much as did the weapons, a deadly combination to both the Cowboys and to me, for I found Wyatt exceedingly attractive in such a situation. My prick hung heavy in my pants. How could I get him to my room?

"Where is Mattie?" I asked to derail the urge.

"Over with Jim and Bessie. She'll be there days, here with me at night."

Well, that sure as hell threw cold water on me. Of course, he was oblivious to this, an Earp wife being a necessity. "You still going to let Jim tend bar?" I asked. Brother Jim had recently taken a job at Vogan's Saloon.

"Yes, but we'll walk him there and back. Nobody else is going to get shot."

"Sounds like a good plan. And now, gentlemen, if you'll excuse me, there are some cards awaiting me at the Alhambra."

As I walked toward my game, I entertained myself with images of Wyatt's gun and his prick as equals. I could see him standing naked, hard cock aimed at me, and in his hand his Buntline Colt. As I entered the Alhambra, I was most amused.

Word soon got around about Wyatt's appointment as Deputy U.S. Marshal, and while Tombstone was predictably divided on the subject, it was a surprise to find the erstwhile *Prescott Democrat* against it:

> *We join with other Territorial papers in calling the attention of Marshal Dake to the impropriety, to say the least, of appointing one of the Earps to the position of Deputy United States Marshal. If he knew the facts, we are satisfied that a decent regard for public opinion would restrain him from placing such a character in so responsible an office.*

I knew Wyatt had seen the editorial when I found him out front of the hotel at two a.m. I'd just allowed the New York boys to give me more money and was looking to fall into bed. Suddenly, I saw I'd have company.

"Have you seen the *Democrat*?" he asked, flushed with rage. I wondered how long he'd been seething.

"I have indeed. They are idiots, Wyatt. You know that."

"Well, there now seem to be more of them than sane people."

"Possibly. Come with me."

He followed me to my room as if we would continue this debate, but once behind a closed door, he saw my intent. “Ah, hell, Doc,” he said and he began to undress.

I liked an angry fuck. Put some meanness into Wyatt and it tapped a great store of power. When we were bare on the bed, he put me on my back, pushed my legs up near my ears, and drilled his prick so deep I swear he poked my gizzard. He held me bent as he drove in and out, eyes blazing, mouth open like he would bite. He grunted and growled but never took his eyes off mine, and I was silently grateful to the *Prescott Democrat* for a damned good fuck.

CHAPTER SIXTEEN

Johnny Ringo became a nuisance to me later that month. The Earp party, five strong, was making its presence known without me one morning as I was otherwise engaged in earning a living at the Alhambra saloon. Having played all night and into the morning, I emerged around ten in less than my usual good spirits due to modest gain. That my opponents found this amusing did not further my mood, although I had stopped short of considering who to shoot. I thus stood on the sidewalk taking fresh winter air when I heard a familiar voice.

"Well, looka here, the lunger has come out of his hole. You done running your game?"

"Johnny Ringo, as I live and breathe."

"How come you ain't with the Earps, lunger?" He stood in the street about halfway across, wearing his gun in defiance of city law. "You boys are always in a herd lately."

"I need no company to face the likes of you," I said. My gun was tucked under my coat as I too refused to go unheeled and Marshal Neagle had, as yet, not attempted enforcement of the ban.

"You are wrong on that score," Ringo called. "Best call for your nursemaids."

"Why is that? Are you planning to make a spectacle and get yourself killed?" My hand hovered near my pistol as I stepped into the street.

"Only spectacle will be you breathing your last."

"Then by all means, let us proceed," I declared.

Silence fell between us and carried down the street until all nearby commerce ceased. While Ringo's fingers fluttered over his pistol and mine remained absolutely still, the town held its collective breath. Johnny's finger tapped his gun while his eyes remained fixed on mine. I in turn waited him out, knowing he'd soon exceed his limit and fire, which would be his last living act. But before this could be accomplished, I was seized from behind just as Dave Neagle grabbed Ringo.

"That's enough, Doc," Wyatt said as he held me back. I attempted to break free but was wrestled away and disarmed while swearing at him. Ringo suffered the same and we were hauled down to Judge Spicer's court, where we were charged with carrying concealed weapons, fined thirty-two dollars each, and released. Wyatt, as we left the court, was not amused.

"You're nothing but trouble, Doc," he fumed as we walked along. "I'm trying to show us as law and order and you're ready to shoot Ringo over words that don't mean a damn."

"They mean something to me."

"You have to stop stirring things up," he went on.

"It was Ringo who did the stirring."

"But you playing into it was the trouble."

"I will not be maligned in public," I declared.

"I didn't hear any maligning, just two fools picking at each other and ready to kill over nothing."

"You call me a fool?"

"In this case, yes."

I stopped in my tracks. "Then good day, Wyatt. I'll trouble you no longer." And I turned toward the Oriental, where I spent the rest of the day and most of the night not causing trouble. When I sought my room around midnight, I found Wyatt out front of the hotel. Without a word, he followed me in.

"You are no fool, Doc," he said soon as he was in the door, "but trouble does follow you, and you have to start holding back due to circumstances."

"I see. Kill a man only when you say?"

He snorted like a pissed-off bull, which he was in a way.

"You've got a goddamn arsenal in your room," I railed. "You walk around town with your posse armed to the teeth, and I'm the one looking for trouble? I will not fail to defend myself when called out, just as you will not."

"I am trying at reason here, Doc."

"As am I, but since I am not an Earp, I must at times survive on my own. You cannot possibly deny me that."

He shook his head. "Fair enough," he said and he left with a slam of the door. We then kept a distance for several days before he caught me at the Alhambra. I was at the bar and he came up alongside.

"I have arrest warrants for Ike and Fin Clanton. Getting up a posse. Are you in?"

"Of course."

"We leave tomorrow morning."

I didn't care anymore about our spat, and Johnny Ringo had not annoyed me further, so I was apparently redeemed in his eyes. Thus, I found promise in the moment. "Buy you a drink?"

"Hell, yes," he said and we headed for the hotel.

Nothing was said this time. No drinks were poured. We stripped and he did me standing, and I let go a gusher as he went at it, spurting come onto the bedpost while he drilled my butthole. He swore when he came, which I think was left over from our spat, the last word so to speak, but I did not care. A fuck righted all.

When he was done and pulled out, I turned to see him far from done. He looked like he wanted to slap me. "You're a troublemaker, Doc," he said, "but I guess I can live with it."

"I'll drink to that."

I poured and we clinked glasses, downed the whiskey, then he pulled me onto the bed.

"Sometimes I think you enjoy pissing people off," he ventured as we lay side by side.

"I will not be degraded by anyone," I said.

"Not even me?"

"Well, I must admit a man is sometimes a fool, although in my case it is not when facing Johnny Ringo." Here I slid a hand onto his soft cock. "I intend to get completely foolish in a minute or two."

He chuckled. "You do me in, Doc," he said.

"Is that permission?"

I didn't wait for a reply but slid down to lick his cock, positioning myself so I could look him in the eye while I fooled around. When I drew my lips to his knob, I saw a bit of swoon in him, which was a treat, coming from the stern and upright lawman. Dick sucking is a great leveler.

He pulled a second pillow up under him so he could better watch, and I played to this audience of one, my tongue now onstage and overacting, fully extended to dramatize the scene. The cock flopped about a while, then began to take note, and soon became a star performer, rising to beckon long licks up and down itself until there appeared the drops of cream common to all enthusiasts. At this point, I raised up and got over it, sucking my way nearly to the root, which got a moan from the audience.

I feasted for a good while, gaze moving between my subject and its owner, who began to squirm and push up at me. When his breathing stepped up, I drew back to reposition myself astride and dropped down onto the prick, which got a near shout out of Wyatt. He attempted to grab me, but I put him off and started to ride, at which he lay back and let himself be taken.

My legs held up well, as did my lungs, though my ever-present cough remained. Wyatt had learned to ignore it, and for that I was grateful, so when I now hacked some, he offered no comment.

How I loved to spear myself with his rod. I raised up his full length, then dropped down over and over until my legs complained. I then settled for a spell of easy canter. My own dick was up again and Wyatt took hold, pumping as I kept at him. I thought ahead to our posse ride and how, when in the saddle, I'd think back to this ride. Maybe Wyatt would too.

It was a good long ride and I was awash in sweat and pleasure when Wyatt raised up, grabbed me, and rolled us over without pulling out, then set to fucking me proper. He called out as he delivered his load, pumping with a fury while I accomplished the same by hand. As I spurted up my belly, he grimaced and groaned until spent, then pulled out and fell over beside me. I lowered my legs, blew out a breath and a cough.

"Holy hell," he rasped. "I have to get out of here, else I'll not be fit on a horse tomorrow."

"Hate to see you go," I said, sliding a hand onto his thigh.

"Leave off, Doc. I am done."

"The hell you are, but I will do as requested since we have important work tomorrow."

"Six a.m.," he said.

"I'll be there."

He lay a bit longer, then sat up and swung his legs over the side of the bed. When he didn't go further, I ran a hand up his back. "This was a good send-off," I said.

He thought on this, then agreed. "A well-fucked man should do fine," he said and stood to dress. "Six," he said again before he left.

At six the next morning, I was in front of the hotel, having gotten my horse from the livery and packed my necessities. Posses were usually given food by local ranchers who appreciated the effort, thus we carried none. Likewise, horses were rested at such stops and on long chases sometimes temporarily replaced. We knew the country well and could go for quite some time if need be. When Wyatt and Morgan arrived, they carried guns and ammunition. Each of us was given a shotgun, rifle, and two pistols as well as a hundred rounds.

"Enough for a goddamn war," I remarked, which Wyatt ignored. "Why no warrant for Stilwell?" I then asked.

"Judge doesn't care what Virgil says; he's going on evidence, which is just Ike's hat at the scene. I'm thinking if we find Ike and Fin, maybe we'll find Stilwell. They've all been seen around Charleston; Ringo too."

People had begun to gather on sidewalks as we prepared to leave. By the time we rode out, they were lined up for a couple of blocks, which I first took as a show of support, then realized was more likely their happiness at us being gone from town. We rode at a good pace and reached Charleston that evening, encountering Ben Maynard, a known troublemaker and Cowboy friend, on the outskirts. Wyatt relieved him of his guns, then forced him to lead us through town at gunpoint as we knocked on doors of buildings where the men we sought might be hiding. Wyatt told Maynard if any shots were fired, he would "not last as long as a snowball in hell."

The search took much of the night and upset residents with our intrusion, and worse, proved a futile effort, as not one of the Cowboys was about. This set some frustration into Wyatt and he began accosting most anyone who strayed into our path. One unfortunate who did turned out to be Deputy Sheriff S. H. Sperry, who Wyatt called a "cattle-thieving son of a bitch" before asking his business and discovering his error. Sperry, to his credit, was reasonable about the mistake, but there was still no holding Wyatt back.

We camped outside of Charleston for a few hours that night, Wyatt gone silent at not finding his prey as expected. He would not settle in and kept fussing with the horses or walking about, and when I suggested he get some rest, warm himself by the fire, he looked at me like I'd suggested we fuck then and there. Wouldn't have been a bad idea, save for the men looking on, as it would have eased his frustration, but I was at a loss as to how to get him off to myself. I don't think he slept at all while I had some whiskey and as reasonable a doze as a man can get on the ground.

At dawn, Wyatt said we would take breakfast in town, then expand our search toward the foothills, which we did, roving long distances to no avail. We returned to town for supper and again camped nearby. We followed such a pattern for two more days before we found Pete Spence holed up in an abandoned cabin about forty miles from Charleston. Wyatt soon had from him the whereabouts of the Clanton brothers, and Pete, with some of Wyatt's good prodding, led us there. Their hideout in a narrow canyon was easily breached and we took them without a fight as they were drunk and thus not alert to our approach.

Wyatt took great pleasure in securing his prisoners, telling them only that he had warrants for their arrest. I do not think they realized these were not for robbing the mail but for attempted murder. Wyatt gave no cause and so we led the men back to Tombstone. The town stood watching as we rode in and placed the men in jail. There seemed to be a positive air among the people, and I had a thread of hope that bringing these men to justice might weigh things toward us.

Once the men were secured, Wyatt was approached by Crawley Dake, his boss. Dake had come to town in our absence and now advised Wyatt that his purpose was to replace Virgil as Deputy U.S. Marshal due to his incapacity from wounds. This had been expected, and Wyatt was most cordial to Dake. "I appointed a five-man committee to recommend a candidate," Dake explained as we walked up Allen Street, "and we held an open citizens meeting the next night at which a good man won endorsement. I am pleased to tell you I have appointed Ben Maynard for the position."

Wyatt went so long in silence that I jumped in. "Ben Maynard? Why on earth?"

Dake seemed surprised. "Your Judge Spicer stood up for him, speaking of knowing him twenty years and vouching for his noble courage and stating he is a gentleman who would represent the solid views of the solid men in town. Others likewise spoke in support."

"Well, Marshal, you have been hoodwinked," I stated, and I then separated from them to leave Wyatt to whatever effort he might make toward righting yet another wrong. I got myself a bath, fresh clothes, and a meal, and was back out and about when I spied Wyatt coming out of the *Epitaph* office. He didn't look like he'd even changed clothes.

"Giving the paper a firsthand account?" I asked.

"Not now, Doc," he replied, brushing past. He stalked off down the street and I knew not to follow. Evidently, he had not been able to get Dake to understand the situation with Maynard which, if the case, would further undermine Wyatt's authority, never mind the Clantons had been captured.

Next day, the Clantons went before a judge and were granted bail of $1,500 each, which was quickly posted by cohorts. They had indeed been surprised to find themselves charged with attempted murder, but they retained counsel and a hearing was scheduled. Meanwhile, I was most surprised when I read the latest *Epitaph*:

> *Draw Your Own Inference/Resignation of Virgil W. Earp and Wyatt S. Earp as Deputy Marshals*
> *Major C. P. Dake, United States Marshal, Grand Hotel, Tombstone*
>
> *Dear Sir:*
>
> *In exercising our official functions as deputy United States marshals in this territory, we have endeavored always unflinchingly to perform the duties entrusted to us. These duties have been exacting and perilous in their character, having to be performed in a community where turbulence and violence could almost at any moment be organized to thwart and resist the enforcement of the processes of the court issued to bring criminals to justice. And while we have a deep sense of obligation to many of the citizens for their hearty cooperation in aiding us to suppress lawlessness, and their faith in our honesty and purpose, we realize that notwithstanding our best efforts and judgment in everything which we have been required to perform, there has arisen so much harsh criticism in relation to our operations, and such a persistent effort been made to misrepresent and misinterpret our acts, we are led to the conclusion that, in order to convince the public it is our sincere purpose to promote the public welfare, independent of any personal emolument or advantages to ourselves, it is our duty to place our resignations as Deputy United States Marshals in your hands, which we now do, thanking you for your continued courtesy and confidence in our integrity, and shall remain subject to your orders in the performance of any duties*

which may be assigned to us, only until our successors are appointed.

If I hadn't seen Wyatt coming out of the *Epitaph* office, I would not have believed my eyes, but here were the Earps handing over their power and thus putting asunder the only law and order in Tombstone. The Maynard appointment had obviously been Wyatt's last straw, which I could understand any man reaching, but still, it was Wyatt and he was not any man. I could not begin to imagine his rage or his disappointment. He'd brought in one of Virgil's attackers and gotten nothing more than a snub for his work.

I did not see him that day. He likely was with Virgil, although I doubted his fuming would be good for his brother's recovery. I could be of no help, so I contented myself with sporting and did not see him until late the following night at the Oriental. He did not sit in on my game, so after a while I cashed out and joined him at the bar.

"Dake refuses the resignation," he said in greeting.

"Smartest thing he's done."

"Maynard's appointment stands," he added.

"How on earth do you figure he got so wrapped up in that man?"

Wyatt considered this a bit, then offered an opinion. "You're always saying the town is full of sheep. Well, he's joined the flock."

"Damned big flock. What will you do now?"

He threw back his drink, then looked at me and I saw his intent. In minutes, we were in my hotel room, stripping. "Only place makes any goddamn sense is here," he said as he peeled off his drawers. His prick was hard and he took hold, stroked some. I could not get onto the bed fast enough.

When he flipped me over to get at my rump, I expected that dick but was not surprised when it was his tongue. He sought the depths, which fired me such that I pumped out a come while he ate my butthole. And I let him know I was doing it, crying out he should eat all of me, as it was driving out my spunk. I carried on far more than usual, spewing filth as I spewed come. When I was done and quieted my oration, he pulled out his tongue and stuck in his dick. He let out a groan as he entered and I knew this was his first good thing in a couple days.

He slapped my bottom as he rode, working himself into a heat to match his rage, and it did not take long to channel that anger into a come that set him roaring. He pounded me to such extent the bed inched forward, hitting the wall in time to his thrusting. Finally, after he'd done all he could—and seemingly then some—he pulled out and fell over beside me, breath a gasp. At that moment, I doubted his lung power equal to mine.

"Feel better?" I asked when he'd settled. I'd rolled onto my side and put a hand to his chest.

"I will after we do that a few more times."

At this good news, I pressed myself to him, humping his thigh for emphasis. "I am liking the sound of that."

"Only good thing a man has is his fucking," he declared, "and I mean to have some good tonight."

He had his good until the sun was up, and I did not concern myself with the wife upstairs. If he didn't, why should I? After the initial go, we had a drink and he speculated on the Clanton hearing the next afternoon. "There should be enough to hold Ike for trial, what with the hat. Not sure we can nail Fin, as I have no proof he was there other than he often stuck close to his brother."

"Any sight of Stilwell?"

"None."

I did not want the Cowboys in bed with us, and yet they did their part in that Wyatt soon had himself angry again. "Suck my dick," he commanded, and when I crawled down there, he pulled me over him to suck me.

The meal was long and pleasurable and as Wyatt fed, he reached around to get a couple fingers into me and proceeded to work me front and back. I, meanwhile, feasted until he bucked and spurted into my throat. With his continued attentions to my entire nether region, I soon gave him just as good. We then fell into a sleep.

I had no idea the time when he rolled me onto my side and stuck his dick in. Still dark, but surely hours had passed. He set up an easy motion in and out, wrapping his arms around me, and I was beyond ecstatic, the embrace as good as the fuck. Contentment seemed with him this time, as if he had no hurry but rather wished simply to be occupied inside me. I welcomed such a change after the angry assaults, even though I thoroughly enjoyed his rage coming out through his dick. But this was special, as he was not often a man at ease.

His thrust was barely that, just a quiet in and out, as if we could remain so engaged for a good long time, allowing the Cowboys and sheep outside to fade away. I wrapped my arms around his and held fast, squeezing my bottom muscle periodically to indicate welcome. It was the most relaxed we had ever been together, a most serene fuck.

After a good while at this, he spoke. "If I could keep on with you…"

He left me to finish the thought. "I know," I said. "Me too."

Feelings rose up in me then, and I had to tamp them down so they wouldn't spill over and complicate things. I wanted to tell him so much more about how I felt and how important he was, but knew better. I had to keep an even keel with him and so made myself content with the feel of him inside me and clutching his arm ever tighter.

The room was getting light when he took me at the hips, rammed his cock a few times, and grunted out a come. He then reached around to find me still hard and worked my dick until I shot a modest load. "Good morning," I then said. He murmured a reply and pulled out of me.

"Did we sleep?" he asked as he sat up.

"Beats me. All I remember is fucking. Don't care about the rest."

"We need to be sharp today. I want you in court with me, as we need to show a strong presence."

"Wyatt, I feel stronger than I have in ages. As you said, a well-fucked man should do fine."

"Hold on to that thought."

I felt us downright invincible when we entered Judge Spicer's courtroom that afternoon. Wyatt and I merely nodded at each other as we met out front while Ike and Fin Clanton strode up with a gang of cohorts, reeking of whiskey and full of bluster. By the time proceedings began, the courtroom was full and I noted it mostly the anti-Earp faction.

Wyatt testified first as to finding Ike's hat at the scene of Virgil's shooting and Sherm McMasters then said that three days after the assassination attempt, he had heard Ike say, in reply to an inquiry about the shooting, that he "would have to go back and do the job over."

While it was good to hear such strong facts stated in open court, they were soon lost to testimony from seven defense witnesses, all stating Ike and Fin Clanton were both in Charleston at the time of the incident. And Ike then testified that he had lost his hat several days before the shooting and had no idea how it got to the scene. Judge Spicer questioned several of the witnesses before announcing his decision on whether the facts merited binding the Clantons over for trial. "As the evidence here presented is circumstantial and therefore inconclusive, the charges are dismissed, and Isaac and Fineas Clanton are hereby discharged."

The Cowboy contingent let out a whoop and started backslapping one another. Ike and Fin hurried to join the others and were all but carried from the courtroom. Soon it was just Wyatt, Judge Spicer, and me. I expected Wyatt to storm out after such a disgraceful failure of justice but he remained fixed. "You go on," he said to me. I saw he wished to speak with Spicer, so I did as asked, figuring the judge was going to get an earful. After I lingered awhile out front, Wyatt appeared. He headed down Fourth Street and I saw he wanted us away from everyone before he spoke.

"Judge Spicer laid it out for me," he said. "Told me I'll never clean up this crowd this way and next time I'd better leave my prisoners out in the brush where alibis don't matter."

"He was in sympathy, then."

"Very much so, but it seems if the culprit is not caught while he is committing the crime, there is little chance of him going to trial."

"Not much incentive to bring them in."

"None. Dammit, Doc, we've risked our lives for nothing. He was telling me it's better to kill a man than bring him in, and that goes against everything I stand for. But if I follow the law and get him into court, a judge will say he's committed no crime, which gives him license to do more of just that."

"It makes me sick to see Clanton and his bunch enjoying a freedom they do not deserve."

"I do not know what to do, Doc. We run up against it at every turn, looked down upon by half the town for attempting law and order, criminals set free over and over."

"Nothing to do but keep on because if you don't, there is no law in Tombstone. You can't let them win."

He shook his head. As we walked, he'd turned us a couple times and we were headed back up Third toward Allen. "What's next?" I asked.

"I do not know. I'm going up to see Virgil and tell him of the latest travesty."

"Maybe see you later?" I asked.

He looked at me hard, but later on, when I sought my hotel long after midnight, I found him out front looking like Judge Spicer had set Ike free all over again. Without a word, he followed me to my room, refusing a drink and letting loose his thoughts rather than his dick. "I should just shoot Ike and be done with it," he ranted. "He is the cause of so much trouble in this town and he is not going to let up until we hang for the killings."

"It would be a service to the community," I observed.

He paced and spewed a bit more, which roused my impatience to such extent, I took up a newspaper. Maybe fueling the fire would get him to boil over.

"You want to see the latest *Nugget*?"

"Now what?"

I read him a quote from Behan stating any call to action against the Cowboys was unnecessary, as the situation was exaggerated. "Due process must be maintained rather than frontier vigilance."

"Due process!" Wyatt railed.

I then read what our new Mayor Carr said about Sheriff Johnny Behan: "I have no doubt that the sheriff of the county is abundantly able and willing to deal with the lawless element. He is emphatic that in all his years experience he has never known a more quiet and law-abiding community than Tombstone."

"Stop quoting me the goddamn *Nugget*," Wyatt said.

"All right. But have a drink; settle yourself."

"I don't want to be settled, Doc. I don't want to let go of what I feel. I want it to burn a hole in my insides, set my whole damn self on fire. Then see what happens."

Maybe he should shoot Ike Clanton. Would do him good, as well as the town. He went on a while longer, then finally saw I'd backed off and he'd become a one-man show. "Listen to me," he said, dropping into a chair. "Running off at the mouth for no good."

"Better to get it out than fester inside."

He blew out a sigh. "Festering," he repeated. "Describes the whole situation."

I went over to him and kneeled. "You get out your dick and I'll detour you a while."

He glared at me, unable to let go his troubles. "It will take one hell of a suck," he finally said.

"That can be managed," I assured him, and I began to unbuckle his gun belt. He allowed me this, then became impatient.

"Get off. I'll do it," he growled. He then stood, dropped the belt, opened his pants, and sat back down.

I found him half-hard and got a hand on him to play around and enjoy watching him fill. When he had a good heft, I did not do as he expected. “Let me try something,” I said and I stood and stripped off everything.

“I want to sit on you,” I said and he considered this about one second before opening his arms in welcome. It took some doing, but I got onto his lap facing him and managed to slide down onto his prick. That he was big-dicked helped anchor him inside me, and I sat for a bit simply squeezing my muscle and swooning not only at him inside me but in our upper bodies so close. I wrapped my arms around him and he put his hands at my waist and we then had us what I would call an upright sort of fuck.

The position did not lend itself to good leverage on my behalf, but Wyatt saw to the engineering by pulling me up and down. For once, my light weight worked to my benefit. “Sitting on your dick,” I said, “I don’t care if the whole damned town goes entirely to hell. I have all I need here and now and, good Christ, Wyatt, you are some good fuck.”

He was stern of expression and I saw it more than his nature. His juice was on the rise. His jaw clenched and the familiar grunts began until he rammed up into me as he spewed his stuff. I hung on for the ride, squeezing him as I received his load. When he had stopped thrusting and I’d settled onto him, he stayed put long enough to take me in hand and pull me to a gusher. He kept his eyes on the spurting while he pumped until I had nothing left.

Once empty, I moved enough to allow him to exit my passage, but I stayed atop him, lying forward to press myself to him. He likewise held me and I nuzzled his neck, basking in our mutual satisfaction. Finally, awash in sweat and come, I climbed off, his spunk running down my leg as I stood.

“We are a filthy mess,” I noted, “but a most desirable filthy.”

Rather than wash up, I fell onto the bed, ignoring the cough that had arrived with my efforts. Wyatt got up and poured drinks, then sat beside me. I clinked my glass to his. “Here’s to fucking,” I said.

“To fucking.”

We drank down the whiskey and Wyatt said, “I may need another.”

“Drink or fuck?”

“What do you think?”

He set aside our glasses and lay beside me, quiet awhile. Then his hand strayed onto my leg. “Raise up,” he said and I did as instructed. He crawled down to where my butthole was displayed and began to finger the thing, rubbing and poking while I gazed upon his face. He seemed to want to play around, which I always liked, and sure enough, he put a finger into me, fucked some with it, then got down and sucked one of my balls, and there we were, me with legs up, him entertaining himself by way of my privates, which he did for some time.

I began to pull at him after a while and he got the idea to slide his lower half my way so I could get to his dick, which was soft to my touch. We lay for a while like that, me working his prick, him licking and prodding until I squirmed in readiness. At last he raised up, lips wet from all his licking. "I am going to put my dick in you and keep it there," he said and he crawled forward and did just that, stuck it in and set to a slow fuck.

Where he was so often rough or rampant, he was now the opposite, scarcely moving, yet his rod remained gun barrel stiff. He was going to make it last, and nothing pleased me more. Keep it in all day and all night or however long nature allowed. Knowing Wyatt's stamina, I figured he could go an hour or two if he chose, and so I secured my arms around my legs, getting comfortable for him while he fucked at leisure.

As we did not overly exert ourselves, my malady went along with things, cough at a minimum. My prick stirred but not so much that it begged attention. That would be for later, when he set to serious work. For now, I savored our communion and the fact that nobody outside this room had any power over us while we were together.

I wondered what passed through Wyatt's mind as he did me with such restraint. His gaze was fixed to mine, but now and then diverted to look down at his prick going in and out. I considered he might be filled with inexpressible feelings and enjoyed such an idea. But he might also have been thinking filthy things since a man's mind gets loose when he fucks. I considered what it would be to hear him utter filthy words, to speak in detail of all he did, and I soon found myself highly aroused though Wyatt had spoken not a word. I took hold of my prick but was unable to exercise restraint and began a spirited pull as Wyatt looked on.

"I cannot hold back," I rasped. "Your dick is going to drive it out of me." I then unleashed a come that felt drawn up not only from my balls but my entire being, all my life fluids gathered into a torrent that spurted up my front. While in my throes, I saw Wyatt's tongue run along his lower lip and knew his restraint was at an end. His eyes widened, his calm faded, and his expression turned determined.

"You got me going," he said as he pushed my legs back and drove his dick in to the root. He then began a hard ride, accompanied with the usual grunts and such until at last he cried out, shook his head, and let go his stuff. His stamina was impressive as he kept at me a good while, then fell back across the bed. I lowered my legs and crawled over beside him.

"This is good," I said. "I have no recollection whatsoever of the morning nor any anticipation of life beyond this room. We are adrift in a wallow beyond compare."

He chuckled. "Wallow. Couple of pigs."

"Oink."

I lay somewhat across him, content beyond words. His fingers lazed over my chest, stopping now and then to rub a tit. After a while, I drew my hand over his. We then dozed a bit.

The following day, I was at the Alhambra Saloon when Wyatt joined my game. Two men vacated at this while two remained. We played for less than an hour before Wyatt made it clear he wanted some privacy so I cashed out, as did he. We then wandered outside, where he seemed uneasy.

"What's up?" I asked.

"Milt Joyce is taking back my percentage of the Oriental. I'm out of the gambling business."

"Sorry to hear that."

"It was a good little moneymaker."

"Can't beat sporting."

"Nothing is going my way, Doc. The law is full of holes. I am trying to make a living, but am set back at every turn. Only good thing is we are not in jail for murder."

"Small favors."

Soon after this, we learned that the governor's request for assistance with the lawlessness in Tombstone had prompted Congress to request President Arthur to begin discussions with Mexico to improve enforcement and extradition procedures between the two countries. While this was good news to us, most people saw our troubles played on the national stage as embarrassing, all of which was somehow blamed on the Earps. Around this time, a quiet began to settle over the town, and in Tombstone, quiet was usually suspect.

While businesses thrived and the stage brought still more opportunists, the hustle and bustle seemed almost a disguise because underneath there lurked a tension that seemed to be building toward something. It drove us nuts that we could not figure what was up, but we could only continue our show of force, Wyatt and Morgan accompanied by at least three men wherever they went. I moved somewhat easier, being notorious, but I did carry my pistol and knife. Wyatt and Morgan, whom he had deputized, were allowed weapons since they were the law.

By the end of February, the tension began to weigh upon Morgan, and further, upon his wife. "I am going to send Louisa to California," he said one evening at the Alhambra. The three of us had been playing poker for some time and were now at the bar. "She is unhappy living under such confinement and I think she would do better with the folks."

"Probably a good idea," Wyatt said. "We'd all be better off in California if we didn't have roots laid down here."

"Pretty shallow roots," Morgan declared.

"That's true, but I am not going to give up our investments to hightail it out of here just because the air doesn't feel right. You go with Louisa if you want, Morg. I'll understand."

"No, I'll stay on here and once we get things sorted out, I'll bring her back."

We then walked out of the saloon and stood taking the night air. It was windy, dusty, and inhospitable. "Maybe one day we can take our money and go to California," Morgan said.

"Not a bad idea," Wyatt replied.

Their parents lived in Colton, California, and would undoubtedly welcome the whole clan into the fold. Thoughts of such a move caused me to seize up somewhat, so I took my leave and headed to my room. I had thought to have Wyatt join me, but Morgan's presence had put down such a notion. Once settled under the covers, I let all slip away but thoughts of Wyatt, who I saw naked and ready to put his dick to me. It didn't take me long to bring myself off and fall asleep.

CHAPTER SEVENTEEN

Something is afoot," Wyatt said. "I can feel it."

It was a Friday night in March and we were making our presence known, accompanied by Texas Jack Vermillion and Sherm McMasters.

"You've been feeling that for weeks," I remarked.

"No, this is different."

Just then, as we neared Hafford's, we ran into Briggs Goodrich, lawyer for the Cowboys but still a fair man. Wyatt stopped him to ask if he knew of any plans for trouble.

"Nothing definite, but you are liable to get it in the neck anytime."

"I don't see any of the Cowboy crowd in town," Wyatt said.

"They're around," Goodrich said. "Watch yourself." And he moved on.

I did not play cards that night but remained part of Wyatt's town posse. We patrolled the streets, up and down Allen, then Fremont and Toughnut and all the numbered cross streets, four abreast much of the time as a show of force. Though music and men's hoots and calls spilled from the saloons, the streets were more deserted than usual, as if the stage had been set for some show. More than once, pistols were drawn toward some encroaching noise only to find it a drunk or frightened dog.

"We're getting spooked," I noted after one such incident nearly cost a drunken miner his life.

"Better spooked than dead," Wyatt declared.

We kept to the streets until Wyatt finally called it a night. Jack and Sherm left us at the hotel, and when it was just us two, I asked Wyatt to my room. He hesitated. "You are the devil, Doc," he said. He always uttered some such nonsense, which I saw as his efforts to justify the detour on his way home.

"Lucifer himself," I replied, willing to play along with most anything to get what I wanted.

"Mattie is sick again," he then said.

"I am sorry to hear that. You need not stay long and you can then go and comfort her."

I could see him trying to work up a better denial and discarding each effort. "Just for a little while," he finally said and he followed me inside. There was no talk as we stripped naked and got onto the bed. He put me on my side, got in behind, shoved in, and did it slowly with his arms around me. It was almost gentle, and as I took him he spoke.

"I don't like it out there," he said.

"Better you're in here, then."

"We can't fuck forever."

"If only."

"I am serious, Doc. I fear for us. No matter how vigilant, we are still vulnerable."

I squeezed my bottom muscle to shut him up, which got a groan out of him. "Okay, I'll quit talking." And with that, he rolled me onto my stomach and set up a serious thrusting that got him off all too quickly. Once he was empty and flipped me over to see me hard, he wrapped a hand around my dick and proceeded to work me until I spurted all up my front. It was most pleasurable to watch him do to me what every man did to himself, and I lay swooning until he jumped up and said he had to leave.

I made no comment as he washed and dressed, figuring he feared Mattie might again take too much laudanum. "Illness" remained the word Wyatt used for her indulgence, and I knew if he was this concerned, things must be bad. Much as I wanted to wish him well, I said nothing as he was now almost back in her world, and I knew it pained him when the two ran against each other.

"Good night, Wyatt," I said.

He looked at me lying naked, paused to consider, then said, "Night, Doc," and left. I lay for some time thinking on him upstairs playing the dutiful husband when his come was still inside me.

The next afternoon, Morgan, Wyatt, Sherm McMasters, and Dan Tipton found me at the Alhambra Saloon. I took a break from faro to join them for a drink.

"Morgan's got an idea to see a show at the Birdcage tonight," Wyatt said with some annoyance. "I told him he's not going alone, but I am not interested in it."

"Will you go with me, Doc?" Morgan asked. "I really want to see this. It's a one-night showing of *Stolen Kisses* by the Lingard Theater Company."

"Sounds good to me," I said since Morgan was a most entertaining companion and a welcome contrast to his stern brother. We agreed to have dinner with all present and be escorted to the theater.

That night we had a fine meal, after which Morgan and I were taken to the show. We were walking toward the Birdcage when we ran into Briggs Goodrich, who said, "I saw some men with guns. You fellows will catch it if you don't watch out."

"Which men?" Wyatt demanded.

"Can't say. Just be careful."

Wyatt let him move on but then stood so fixed I thought for sure he'd tell Morgan no theater. A few seconds passed, but he finally relented as he usually indulged his little brother. We started again to our destination where we were left to enjoy the show. Wyatt said they'd be back to get us at ten o'clock.

Stolen Kisses proved a delightful romp that gave Morgan and me a good time. It ran until after ten, and when we emerged, there stood Wyatt, Sherm, and Dan. When Wyatt started us toward the hotel, Morgan balked. "It's too early to turn in," he said. "I want to shoot some pool at Hatch's."

Wyatt bristled. "No," he said. "I saw Indian Charlie and Hank Swilling a while ago, and that means others may be around. I don't think you should stay out."

"Then you come with me. Just one game, have a beer, relax a while. Come on, Wyatt, loosen up."

Morgan was probably the only person who could get around Wyatt, but Morgan was a sweetheart few could resist. I watched as Wyatt let himself give way. "One game," he said and we turned up the other way to Hatch & Campbell's Pool Hall.

Hatch was always happy to see Morgan, as the two liked to square off and provide entertainment with their expertise. While Sherm and Wyatt sat in chairs to watch, Dan and I stood at the bar. It was nearly eleven, as Morgan bent to line up a shot, when gunfire blasted through rear window glass and caught Morgan in the back. As he crumpled, a second shot rang out, and we all hit the floor except for Wyatt, who rushed to his brother.

"Morg! Morg!" Wyatt cried, holding the bleeding Morgan, who

bore a stunned expression. "Dan, help me get him to the lounge. Sherm, Hatch, go see who's out back. Doc, go get Doc Goodfellow."

All did as instructed. I ran out as Morgan was carried to a sofa in the lounge. Doc Goodfellow had gone to bed when I pounded on his door but was most responsive to the urgency, throwing on pants and coat over his bedclothes. At Hatch's, he had to pull Wyatt away to get to Morgan, who cried out when he was turned so the wound could be examined. After a good look front and back, Doc Goodfellow took Wyatt aside. "The bullet has severed his spine and come out his groin, possibly hitting his kidney," Wyatt was told. "Make him comfortable, as I'm afraid nothing can be done."

This was not acceptable to Wyatt. "Do something!" he cried. "You can't just let him die!"

"I am sorry, Wyatt, but there is too much damage."

Sherm and Hatch then came in and said there was no sight of anyone out back. Wyatt just stared at them, then looked back to Morgan. I had never seen him so undone. He pushed the doctor aside and kneeled beside his brother, taking his hand and leaning in close to offer words of comfort. He was like that for some minutes before telling me to go get Virgil and Jim.

I assured him I'd take care of this and was at Virgil's door before I realized the weight of my mission. Allie answered. "Doc. It's awful late to call. Virgil is asleep."

"Allie," I said, pushing past. "You have to wake him. Something has happened and Wyatt said to fetch him."

Aware of the threats against us, her face went pale. She nudged Virgil until he opened his eyes. "What?" he demanded.

"Doc is here. Wyatt said to fetch you as something has happened."

"What is it, Doc?" Virgil said as Allie helped him sit up. He was still recovering from his wounds and had difficulty moving about. His arm was bandaged against his body to render it immobile.

I stepped forward and looked him in the eye. "I am sorry to tell you Morgan has been shot down at Hatch's and will not survive his wound."

"Help me up," Virgil said to Allie, and I thought to assist until I saw she was well practiced at such things. She helped Virgil into pants and boots and threw a coat around him. As we went out, he asked for details. "Where was Wyatt?"

"Sitting not ten feet away. A second shot was probably meant for him but missed. They fired from out back, shattered the window, but got away."

As we passed Jim's room, Allie knocked and gave him the bad news. We then reached Wyatt's room where Allie knocked, and after a minute, Mattie answered looking quite disheveled. "What?" she said, bleary-eyed.

"Morgan has been shot and we are going down to Hatch's where he is dying. Wyatt is there. They missed him. You'll want to come along."

"Yes," Mattie said. "Let me get my coat. I'll follow."

When we reached Hatch's a crowd had formed outside while the vigilance committee was now inside. Wyatt remained beside Morgan, clasping his hand, both men bloody. "Wyatt," Virgil called as he entered the lounge and Wyatt turned and stood looking about to come apart.

"Virg," he said. "Hurry."

He helped Virgil kneel down to speak to Morgan, whose eyes had now closed. Jim got down next to Virgil. I couldn't tell if Morgan was talking, but his brothers were most persistent and loving in their efforts toward his comfort and assurance. Some time passed in this manner and then Virgil bowed his head and attempted to stand. Allie stepped in to assist him to a nearby chair while Jim stood and fell into Bessie's arms. Wyatt, ashen, moved in close to Morgan. "Morg! Morg!" He ran a bloody hand over Morgan's cheek, then stood and turned toward me. "He's gone," he said, mouth working to say more but issuing not a sound.

Mattie stepped toward him but Wyatt pushed her aside, staggering toward the door. He looked dazed as he pushed through the crowd and out into the street. I caught up with him halfway across.

"Wyatt, you can't be out here. They'll kill you."

"Leave me alone, Doc!" he shouted, pushing me so hard I fell back into the street. The sight of me on the ground stopped him and he offered a hand to help me up. "I'm sorry," he said as he got me to my feet.

"That's all right, but you need to get inside. You're a target out here."

"I have to do something. Go after them."

"We will go after them, but not now. Nobody was seen out back. There's nobody to go get right now, so you need to come inside."

"But Morgan. I can't...I have to..." He was turning in place, looking for where he should be, his world upside down.

"He'll be taken care of. You can see him later. Right now, you come with me. You need to get inside."

He looked at me like he finally understood. "All right," he said.

I should have led him upstairs, as I knew his family would soon return, but instead I took him to my room because I honestly believed he would not want Mattie's attentions at such a time. We walked side by side through throngs of people that gawked and whispered. I didn't care about what any of them thought anymore. I wanted to give Wyatt privacy.

In my room, he was lost. He refused to sit or drink, and I wasn't about to suggest he lie down. His shirt and coat were soaked with blood and it had dried on his hands and face.

"You need to wash up," I said, more to occupy him, but this proved a mistake as he looked at his hands, which bore the grisly reminder. He traced fingers of one hand over the palm of the other, as if to feel Morgan's essence, and I thought my heart would break.

"It's the last of him," he said. "The last of his life. Christ, Doc, he's dead. They killed him for no reason but his name. I can't...I can't..."

He stood with both palms upturned, and I have never seen a more anguished sight. This man of strength in such pain brought on my own tears, which I fought back. I went to him, put my arm around him, and as I tightened my grip, he broke. A wail came out of him and a flood of tears, at which I folded him into my arms and simply held on, crying along with him, for I had loved Morgan too.

After a while, he regained himself and pushed me off, pacing the room again. I poured us a drink and when he said no I insisted. "Take it. You need fortification against this awful night."

This got through and he drank the whiskey down and followed with a second. "You need to sit and calm yourself," I said. "You do no good pacing the floor."

"I won't curl up for you."

"I am not asking that, but you'll wear yourself out and be no good to anyone if you don't get hold of yourself."

He glared at me but he did sit on the edge of the bed and didn't object when I sat beside him. We were quiet awhile, but then he started looking at his palms again. "I can't believe he's gone," he said. "I let him go over there when I knew better. I had that bad feeling, but I let him go over there."

"It's hard to say no to Morgan."

He nodded. "Everybody's favorite and oh, Christ, this is going to kill Ma. She dotes on him something terrible, her sweet boy. And Louisa. I have to wire her that her husband is dead."

"Not tonight. You can tend to things tomorrow. Right now you need to tend to yourself."

"What about Virgil?"

"He is likely back upstairs by now. I can go up and tell him you're down here and I can find out where Morgan has been taken. You can see him tomorrow when he's cleaned up."

He looked at me blankly, like things weren't getting all the way through, but nodded. "All right, do that. I'll stay here a while and take care of things tomorrow. Arrangements and such."

"Good. That's good. Now I'll go up and see to Virgil. You rest. Have another drink."

As I reached the lobby, an awful sight met me. Men carrying Morgan's body were starting up the stairs. I moved to join the procession and found Allie helping Virgil along. Mattie was unseen.

Morgan was taken into his room and placed on the bed. Allie settled Virgil into a chair while Bessie sank into another, Jim at her side. Allie then began removing bloodied clothing and washing the deceased. I went to Virgil, who looked to have aged a year in one night. He had already endured so much, and this latest was more than any man should have to bear.

"I am so sorry for your loss," I said as I squatted beside him. "I wanted you to know Wyatt is down in my room. I had to corral him, as he was bent on going after somebody when he doesn't even know who the somebody is. He's badly undone, so I'm going to keep him inside awhile if that meets with your approval."

Virgil considered this and agreed. "Thank you, Doc. He's probably best off with you. Sometimes I think you have greater sway with him than any of us."

"If you need us, send down word," I said. As I retreated, Mattie came in and caught sight of me.

"Where is Wyatt?" she demanded.

"Downstairs in my room. I had to stop him running after the gunmen."

"He should be here with me," she said.

Before I could respond, Virgil entered the fray. "He's best off with Doc right now," he told her in his most commanding voice. "You couldn't stop him from going out and getting himself killed. Doc can."

She protested no further but threw me an awful look as I fled the scene. Back in my room, I found Wyatt lying crosswise on the bed. "Virgil and Jim are upstairs and so is Morgan," I said. "He is being seen to, so there is nothing you need presently do."

He gave no reply, eyes fixed on the ceiling.

"How about you take off your coat?" I suggested and he looked at me like I spoke a foreign tongue. "Sit up and take off your coat," I said, putting a hand to his shoulder. "Come on."

He raised up and allowed me to pull off the bloodied coat, but once I had it off him I realized it was the wrong move, as it revealed the bloodied shirt, the white of the cloth a stark contrast to the awful bright of the red. The sight caused me to choke back a cry as I thought how this man now endured a second bath of a brother's blood when all he sought was to uphold the law. Wyatt, on the other hand, didn't seem to connect this, which was just as well. As I attempted to reel in my feelings, I urged him out of the shirt, then saw the blood had gone through to his undershirt. I let it alone and poured us drinks.

My cough was the only sound for a while. Agitation at events had set it off, and I kept to a corner chair while I did battle. Wyatt had swallowed his drink and lain back down across the bed while I contented myself with knowledge that I had kept him from certain harm had he remained outside.

"Did he enjoy the show?" Wyatt asked after a while.

"He did. It was a romantic romp, lots of funny lines, some good laughs. He had a fine time."

"He was beating Hatch too."

"Was he? That's good. He was a fine player."

Wyatt went quiet again and I saw he was in search of better times. "I always looked out for him," he said. "Taught him to shoot, kept him from drowning once. Only four years between us, but I always felt so much older. Or maybe he felt that much younger, being babied by our ma. Pa had little time for him, so Ma made up for it. I guess we all did."

"He had a great sense of humor," I said. "You suppose he got that from your ma?"

"Absolutely. She's got a big laugh, which is much needed as Pa is not given to humor."

"So your pa is where the rest of you get your stern outlook."

"He's a good man, did right by us, taught us well. No nonsense, which meant Morgan was a puzzle to him."

"You sound like the go-between."

"Some, yes, but Morgan was feisty too, understood Pa and saw how to get around him."

Again, he went quiet and laid his forearm across his eyes, stricken again by the loss. "It is unfair for a father and mother to outlive their child."

"That is true."

"Life makes no sense, Doc. We have tried our best and seen only the worst. Tried for murder, Virgil maimed, Morgan killed. We did no wrong yet suffer retribution."

"I cannot argue. Life here has become perilous."

"I do not know what to do," he said.

"You need not figure that out right now. It's late and you are exhausted. You need to try and sleep."

"What time is it?"

"Two fifteen."

"I'll have to wire Louisa and the folks."

"Later. You need to rest so you'll have strength to carry on."

"You're right, Doc."

"Why don't you get undressed and into bed? I told Virgil you were staying down here and he's fine with that."

"And Mattie?"

"Not so fine."

He stripped off his bloody undershirt and his pants, socks, and boots but left on his underdrawers, then slid beneath the covers. In his anguished state, he correctly saw no designs in my suggestion, and I underscored the innocence by not hopping into bed beside him. I put myself into a chair with a drink, turned the lamp out, and sat sipping whiskey until I heard his soft snore. Only then did I strip and climb in beside him.

Dawn colored the room a soft yellow when I awakened to Wyatt at my ear. "Lie still," he said as his hard dick prodded my backside. I lay with my back to him and he parted my buttocks, then guided his prick into me. Once inside, he slipped an arm around my chest and held on as he began an easy thrust. I sucked in a breath, which brought on a cough, but Wyatt took no notice. As I hacked, he fucked, and before long, one had given way to the other, the two of us in silent communion, cock and bottom.

Though it pleased me to start his awful day with pleasure, it still felt a most wrenching encounter. Not in my crotch but in my gut and my heart. In doing me he was attempting to right his world, even for the briefest time, and he deserved such a thing more than any man I knew. I slid a hand onto his forearm and gripped him tightly while I enjoyed the steady presence of his prick. That he went slow told me how he dreaded the day ahead and how he wished to remain in this state as long as possible.

I worked myself as I enjoyed his quiet assault, and when his breathing increased and his thrust quickened, I picked up my own pace so that when he began to grunt and come, I did the same, spurting into the bedding as he let go.

Sharing the climax set us free for a few glorious moments. Sharing Wyatt in such throes eased my heartache, as I hoped it did his. When he'd finished, he nuzzled my neck and I rubbed my cheek against his, much like horses in the field who dote on one another. He nibbled and nipped as his dick softened and slid out, then he laid his head next to mine for some time before rolling onto his back. I turned to face him.

"My brother is dead and here I am fucking," he said as he looked heavenward.

"I am sure the Lord will make allowances."

"Your Lord is mighty forgiving."

"My Lord has, of necessity, embraced generosity."

"I am not sure you even have a Lord, Doc."

"You are probably right. Lucifer likely looks out for me."

He blew out a sigh and sat up. "I'd best get on with the day," he said and he began to gather his clothes. "Thanks for reeling me in last night," he added. "I was off my head."

"I was glad to help, and if I can assist you today, just ask."

I dressed, as did he, hoping to continue with him. I was pleased when he asked me to accompany him to the telegraph office.

"You should have some breakfast," I suggested as we walked there.

"Don't think I could stomach food right now."

Watching him write the wire to Louisa and the family pained me something awful. I saw what it took for him to remain composed, and my heart went out to such effort. Once the wire was sent, we were off to the undertaker for a coffin. "I am going to ship him to the folks in California. I'll ask Jim and Bessie to go along. I want the families out of here."

Wyatt the general had now overcome Wyatt the stricken brother. Taking charge assured him the world he knew still turned. I stood by as he made arrangements for Morgan, who would be transported to the train at Benson, then on to California. Walking back to the hotel, Wyatt asked me to go along. "We are still not safe, so I want you to round up some of the boys to ride with us. I'm going up to Virgil's. Come up when you've got us set. We'll leave at noon to catch the six o'clock train."

At the hotel, he stopped out front. "You know, Doc, today is my thirty-fourth birthday. I feel so bad gaining another year when Morgan will not."

"My good wishes, in that case, will be for your continued safety. I'll see you later on."

The entire vigilance committee, along with all Wyatt's friends, would have gone along if I'd let them. As it was, I settled upon Dan Tipton, Sherm McMasters, Turkey Creek Jack Johnson, and Texas Jack Vermillion. They were the men who stood most closely by, who had known Morgan well, and who deserved the chance to pay respects in the best way they knew. Our first task was getting the coffin up to the hotel room, which we did later that morning. I watched as Morgan, now dressed in a good suit, was laid out inside it and the lid nailed closed. Wyatt, commanding everything, held up well while Virgil, seated, shook his head as tears rolled down his face. Allie kept to his side, also in tears, while Bessie and Jim clung to each other. Mattie sat in a chair looking quite grim. She shed no tears.

Chapter Eighteen

The fire bell rang a slow cadence as Morgan was brought down and put into the wagon. His coffin was unadorned, as the Earps refused to provide even a hint of ceremony for a town they saw as responsible for taking this young life. An erstwhile supporter was undoubtedly ringing the bell, but it was not at the family's behest.

People lined the sidewalks, everything hushed, save for the bell. Once Jim and Bessie were settled into the driver's seat, we mounted our horses, Wyatt and me ahead of the wagon, Dan Tipton, Sherm McMasters, Texas Jack, and Creek Johnson behind. Though a solemn and respectful procession, we still rode with shotguns across our saddles and pistols on our hips as we would be in open country and therefore targets.

I had eaten some breakfast while Wyatt had not. I knew how difficult it could be to take food when upset, but I also knew Wyatt carried a powerful guilt and likely saw himself as undeserving of nourishment. I would try to get him to eat at Benson.

As we made our way down Allen Street, I saw Curly Bill Brocious and Johnny Ringo kicked back in chairs out front of Hafford's, feet up on the railing as if most satisfied with themselves. Wyatt undoubtedly saw them, though he moved not a muscle since acknowledging their presence was surely what they wanted. I wondered if one of them had pulled the trigger the night before.

The entire population seemed to be watching us depart, but I doubted many troubled themselves with sympathy. We were a curiosity now, the detested Earps, down by one. Even Johnny Behan came out to stand with his two useless deputies. He might well have been down with Curly Bill and Ringo, since they were much the same.

When I began to cough, I felt most disrespectful in breaking the solemn tone of the occasion, but events of late had got my malady up. I sought my flask, which was undoubtedly seen by onlookers as drunkenness. Wyatt took no notice. He sat tall and grim, and I did not wish to consider what ran through his mind.

Benson lay about twenty miles north, and beyond Tombstone, the land was flat and uneventful. Clouds kept the sky appropriately gray, the air cool. We all wore our long coats, as Arizona weather, even with spring's imminent arrival, was unpredictable. Not a word was said the whole twenty miles and not a shot was fired. We carried Morgan to the train without incident and saw him loaded into a freight car. Wyatt showed some reluctance at that point, inside the car next to the coffin. I let him alone but found it a wrenching sight as he stood rigid at the coffin, not reaching to touch the last of Morgan. Finally, he climbed down, catching my eye with a wounded determination. I held his gaze, holding back even as I longed to rush forward.

Our posse kept close, always alert to danger that was never truly absent, no matter how things might appear. Wyatt bid good-bye to Jim and Bessie and saw them settled into a passenger car, then returned to us near the freights. He watched as the door was closed, Morgan's coffin now out of sight, and we stood until the train departed and gradually shrank from view.

"We are going to get supper before we start back," Creek Johnson said and I nodded. The four walked over to the station restaurant while I stood with Wyatt on the deserted platform. After some silence, I suggested we also get supper.

"I cannot eat," he said.

"You need to try," I urged him. "Come on." I started toward the restaurant slow enough for him to catch up.

We sat at a small corner table removed from the others. I ordered coffee and beef stew for us both, as stew was a favorite of Wyatt's. We said nothing, and when the food was put before us, he looked at it as if it too was bloodied, and I saw how the killing would color everything for some time.

"It's good," I said as I began to eat. "Try some."

He poked at the beef chunks, but it was potato that he put into his mouth. He chewed so slowly I saw even this was an effort.

"Coffee's good," I said and he took some and then some more. Possibly the bitter heat suited him more than comfort food.

He ate a few vegetables and finished his coffee, after which we joined the others outside. "I want to thank you boys," Wyatt told them. "Morgan would have appreciated your company. I do too."

He then mounted his horse and the rest of us followed, shotguns still at the ready. Dark was soon upon us, but the clouds gave way to clear skies and a full moon. Though I had but thin belief in God, I did consider as we rode along that Morgan might be looking down from above rather than boxed up on a train.

Wyatt rode tall in the saddle, which I admired, as I felt most washed out. My cough persisted, which seemed to stretch the miles, but at last we arrived in Tombstone, a place I was coming to thoroughly dislike. Sherm McMasters took our horses to the livery, leaving us at the hotel. Inside the lobby, Wyatt said he was going to tell Virgil he had to go to California. "All of them, Virg, Allie, Mattie. I am going to go after the men who killed Morgan, and I can't do it if the family is around."

"That's a good idea," I said, "but it's too late to discuss it now. Let him sleep. Talk to him tomorrow."

"I suppose."

"You are welcome in my room,"

"I am tired, Doc, more tired than ever in my whole life."

"I am offering you quiet and nothing more. If you think that awaits you upstairs, then go on up."

He put a hand on the banister but took no step. I saw it cruel of me to make him choose, but once again, I believed I could provide more comfort. A few seconds passed before he started down the hall.

In my room, he undressed, but as he did so he said he didn't want to do anything. "Not even talk," he added. Down to drawers and undershirt, he crawled into bed, lay on his back with an arm across his eyes, and that was it. As I was coughing, I poured a drink, turned out the lamp, and sat in a chair. Quiet descended soon as I had myself under reasonable control, and I looked back over all that had come down upon Wyatt and felt a wave of sorrow rise up in me. He suffered such great loss through no fault of his own. I wished I could lie with my arms around him but, knowing this chancy, I contented myself with imagining such comfort. After a while, I dozed in the chair.

Wyatt woke me shortly after dawn. He was dressed when he nudged me awake. I lay splayed in the chair, neck cricked from the night. "You should have come to bed," he said.

"Guess I fell asleep before I could get there," I managed before my cough took away speech. I sought my whiskey but still hacked and spat. Wyatt gave me a few minutes, and when I managed an interlude of silence, he said he was going down to Hatch's to view the scene. "Do you want to come along?"

"Yes, soon as I can get settled. And we need breakfast. Why don't you go down to Pearl's Restaurant and order us both a meal? I'll be down shortly."

I could see he was more himself now and, when he did not resist the suggestion of a meal, I was most heartened. He left and I set about washing up, dressing, and attempting to corral the cough. After a while, I was presentable and went down to join him over steak and eggs. We both ate like we'd been on open range for a week.

After breakfast we walked over to Hatch's, where Wyatt looked around out back for some time. "Nothing," he said when he came in. "Ike didn't leave his hat this time."

Hatch then came up and said he wanted to show us something. He led us to the chair where Wyatt had sat watching Morgan play and pointed to a bullet hole in the wall not three feet above. "There's the second shot," he said. "Thank the Lord it missed."

I hated to think what viewing the evidence brought up in Wyatt, him standing there and Morgan in a box on the way to California. If there was a Lord, why did he make such a choice? Grateful as I was that Wyatt survived, I still had to question something that seemed more a gamble than any grand design.

Hatch, backing off once he saw he'd stirred something in Wyatt, offered that Dan Tipton had word that the killers had been seen. This snapped Wyatt to attention and he turned with eyes blazing. "Who?" he asked.

"Frank Stilwell was the trigger man," Hatch said. "Bob Fritsch was taking a piss in the alley and saw Stilwell and some others come up, saw Stilwell fire."

Wyatt took this in, then asked, "Did you see Fritsch when you ran out there last night?"

"No. He told Dan he'd run at first shot, afraid they'd hit him with his dick out."

"Who else was it?"

"Bob is not sure but thinks Pete Spence and Indian Charlie, maybe Hank Swilling."

"What about Ike?"

"Don't think so."

"Curly Bill?"

"He wasn't seen, but you know how it is; he and Ringo are probably behind it."

Wyatt nodded, then turned and stood looking at the pool table where Morgan had been enjoying a game. It now bore Morgan's blood at the edge, while below, a dark stain colored the floor. "I told Morgan I would get the men who shot him," Wyatt said, eyes fixed on the table. "And I mean to do just that. Thanks, Hatch. You have been most helpful."

We then walked back to the hotel, where Wyatt said he would go up and convince Virgil and the others that they must leave town. "I'll do this on my own," he said and I agreed. It was a family matter, so I made myself scarce by way of the Oriental, where a poker game had been going all night. Bleary players were good for the likes of me, so I settled in to earn my keep. I didn't see Wyatt until I emerged later on to find him and his posse out front. When I consulted my pocket watch, I found it after midnight. Allen Street again had that eerie quiet.

"I am going to call it a night," Wyatt announced. "Doc, we'll walk you to the hotel."

It was clear to me that his confidence had been regained and also that he had designs on my body. My step quickened, and at the hotel, we bid good night to the others, then went to my room. I wanted to ask how things had gone with Virgil, but Wyatt would have none of that. When he began to tear at my clothes, I had to stop him. "See to your own," I said and he relented to quickly strip. When I'd undressed, I turned to see him standing with a hard prick, and the sight caused me to suck in a breath, which stirred my cough. I thus stood naked and hacking for a second before Wyatt shoved me onto the bed, cough be damned, and drove his prick up my bottom.

He did me from behind, back to his old rough self, and I found this self most welcome. His need was fierce and the bed squeaked and squawked, hitting the wall and carrying on while I was most wonderfully fucked. It took but seconds for me to shoot a load into the bedding, as I was highly primed. Wyatt grunted and growled while pumping out a good come, and when he finished and pulled out, he kept my ass high, buttocks parted, and I knew he had not gotten enough.

I have never known a man who could be so voracious seconds after he'd come, but that was Wyatt when life had him worked up. He began to lick my bottom, running his tongue up and down my crack, then finding my pucker and prodding it until I begged him to stick it in. Finally, when he had me squirming, he did as asked, driving his tongue into my hole and fucking me with it, mouth plastered on my buttocks. I grabbed my prick as it rose up to celebrate the renewed assault.

There came snorfling and such as Wyatt went at me pig-like, the two of us most pleased to wallow in our filth. His fingers dug into my hips as he fed and fucked, tongue backing off at times to run up and down the crack and lick all around my bottom before driving back in. At times he bit my buttocks, and I was hoping to retain teeth marks back there as evidence of such attention. How long we continued in this manner is unknown to me, but I did commence to coughing at one point, which was ignored by the pig in my hole. I buried my face in the pillow as much as I could without smothering.

When Wyatt finally relented, it was only to flip me over and devour my cock. I was stiff, of course, wound up as if I hadn't already come, and as he began a fierce suck, he switched around to climb over me and drop his stiff prick into my mouth. Didn't matter I coughed on the thing. I soon managed to suck and cough, then finally just suck, as feeding on his prick always seemed to gain on the malady. At last, we quietly fed on each other, and it was a long feast since we'd both already had a first go. I even grew bold enough to get a hand on his balls and roll them around in my palm, which he seemed to like as he shoved his dick into my throat, which unfortunately set off the cough.

We were awash in sweat when he began to pump into me and I to thrust up at him. I knew my man well enough to pick up my own pace so as to spurt along with him and we did just that this time around, coming into each other's mouths. I sucked and swallowed his stuff, happy to be taking him both above and below, awash in sweat but also awash in come.

When Wyatt climbed off and fell over beside me, he lay in reverse, feet at my head, which I found amusing. I did my best not to cough but lost the battle and had to seek my whiskey. I downed a couple shots and managed to settle, then lay back down next to Wyatt, my head now at the foot of the bed alongside his. He lay with eyes closed, but his hand slid down to his dick and held it, which caused me to call up an old observation that with all the hell and damnation the world presents, a man always has his privates for comfort. That Wyatt succumbed to such warmed my heart.

"I want to fuck the whole goddamn night," he said after a while. "Things get so bad I think life is almost not worth it, then I get in here with you and am reminded otherwise. You are good for me, Doc. You know that."

"Yes, Wyatt. I know that and it makes me most happy."

He rolled over and laid his arm across my chest, his hand gripping my shoulder in a rare show of affection. I slid my hand up onto his forearm and held on and we lay for some time in this quiet, punctuated by my cough, which seemed to gradually give way to the moment. "You are good for me too," I said. "Times like this, my malady subsides."

"Probably worn out."

I chuckled. "I do not doubt that, as the whole of me is quite done in. And yet…" I got a hand onto his prick and settled the soft meat into my palm. "I like what you said about fucking the whole night."

"You think you can handle that?"

"If I can't, I will expire a happy man."

In our mellowed state, he was, after a while, able to talk about other things. "Virgil has agreed to go to California and Allie is most happy about it."

"And Mattie?"

"Not so happy, but she understands. I told her I can't do what I mean to do if I have to worry after her. Virgil helped her see it is the only way and she finally agreed. They'll leave in a day or two, as it is going to be rough on Virgil to travel in his condition. We talked about how to do it and decided we'll have them catch the train at Contention and ride with them to Tucson, where they'll change to the California train. This will mean less wagon time."

"Sounds like a plan."

"I'll miss having my brothers around, but anymore I see that as a luxury we cannot afford."

"So it will be just the two of us," I noted, pulling his dick.

"Doc, you are a devil," he said. "Now turn on your side."

We rearranged ourselves so my back was to him, and he put a couple fingers up my bottom. "If this is hell, I am happy to burn," I said as I swooned from his attentions. He prodded and played and we went like this much of the night, poking and pulling, then getting back to licking and squeezing and, finally, in what had to be the early morning hours, fucking.

By this time, my malady had fled the scene. I was in such complete repose that my lungs regained substance, which allowed my prick a command performance. Wyatt's expert attentions to my butthole got me stiff and he finally put me on my back, threw my legs up over his shoulders, and stuck his cock into me. The lamp had burned low but still flickered enough to illuminate this grand coupling and I thrilled to the sight of him going at me steadily, underscoring the perfection our bodies enjoyed in communion.

It was a good long fuck, and Wyatt at times had his eyes shut, his head lolling from side to side as he allowed himself full indulgence.

Other times he looked down at what he was doing, pulling almost out of me and shoving back in to watch himself fuck. A couple times he popped out entirely, which he seemed to like, running his prick up between my balls, looking at it all flushed and wet before guiding it back inside where I squeezed in welcome.

When he began to quicken his thrust, I was grateful that we were going to come again yet hated to see this glorious night end, and this surely would be the end. Wyatt set his jaw as he began to pump in and out, and I grabbed my prick and began to stroke it, working in unison now although I came before he hit his peak. He watched my modest spurts, and it fired him to such extent that he grimaced and grunted and started to pound me with the purpose of a man in the throes of ecstasy. By the time he finished, he was gasping for breath and I was coughing.

He pulled out and my legs fell to each side of him and he laughed. "We never slept," he noted and I too laughed.

"We are going to be no use to anyone today," I added.

"Maybe that's what we need."

I loved the idea of such a thing, a day to indulge ourselves with rest and basking in the pleasure we had taken, but suspected that soon as he righted himself, the general would emerge and the night would be asunder. Still, for him to voice the idea gave me hope.

He sat up, swung his legs over the side of the bed, and I ran a hand up his back. "It was a good night," I said. "I may not be able to walk, but who cares. I am well fucked, and for that I am most grateful."

"My pleasure," he said. When he got up and started for his clothes I could tell he was already out the door. I lay sprawled amid tangled covers. When he was dressed he sat beside me, hat in hand. "I'm going to go help the family start packing. Now that they've agreed to go, I don't dare let up."

"Of course," I said, happy that he seemed refreshed and somewhat recovered from his ordeal. "Let me know if I can help," I added. "I'll be around."

He reached over and squeezed my thigh. "Thanks for being there, Doc. In all different ways."

"You are most welcome, Wyatt."

Chapter Nineteen

Virgil had admitted to Wyatt that his pain was constant. The arm, minus five inches of upper bone, was slow to heal, which robbed him of both strength and spirit. Allie, a most remarkable woman, saw to his every need, and when pain overcame him, she sat holding his good hand. He refused laudanum in favor of whiskey, which we all understood.

It took some persuading for him to agree to stretch out in the wagon's back rather than ride up front alongside Wyatt. It was Allie who finally made him see that she could not assist him if he sat up top, and so Mattie gained that spot while a bed was made up in back for Virgil. As Contention was about halfway to Benson, his situation would not be endured for long.

On the appointed day, blankets were laid next to luggage and Virgil was helped in. Mattie was assisted up front while the posse, minus Dan Tipton, who had business elsewhere, mounted our horses. When Wyatt climbed on board and took up the reins, I rode my horse up beside him, where I intended to remain. Mattie purposely took no notice of my presence. Once again, the town turned out to watch us depart, but this time I saw none of the Cowboys.

I had to wonder at Mattie's thoughts as we started out. If, as Wyatt said, a woman's instinct tells all, she knew she was losing him to me, and I must confess this pleased the hell out of me. As we rode along, I envisioned our posse work punctuated by vigorous bouts in my bed and also in Wyatt's. We could even share a room, as it was common for bachelors to double up to cut costs. I also considered that once this journey ended in Tucson, we might stay over there. I would suggest this, and surely the boys would double up. I would then offer Wyatt comfort in his loss of the family and undoubtedly get him to fuck me. My dick stirred at such thoughts.

The day was bright and warm, spring having sprung. A few

wildflowers poked their heads up through the grass, and it wasn't long before we were all down to shirtsleeves. I forgot entirely that Mattie sat beside my man and contented myself with keeping watch and getting myself as close as the situation allowed. Wyatt stopped once to check on Virgil, who was understandably cranky with both the trip and having to give up a life he wanted, not to mention doing all this missing some arm bone. He even snapped at Allie, who had to hold the piss pot for him.

"He's fine," Wyatt declared when Virgil was again settled. "I'll worry when he stops complaining."

The station at Contention was smaller than the one at Benson, but served us well. While Wyatt saw to getting tickets and assisted Virgil and Allie on board, Sherm and the others stabled our horses at a local livery, after which they joined me on the platform. As Wyatt came out of the train to bid us now board, Alden Carp, deputy to Pima County Sheriff Bob Paul, came up. He told Wyatt he'd been sent with a message from the sheriff. "Ike Clanton and Frank Stilwell are in Tucson and know you are headed there. They say they are going to finish the job, so Sheriff Paul wants you to be on the lookout."

"Send my thanks to Sheriff Paul," Wyatt said. "We'll take care of those two."

We were well armed, as always, pistols upon our persons and shotguns in hand. We boarded, and while Wyatt and Mattie sat opposite Virgil and Allie, the rest of us took up a similar formation across the aisle. From where I sat I could look upon Wyatt, and once we were under way, I entertained myself by catching his eye more than once.

We had not before traveled by train together, and had it not been such a solemn occasion, the steady rock and hum of the wheels below would have proven most enjoyable. I pushed aside thoughts of Stilwell and Clanton looking to kill us in favor of consideration of a night in a hotel room with Wyatt. With Mattie on her way to California, he would at last be free of the husbandly charade. I saw him as a stallion broken free of his reins, big dick at the ready. My cock was excited for much of the trip, though Wyatt did not allow himself a glance down that way.

At Tucson, we did not allow Virgil off the train until the platform had been scoured for assassins, and even then we moved Virgil and thc women under full guard. We entered the other train as one large party, shotguns at the ready, and saw the family into a car where Virgil insisted on taking a window seat. Wyatt then strapped Virgil's six-shooter to tiny Allie's waist so Virgil could draw it if needed, as he could not yet manage to carry a pistol on his own. Once all were secured, farewells were shared, but as we were about to depart the car, Wyatt said he saw Stilwell and Clanton lying on a nearby flatcar, shotguns in hand. "You go out onto the platform," he commanded us. "I'm going out around by the back."

He did just that, jumping down and slipping around near the flatcar, at which the two men saw him and fled out onto the platform. Wyatt followed and we caught sight of him as one man stumbled and fell, dropping his weapon while the other escaped. We rushed up there to see it was Frank Stilwell, who had by then gotten to his feet and had his arms raised in a plea for his life. I could not believe my eyes when Wyatt took no regard and let go both barrels. As we came up, Frank Stilwell, who had murdered Morgan Earp, was blown to a bloody hell. We were so pleased with this turn of events that we all drew our pistols and fired more shots into him, so by the end there was not a whole lot left.

When the shooting stopped, the train began to move and Wyatt caught sight of Virgil looking on. He had witnessed the killing. Wyatt raised up a finger to indicate the first man had paid the price and Virgil nodded in approval.

We did not remain. The body was pushed off the platform's end, which left it in a spot not immediately noticeable, and we returned to the station, where we waited on the train back to Contention. Nobody said a word to us about any gunfire, nor did we see any scrambling of officials. I couldn't believe no one heard the commotion, but then I saw that everybody kept a distance from us, so we were perhaps seen as trouble not to be stirred yet. Amusing since we had just reduced the criminal population by one.

Wyatt was restless once aboard the train to Contention. Killing Stilwell had done him good but had also gotten his blood up to such extent I knew him ready to set out after the rest of the gang and kill them all. He might also be ready for a good fuck.

Ike Clanton had gotten away again, which seemed an oddity in that he was a stupid man, but sometimes stupidity works in the fellow's favor by way of saving him certain cautions. Ike was likely riding hard toward the Clanton ranch near Charleston. We would surely see to him later on.

Wyatt paced the car, then went out onto the rear platform for a smoke. After a minute, I joined him. Smoking was not favorable to me, but I took the cigar he offered and coughed some as we smoked in relative silence. I also noted that storm of need swirling around him. Had it been anywhere near reasonable, he'd have fucked me then and there, I had no doubt, but since others were just inside the car and could come out at any second, it wouldn't do for the marshal to have his dick up his friend's bottom. Still, I knew we were both thinking the same, especially when Wyatt reached down to adjust the heft at his crotch.

At Contention, we left the train, got the horses, and rode hard for Tombstone. There was no urgency, but Wyatt still drove us full out. As the horses were well rested, it made no difference, and we soon roared into town as if in pursuit.

Wyatt thanked the men, who again left us at the hotel and took the horses to the livery. Wyatt said nothing except "upstairs" and I followed him to his room. Once inside, he threw off coat and gun belt, then looked at me. "I mean to fuck in my own goddamn bed," he said as he undid his pants. Out sprang his dick, wet with anticipation. "Strip," he commanded when I stood gaping.

Once naked, he pushed me onto the bed he had shared with Mattie, threw my legs up onto his shoulders, drove into me, and never let up, giving me his every inch while carrying on with verbal filth such as he had never previously uttered. It was apparent that now the wife was gone, he was at last free to unleash the worst. After a decidedly nasty outpouring, he got around to specifics.

"When I shot Stilwell, I wanted to turn around and fuck you," he rasped. "Rip down your pants and shove into your butthole and not give a damn who saw. Christ, Doc, killing and fucking feel the same, and I am going to drill you until you choke on my prick and I am then going to eat your asshole, get my tongue in there, and suck out my come, shit be damned. I am going to fuck until I expire, then rise up and fuck some more, and Christ, Doc, I am…" Here he was reduced to grunts and grimaces, eyes wide as if he could not himself believe the flood of come he shot up into my bowels.

I was hard as steel but did not work my cock. I wanted only to satisfy my man, to have him dirty me so he could lick me clean. I reeled in his assault, and when he finally relented, I saw him reluctant to let go, still pumping into me, trying to call up more spunk. He persisted until nature finally declared him done and the mighty prick began to soften. Only when it slipped out did he discover me stiff and dripping. He pushed down my legs, got between them, and dove onto me, sucking so hard I immediately bucked and spurted. He pulled and swallowed, and when I went soft, still sucked, feeding upon my morsel until at last he saw things were over. He then sat back on his haunches looking far from satisfied.

When I began to cough, he sought the bottle and glasses, poured, and sat on the bed's edge. I pulled myself up onto pillows and drank my whiskey. I could not believe tension remained in him, but he truly did not settle. While I felt quite done in, he remained straight-backed and rigid, taking a second drink, which seemed to have no more effect than the first.

"Lie down, Wyatt," I suggested.

"I can't."

What to do? I pondered the situation as I finished my whiskey, the cough subsiding. He was still breathing hard, still pent up, and I saw there were only two things that could help him now. Kill or fuck, and since his dick was likely not to raise up for a bit, I thought to offer an alternative. I set my glass aside, turned over, and stuck my butt up in the air. He looked over. "Hell, yes," he said, and he got behind me and dove in.

He bit me some and left some claw marks as well, such was his need, but that mouth set to work at appeasing him and did not relent for quite a while. His tongue tried to get up where his dick had been, and at times felt like it succeeded, such was the thrust, and when he wasn't fucking me with it, he was licking my passage like he needed some shit on his tongue to confirm what he'd done this day. When he withdrew now and then, it was only to lick up and down my crack or get his fingers into me to prod somewhat roughly until the need to taste me overcame him. At one point, he had a hand around front tugging on my spent cock while his tongue fucked me at the back, and I got stiff due to such attention. When I cried out that he was going to make me come, he flipped me over, pounced on my prick, sucked the cream out of me, then flipped me over and went back to the filthy hole.

Having now come twice, I was thoroughly spent and most pliable, thus I quietly savored him going at me back there. I even smugly contented myself with thoughts that the great Wyatt Earp, lawman of renown, had his tongue up my butt. And in one last thought of the departed Mattie, I told myself she certainly had never allowed such an intrusion upon her person. I was pleased with my ability to offer him filth if that was what he needed and comfort if that was required. Full-service friend, John H. Holliday.

Wyatt didn't wear himself out, but he did wear himself down. When he pulled off, he got out of bed and poured us more whiskey, but he stood to drink this time, lighting the lamp because dark was upon us. I lay on my side having no idea how to settle him, as I had never seen him in quite this state. He was still worked up in some way that fucking was not going to solve, and when he caught himself in the mirror, I began to realize he was taking note of the fact that he had crossed over to my side. He had killed a man with little compunction, and it didn't matter how deserved that killing was. All his years of avoiding such piled onto his shoulders, as even the judge's suggestion to kill by way of leaving his prey out where alibis don't matter could not erase the fact that Stilwell had been unarmed and begging for his life when Wyatt shot him. It was indeed revenge, and while that allowed the act, it did not lessen the impact. I also saw that Wyatt had not anticipated how such a thing would feel.

"You were justified," I said as he stared at himself in the mirror.

"Like you," he replied. "I have come over to your side, Doc."

The words cut into me not because they were true but because I saw in that instant that our biggest difference, lawman and killer, had now been erased. Should I welcome him to hell and damnation? I did not lead him to the dark side, but I was surely there to greet him, having been in residence for some time. All I could do, I realized, was ease the way. He was still a believer in law and order. He killed for the greater good as well as for revenge of his brother, and I reminded him of this, which caused him to come back to the bed. He sat on the edge and turned to me, stern-faced as always, yet with anguish in his eyes.

"There is one less to terrorize Tombstone," I said, "one less to wound and kill. You have done a service, Wyatt. You have avenged Morgan, but you have also avenged a whole town."

"Thanks, Doc," he said and he lay down next to me on his back with an arm thrown over his eyes. Rest was all he could summon, and I lay there with him until he gained the quiet he needed. The lamp was low when I finally heard his soft snore.

I woke early next morning and set to coughing, so I hopped out of bed to see to my daily battle. Wyatt slept on, exhausted, and I hoped I could gain control of myself to allow him to snooze awhile longer. As I downed some whiskey, then took a good piss, it occurred to me that we need not rush out to chase the others, as one day more would not matter. We could pass some quiet right here if we so desired. We could go out and get a meal, then come back here for a good long fuck, maybe fuck the whole damned day. Much as I knew he loved his family and much as I liked and respected them, I was glad as hell to see them gone. Such was my selfish nature. I wanted this man.

When I was quieted and had completed minor ablutions, I went over to the bed and drew back the covers to reveal Wyatt's morning erection. He lay on his side, one arm outstretched, the other across him, fingers inches from the promising rod, and when he stirred, those fingers slid down to grasp the prick and hold on. He then fell back asleep, leaving me to feast on the sight. I did not wake him, nor did I begin the day. I sat naked in a chair, sipping whiskey, and thinking that at some point the general would emerge and began to plan the chase. Still, I hoped this could be put off for at least a day. How I was to convince such a determined man occupied me until the sun was well up and Wyatt finally woke.

"I feel like a herd has run me over," he said without moving, hand still on his dick.

I grinned. "And I feel like a herd has fucked me."

He paused in recall of the night, then blew out a sigh and turned onto his back, letting go of his prick. It stood tall and promising, so I vacated my chair, eased onto the bed, and climbed over him. "You'd think I'd have had enough," I said as I applied spit to him and dropped down to spear my butthole. "You would be wrong."

He drew an extra pillow under his head as I set to riding him, easy canter at first, rocking back and forth while savoring the feel of that prick up inside me, then raising up to his full length and dropping down, which caused me each time to groan with pleasure. "I could ride a thousand miles like this," I declared.

"One-man posse," he observed, thrusting up at me. I could see his juice was starting to boil, never mind how tired he was, but I did not step up my pace, as I wished this to last a while. My legs held up surprisingly well, though I did begin to cough, but we were used to hacking along with fucking. "Faster," he finally said, "or I am going to roll you over and do it."

I picked up the pace, as I wanted to make him come while astride him, and his arms flailed at his sides when he hit the rise. He thrashed on the pillow, his mouth opened, but at the moment when the climax hit he fixed his eyes on mine, as if he could look the stuff into me as well as spurt it up my chute. He let out a cry as he let go, and I liked that he didn't try to restrain anything about himself, driving his spunk into me where it belonged. Finally emptied, he settled back, breathing heavily. I remained upon him as the dick was slow to lose its girth, and after a few seconds he took hold of my hard prick and began to pull. This caused me to hoot and holler and ride his cock as I shot cream all up him, gobs landing in his chest hair, which was a most appetizing sight.

His spent cock slipped out, but I remained atop him, easing back enough to get my tongue into his pelt and lap my own come. I strayed around to include a tit in my cleaning, lingering to nip and then suck until it became a persistent little nub. As I played, my hand strayed to the other and began to pinch and rub as I resumed my grooming.

Wyatt issued soft and agreeable murmurs, and when I'd consumed all my spunk, my tongue followed the chest hair as it descended onto his stomach, then inched down to where things thickened around his prick. There I teased, bringing my nose into the bushy thicket, tongue poking and licking until Wyatt spread his legs and succumbed with invitation.

When I strayed between the legs to get under to his balls, he raised up some and I sucked a fat nut into my mouth. As this seemed most agreeable to him, I rolled it around on my tongue before releasing it in favor of taking up the other. I was tempted to stray toward the back, but Wyatt, as if reading my thoughts, pressed his thighs in against me to push me back up to his prick, which I then took into my mouth.

He was soft and delicious, pungent and salty, and I settled in to make him a meal. After a bit, when the prick did not rise, I moved to his thighs to nibble and lick, the hair finer here but still plentiful. Wyatt seemed much the beast when approached this way, furry animal tamed for the moment, and I kept at him, gradually moving back up until my malady jumped in and set me coughing. I turned my head to the side and lay on his chest until I'd somewhat subsided, then licked my way around his neck, where I nuzzled some. As I busied myself there, Wyatt laid a hand on my bottom and began to squeeze and knead, starting in on me much as I had him. I rolled over to allow him to nip at my tits and to lick and play his way down to my cock, which he fed on a good long while.

The day was well along when Wyatt finally put me onto my stomach, raised my butt, and shoved his cock into me. By then we stank of sweat and fluids, and the room had grown hot and stuffy, as if we'd sucked out far more than come. The fuck announced the day, and Wyatt took his sweet time in urging the rise, my butthole well chafed before; at last, he issued his grunts and came.

When done, he fell onto his back, but as I was still hard, he allowed me to crawl up and drop my dick into his mouth and I could not keep from thrusting into his throat, which he seemed to welcome. Looking down to see my prick fucking that mouth sent me over all too soon, and it wasn't but seconds before I lay beside him, more than spent.

"I'm hungry," he said at last.

"Me too, but I doubt I can walk."

We lay awhile longer, stomachs growling in near unison, which made me laugh. With some effort we then rose, washed, and dressed. Wyatt no longer insisted on us being accompanied while in town. "The assassins are likely scattered all over hell," he declared, which was probably the case so we proceeded from the hotel as two.

"Good morning," I said to him when we hit the street. It was half past noon.

We ate a huge breakfast at the restaurant next door and were just finishing when Dan Tipton came in. It pleased me to greet our friend while my butthole still tingled from Wyatt's assault. The fact that I once again carried his come also pushed me toward a sunnier disposition than usual, something Dan noticed. "You are in fine fettle today, Doc," he said.

"A good night," I replied, glancing at Wyatt, who remained stone-faced.

"I am getting up a posse to go after Morgan's killers," Wyatt said to Dan. "Will you join?"

"Afraid not. Circumstances don't permit me to leave right now, but I can still help. I'll be your contact in town, keep an ear out for information and get it to you so you're not chasing your tail out there."

"Good idea," Wyatt said.

"And I have something for you already. Zach White, who you know is one of the Cowboys, is saying they went too far in killing Morgan, and he is ready to bolt, but I told him he can do us more good by staying and feeding me information. He said Indian Charlie is holed up at a camp in the South Pass of the Dragoons, so you might want to start there."

"That we will," said Wyatt, sitting forward in his chair with new energy. This caused me to think that an indulgent day might be off, but I remained hopeful the posse could be got up for tomorrow. The promise of a hard ride also might get Wyatt worked up enough for, well, a hard ride. My dick stirred in agreement.

He and Dan discussed how best to stay in touch once we were

out on the chase, and Wyatt slipped on his general suit, making plans to meet in various places and, if necessary, to telegraph each other. "Hooker's place can be a main stop for us, as he supports our cause," Wyatt went on. "Other ranchers will assist as well."

"You'll find plenty of men on your side," Dan replied. "You let me know if there is anything else I can do for you here in town."

"Much obliged, Dan," Wyatt said and Dan left us. Wyatt finished his coffee, issued a good sigh, and sat back. "Feeling right good," he said.

"You are welcome," I replied, which got a chuckle out of him.

"I'd like to walk around town, see who is around, see if we can pick up anything, and get our men for the posse."

"Sounds like a plan."

And so we walked out into a blustery day, the ever-present dust swirling about and sending bits of man's debris into the air to blow around. As the weather had warmed, we did not have our long coats, which was a welcome change. We both could have used a bath, as we bore the stink of sexual indulgence, but I was happy to wear the evidence.

At Hafford's, Wyatt talked with the bartender but gained little. He bought us cigars and we sat out front for a while. I enjoyed the smoke between coughs but finally had to give up and go inside for a whiskey. When I returned, Johnny Behan was standing in the street just beyond Wyatt, looking satisfied with himself.

"The inquest is tomorrow," he was telling Wyatt. "Judge Spicer will preside."

Wyatt nodded and Behan, knowing Wyatt's inclinations, advised that he had best let the law handle things. "We want no vigilance here," Behan said. Wyatt was agreeable by way of saying nothing and Behan finally moved on.

"He doesn't know about Stilwell," I said.

"Not yet."

"Maybe you weren't seen. Without witnesses—"

"There was a whole goddamn train of witnesses, Doc. It is just a matter of time."

"I suppose."

He went quiet and I saw he was considering that we, in our pursuit of the killers, might also be pursued. And if that came to pass, it would be Johnny Behan doing the pursuing, which would honestly work to our favor as Behan was not a man to seek confrontation. So much lay ahead, the inquest with the most weight. I knew Wyatt would want to attend, as information presented as to Morgan's killers would assist us in our efforts toward revenge. On the other hand, if word of Stilwell's killing reached Tombstone, things might get dicey.

CHAPTER TWENTY

We found Turkey Creek Jack Johnson and Texas Jack Vermillion arguing outside the Oriental saloon, their difference of opinion on a faro game having spilled into the street. They kept on squabbling, as good friends often do, until they saw Wyatt, at which they greeted him and forgot their spat.

"I am getting up a posse to go after Morgan's killers," Wyatt told them. "Will you ride with me again?"

The two readily agreed, as they never turned down their friend. "Sherm is inside, winning. He'll want to go too," Creek Johnson said.

"Good," Wyatt replied and we stepped inside to confirm the offer. McMasters proved as enthusiastic as the others. "We'll leave tomorrow after the inquest," Wyatt said. "As we're all staying at the hotel, we'll meet up there."

After this, Wyatt and I walked about town, and while people who were his supporters stopped him to offer condolences, those who had decided they belonged to a more respectable class of citizen shied away. I suspected that on this day they carried some guilt, since their lack of support for the Earps had undoubtedly contributed to Morgan's death.

Wyatt paid no attention to such slights, though I doubted he failed to notice. When Ken Drucker, proprietor of Drucker's Ice Cream Parlor, stepped out to speak fondly of Morgan, I could feel Wyatt give way a little.

"Morgan always got the vanilla," Drucker said, "and I would sometimes kid him about not trying other flavors, but he knew what he liked. He always had a good word and a smile. He will be missed."

"Thank you, Ken. You are right on that. He is already missed."

As we walked on, I thought to suggest we play some cards but decided against it, as gaming just two days after Morgan's death could be seen as disrespectful. Thus we passed by the Alhambra, Hafford's, and others. I then thought to suggest a ride out to that comfortable little notch where we'd gone at each other a while back but decided against that too, as we'd soon be all but living in the saddle.

"Bonner's ranch is near the Dragoons," Wyatt noted as we turned up Toughnut Street.

"That it is."

He was already thinking ahead to where we'd spend the night once we'd completed our business with Indian Charlie. He was walking alongside me, but in his mind was already on the chase. This annoyed me, as he lost sight of the opportunity at hand while I thought of little else. Never mind all we'd done that morning. It was getting on toward suppertime and I wanted, before we got our night's rest in preparation for our chase, a fuck.

"I want to see to the weapons," Wyatt suddenly said, and he turned and started back to the hotel. We had left the shotguns there upon our return from Tucson, and it did seem prudent to clean them and make sure we had adequate shells. Thus we were soon in Wyatt's room, which still resembled a small armory.

I assisted with cleaning the guns while sipping whiskey and enjoying Wyatt with sleeves rolled up. I liked the way the forearm flexed as he worked and was most taken with the shine of gun oil on the same hand that had wrapped around my dick. It was testament to his prowess that he could arouse me by doing no more than clean a gun. When he ran a cloth down the long barrel, I started thinking of his dick, since that could also be seen as a weapon.

I sought my flask to quiet myself—not just the cough—and continued the work at hand. It pleased me to have him alone in the room that had so often been crowded with family. The rightness of our pairing seemed confirmed by the new arrangement, and I thought how once we'd dispatched Morgan's killers, we could return here and batch together, or at least fuck regular.

Our chore was at last done to Wyatt's satisfaction. He declared all ready for our task ahead, then said he was hungry, so we went down to the restaurant next door and had a meal. Johnny Behan was there glad-handing around, and he made a point of coming over to spew tripe about the wheels of justice. Wyatt and I kept eating as if we'd taken no notice.

"Well then, gentlemen," Behan said, "I will see you at the inquest tomorrow. Two p.m. sharp."

Wyatt issued a loud belch in reply, then picked up his coffee. I could not contain a snort as the dandified sheriff made his exit.

"County sheriff," Wyatt said when Behan was gone, "city marshal, and neither raises a finger to go after Morgan's killers. If we don't do it, nobody will, which is a sad state of affairs."

"We will set things right," I assured him. He looked to me at length. "We will get them all," I added to extend the moment now that I'd gained his attention.

He nodded and I wanted to suggest we go upstairs then and there, but he stood and said, "Ate too much. Let's walk it off."

Damn, I thought. Rather fuck it off, but I joined him as we paid and stepped out into the night. Tombstone was calm, the tinkle of a nearby piano and men's laughter the only sounds. It was a fine evening, full of stars, and I enjoyed looking up at the sparkling canopy. "Impressive," I said and turned to find Wyatt also looking heavenward.

"Warm," he said. He'd come out without his coat, as had I, and as we began to walk along, I noted the gusty wind had disappeared. Man's debris remained on the ground, which gave us a most amenable setting.

I soon realized Wyatt was restless. Much was to happen next day, and the present idleness served no purpose but to delay getting on with things. He needed occupation, and if we were not to play cards or take a ride, there was only one other thing to fill the time. "How about a drink?" I suggested and before he could reply I added, "Upstairs."

He said nothing, just stepped into the Alhambra and bought a bottle, then strode to the Cosmopolitan. Up the stairs he went, me hurrying behind, and once in his room, he poured the drinks.

"A fine idea," he said as we clinked glasses and threw back the first. He poured us seconds, then sat in a chair, legs outstretched. "We need a good sleep tonight," he informed me as he set aside his glass, "but right now, how about you get down here and suck my dick."

He unbuttoned his pants and pulled it out, and I saw he was about halfway along, which was a most delicious state. I tossed off the rest of my whiskey and fell to my knees. He was hefty yet pliable on my tongue, and as I sucked in that pungent odor particular to a man's crotch, I set about a feeding meant to last. Wyatt pushed up at me, squirming a bit while I licked and sucked, playing my tongue about his knob, poking his piss slit until he stood tall. I wrapped a hand around him and pumped a few strokes, but, much as he seemed to enjoy this, he told me to get my mouth back on him, and I did as asked.

I thought I would soon receive a load of spunk but was mistaken. Suddenly, he threw me off, pulled down my pants and drawers, bent me at the bedpost, and shoved in. He then set to a rigorous fuck that had him grinding like this would be his last. Finally, he cried out and came. I held on, as he was quite rough, my knees nearly buckling from the assault, but at last he was done and pulled out. When he flipped me around and found me still primed, he dropped down to suck me, at which I shot my stuff into his throat. As I unloaded, I looked down to see his lips around my prick, his mouth working me, all of which made the come most savory.

We then undressed and stretched out with the bottle nearby. "We'll be out on the trail a while," I said. "I am looking to stock up on you." Here I slid a hand onto his thigh, a finger onto his cock.

"You are the devil, Doc, but hell is starting to look right good."

From there, we groped and grabbed, rubbed and licked for what may have been hours, getting up to another fuck at what time I had no idea. My legs up over his shoulders, he went at me for a good long one while I pumped my dick to entice him further. A fine climax was had by all, after which we fell into a heavy sleep. We did not wake until somebody pounded on the door next morning. Wyatt was up in an instant, leaping from the bed to call out, "Who is it?"

"Vince Fowler, and it is most urgent," came the reply.

Wyatt pulled on his pants, motioned for me to stay put, and opened the door to admit the man. Fowler was manager of the telegraph office and a friend of Wyatt's. "A wire just came in from Sheriff Paul in Tucson," Fowler said. "Stilwell's body was found and arrest warrants have been issued for you both, along with Texas Jack and Creek Johnson. I can hold off giving this to Behan for a little so you can get away."

"Then I was seen."

"Yes. Railroad workers say they saw you do it and the others finish the job."

"The others shot a dead man," Wyatt snapped.

"Maybe so, but the warrants have you equal."

"Thank you, Vince. You are a good friend."

Fowler left, and I scrambled to dress while Wyatt stood in thought. "We'll have to leave now," he said. "I'll tell the others, you pack up, and we'll all go down and get the horses as an armed party in case Behan gets word too quickly."

While Wyatt packed his own belongings and went to round up the others, I ran down to my room to change clothes and grab things for travel. As we were now wanted men, I knew we'd not be back soon, but

I still had to leave much behind. I pocketed my diamond stickpin and other valuables, filled my flask, put a bottle and change of clothes into my bedroll, and checked my pistols and knife. I also took my long coat as we'd be sleeping out more than not.

When I met Wyatt and the others in the hotel lobby, I was handed a shotgun. We then went out and walked toward the livery to get our horses. We'd gone about a block when Behan approached.

"Wyatt, I want to see you," he said.

"You can't see me," Wyatt replied. "You have seen me once too often." He passed the sheriff by, the rest of us following. We were not disturbed as we got our horses and rode from town.

Our pace was brisk as we headed for the Dragoon Mountains, and I could not help but wonder how Wyatt felt being a wanted man. The fact that he'd been charged as such on a previous occasion did not matter, as that was a trumped-up travesty over a fair fight. This time he had shot an unarmed man, and while he and I and many others saw it justified, Behan had the law with him. How long until a posse formed to chase a posse?

By the time we reached the southern Dragoons, heat was upon us. Coats were removed and tied to saddles and I saw Wyatt all but consumed with the task at hand. Arrest warrants meant little now.

Near the south pass we encountered a band of Mexicans that included one American who Wyatt set upon for information. The fellow said he'd seen some men up in the hills but did not know them. Wyatt persisted.

"Indian Charlie, Pete Spence, Hank Swilling?"

"Sorry, don't know them. It was just some men."

The party was allowed to pass and we went up a trail that led us around, up and down, before bringing us onto a bluff where we spotted a campfire burning low. One man squatted beside it and when he saw us, he began to run. Wyatt charged ahead and knocked the man down. Jumping off his horse, the marshal got the man by the neck. It was Indian Charlie, who was in reality a Mexican named Cruz. Why the Cowboys had dubbed him an Indian was unknown, but once a man had been given a nickname, his true identity was forever lost.

Indian Charlie was disarmed and made to kneel while Wyatt interrogated him. "I know you were in on my brother's murder. If you value your life, you will tell me all I want to know. Who was with you?"

Charlie's mouth worked for a second with no words, then he found his voice. "I did nothing," he said. "I was paid twenty-five dollars to stand watch while the others… I did nothing."

"Who else?"

"Ringo, Curly Bill, Frank Stilwell, Hank Swilling."

"What about Pete Spence?"

Charlie shook his head. "No, he wasn't there."

"Where have they gone?" Wyatt demanded.

"Don't know. We split up."

"You were seen with others up here."

"They left. I don't know to where."

Wyatt pulled Charlie to his feet. "You goddamn son of a bitch, you took money to see to Morgan's killing, so you might as well have pulled the trigger."

"No," Charlie pleaded. "I was a lookout. I did nothing."

"You looked on," Wyatt countered. "You did nothing to stop my brother's killing."

Here Wyatt dropped his shotgun and took out his Colt. "Bullets are your way," he said before he shoved Charlie back and shot him dead, at which we all joined in with pistols until the criminal was full of holes.

"That's two," Wyatt said as he holstered his weapon. He took Charlie's gun and threw it some distance. "The others may still be up here," he added. "I want to keep on looking." We thus mounted up and rode on, keeping sharp watch while Wyatt saw to tracking. His skill at this was such that he might well have borne the Indian name.

Trails were sketchy, and after a good while, we rested beside a little stream running down from the rocks. As it was now hot, we splashed ourselves both to cool and to remove a layer of dust. Kerchiefs were soaked and tied around necks in an attempt to further escape the heat. Canteens were filled, horses watered, pisses taken. Wyatt, after cooling off, said we'd keep on until sunset, then ride over to the Bonner place, where Alma Bonner would give us a meal. He then climbed up onto a rock that allowed a view to the west. I followed.

The brown plain bore a haze of green and looked most innocent. Nothing seemed to stir, which was not what Wyatt wanted. "They could have gone east," he remarked.

"Or north or south," I added.

"There is no good trail. Like they flew off."

"If Indian Charlie told the truth."

"Why would he lie?" Wyatt asked. "He was bargaining for his life."

"Not all men will give way at such a time," I replied. "You wouldn't."

This annoyed him, but I wanted him to look beyond what he wished. We had no trail and weak information. "He said Spence wasn't in on it," I pointed out, "yet Bob Fritsch said he was there, so that's an indication Charlie's information is shaky."

Wyatt huffed. "That may be, but right now it's all we have."

He said this with such finality that I shut up and we stood a bit more looking down upon the tranquil illusion before he declared we must press on. We rode a good distance before he stopped us and hopped down to examine something.

"What is it?" I asked.

"Spur rowel. Not weathered, so it's recent."

He showed me the find and I agreed with his assessment while not mentioning that any man could have come through here and lost it. There was no way to tie it to our prey, but if it pleased him, so be it. He mounted up and we rode on with him looking more at the ground than ahead.

We gained nothing more for our day's work, and at dusk started back down to the flat, then over to the Bonner ranch. Matt, the eldest son, waved to us from amid a cattle herd, then rode over. His father, Lester, soon followed. "You boys on the chase?" Lester asked.

"We are," Wyatt said. "Looking for the men who killed my brother Morgan on Saturday."

Lester's jaw dropped. He had not heard, as he seldom got to town. "I am sorry on your loss, Wyatt. Suppose it was the Cowboys."

"None other."

"How are you going?"

"Got two so far, Frank Stilwell and Indian Charlie, but there are more to get, Ringo and some others. Can we put up here tonight?"

"Yes, you can. There's room in the bunkhouse for some, and the rest can sleep in the barn. Alma will feed you all just fine."

We rode on into Lester's place and took down our bedrolls and such while his sons saw to the horses. In the house, we were warmly greeted by Alma, who looked us over and said, "Supper is about ready. Have a seat."

A long table accommodated the family, three ranch hands, and us. Beef stew with biscuits was most filling, as was lots of coffee. As we ate, Lester asked for news and was made current on recent unfortunate incidents in Tombstone.

After supper, Wyatt and I sat on the front porch with Lester, enjoying some whiskey and a smoke while the rest of our party sought a card game in the bunkhouse. While Wyatt and Lester kept on about the law, or lack thereof, I looked ahead to Wyatt and me getting up to something. As the night was warm, we could sleep under the stars. There were lots of good places in the grass a little way out so we could get away from the sprawling house that looked as if a room had been tacked on every time a child arrived. Wyatt finally called it a day and declared it such a fine night he would sleep out of doors. "There is a good spot about a hundred yards beyond the barn," Lester said. "Little stream, a few trees, fine grass to bed down upon. Have a good rest and come up for breakfast."

"Thank you, Lester," Wyatt said. "You are a good friend."

I tried to conceal my excitement at this turn, but Wyatt caught wind. "Okay, Doc, settle down," he said as we sought bedrolls and started toward the spot which was just as Lester said, most hospitable. We made our beds beside the stream, then stripped naked and had us a bath which, even in weak moonlight, was most entertaining. As Wyatt stood washing, his dick rose up, but he kept to his ablutions as if not in the least aroused, while I pulled on myself, as I was too wound up to leave off. Finally, Wyatt took note.

"Come here, Doc," he said and I went to him. He turned me around, bent me over, and shoved in. "That what you want?"

"Surely is."

He then set to fucking me there on the Bonner ranch. As I had anticipated this for much of the day, I took hold of my prick and pumped out a quick come, which Wyatt noticed. "Letting go, are you?" he said, ramming me for emphasis. "Well, goddamn, so am I." And he drove in so hard I nearly buckled but managed to receive him as he held me fast at the waist.

When his dick slipped out, he wrapped his arms around me and nuzzled my neck. Standing there in the water in his embrace, I felt gone to heaven, such was my reward. His cream dripped down my leg in confirmation.

"Some good night," I said, pressing back against him.

"Not over yet," he replied and I raised a hand to grip his forearm, basking in the moment.

My cough asserted itself, damn it to hell, and I sought the bottle that had been in my bedroll. I took a couple good swallows and we then lay down on our bedding. "Not a bad day," I declared.

"Could have been better," Wyatt noted as he stretched out. "Could have got more than one."

"We will. Might take us a while, but we will get them all."

"Kill and fuck," he said.

"I suppose," I replied, "if you want to look at it that way."

"Not much in between."

This threw me, as I could not tell if it was acceptance or condemnation, so I decided not to think upon the statement and turned my thoughts to the night and the naked man beside me.

"I would go to the Chiricahuas," he said of another batch of mountains. "Lose myself up there for a while, come down into Galeyville if need be. That is what I would do if I was running from me."

I did not want to talk about the chase but had no choice as he was already gone in mind. "Why there? Why not the Whetstones? Or New Mexico?"

"Too far afield," he said. "We'll head over there tomorrow, and if we don't see anyone we'll get back around Tombstone and get hold of Tipton to see if he's picked up anything. I'd also like to hear what happened at the inquest."

"Sounds like a plan," I said. I then crawled down and scooped his soft prick into my mouth.

"Doc," was all he said.

We fucked half the night. By the time we slept, we were sticky with come, and when dawn crept upon us, Wyatt got onto me and put it in to have himself a breakfast fuck of some length. When I did not unload into the bedding, he sucked out my cream, and after this we washed our residue in the stream and dressed. At the house Alma remarked on how refreshed we appeared.

"Good night air," Wyatt said. "Can't beat it."

Over breakfast, he laid out his plan, surprising me that it did not include the Chiricahuas. Galeyville would be our first destination. We then emerged well fed—and well fucked, in my case—and Lester bid us Godspeed.

It was late afternoon and hot as hell when we reached Galeyville, a known habitat of the Cowboys. "Pick up some information and get a meal," Wyatt said, "but we'll go in quiet to not draw attention."

Food was the first business, but Wyatt fairly bolted his meal as he was anxious to see Fred Bullard, a store owner usually willing to help the law. I shoveled down my food and joined him toward the store while the others lingered at the restaurant. We found Fred sitting grim faced out front of his store, arm in a sling. "Wyatt," he said. "Could have used you a couple nights ago."

"What happened?" Wyatt asked.

"Damned Cowboys hurrahing the town, shot out my window, which set me off, and I took my shotgun out into the street and fired over their heads, told them they'd have to pay the damage. Well, this was foolish of me, as Worley, that pig of a man, came over and shot out the other window. Then a bunch were upon me and I was pulled into their crowd and made a fool of before they shot me. At least I survived."

"I am sorry to hear this," Wyatt said. "Who was it?"

"Like I said, Worley, and there was Claude Langston and Johnny Bain, Doyle Eastman, and I don't know who else, there were so many. Finn Coombs. I'd know that laugh anywhere."

"Anybody come to help you?"

Bullard huffed. "Not a soul. Town marshal is a drunk, and when sober he is in with the Cowboys. No deputy anymore, but that's no matter as he was useless. They shot him last week and there's been no replacement."

"A sorry state," I said.

"I may close up and head east. Came out from Springfield looking for better, but this is not better, not anymore."

"Any idea where they've gone?" Wyatt asked.

"I hear they've got a camp in the northern Peloncillo Mountains, just into New Mexico, where they have a setup to rebrand rustled cattle. Likely they are down there."

Wyatt drew a big breath, as if fresh air had finally come his way. "This is most helpful, Fred. We'll go down there, get justice done."

"Courts won't hold them," Fred replied.

"My kind of justice," Wyatt countered, slapping his pistol.

Fred nodded. "Without those men, it would be a fine little town."

"I'll see what we can do toward that."

As we walked back to the restaurant, Wyatt said we would ride hard for the Peloncillos. "You up for that, Doc?" he asked.

"That I am," I said. Wyatt politely ignored the cough that followed.

When we met the others, Wyatt laid out his plan—or lack of. "I do not know these mountains, so we'll approach with caution. With that many men, we should have good tracks. They also are not likely expecting us down that way, so may not be alert."

"And less than that if they are drinking," I added, which Wyatt ignored.

"If we can get close without being seen," he went on, "we may get the drop on them, but if not, we'll shoot the whole damn bunch."

He was stirring the killer in himself. Though he was now ready to shoot without questions, there did remain the law-abiding character of him, unlike me, who had long ago cast aside such notions. Thus it pleased me to listen to him and know we rode as one.

The Peloncillos were about thirty miles south of Galeyville, and we set out with little notice of the local population, riding hard until the low peaks rose up in the distance. They had not the sharpness of the Dragoons but still appeared formidable. Wyatt stopped us a couple miles out, as we were on a wagon road and he was looking around.

"We'll go easy from here," he said, dismounting to scuff the dirt. I could not imagine what he could see beyond hoofprints by the dozen, but he seemed pleased when he got back on his horse. As we approached, we saw smoke rising from behind a bluff.

"Damn fools light up a come-and-get-me," I noted. "Must be drunk."

"Don't count on it," Wyatt said. "One lookout is all it takes."

Things appeared calm ahead, the area deserted, but we knew not to trust such things since we could not tell what lay beyond that bluff. Oak trees scattered among the nearby grass and rocks, giving the place a peaceful look. If the Cowboys had a rustling operation here, it was not highly visible. I began to appreciate Wyatt's caution.

Ever the scout, Wyatt insisted on climbing up onto the bluff to view our prey while we waited at some distance. The rising smoke had determined the camp located just beyond this modest rock, the big square chunk of granite providing cover from anyone coming up the road.

Wyatt scrabbled up to the flat top, where we lost sight of him as he hunkered down for a look. We waited, still astride our horses in case a charge or swift retreat was needed. All was quiet save for the bray of cattle that told us the Cowboys were tending a rustled herd, the fire needed to heat a branding iron. This worked in our favor, as they would likely be occupied.

As we waited, I could not help but consider how we were straying from our initial purpose of avenging Morgan. It seemed we were now out to avenge all of Tombstone, and maybe Galeyville as well, by way of eliminating the Cowboys. A tall order, but if there was a man to do it, it was Wyatt Earp.

He was on the bluff some time, no doubt planning his attack. When he finally came down, he said the bluff was a lone outcropping that eased down on the other side where the Cowboys had about thirty head of cattle penned and were doing some branding. "I count eight men," Wyatt told us, "and if we position ourselves well, we can get the drop on them all."

Did he mean to kill by way of harking back to Judge Spicer's pronouncement about leaving prisoners out where no alibis are needed? As Deputy U.S. Marshal, he had authority to arrest them, but I knew he was not going to herd a bunch of rustlers back to Tombstone for questionable justice. This was confirmed when he laid out his plan.

"Doc, you and I will go in from the front while the rest will be positioned behind them. Creek, you and Jack climb up onto the bluff and work your way around behind the cattle, and, Sherm, you keep on to the other side so we have their backs at three points. We will ride in and challenge them, and from there it is up to them if they wish to live or not."

He gave us a second to take this in and when all expressed agreement with the plan, he said, "Let's go." We tied the three horses nearby, then allowed time for the men to climb the bluff and position themselves. I checked my pistol while we waited, finding myself itchy to get on with it. "That's enough time," Wyatt then declared. "We'll go in hard."

We roared into their camp as a pair, guns drawn. "Throw up your hands!" Wyatt shouted, at which two men at the fire raised up, one dropping his branding iron in favor of his gun. He was quickly dispatched by my bullet while Wyatt fired on the other before he got his gun out of its holster. Others who had been standing about or near the cattle pens sought cover or sought to draw. None threw up their hands. Gunfire then erupted from behind the herd, which set the cattle attempting escape from their pens, braying as they pushed one another and the fence. Creek Johnson emerged, firing at a man attempting to run in with the cattle while Texas Jack shot a man in the back as he attempted to run the other way. When one fellow reached for a rifle, Wyatt blasted it from his hand, then put a bullet into the man's chest while I did in another who made the mistake of taking aim on Wyatt. Wyatt shot the last culprit amid the fellow's straying shots.

The air grew rank from gun smoke and dust stirred by the panicked cattle, who soon managed to trample part of their fence and make a run for it. About twenty of them charged by, taking down two tents, one of which revealed a man in underdrawers who had attempted to remain out of sight. As he had no gun, he threw up his hands, but in the melee he had been shot, blood staining his dirty whites as he staggered and fell. The whole battle took maybe two minutes. The freed cattle dispersed while their still-penned brethren carried on something awful until Wyatt rode over and leaned down to unhook their gate, at which they charged from the camp. Once the cattle were gone, quiet came over the place.

Wyatt, still astride, moved around to make certain all were accounted for while I, beset by coughing, hopped from my horse and spent some minutes attempting to right myself. The others poked around, looking at the dead men, calling out names. "Worley," Creek said.

"Eastman, Coombs," added Texas Jack.

Sherm rolled over another. "Ah hell, it's Reed Garrity. His old man is going to take this hard."

Wyatt joined us then, down off his horse and striding around, still much the general. "That Otto Maltby?" he asked of one fellow shot in the face.

"Was," I said.

"This one's alive," Creek called out and we went to look upon Johnny Bain, who was clutching his middle as if he could keep the life from running out. Wyatt leaned down and put his pistol to Bain's forehead. "You can join your friends right this minute or you can buy some time and tell me the whereabouts of Johnny Ringo and Curly Bill."

"Last I saw they were at the McLaury place, but that was a while back. Ain't seen 'em since. Honest."

"Honesty is not your strong suit," Wyatt countered as he eased his pistol from the man's sweating forehead. "You are guilty of a federal offense in bringing stolen cattle from one country to another. As a Deputy U.S. Marshal, I have authority to bring you in to stand trial. Do you understand that?"

"Yes, I do," said Bain, grimacing in pain.

"Good. I want to be clear on the law and the fact that you are a sorry son of a bitch who has broken it to such extent you do not deserve to stand in any court." And with this, Wyatt brought the pistol back up and put his bullet into Bain's heart. Bain looked puzzled as he expired.

"A few less to contend with," Wyatt said as I came over.

"What now?" I asked.

"I want to ride over toward the McLaurys'. Since it's on the way to Tombstone, no reason not to take a look. With Frank and Tom dead, I thought that operation done, but Bain makes me think that may not be. Could be a good spot to hide or maybe even keep doing business. We need to see what is going on."

"How about a rest between campaigns?" I suggested; he looked at me like I'd called for mutiny. He was charged from the gunplay and allowed not half an hour before we set out for McLaury's.

Frank and Tom McLaury, deceased, had a fine spread in the Sulphur Springs Valley about fifteen miles southeast of Tombstone. Their surviving brother, attorney William, resident of Texas, had likely inherited their ranch, but it was doubtful he'd be on the premises, being a city man. We were thus surprised to see cattle in the pens.

The area was inhospitable, as trees were mostly absent. Water was also scarce, a lone well serving the ranch. Grass was thin, giving the place a homestead look, like it had plunked down but not taken root.

"Someone is about," Wyatt said, and before I could comment, hoofbeats were heard behind us, followed by gunfire. When a bullet whizzed past my ear, I spurred my horse to full gallop, as did the others. By then it was clear we had more than one man after us, and as we hightailed it, Wyatt shouted, "Peel off, Doc." I did as told, reining my horse to the right, Wyatt following. This left our other three headed toward the ranch house and gave the shooters a problem, which is what many an impulsive lowlife does not anticipate.

Once turned, we saw we had about ten in pursuit, which could have been cause for concern had not the general been in charge. Our unexpected move gave us valuable seconds in which not only to assess the situation but to start firing at our pursuers as we rode toward them from their side. As is often the case, they proved to be lousy shots.

They did not apparently think to split in two, which confirmed them as more ragtag than organized. It also gave us an upper hand as we came at them from the side, shooting two at first crack with a third going down when a bullet caught his horse.

We turned as we rode, now behind the men who were behind the rest of our party. In no time, we began to close in and their shots went astray as they fired awkwardly. It is not easy to shoot someone when you must aim behind you. Creek, Jack, and Sherm then split up so there was no party for the men to chase, just five individuals now coming after them. Still, they kept on as they knew to stop meant death. They could not help but know the man sitting tall in the saddle was the legendary marshal.

The fleeing Cowboys bypassed the ranch in favor of open country, which was a fatal mistake as Wyatt would ride forever to catch a criminal. As it was, we did some hard miles, horses lathered with the heat and us not much better. My chest complained by way of searing pain while I attempted to draw enough breath to keep on. Fortunately, the Cowboys' horses began to tire enough for us to gain shooting range. Wyatt was a sight to behold as he rode hell-bent while firing a rifle to drop the men one, two, three. Creek and the others finished it while I, coughing and spitting, was useless.

When the last man had fallen, his horse still running, Wyatt came over and saw my difficulty. "Doc, you all right?"

"In a minute, yes. I just need to goddamn stop."

I slid from my horse and leaned against him until I'd gained enough to get at my flask. While the others dismounted, Wyatt took my reins and stood apprehensive as I swigged between hacks. At last, I quieted, though the chest pain did not.

"Got 'em all," Sherm noted.

"Did you see who all it was?" Wyatt asked. "I thought Don Bradshaw."

"Yep. And that's Bill Langer over there."

"Bill Tatom and Sam Kroger," Creek Johnson chimed in. "And some we ain't ever seen."

"Fair enough. We ran some miles out of our way," Wyatt said as he noted our surroundings. "But Tombstone isn't all that far. Can you ride the rest of the way, Doc? Maybe fifteen miles."

"If I can lie down when we get there, yes."

He thought on this. "We'll go over to the San Pedro and set up camp and you can rest all you want. Sherm can go into town for us."

I did not answer as I was coughing again. Soon as I caught a break, I climbed into the saddle, a place I truly did not wish to be, and we set out at a walk. After a while, I suggested we speed up as I preferred a hard ride to an extended one. We thus rode a good clip, bypassed Tombstone to the north, and finally reached the San Pedro River. Never had I been more pleased to step down off my horse.

Chapter Twenty-one

Wyatt became a regular nursemaid, which I found most endearing. He laid out my bedroll in a shady spot, rolled my coat as a pillow, and set my whiskey bottle close by. When I was stretched out, he took a kerchief to the river, wet it, brought it up, and handed it to me, and in that small offering, captured any corner of my heart he didn't already own. As I wiped my dusty brow, he squatted beside me, saying nothing since there was no need. While the others set up camp, he remained with me and I drank a good bit, then closed my eyes.

I did not sleep. Eyes shut, I hovered just short of that state, so I heard Wyatt's instructions to Sherm. "Find Dan Tipton and bring him out here. Once it is dark, we'll go eat at the Mexican place at the edge of town."

Sherm rode out and, as things settled, I listened to the San Pedro lapping while birds sang in the trees above. The horses, which were tied at the water, slopped noisily, which I found oddly reassuring, everyone easing up except Wyatt.

He walked with authority even when at loose ends. The others bustled about, but he strode, coming over my way, pausing, then walking off only to return minutes later. Finally, he sat beside me and I opened my eyes.

"You're not sleeping?"

"Rest is what I need," I said. "Sleeping is extra."

This did not amuse him as intended, and I saw his concern for me. "What can I do, Doc?" he asked.

"Nothing, Wyatt. Nobody can. Not even me."

This was a mistake. His expression turned stricken, and I realized I could not play my illness to him as I did to myself. He was still new with the malady, whereas it was an old and crotchety companion to me. "I'll be all right," I assured him. "Rest will do me fine."

I don't know if he believed me, but he nodded and stretched out on his bed, which he had again laid beside mine, and while Creek and Jack smoked and guffawed in their own raw friendship, Wyatt's hand stole onto my forearm, where it remained until Creek asked if we could have a fire.

"Hell, yes," Wyatt said, getting to his feet. "We've killed the threat around here."

I opened an eye to see him join the others in gathering firewood and was pleased at seeing him occupied. The fire was burning well when Sherm and Dan arrived.

Wyatt shook Dan's hand and asked for news. "Behan's got up a posse to go after you," he said. "Left yesterday. Mostly Cowboys."

"Where's he headed?" Wyatt asked.

"Not sure. Whetstones maybe."

"Good to know. Tell me about the inquest."

"Pete Spence's wife testified that Pete and Hank Stilwell came home that night as if they'd got up to something, fiddling with their guns and talking low. She also told how some days earlier, when Spence was talking to Indian Charlie or Hank Swilling, she wasn't sure which, and Morgan walked by, Spence nudged the other and said, 'That's him.'"

"Makes no sense," Wyatt said. "We found Indian Charlie in the Dragoons and he said Spence had no part, but Swilling was in on it."

"Swilling is in jail in Charleston, had some trouble in a saloon and got a twenty-day sentence. Spence gave himself up to Behan in fear of his life, saying you'll kill him. He is in jail, but Behan allows him a weapon."

"If I find he had a part, I will kill him. I have already dispatched Indian Charlie."

Dan considered this a moment, then went on. "Wells Fargo has come out in your support. Hume gave an interview to the *San Francisco Examiner* telling how the Cowboys terrorize the county and how the best citizens of Tombstone are in favor of the Earps, as is Wells Fargo. He went to great length to defend you in the Clanton-McLaury shooting and told how they never got the strongbox on that stage you were said to have robbed. It was a fine statement, Wyatt. It said you were justified in all your lawful efforts."

Wyatt, squatting at the fire beside Dan, blew out a long breath. "Nice to know, but it is a tad late. Back to the inquest. What was decided?"

"Spence, Swilling, Indian Charlie, and Stilwell were said to likely have done the murder, but nobody is sure of anything."

Wyatt nodded as he took this in, then said, "Dan, I need you to do something for me. We're going to need money to continue our posse. I want you to see Gage, the mine operator, on my behalf, explain our mission, and ask for a loan of one thousand dollars to finance us. If he is agreeable and has the cash on hand, try to get it to us here tomorrow morning; otherwise, we can arrange to pick it up later on."

"Will do," Dan said. He then paused, as if his next words had to be carefully chosen. "I don't know if you want to see, but you are all over the newspapers. The Stilwell killing got a lot of press, but Morgan's killing didn't. The *Star* is calling your mission a Vendetta, capital letter, and now the San Francisco papers have picked up the story. And the *Nugget*, well, you know how they are. I brought the papers if you'd like them."

"Might as well."

Dan retrieved a bundle from his saddlebag and said he'd best be off. "You can come into town if you want. Behan has most of the Cowboys with him, and the new marshal is of no consequence."

"Thanks, Dan, but we'll stay on the outskirts."

"Probably wise. I guess there still might be somebody about."

Wyatt walked Dan to his horse, and once he was in the saddle, asked him if he'd seen Ringo or Curly Bill.

"Nope. Making themselves scarce from Tombstone, but I did hear Ringo made some trouble up in Contention."

"Good to know. Thanks again, Dan."

When Dan had departed, Wyatt tucked the newspaper bundle into a saddlebag, then declared it supper time. "Doc, you up for a meal at the Mexicans'?"

"Rather not. Bring me some tortillas and beans."

"Will do. Sherm, you stay here and we'll bring you supper too."

Once it was just the two of us, Sherm fed the fire and sat quiet beside it while I almost dozed. My chest had eased some, but I knew soon as I began to move about it would ambush me, so I stayed put. Worst thing about the malady was the occasional need of lying quiet.

I did not sleep but again hovered in the vicinity, retaining enough conscious thought to amuse myself in recall of Wyatt putting his dick to me. I replayed a goodly amount of fucking, and when not viewing that, I sought images of my man naked in that shallow stream where he bathed while fully erect. These thoughts got my dick stiff, and I slid a hand down to massage the thing, which was likely as much action that region would see this night.

When the men returned later, they were in good spirits. Wyatt brought a little bucket of beans, which he set on the coals to warm while he took tortillas from their paper package and hung a couple on a stick above the fire. A fine meal was then had by Sherm and me, and Wyatt was pleased with my appetite.

"Feeling better?" he asked.

"Much," I said, which was mostly true.

He took off his hat and gun belt and stretched out beside me. The others bedded down, and soon Texas Jack had a buzz saw snore going. "You want to move?" Wyatt asked.

"Too tired. I think I could sleep inside a sawmill tonight."

Jack's snore grew louder at this point, as if to challenge such a notion, and this made Wyatt chuckle. "Sounds like you may get the chance."

He turned toward me and was most handsome in the fading firelight. I warmed to his gaze, and I swear my malady also took note as my body seemed to ease its entire self by way of his company. Either that or I was in enough swoon not to notice such troubles. In any case, the devil in me rose up along with my cock and I decided mischief could be got up to.

The others were now asleep, thus we lay in most hospitable circumstances. My cough had relented due to my remaining prone, thus I ventured ahead by reaching down to unbutton my pants and pull out my dick. Wyatt looked at what I'd revealed, then back up to challenge the notion, at which I whispered, "The illness lies in my chest. The rest of me works just fine, and if you don't do me some good, I'm going to do myself."

He raised up to look at the others, then eased back down and undid his own pants. His dick was coming up, as I knew it would, what with him worked up from the day's activities. "I could use a good come," he whispered as his hand slid onto me. I reciprocated, reaching down for him, and we were soon pulling dicks in the quiet of our little camp.

Wyatt was generous in not starting for Contention at the crack of dawn. He was enthused about the Ringo sighting and already exhibiting agitation brought on by the possibility of bringing down another of the Cowboys. But much as he was ready to step into his general role, he kept to some of the nursemaid, which I much appreciated, helping me to my feet and hovering while I hacked and spat my way into the morning. A fire had been started, as a chill had descended upon us.

This change was welcome after all the heat we'd lately endured. Once righted, I took a long piss, then washed up at the river with Wyatt so close by I finally had to comment.

"I am not going to drop over on you," I said. "I can get myself into the day, thank you."

He backed away. "Just trying to be helpful."

"Which is appreciated, but I have navigated this road a long time, Wyatt, and I know the bumps well. I'll be all right. Just let me greet the day at my own pace."

"Fair enough."

When Dan Tipton rode up, I was gratified as Wyatt needed occupation. In Dan's presence the general emerged and the tone turned hard-edged. While I listened, I enjoyed recall of us bringing each other off in the night.

Dan handed Wyatt a wad of cash. "Hatch insisted on putting up five hundred," he said. "The rest is from Gage, who says it is not a loan but pay for your work. You have full support of some good people."

Wyatt was speechless for a few seconds. "You send them my thanks," he finally managed. "Tell them we are getting the work done, but there is more to go."

"Anything else you need?"

"If I do, we'll send word. You are a good friend, Dan."

"Where you heading next?"

"Contention, but first we're going by the Mexicans', get some breakfast. Care to join us?"

"Thanks, but no, I have to get back to town. Business doesn't wait."

"Fair enough. We'll be seeing you."

We bid him good-bye, after which Wyatt was too restless to allow further leisure. "Let's pack up and get on," he said and we broke camp. He saddled my horse, but aside from that left me on my own, and we were soon riding over to get breakfast, which my growling stomach would appreciate.

The Mexicans were an enterprising family who had put out a sign at their adobe residence offering hearty food. Being so close to the border, their fare was common, although the blue noses of Tombstone thought it beneath them. As for me, I found it most hospitable and ate a good plate of huevos rancheros, bacon, and tortillas, plus what felt a gallon of coffee. Over the meal, Wyatt laid out his plan.

"We'll see what's up in Contention, and if Ringo's not there we'll go on up to Benson, then maybe over to Hooker's place. He may know something, as he gets around a lot."

I did well for most of the ride to Contention, as the general allowed us along at a walk. He bore a measure of contentment at possible prey ahead, although I'd venture his mind was buzzing with anticipation. I appreciated the slow pace, as did my body, my two selves in rare conformation, which eased my chest discomfort and got me back to mere cough.

Going along, I tried to establish if it was Monday or Tuesday but found I'd lost track, and if anyone had asked the date I would have given March and nothing more. April, I believed, lay close ahead, but I had no idea how close.

We were not halfway to Contention when Wyatt snapped to attention and called out "trouble ahead." I hadn't been paying attention, lingering in the calendar as I was, but I looked up to see the Benson stage stopped up ahead and surrounded by a bunch of Cowboys. As Johnny Ringo was known to rob stages, I knew Wyatt was hopeful toward an encounter.

"Let's let them know we are here," he called and he pulled up his shotgun, spurred his horse, and charged ahead. The rest of us did likewise, at which the robbers took note and began to fire. Wyatt emptied his shotgun, taking one man to hell, while I caught another, but neither was Johnny Ringo. The others scattered and we gave chase, Wyatt catching one in the back with a bullet from that Buntline Colt. Jack and Sherm each rode after another, going a good distance before bring them down while I, after too long a pursuit, overtook one sorry son of a bitch and nailed his gun hand and then his gut. Riding up to the fallen man, who lay shivering with his wounds, I saw it was Ross Webb.

"It is fortunate for you that Marshal Earp is not the one looking down upon you, as he lacks my patience," I said. "Now tell me where I can find Johnny Ringo."

Here I cocked my pistol and waited. When Ross blubbered that he did not know, I said this was most unfortunate. "Then you are a daisy," I added and I pulled the trigger to end his misery. The shot entered his forehead, so his exit was quick.

When I rode back to the stage, I was coughing. "Hello, Doc," called the driver. It was Tom Leaver, who had lost a good amount of money to me at faro.

"Tom," I said. I saw his shotgun messenger laid out on the ground, shoulder bloodied. "Ben took a shot," Tom said, "but the rest are fine, thanks to you all."

"Was it Ringo?" I asked as Wyatt and the others rode up from all directions.

"No. I saw Ross Webb and Garth Sykes and some others I don't know."

"Well, they are no more."

"Two got away," Wyatt said with some disgust, "but the rest are done."

I tried to tell him who I had dispatched but had a coughing fit, and he held up a hand to stop me from attempting to speak. He then got down to inspect things, talk with the passengers about what they had seen, and ask about Johnny Ringo. Nobody had seen him. After this discussion, Wyatt looked to me. "You all right, Doc?"

"I am doing fine but would appreciate a modest pace."

He studied me further, then looked at the departing stagecoach. When it was some distance away, he declared we would not go on to Contention but to Hooker's place for a rest due to our unexpected activity. My gratitude at this turn went unspoken, but Wyatt knew anyway.

We rode northeast to Henry Hooker's Sierra Bonita Ranch, which was just across the line in Graham County. Hooker welcomed us with an invitation to make his place our base. "Plenty of room, plenty of food, plenty of company," he said. "Stay as long as you like."

"We'll take you up on the offer, as the trail has gone cold," Wyatt said. This plan was sealed with drinks all around as Hooker was most eager and had a steady pouring hand. As we enjoyed some leisure, he had his men see our horses comfortable, then set about the same for us. He employed a Mexican couple, Jose and Maria, to cook and clean for him, and a fine table was laid over which Wyatt related our recent exploits. When Hooker heard Stilwell and Indian Charlie were dead, he was most pleased, and when we gave him other names, he poured more drinks.

By late afternoon, we were well fed and slightly sozzled, even Wyatt, who always drank less than the rest of us. "How about I show you your accommodations?" Hooker said. "You can double up as you wish. There are three rooms upstairs, and you can have them all, as my room and that of my foreman are down here at the back"

Upstairs, Wyatt chose the largest and said he and I would double up. "Texas Jack needs a room to himself, as he snores like a buzz saw," Wyatt told Hooker, which got a laugh out of everyone, even Jack. Sherm and Creek were fine sharing a room. As we made these arrangements, Hooker made another offer. "Anybody want a bath? It can be arranged."

"Hell, yes," Wyatt said and all agreed.

A procession took place over the next couple hours as water was heated and poured into a big tub in the kitchen. Towels and soap were laid out, the servants then departing. "You first," Jack told Wyatt. "You're in charge; you get the clean water."

I did not care to bathe in used water, even Wyatt's, thus I deferred to last and asked that the tub be emptied and refilled. "I'll help with the filling if this is a hardship," I told the Mexicans, but they insisted on doing it themselves "for the good friend of Don Hooker."

Wyatt kidded me no end about my fastidious habits, and I accepted his jibes as all were true. We had acquired a layer of dirt and sweat which dried upon us and allowed additional layers of dirt and sweat to accumulate until we were a truly rank bunch. I suspected our collective smell had driven Hooker to offer baths.

Once into the tub, I lingered, feeling good from the liquor, the meal, the company, and being off the damned horse. I coughed some, but the chest pain had eased, thus I soaked for some time. Finally, Wyatt came in.

"You going to swim in that all night?" he said. It was late and he wore only underdrawers, looking a fine specimen with his dick tenting the front. He stood with hands on hips and all but sparkled in his cleanliness, which I knew enticed him toward another kind of dirty. Get a man naked, even for a bath, and he will consider that he might as well get up to something, being already undressed.

"I am enjoying myself," I said, unable to suppress a smile.

He looked around to confirm us alone, then came over, kneeled down, and dropped a hand into the water to grab my dick. "You can have it here or in that fine big bed," he said with a tug.

"Not both?"

"Ah, hell, Doc," he said and he began to pump my dick. As I'd already been playing around with the thing, it took but a few strokes before I splashed and came, my white gobs rising to float on the water. That I did not cough pleased me no end and Wyatt took note.

"You must be feeling better," he remarked.

"I am now."

"Come on to bed."

I stepped from the tub and he handed me a towel. "Don't bother with your drawers," he said. "They'll just be coming off."

In our room, the lamp burned, the covers had been turned back, and a full whiskey bottle sat on the bedside table with two glasses. He poured both, taking such time you'd have thought that dick of his wasn't trying to get past its confinement. I sat on the bed while he remained standing. "You've been a big help on this run, Doc," he said after we'd had a swallow. "I know it costs you to ride with me and I appreciate that."

"Thank you, Wyatt. I would not consider staying behind."

"We'll stay here a few days," he said.

"Because of me? I can keep up."

"I know you can. That's not it. Even I can use a rest now and then, and this is a most hospitable place."

I hadn't really looked around the room until then, my earlier glance at it caught up in the big bed. Now I saw Hooker had spent well on fine furnishings, which were heavy and ornate with dark green drapes, tufted chairs, and rich bedding. The dresser and bureau were impressive with their heft, as if everything in the room was to last a century. The mattress on which I sat was not coarse like most. I had no idea its filling but it was soft yet firm, which seemed impossible in mind. My buttocks, however, confirmed a welcome state.

When we finished our drinks Wyatt pushed down his drawers and kicked them off. "Now," he said as he climbed onto the bed, put me onto all fours, and drove his prick into me. His thrust was urgent, as if his come was already on the rise, which I guess it was because he pounded me terrible, grunting and growling as he quickly let go, then, once empty, pulled out and fell over onto his back. "Goddamn," he gasped and it was some seconds before he added, "been thinking on that the whole way here."

"Me too. My mind is no longer my own, having been taken over by my dick."

He rolled over to face me. "We have this big bed, this big room, all to ourselves and no purpose but to use it."

"We are going to fuck to excess?" I asked.

"We are going to fuck to kingdom come."

The chases of late, the shootings, the satisfaction at reducing the Cowboy population fueled him to my benefit. After this first release, he paced himself, using tongue and fingers to prod and poke me until he was again primed. The second round put me on my back, legs up over his shoulders as he gave me a good long one. I shot a meager come long before he told me he was going to give me enough to choke a horse, an idea which entertained me as he seemed much the stallion. As he rode me, I managed to marvel that all our miles in the saddle had taken no toll upon him, his prowess possibly aided by such effort. If only those who saw him as the formidable lawman could know the description might well apply to his dick.

When this horse of mine had unloaded his gusher, he eased out and lay on his side. "Getting you dirty," he said, as we were shiny with sweat.

"Filthy," I added.

He considered this. "I like that. Filth." And he eased me onto my side facing away from him and got a couple fingers in where his prick had just been.

We did not sleep until Wyatt had come one more time, which he managed by way of licking my butthole at length. Due to our long day, I issued nothing more, content at being well used. Wyatt, sweating like a pig when finally done, declared he'd need another bath. He then fell asleep. I lay listening to his breathing, and when a cough caught me, I muffled myself into the pillow. After a while, I managed to doze off.

Sunshine woke me next morning, insisting on a new day. I did not consult my watch, as I did not wish intrusions by such nonsense as minutes or hours. Instead, I curled onto my side and enjoyed Wyatt's steady slumber. I confess to peeking under the covers to see if he was stiff, which he was, but I decided to refrain from climbing on. Best not to challenge my malady since some of the purpose in being here was to give it rest.

When Wyatt woke, it was with a start, his arm slashing the air as he uttered some gibberish. I could see it took him a second to determine his whereabouts.

"Good morning," I said.

His hand slid beneath the covers to attend his prick. "Morning,"

"Beautiful here."

"That it is."

"You going to make use of that thing?" I asked.

"If you'll roll over, I surely am."

I got onto my side, butt to him, and he spread me and eased in, at which I was compelled to tell him it was indeed a fine morning. "Didn't you once say the best days begin with a fuck?" I asked.

"May have," he replied, gently thrusting. He wrapped his arm around me and I took hold of it, content to have my man inside me and to know we need not go chasing around later on.

Lying easy, Wyatt could fuck for hours, and I basked and swooned with his attentions. My own dick finally woke, so I worked it until Wyatt's hand pushed mine away. He then stroked me steadily while pumping into my bottom, which caused me to cry out and shoot a load into the bedding. When I was done, he rolled us over so he was atop my back and he then got to serious work, a proper goddamn fuck that had the big bed creaking like it had not been used in such manner. At last, he shot his spunk, riding me vigorously until empty, at which he fell onto his back and immediately slept. I curled up and joined him.

When we again woke it was to noise in the hallway. Creek and Jack were arguing about whether or not to wake us and we lay listening until Wyatt finally got up, put on drawers, and opened the door. "What is the goddamn matter out here?" he demanded with mock anger. "We are trying to sleep in here."

"I'm sorry, Wyatt," Jack said. "I didn't want to bother you, but Creek said we should. Hooker is going to ride over to Benson on business and we're going along, didn't know if you'd want to join us."

"What time is it?"

"Almost noon."

"We'll pass. You go on."

"Sorry to wake you," Jack said and they hurried away.

"Good thing they have a late start," I noted, which made Wyatt chuckle. "Would have been awful to get interrupted before."

"Wouldn't have been interrupted," he replied as he fell back onto the bed crosswise. "When I get my dick into you, I do not stop until I've done my business."

"For which I remain grateful."

"I am hungry, though. How about we get ourselves upright and find breakfast?"

As we dressed, I savored our circumstance. For the first time since we'd taken up with each other, we were unencumbered. The day had no demands beyond those we desired. I noted myself not presently in the grip of my malady, and I attributed this respite to the calm—and the fuck.

Though breakfast was long past, the cook fixed us a fine spread of steak, eggs, potatoes, tortillas, and coffee. We ate like we'd just come in off the range, but a good roll in the sack was known to result in the same appetite. When we had stuffed ourselves, we took our coffee out onto the porch that fronted the house. Shaded and with comfortable chairs and a small table, it was a fine place to avoid exertion, and I settled in while Wyatt perched on the railing.

After a while, he took a cigar from his pocket, offered me one, which I declined, and enjoyed a quiet smoke. The day was clear and already hot, the breeze absent, a sweetness persisting. Looking around, I saw flowers nearby and wondered if the Mexican had planted them or if Hooker was possessed of a green thumb. In either case, they gave the day a fine fragrance.

When Wyatt had finished his smoke, he went inside and came back with the bundle of newspapers Dan had brought. "Might as well see what is being said," he remarked.

"Why?" I countered. "It's a peaceful day, and if you read that malarkey you are going to get pissed off and want to go riding off steam on something other than me."

"You make a point, Doc, but I still want to know," he said and he began to sort the various papers. The *Nugget* was first. He read for a bit, then handed it to me, but when I declined, he read me the headline. "Cowardly and Brutal Assassination of Frank Stilwell—His body filled with Bullets and Buckshot."

"Except for the 'cowardly,' it seems accurate," I noted.

"Nothing about his killing Morgan, just a rant on us." He tossed aside the *Nugget* and took up the *Arizona Daily Star*. "A Dark Deal, Murder in Cold Blood of a Supposed Innocent Man—The Shadow of Tombstone's Bloody Feud Reaches Tucson," was the headline he read. "Feud?" he railed. "That is downright silly. They forget I am a lawman."

He was starting to get upset, so I made no comment as he read the article, then looked for another paper. "Another *Star* and goddamn, Ike Clanton has given them an interview. Holy hell, what are we coming to?"

He began to read me how Ike said he had been in Tucson in support of Stilwell, who was there only to appear in court on charges of stage robbery. Ike said he was at his hotel when he heard shots and asked about them and was told that it was the locals celebrating the city firing up new gaslights. "Horse shit," Wyatt declared, "all of it."

"You saw him on that flatcar with Stilwell."

"But that is the truth, which has no weight these days. Ike also says Stilwell had an alibi for the night Morgan was shot." Here he threw the paper aside and I hoped that was the end of his reading, but seconds later he took up another *Star* and read out the next article:

"The assassination of Morgan Earp in Tombstone was a foul crime but was the natural outgrowth of the cowardly assassination of William Clanton and the McLaury brothers by the Earps and Holliday, under the guise of official authority. Both crimes were equally heinous, and the perpetrators should have been made to pay the severest penalty of law. But worse than all this was the deep-dyed assassination of Frank Stilwell at the depot, when without any provocation, a band of four or five slayers pursued a lonely man in the dark, and without a word of warning murdered him in cold blood and then hied to their stomping grounds as unconcerned as though they had been out on a hunting expedition, or like so many bloodthirsty Apaches rejoice over their crime."

He stopped to allow this foul piece to hover between us, then found an editorial. "It says we are a roving band, our path strewn with blood, and whenever we halt in a settlement, stage robberies follow and human life ceases to be sacred."

I did not comment, as part of the statement was true. Our path was strewn with blood, but it was still a stretch to add stage robbing, which we had never done. I began to silently curse Dan Tipton for bringing us the papers, especially when Wyatt took up the *San Francisco Exchange* and found a piece on the so-called Vendetta. "Well, here it is," he said, pausing before he began to read it out to me.

"The Earp Vendetta still looms. The latest dispatch from the seat of war tells of another murder by the Earp party—a Mexican named Cruz, whom the Earps suspected of being concerned in Morgan's murder. The sheriff has enlisted the Cowboys under his banner, as he himself evidently has no stomach for the job. Still, the outlook is hopeful for the people of the territory. When the Cowboys and the Earps meet, a sanguinary conflict is inevitable. It may fortunately happen that the slaughter on both sides will leave but a few survivors, and a big funeral, with the Earps and Cowboys to furnish the remains, would be the lifting of a great weight from the minds of the citizens of Tombstone."

"Will you stop ruining what was a fine day," I said, gathering the papers he had tossed my way and getting up to pull the *Exchange* from his hand. "Enough. This is not new."

"No, but it is growing. We are out here risking our lives to rid the county of a band of criminals, and we are made to be the worst of it."

I shook my head. "I give up. You'd rather get all pissed off, be my guest. Why don't you go ride your horse for a couple hundred miles and get it out of your system so I can sit here and enjoy the day in peace."

This rankled him further, even though I could see he took my words to heart. He attempted to settle himself into a chair but still fidgeted. "You should have gone with the others," I remarked. "Idleness doesn't suit you." This comment, which simply fell from my mouth, caused me to consider we had never had much opportunity to idle together. Always there had been the work of earning a living or threats from the Cowboys or trumped up court proceeding. Wyatt had always been coming from something and going toward something else. I had been a pleasurable interlude between events, but now there were no events, save the stories just read. Unfortunately, they gave him no purpose beyond upset, and I saw there was nothing I could do, as we'd already had a fuck.

"You have a better grip on doing nothing," he observed.

"Of necessity, but still, it hurts no man to sit a spell, look on the view, consider the flowers, the blue sky, and the fact that he is at relative peace."

He said only, "I suppose."

Chapter Twenty-two

Behan's posse is in the area," Hooker said that night when he and the men returned from Benson. "You may have been seen coming over here, so we need to be on the lookout."

This perked Wyatt up to such extent I could almost feel the general massing his troops for battle. "If he shows up, we are going to set things right," he declared.

Nobody asked how this was to be done, as all knew we would be instructed when the time came. As it was, everyone was hungry, and we had a fine supper, after which we played poker until late. This also entertained Wyatt until we went to bed, at which he got at me something fierce. He took my every inch and then some, which, when he was done, put me into a welcome sleep. Next day, he was up and gone with the sun, riding out with Hooker to look over the stock.

The others were not so eager for occupation, thus they sat with me to enjoy some leisure by way of telling stories, cleaning guns, and snoozing on the porch. We were easing along into the afternoon when Hooker and Wyatt rode up and called out that Behan's posse was in sight. "Saddle up, boys, and hurry," Wyatt told us. "I do not mean to make a battle here. We'll ride up onto a bluff a few miles out and settle it there."

We did as told, despite Hooker's insistence that remaining at the house was perfectly acceptable. Wyatt would have none of that. "I am not going to be shooting near your home. You tell Behan where we are, as I want him to come for us. We'll then end it." Well armed, we followed Wyatt for about three miles to where we climbed to a bluff that offered a view of the ranch and a good distance beyond. Soon a cloud of dust appeared on the horizon.

"There they are," Jack called.

The posse looked to be about twenty men, and we watched as they rode up to Hooker's porch. After some time, all movement stopped, which puzzled us. "Would he feed them?" Creek asked.

"Possibly," Wyatt replied. "He needs to remain in good with Behan, as he is still the law."

We got off our horses and milled around for quite some time, Wyatt pacing about, me sipping my whiskey as the sudden flight from the house had set me to coughing. It was a good two hours before we saw the posse ride out. "They're going the other way," I noted.

"Son of a bitch," Wyatt said. "He won't fight."

We hopped into our saddles and rode back to the ranch, eager to hear what had transpired. Hooker sat kicked back on his porch, looking like a king and grinning from ear to ear. "Did you tell them we were on the bluff?" Wyatt asked.

"Sure as hell did, but it seems Behan is willing to ride any direction except where you are waiting for him. He said they are going back to Tombstone, as expenses of the trip are running high. He has a bill against the county for thirteen thousand dollars for his work. He didn't stay long after he learned what I thought about that expense bill."

Wyatt began to laugh. He went over and shook hands with this man who had said to Behan just the kind of thing we would have. "Seems nobody is chasing us anymore, boys," Wyatt announced. Hooker said we should celebrate and brought out a fine whiskey for us all to enjoy. We stayed on the porch for some time, talking of Behan returning home empty-handed.

"All he has is his bill to the county," I noted.

"I want to go to Contention tomorrow," Wyatt said in our room later that night. We had played poker into the evening, but he called it a night earlier than expected. I assumed he was worked up with his victory over Behan as well as plans for our next move.

"I hate to leave the peace and quiet," I replied.

"You appear well rested, Doc, and I am tired of sitting around. We still have to find Ringo and Curly Bill."

Our conversation took place as we undressed, and I did not challenge Wyatt's statement as he was naked and his dick was hard. "Come over here and suck this thing," he said. I did as told, kneeling before him to draw out a mouthful of spunk. Once I sat back licking my lips, he pulled me up and shoved me onto the bed. "I need some dessert," he said before rolling me over and getting his mouth onto my bottom.

He was as thorough as always in his attentions to my backside, tongue teasing up and down my crack until he finally spread me, paused for a look, then pushed into my hole. At this, I took hold of my cock and stroked it about twice before letting go into the bedding. Wyatt took little notice as he snorfled in my bottom. My come was enhanced by his tongue work, and I cried out with my pleasure, not caring if the others heard. His tongue fucked me as good as a little cock, and when I had spent and became most pliable, he still went at me. I thought I might dissolve entirely with such attentions until at least he retreated and sat back. I rolled over to see him wipe his arm across his mouth. He looked far from satisfied.

"We'll be in the saddle tomorrow," he said, "so I mean to get my fill." He then crawled down and got my soft dick into his mouth and proceeded to suck and play until his own was up again, at which he put me on my back, legs on his shoulders, and gave me a good long fuck. Night was well along when he came and then collapsed beside me. "You are holding up right well," he said when his breathing quieted.

"Like I said before, the malady is in my lungs. Lower territory is unaffected, although right now it is in somewhat of a swoon."

"You ready to get back out there on the chase?" he asked, squeezing my arm.

"Most ready. I have not lost sight of our purpose."

This apparently got him thinking. I never knew when that would kick in. "I miss Morgan something fierce," he said wistfully. "Miss the others too. I'll see them one day when I visit California, but Morgan won't be there. It is the saddest thing I have ever known."

"Morgan was a fine man and good friend," I said. "Those men will pay."

"Not enough."

"That is true. Robbing a man of life has no penalty strong enough, even death. It is the most unfair circumstance."

He rolled over onto his side and looked at me. "Do you have any people still around, Doc?"

This surprised me. In all our time together, he'd never asked who I had left behind. "No brothers or sisters," I said. "I was the sole child. I believe my father still lives, and I have a stepmother I am not fond of. A pair of cousins were close to me, brothers who I would like to see one day. One was going to go into dental practice with me in Atlanta, and I hope he has gone ahead with that. Their father, my uncle John, a doctor who I am named after, also favored me. Mostly, I don't think about them as it serves no purpose. I only hope they have not heard about my reputation since it is greatly exaggerated."

"Will you ever go back?"

"Doubtful. The weather is against me."

We fell to quiet, gazing into each other's eyes until he said we'd best get some sleep. "Contention tomorrow. Work ahead."

Hooker saw us off the next morning with a good breakfast and wishes for our success in bringing in the last two murderers. "Come back if need be," he said as we climbed onto our horses, who were well rested and eager to get moving. We rode to Contention at a good clip, Wyatt stopping us a couple miles from town.

"I want to go in quiet rather than make a show," he said. "Creek, you, Jack, and Sherm wander in ahead of us, start poking around. Doc and I will amble in after a bit and do the same. We will all meet at the bank at noon and see if we have anything of substance. If something of merit jumps out at you, come find me."

We watched as they rode off. I hopped down to take a piss and Wyatt did likewise. We then stood looking around but saw not a soul. "Usually somebody on the road," Wyatt remarked. "Prospector or freight wagon or the goddamn Cowboys."

"Maybe everybody slept late," I replied, as I liked us being untroubled by others. We passed some minutes with me sipping whiskey and Wyatt scuffing around before he declared it long enough and we started out.

Contention did not thrive as did Tombstone. Supported mainly by a mill and a host of saloons, it persisted in spite of itself. There was only modest new construction. We went first to the Flying Horse Saloon where Wyatt saw a man he knew and headed back into the gaming room. I went to the bar, got myself a drink, and took up conversation with the bartender, who knew who I was. "Your friend is scaring off business," he said, leaning over to me. "This Vendetta of his has the Cowboys running off to Mexico or California."

"How do you know where they are headed?"

"Some told me when they last came in here. They had friends killed by Earp and by you, I suppose. They realize he is not going to stop, so they hightailed it out of here. 'Arizona is done for,' one told me, and I am starting to think that may apply to my business. They may be the worst of men, but they have been good customers."

"This is most enlightening and I am sorry for your trouble," I said.

"The marshal's intention is not to have honest businessmen suffer. He is only concerned with law and order and cleaning out the criminal element from this county. I'd venture once they are gone, respectable people will come to your town and your business will pick up more than ever."

"You think?"

"I surely do. Now tell me, have you seen Johnny Ringo or Curly Bill lately?"

"Bill is said to be over in the Whetstones, but Ringo was drunk in here last night. I haven't seen him today. Figure he's sleeping it off in a shack they've got south of town, over across the river. Belonged to Ed Freeman till they ran him off."

I finished my drink and paid the man a fine tip, then headed back to find Wyatt. He was talking to some men and I did not interrupt. When he saw me, he left them and came over. "Anything?" I asked.

"Ringo has been seen recently, but nobody knows where he is."

"I may. The bartender said the Cowboys have a shack just across the river south of town. And Ringo was drunk in here last night, so maybe he's down there now."

"Let's walk around some. If we don't spot him, we'll go out there. It's almost noon, so we can go on to the bank presently."

As we walked about, nobody spoke or made any sort of move toward us, good or bad. Going along, I told Wyatt how the bartender said the Vendetta was driving the Cowboys out of Arizona. "That is good to hear," he said. "Infamy may serve a purpose."

We wandered in and out of several sporting establishments but saw no Ringo nor any Cowboys we knew. At noon, we crossed to the bank where the others waited. "Shack south of town," Creek said, and I told him I had gained the same information. We then left it to the general as to our next move.

"We'll ride out there and see what we're up against," he said. "Make a plan then." And we did just that, crossing the San Pedro once well south of town. In the distance, near a dead oak tree, sat what appeared to be an old miner's shack, implements rusting out front. Horses stood unsaddled, which was good as it meant the men were likely sleeping off their night. Still, we scouted around.

Wyatt rode a large circle while we waited at a distance and he came back to tell us there was but the one window in front. "We need to bring them out," he decided. "Creek, we passed a few trees back some. Go cut me a good branch. We'll set it afire and throw it onto the roof."

Creek took Sherm and they did as told, returning with a long and bushy branch. Nearly dead, it was highly brittle and thus good fire starter. "I'll do it," Creek volunteered.

Wyatt positioned us back some, spread out so as not to be easy targets. He then gave Creek the sign at which Creek lit the branch. Once it was aflame, he carried it behind the shack and threw it onto the roof, where it immediately caught in the aged wood. Creek then rode back out among us and we all waited. It was not long until the entire roof was ablaze and the door burst open. Spilling out were men in drawers, some staggering with hangovers, others with their wits intact and guns blazing. We returned fire, hitting some, missing some, and then I saw Johnny Ringo come out in just his pants. He fired his pistol as he ran for his horse and hopped aboard, no saddle required. I shot and missed, then turned my horse after him as he spurred and took off. As I went by Sherm, I saw him get hit and fall, but I could not be troubled by this. Ringo was our purpose and I meant to bring him down.

He made no effort to shoot at me while running his horse. He got the creature into full gallop, going upriver hell for election, me not far behind. I fired some shots and saw him nearly fall, but he righted himself and kept on. He was a tough son of a bitch who was going to fight to the last breath.

I suffered some pain with the ride but did not let it slow me. Finally, I shot Ringo's horse, which I hated to do, but there seemed no recourse. Either the animal paid the price or I did, as my malady was rearing its head something awful. When the horse went down, Ringo was thrown and I took advantage of this, riding up and getting the drop on him. That I coughed proved entertaining to him.

"Well, if it ain't the lunger thinking he has got me," he said with a wicked smile.

"Knowing he has got you," I replied, getting down off my horse. "You are going to pay the price at last," I added as I took his guns, emptied them, and tossed them away. Just then Wyatt rode up and hopped off his horse.

"Damn fine work, Doc," he said and I coughed a reply, then managed to speak.

"I have saved him for you, Wyatt. You alone deserve to avenge your dear brother."

Wyatt unholstered his Buntline and paused to savor the moment. And why not? We'd chased all over hell for this varmint, and now we had him. He should squirm with the knowledge his life was about to end as payment for the one he took. "You murdered my brother," Wyatt said to him.

"I did no such thing. Frank Stilwell shot him and you know that."

"I also know you were in on it. You and Indian Charlie and Curly Bill and Hank Swilling. I am sending you all to hell."

Ringo's defiance here lost some power. His expression turned to concern, his eyes widened. When Wyatt put the Buntline to Ringo's forehead, Ringo sucked in a long breath. "Enjoy that. It is your last," Wyatt said and he pulled the trigger. Ringo fell back, a red hole marking his end.

I said nothing, as it seemed a sort of holy moment for Wyatt. I knew Morgan was with him in spirit, little brother deserving far more than this, but it was all Wyatt had power to do. He had done it well, and I hoped he would soon come to feel satisfaction. As it was, he pulled Ringo's body over to a tree and sat it up against the trunk. "There for all to see," he said before walking away.

Back at the shack, we found Sherm McMasters dead. Creek and Jack stood over him and Wyatt and I joined them, Wyatt kneeling down over his friend. "All this way he's come. Not fair. Not fair at all."

The bullet had gotten him in the neck, severing his jugular. Blood was all down his front, life literally run out of him. "We'll take him to Hooker's," Wyatt said. "I will not bury him here."

We noted which of the Cowboys we had gotten, but some were unknown to us. This mattered little. They had been with the outlaws and they had fired on us, thus they met their end. We left them for the buzzards, put Sherm over his saddle, and took our time getting back to Hooker's.

Our friend was most hospitable. Happy that Ringo was gone, sad we'd lost Sherm. "We'll bury him here on the ranch," he declared. "My wife, Sara, is in a fine spot a little north and we'll put him up there. Nice shady spot, some trees. If you have to face eternal rest, might as well make it comfortable."

"That is big of you, Henry," Wyatt said.

Hooker's men dug the grave and lowered Sherm in, after which Wyatt said words of gratitude over his friend. It was a sobering time for us all, the first casualty in our war of revenge. "He had no family that is known to us," Wyatt concluded. "We did our best by him in that regard and now wish him peace."

We then went back up to the house where we were invited to stay the night, which we did. I was suffering some pain and a revived cough, so I sought the big bed rather than a meal. Wyatt was most concerned, but I assured him it was simply the day's exertion that had brought on the spell. He sat on the bed wearing a frown. "Go eat some supper," I said. "Let me rest. I will be fine with a quiet night."

"I can bring you something to eat," he said.

"I am not hungry. Get me my whiskey and a glass and leave me be. Please, Wyatt. I will recover with the morning."

He was still reluctant but honored my wishes and left me alone. I stripped to my drawers, pulled back the covers, and sat drinking to calm things. Finally, I slid into bed and lay wondering how many days had passed in our pursuit. Much as I assured Wyatt of my recovery by morning, I knew I was trading something I might not get back. But this made no matter as we still had work to do. One more and then I could rest. One more.

Chapter Twenty-three

Wyatt's presence remained in the bed next morning even though he was absent. The smell of him lingered, and I would swear I could, in the cold of the room, feel his wake.

Rest had not repaired me as much as anticipated, so it took time to get into the day. Already quite bright, the room grew still brighter as I coughed and sputtered through my ablutions, downing whiskey to attempt calm. A compromise was finally achieved and I dressed and descended.

The cook fixed me breakfast, which took time to eat due to the cough. My chest complained at my being upright, but I was not about to lie in bed when we had work to do. The last thing I wished, the very last thing, was to be a burden on anyone.

"Here's the lazybones," kidded Texas Jack when I stepped out onto the porch around noon.

"Sleep like a baby absent your hellacious snore," I countered, which caused the others to laugh and me to cough. Wyatt, smoking a cigar while perched on the railing, looked uneasy. This I understood, given yesterday's activity and his leaving me alone both night and morning. He was pent up and in need of either more posse work or a good fuck. As I knew myself not yet up to the latter, I encouraged the former.

"That bartender in Charleston told me Curly Bill may be over in the Whetstones," I said. "We should go there and see."

Wyatt came over. "You up for that?"

"I surely am."

He studied me for a few seconds and, as I managed not to cough, saw me fit. "Fine, then. Boys, we are headed to the Whetstones. Saddle up and let's go."

When we reached our room, Wyatt asked if I was sure about this.

"Curly Bill? Only one way to find out."

"I mean you and another ride."

"Yes, Wyatt, I am sure. If I was not sure I would not suggest going."

He looked at me like he wasn't buying this.

"You need not be concerned," I said, at which I began to cough. "I am my usual ornery self."

The Whetstone Mountains lay west of Tombstone and were a larger range than the Dragoons. Known best for several hospitable springs, they had often played host to various outlaws on the run. By the time we started there, the day had clouded over and gone cold. We donned our long coats and, after a brisk ride, we reached our destination late that afternoon. Our journey took some out of me, so I was most pleased when Wyatt said we would ride up into Iron Springs for a rest.

We threaded up a narrow trail that led us among trees and boulders until the water hole was in sight. It looked a fine break from open plain and led me to contemplating leisure, but such thoughts were suddenly asunder as gunfire pierced the silence and bullets flew our way. The attack came from across the pond and from too many guns to count, leaving us no time to think on a next move. I reined my horse to turn and saw Creek and Jack doing same. There are times to fight and times to run. As we fled, I looked back to see Wyatt charging into the water amid the barrage of bullets. My gut seized, as did my lungs, but no cough came. Instead, my body was gripped by a fear unlike any I had known, and when Wyatt jumped down off his horse, holding the reins in one hand and his shotgun in the other, I knew him a goner. We three cowards, now off our horses and hidden in brush, watched as none other than Curly Bill Brocius splashed into the foot-high water from the opposite shore. I could not hear what he called to Wyatt but saw him raise his pistols. Before he could fire, Wyatt raised his shotgun, shouted "This is for Morgan," and pulled the trigger to blast open Curly Bill's gut. The impact threw him back several feet and into the water.

As others continued to fire, Wyatt tossed aside the spent shotgun and sought his rifle, but by now we were all firing and his horse spooked and reared so he couldn't get to the rifle. He drew his pistol instead and began shooting at those concealed in the brush until they turned and fled. Things then fell to an eerie quiet and I jumped up to see how Wyatt had fared, as no mortal man could have escaped such a battle unscathed. I was encouraged when I saw him get back onto his horse and ride our way, but still feared bravery carried a wounded man. When he reached our shore, I rushed to him. "You must be shot all to pieces," I said as he climbed down.

"Don't think so," he replied, "but look at this." He held out the skirts of his long coat, which were in shreds.

"Hit the saddle too," said Creek and we saw several bullet holes in the leather.

"How in hell you escaped…" I could not finish the statement as I was gripped by both powerful emotions and a coughing jag that had me hunting my flask. Once I'd swallowed a good bit, I settled enough to speak, even as the pain in my chest tightened its grip. No matter my malady, an anger rose up in me. "Let's go after the sons of bitches," I cried. "They could have killed you."

Wyatt shook his head. "No. If you are hungry for a fight you can go and get your fill. I have had enough." And he turned and walked away.

Texas Jack was upset that his faithful horse had taken a bullet and faltered. Jack had no choice but to end the animal's misery. Jack then slumped at the loss, saying the animal had served him well for many years. Creek threw an arm around Jack and began to console him as the two moved away from us. I stretched out under a tree to rest, but Wyatt would not sit. He stood at the spring's edge as if in contemplation and I hoped it was on the good he had just done rather than questioning himself going unscathed. That kind of survival could come to haunt a man, and in looking back, I saw that Wyatt had cheated death many times. Still, Wyatt was not any man, as this fight had proven. Never had I seen such total fearlessness. Never. As I lay resting, I also considered that he might be looking ahead, but to what? The posse had been our purpose for how long I did not know. What was now to become of us? What was a general to do without a battle?

Creek and Jack saw to unsaddling and watering the horses while we reloaded guns. When Wyatt finally joined us, he said, "How about we go back to Hooker's for a bit?"

"Fine idea," I replied. "He will be pleased with the outcome here."

Wyatt said no more and I saw him still restless. We could not go back to Tombstone as murder warrants remained in force. In fact, all of Arizona was legally inhospitable. Consideration needed to be given toward our next spot, but that could be put off a bit. After an hour or so

I sat up and said we should get on to Hooker's. "If we leave now, we can be there for supper."

This required a spirited ride, which was a mistake on my part. I had apparently overestimated my resilience, and partway began to suffer something fierce, allowing my horse to fall behind the others and then stop, at which I slid off. When I regained consciousness, I was on the ground, Wyatt's hand under my head, his kerchief at my lips. When he pulled it back, I saw the blood.

He looked down at me, but I had trouble seeing him as dizziness swept in to send me reeling. My stomach rolled, my body sweated, my chest heaved, and when I began to cough, Wyatt held the kerchief to my mouth.

"Doc," Wyatt said, "we need to get you to Hooker's. It's ten more miles. Can you make it?"

"I will try. Put me on my horse."

My coat was buttoned up and I was helped into the saddle, which was the last place I wished to be. Wyatt rode so closely our legs slapped against each other at times, and once, when I began to fail, he grabbed me, shook me, and got me upright enough to continue. In this manner we got to Hooker's, where I fell from my horse into Wyatt's arms. I was carried upstairs and put into the big bed. Wyatt undressed me, the cook brought me broth, and all were most concerned. "Let me rest," I finally begged and all retreated save Wyatt, who bathed my dusty face, fed me a little broth and more whiskey, and mopped the blood I expelled on a cough that was now most painful.

"You should not have gone over there with us," he said.

"It is over, Wyatt. Let it go. I'll be fine with a good rest."

He refused to join the others downstairs. When I accused him of playing nursemaid, he did not bristle. He simply removed himself to a chair. The lamp burned low as I dozed and woke, unable to get a grip on sleep. It was Wyatt's soft snore finally brought me calm.

Dawn had not arrived when I woke to a coughing fit. Wyatt, who now lay beside me, fully clothed, got up and lit the lamp in time to see me bring up still more blood. He sought water and a towel and tended me until I quieted enough to lie back. The chest pain was severe but bearable. Wyatt poured me whiskey, which I took, and in time I lay spent and sweaty, my breathing labored. Wyatt sat beside me on the bed, bloody towel in hand. He looked most stricken.

"I am not dying," I said.

"How do you know?"

"I watched my mother die of consumption when I was fifteen. I know what the end looks like. This is not it."

He shut his eyes and I suffered a rush of feeling for this man who held great stores of compassion yet had little means to spend it. I put a hand on his and gripped as tightly as my weakened condition allowed. He held on and after a bit seemed to gain himself.

"You are a brave man, Doc," he said. "Braver than all the rest of us put together."

"Thank you, Wyatt. That means a great deal. Now, why don't you lie back down and sleep. I think the worst is past."

I was wrong about this, but we did manage to doze until the sun was up. Unfortunately, my malady—it now seemed the general—attempted another foothold, and I had a bad time of it for what seemed hours but was likely minutes. This left me greatly reduced, and once quieted, I fell into a heavy sleep.

The day went on without me. I took little note of time's passage beyond the rise and fall of my malady. I was drowsy from fatigue yet slept little and when people came up to hover, Wyatt mostly, I grew short-tempered, upset more with my failure than their attentions. Finally, I was left alone for a time. Even whiskey did little good.

"Three days," Wyatt said when I asked him how long I'd been sick. I was rank and unshaven, bedcovers a sweat-soaked tangle, but I seemed to be past the worst. Caring how many days had passed was a good sign. Caring about much of anything. I had also stopped coughing up blood.

"If you can manage a chair," Wyatt said, "Maria will change the sheets and wash your clothes. And if you can get downstairs, a bath is on the boil."

He helped me to my feet, removed my underdrawers, and put a blanket around me. "Can you make it downstairs?" he asked.

"For a bath, I will give it my all."

It was slow going, but I made it to the kitchen where Jose was pouring hot water into the tub. Wyatt eased me in and I immediately felt much improved. "We'll leave you to it," he said and I thanked him and lay back to savor the warmth. After a while, I began to wash my sorry body. Jose periodically came in to add hot water, for which I was most grateful. Finally, Wyatt came back and said I would shrivel to nothing if I didn't get out of the water. He helped me up and into a towel, patting me dry. The trek back upstairs was slow, and I began to cough on the way, but we managed to get me back to the bed that was now freshly made.

"Maria is washing all your clothes and brushing your suit. You are getting better treatment than any of us," he said, seeming much amused. This warmed me, as he did better when occupied, and if I had to be that occupation, all the better. "I am going to be away for a few days," he continued. "I have things to attend to. The property and business interests in Tombstone can't be neglected, so I am going to see toward some arrangement."

"Will you take the men with you?" I asked, mindful he was a wanted man.

"Creek will go. Jack will stay to look after you."

"God help me."

Wyatt chuckled. "You are getting better."

I was determined to be, if not a new man, at least an improved one at Wyatt's return. Maria saw to me more than Jack, which was a welcome substitution, fussing and doting in such a way as to nudge me toward small steps. It was she who encouraged a shave by holding a small mirror as I sat in bed, bowl of water in my lap. It was she who giggled and asked for my underdrawers so she could wash them. It was she who admired my suit and treated it with as much care as she did me. She also insisted I eat more than I wanted, plying me with broth, then soup, and finally the ranch hand's staple of beef and beans. I was ambulatory when Wyatt returned a week later, but not overtly so. The porch was an effort, but the weather had turned hot again, so sitting outside was most beneficial. The wind even quieted down, for which I was grateful.

The rush of feelings that rose up when Wyatt rode in surprised me. I had read of hearts leaping but until then had dismissed such as fanciful. As he hopped down off his horse and bent and stretched himself, my breath caught most pleasurably for a change while my heart set to beating so fast it seemed it was indeed attempting to leap from me. Had I been more able, I would have bounded up to him for an embrace. As it was, I sat forward in my porch chair and let him come to me.

His eyes were quickly upon me, but he made a point of greeting the others, as Hooker and McKinstry both welcomed him. They talked a bit, then he and Creek came up to Jack.

"Jack, how the hell are you?" Wyatt asked.

Jack went into some detail about helping with the stock and

winning at cards in the bunkhouse. Wyatt listened attentively, then he came over to me and sat down. "Doc, you are looking right good."

How thrilled I was to again be in his company. Though I knew I had missed him, I did not see how much until then. I felt nearly foolish with such sudden happiness, but must say, I welcomed it. "I have been well cared for in your absence," I said, "though not by Jack here. It is the dear Maria who has seen to my every need."

He hinted at a smile and I added, "Well, not every one." My dick, indisposed of late, made itself known by way of crowding me at the crotch, and all I could think from then on was Wyatt sucking the thing. This had to mean my recovery was further along than I had realized. "How did your business go?" I asked.

"Well enough, though I had a close call at Fort Grant. I went there to see a notary about some papers, and Colonel Biddle, who is the law, said he would have to hold me since there are warrants out for my arrest. But then in the next breath he said we should eat first, so we joined him for a meal with me expecting arrest with dessert."

"How did you escape?" I asked.

"Near the end of the meal he called his orderly to prepare our mounts and leave them at a certain gate. He then excused himself, leaving us to finish supper and leave, which we did. I do not think he had any intention toward arrest but felt it his duty to give that impression."

"Well, that is downright amazing," I said.

"And now, if you gentlemen will excuse me," Wyatt said, "I am tired and need a wash and a rest. I will see you later."

He took his saddlebags and went inside, and after some minutes I followed. When I reached our room he was bare-chested, washing at the basin. I ambled to the bed and sat on the edge. "You were missed," I said as I gazed upon him.

"Now, Doc, you're not going to get up to something."

"It is a consideration," I replied. "My dick has been in slumber for some time, but has, with your arrival, enjoyed a most pleasant awakening."

"How is the rest of you?" he asked as he dried himself.

"Much improved. The heat has helped, as has the quiet."

He shook his head.

"Is that a rebuff?" I asked.

"No, it is wonder at your determination to indulge yourself."

"Not just me. Tell me you're not up for it and I will retreat and play invalid."

"The devil in you seems most healthy."

"Lucifer suffers no mortal malady, God bless him—if such a thing is possible."

"You were missed too," Wyatt said as he began to undo his pants. I could not help but smile at sight of his lower half emerging.

"I am suddenly much improved," I declared, "or at least much inspired."

When he stood at the bed, I wrapped a hand around his cock and looked up at him. "Welcome home," I said with a tug. He then began to undress me so carefully I had to remind him I would not break. Once naked, he eased me back and lay down to face me. He ran his hand onto my chest.

"You worry me at times," he said.

"I know. I wish things were otherwise but, as they are not, we'd best make do."

"That what you call it?"

I chuckled. "I call it a fuck, and I wish you would get on with it."

Here I rolled onto my stomach and stuck my bottom in the air, which caused him to issue a happy growl and get in behind. When his dick went into me, I let out a moan as I was in ecstasy simply at receiving him into my passage. His thrust soon commenced and was most urgent. As he went at me, he announced he could not hold back, to which I replied, "Fuck hell out of me." This set him to doing just that and quickly coming. The ride was rough as he filled me with his stored up spunk, but I suffered nothing more than pleasure.

Once spent, he grew concerned at my condition and I had to assure him his assault did no damage. "I have not felt this good in days," I said as I rolled onto my back. Though I coughed some, it was the kind he had seen early on and of little consequence. My dick was still up as I, though primed, had not the energy to get off without assistance. Wyatt looked down at the cock, then up at me, then went down and got his mouth onto me. I pulled a second pillow under my head to give better view to his bobbing and licking until at last my juice boiled over and spurted into his throat. He sucked down every drop and still kept at me, feeding on the softening morsel as if his hunger might never be appeased. At last, he pulled off and crawled up to me, hand on my shoulder.

"Welcome home," I said again, which made him chuckle.

"Damn welcome," he replied.

Everything was better from then on. Rose-colored lenses, to be sure, but who cared? Over supper that night I was more than enthralled as Wyatt explained what he'd been up to.

"I thought this new Governor Tritle might help us, as he is not tainted as much as his predecessors, so I wired him to ask if he might assist us out of our current predicament in Arizona. Well, he was receptive and a few days later wired that he had been in touch with Pitkin, governor of Colorado, who says we will be welcome there and who assures us he will not honor any extradition order without full due process."

We all took a moment to take this in and I, even in my enraptured state, saw it flawed. "What makes you think due process will suddenly be granted us when it never has been before?" I asked.

"We have always either stood before corrupt officials or suffered lying witnesses," Wyatt replied. "In Colorado, we would face impartial judges who could be made to understand our justification."

"How can you be certain?" I asked.

Wyatt set down his coffee cup and looked at me. "Doc, we have nowhere else to go. New Mexico, California, doesn't matter. We are wanted men and, territory or state, they will honor extradition. We have something favorable in Colorado, a leg up, and we'd best take it."

I had spent time in Denver in years past, a thriving city where I could get back to my gaming. And our friend Bat Masterson was up there somewhere, but it was still sad to acknowledge Tombstone, which we had essentially tamed, was no longer ours. "I suppose," I said at last.

Jack and Creek, also suffering murder warrants, agreed. Colorado was the place for us all, and even Hooker got on board. "Fine country," he said. "Ranching, mining, lots of commerce and opportunity. Denver and Leadville are thriving."

Talk continued on the subject until I excused myself and went up to rest, though this reason was but partly true. Turns out I was the unsettled one when confronted with the next move, me, the vagabond gambler who had followed the circuit for several years before meeting Wyatt. Funny how he had changed things.

It was late when he joined me in bed. He undressed in the dark until I asked him to light the lamp. "I am not sleeping," I added.

He finished stripping in the soft light and got into bed where I lay full naked. But I did not devil him this time and he took note. He lay propped on one elbow, gazing upon me like I would eventually spill. Finally, he asked, "Don't you want to go?"

"Colorado is fine. I just…I don't know. Something is nagging at me, something I can't pin down. So much has happened. Part of me is looking back even as I try and look ahead."

"Back where?"

"I don't know. Year or so maybe, before it all went to hell, before the Clanton-McLaury thing. It was good back then, only we didn't know how good. I see it now and maybe I am sort of digging in."

"Maybe the best lies up ahead."

"In Colorado."

"Why not?"

Here he began to run his fingers over my tit nubs, which put asunder concerns about much of anything. "How about I take your mind off your troubles?" he said. He pushed his hard cock up against my leg. "Roll onto your side." When he put it to me he said, "Nice and easy."

For such a rough and rugged man, he surely had his gentle side. Where earlier there had been urgency, there was now calm, as if he could keep stiff for hours. I welcomed his effort to go all night if he wished, as his attention made no strain on me but the exercise of my heart. My bottom knew him well and was thus most accommodating, welcoming both his occupation and his exercise. I lay in his embrace for a good long while as he pumped in and out, my body at last more pleasure than pain. I scarcely coughed. It was bliss.

"I am going to come," he said at last. "Just lie still." He picked up speed yet remained gentle as he let go with a series of muffled grunts. It seemed he thought quiet appropriate, even at the point of release. When he was done and pulled out, he kissed my neck. "We'll fuck our way to Colorado," he said.

"I'll hold you to that."

Next morning, I woke before him and tried my best to be quiet but seldom won that battle. The sun was well up and the room warm but, hospitable as it was, I still hacked and spat. I knew I'd awakened Wyatt, but he was courteous in not drawing attention to the fact, lying with eyes closed as I got up to get my whiskey. I pissed the pot and washed up, which occupied me until I was righted. I then sat on the bed. "I woke you," I said.

"Don't care. Not done sleeping yet."

But, of course, he was. His eyes opened and he ran a hand up my back. "How are you feeling?" he asked.

"My old self," I said.

"How about the truth."

"Almost my old self. A few more days."

"Fair enough."

I eased down beside him, his arm around me. "Tucked up with you like this, I have no incentive to even walk upright," I said.

He squeezed me. "Tucked up is mighty fine."

We lay for a while longer before he told me what else he'd been up to while away.

"I had papers drawn up to deed all my Tombstone property to Virgil. I have to try and hold on there. Once we're in Colorado, I plan to request a pardon for us all. This new governor seems like a reasonable man."

"Would you go back to Tombstone if you were pardoned, knowing how those people feel and Behan still the law?"

"He won't be the law forever, and it is my home, Doc, until I decide it is not."

I couldn't see it. They had all but run us out of town, but then I had not a single root there nor one stick of property. Wyatt was the hold. He alone.

CHAPTER TWENTY-FOUR

Turned out a general was still a general, even without a battle. Wyatt planned our route to Colorado with great care, saying we must not go directly there but wander a bit so as to elude the law. And once in Colorado, we must exercise caution.

"Wells Fargo has also provided us funds," he added. "I picked up the money at Fort Grant. Jim Hume said they are most grateful at our ridding the county of a criminal element."

"How many funds?" I asked.

"Two thousand. That should see us well settled in Colorado."

"Nice to be rewarded for a change," Creek said. "I may become a new man in Colorado."

"You are too old to be a new man," I chided him, which drew a laugh. Texas Jack punched him in the arm, as good friends will do.

We were at Hooker's supper table, kicked back after a fine meal. "When will you start out?" he asked Wyatt.

Wyatt glanced my way. A week had passed since his return, and I felt much improved. As a result, we'd been fucking like rabbits, so his inquiring glance surprised me. "Day or two," he replied. "I am still deciding on a route."

After supper he and Hooker pored over a map, tossing around towns and mountains like poker chips. I lost patience with this and got up a game in the dining room, Creek, Jack, McKinstry, and me. It felt good to get cards in hand. Another sign of improved health was winning.

"Dammit, Doc," Creek complained. "No luck with you sitting in."

"Sorry, boys. Winning is an old habit."

Maria insisted on washing our clothes before we left. In the hot sun they dried almost before she got them hung up. We all enjoyed a final bath as well, and the night before we left, Wyatt was at me half the night. "Having you well pleases me no end," he said after a he'd pumped a load of come into me.

"That is most obvious," I replied. I had shot a gusher into the bedding as he did me but was still looking for more. "I am in good shape for our journey, save for a sore bottom."

This got him to playing nursemaid by way of rolling me over and licking the area. "That better?" he asked when he'd driven me near crazy.

"Getting there," I said.

This set him to serious tongue work, and before long my backside was awash in spit and he was giving me thorough attention, which got him so worked up he pulled out his tongue and put in his prick. "Goddamn, Doc, you are the devil reborn," he said as he rode me. He slapped my bottom for emphasis and I managed a "hallelujah" in encouragement. Once he'd enjoyed another come and sucked a dollop of cream from me, we lay splayed across each other, sweating like the pigs we were.

"I will miss this bed," I observed.

"We'll manage a hotel now and then."

"Where are we headed first?" I asked.

"Silver City, New Mexico. From there, Santa Fe and Albuquerque, then Trinidad, Colorado, where Bat Masterson is marshal. That can work in our favor, so it is a good place to land."

I offered no comment on Trinidad, as I would never take up residence in Bat Masterson's town. What Wyatt had failed to see in our so-called friendship with Bat was that it was actually a two-man deal because Bat did not like me. He tolerated me only because he wished to remain friends with Wyatt. Though he had never once done wrong by me and always offered his hand in greeting, he gave off a disdain that could not be missed—except by Wyatt, whose oblivion toward things nuanced remained constant.

I did not expect all men to be my friend. Few took the step, Wyatt the longest stride. My reputation and my temper were objectionable to many, and I usually took wide berth of such people, but sometimes, by way of Wyatt, I was forced to go along. It was that way with Virgil Earp and more so with Bat Masterson. But this problem could be addressed in Colorado. I therefore asked questions about various places, as I knew Denver but not much else. It was a fine talk, and I enjoyed his enthusiasm which, once I'd set aside Bat Masterson, was starting to rub off onto me. The two of us in new territory, unencumbered by politics,

Cowboys, women, or much of anything save for those pesky murder warrants. Maybe we could settle somewhere and batch together, have a saloon or some business that would interest Wyatt. No reason he couldn't do in Denver or Leadville what he'd done in Tombstone—without the killing.

"We'll do just fine, Doc," he said.

"I expect we will."

"I am not hearing much coughing lately," he noted.

"It is called remission. The malady can, if babied enough, make itself scarce. I believe such a state is at hand."

"That is good to hear. We don't need to hurry on our way, so the ride shouldn't bother you."

"I almost look forward to it."

"Almost."

"It means we must leave this big and most hospitable bed." Here I slid down and sucked his cock into my mouth to make my point.

We set out early next morning after good-byes and thanks to Hooker. I found Maria and slipped her a few dollars in appreciation of her attentions during my convalescence. *"Muchas gracias,"* I said as she hugged the bills to her ample chest.

The day was hospitable and we headed northeast to the Gila River, which we followed east to Silver City, New Mexico, arriving around ten that night. Wyatt surprised me by taking rooms at the Exchange Hotel where we cleaned up, then had a fine meal at the Broadway Restaurant. The four of us were in high spirits at leaving behind old concerns in favor of a new opportunities. After supper, we sought our rooms as Wyatt said he wanted to start early for Santa Fe. I alone knew what else he wanted. As we undressed I said he surprised me at staying in a hotel.

"I've got something else to surprise you," he said, at which he pushed me onto the bed and fucked me most thoroughly.

We did not do our rabbit imitation as we'd soon be back in the saddle and needed our rest. Wyatt contented himself with coming once, which gave us a fine night, though my cough returned to interfere some. Next morning after a big breakfast, we hit the trail again, forgoing hotels in Santa Fe and Albuquerque, where we camped under hospitable skies. After that, we rode into Trinidad, Colorado, our first stop the marshal's office, where we found Bat Masterson in conversation with a deputy. Bat was a looker, I'll give him that, handsome to the point of beauty, which he enhanced by spiffy dressing. He was well respected in a way similar to what Wyatt had once been, notable lawman, honest and true.

"Wyatt," he said, breaking off his talk and extending a hand to him. "Good to see you. Welcome to Trinidad." He then glanced at me, put out his hand. "Doc," he said and we shook and parted.

"You know Creek Johnson and Texas Jack Vermillion," Wyatt said and the two stepped up to shake hands.

"How was your ride?" Bat asked. "Any trouble?"

"Nothing," Wyatt replied. "I've been told the Cowboys are mostly gone and am coming to believe it."

"Let me show you around," Bat said and he donned his hat and led us out. We walked up and down Commercial Street, the bustling center of town. "You can get a fair game here," Bat announced, at which I had to hold back a laugh as nobody ever got a fair deal at faro. Poker you maybe had a chance.

It was late afternoon when Bat said he could put us up at his place. "I have a little house at the edge of town where you are welcome. Have to double up, though."

"Fair enough," Wyatt said. "A bed sounds good."

Bat took us there and showed us a guest room. "This can be yours, Wyatt," he said, to which Wyatt declared he'd double up with me.

"Creek, you and Jack will have to take the parlor floor, but at least you are indoors," Bat said and the men agreed. We all then washed up and went to a fine supper at Black Jack's Saloon and Steakhouse. Over the meal, Bat worked at selling the good prospects of his town, then got Wyatt to dredge up their Dodge City days. I kept to myself, sipping whiskey to quiet the cough, but around nine o'clock excused myself to find a poker game. Wyatt frowned at this, but I did not care. I wanted entertainment, and Bat Masterson was not it.

The Black Jack had a large back room where gaming thrived and I sat in at poker, enjoying good whiskey and winning. When it became known I was Doc Holliday, a couple of players deserted, but two others took their places, and one of these I saw was looking for trouble.

The way a man carries himself tells all, and this young fellow reeked of arrogance. He wore a fine black leather hat and vest, both much ornamented in silver, and two pistols in a fancy rig that likely cost more than the guns it carried. As we played, he kept looking my way, as if trying to get under my skin, and I could see it bothered him that I found him of no consequence. When he began to lose, he decided something was amiss and spoke upon the dangers of cheating and then in particular of cheating him.

"If you are attempting an accusation," I said, "you had best be more specific."

A player fled and those remaining froze.

"You calling me out?" asked the fool.

"I would not dream of doing such a thing. I am merely pointing out that the bullshit you are spilling serves no purpose but to dirty your boots."

Conversation at such a time often throws a man whose trigger finger has the itch. I began to deal another hand. "You in?" I asked him.

That I continued the game was taken as insult. His eyes widened, his face flushed, and he began to steam, chest heaving beneath the fancy vest. When his hand slid off the table, I attempted to prevent the inevitable. "If you wish to play another round or draw another breath, you will put your hand on the table where I can see it."

"And if I don't?"

"You will suffer a shortened life, as you seriously underestimate the peril of your situation."

I set down the deck and waited, and when he wavered, I lost patience. "You are holding up the game. Either you are in or you are out."

That did it. He made the fatal move and I drew my nickel-plated revolver and shot him, his gun firing toward the ceiling as he fell back. By the time I holstered my pistol, Bat Masterson was in the room, followed by Wyatt and the others. "What happened?" Bat asked.

"He drew on me. I had no choice."

Others confirmed it a fair fight, saying I'd gone to great lengths to avoid it, but this did little good. It never did. "You are under arrest," Bat said, demanding my gun and knife.

"You leave me bare," I said as I complied.

"Only way to keep the peace," he snapped. "Come on." He then grabbed my arm rather roughly and pulled me toward the front. Wyatt looked on with his most stern expression.

"Too late to see the judge," Bat said at the jail, where I was pushed into a cell. Wyatt stood watching, and once I was secured, they left. Trinidad was definitely not going to work, I decided as I lay down on the hard cot, my cough hacking agreement.

Jail was not new to me, and I accepted the lawful nature of incarcerating a killer until justice had its say, but this night was not like others because the man locking me up was likely chewing Wyatt's ear on his nefarious association. I wondered how much of Bat's counsel might be embraced.

I had been allowed my flask for medicinal purposes, as Bat was not an unreasonable man. Thus I gradually emptied it to ease both cough and conscience, but a long night still ensued. When Bat came for me next morning, I asked after Wyatt. "Back at the house," he said. "I'm taking you over to Judge Conway's office, where he'll hear your case."

I was surprised to see two of the card players stand up as witnesses on my behalf since men usually avoided such testimony, even if for the good. Based on their word and my own, the killing was found justified, but I was fined for unlawful discharge of a weapon in town and also paid court costs. I was then declared a free man, my weapons returned.

Bat stalked away, but I found Wyatt waiting outside. "Come on," he ordered, which rankled me, but I was in no position to dispute much of anything. I followed him to the Columbia Hotel, where we took a corner table in the saloon. Few were about, so we had some privacy. When I began to cough he looked at me like I was doing it on purpose.

"My flask is empty," I said. "I've started the day with no assistance. Can we get a bottle?"

Without a word, he purchased one and set it on the table with a single glass. I knocked back one drink and poured a second, my malady gradually loosening its grip.

"Goddammit, Doc, we're not in town a day and you get into trouble."

"It was justified, Wyatt. He drew on me."

"It is always justified; I don't doubt that, but you bring trouble. You go into a place and sooner than later a man is dead."

"What would you have me do?" I asked. "Let him shoot me?"

"Tell me you didn't say something to piss him off. I know that temper, Doc. I spend a lot of time with the goddamn thing and go out of my way to give it room, but others are not so generous." Here he studied me. "And I think you enjoy pissing people off."

"Like I am now?"

He blew out a huff and sat back, glaring.

"I make every effort not to kill people, but some insist," I said.

"And you can't turn from it."

"I will not be made a coward," I said. "Wyatt, we have just come from killing a host of men, and I am sorry to have continued, but you know as well as I do that we are going to be challenged on occasion."

"You have too many occasions."

"I do not disagree. How were things at the Masterson house last night?"

"How do you think? Bat is angry at you for coming here and shooting up his town. He opened his home to us and what does he get? I let him rant, then went to bed to avoid the subject, but he was still fuming. Had to double with Creek, as I couldn't very well have the bed to myself. God-awful night."

I could not help but chuckle at the thought of him bedding down with Turkey Creek Johnson, who was a rough character, even though bighearted. "We'll do better tonight," I said, which was a mistake.

"Christ, Doc, don't start deviling me. Here I thought we could make a new start, and now plans are shot to hell."

Until that moment, I had not seen what was underneath his upset. By way of defending myself, I had embarrassed Wyatt to his friend. "I am sorry, Wyatt. I am sorry some hothead drew on me and put me in such a position. I am sorry to complicate your plans. If you'd prefer I go on alone, I will. You can have Trinidad to yourself."

He did not expect this and it wounded him, which I suppose was my intent. Much as I cared, I would go elsewhere rather than make more trouble, and it would surely arrive again as it always did. As he sat in consideration, I felt my heart, which had once leaped in welcome of him, seize like a hand had reached inside to wring out the life. I began to sweat, my stomach to churn, and, of course, the cough hopped on board. An endless and agonizing moment stretched out until Wyatt said, "Now, don't go off half-cocked."

"So what will we do?"

"Move on."

I did not jump on this, as I knew defeat pained him, and that was what I had brought on. But I was through apologizing. We got up and walked out onto Commercial Street, and once some time had passed, I ventured forth. "How about Denver?" I suggested.

"We need to keep a low profile, Doc. You forget we are wanted men, and if we show ourselves too much in too big a town, somebody will surely set upon us."

"Where would you have us, then?"

"I am thinking Gunnison. It is similar to Trinidad in size and nature. There are plenty of saloons for you to earn your living while I see to some enterprise."

"A fine idea," I said. "When do we leave?"

"Today. There is no point staying around here. I'll go tell Bat and we can stop by the house for our things. You find Creek and Jack and tell them our change of plans."

It took three saloons before I found the two. They were having a high time entertaining the locals with tales of our Cowboy exterminating. "And here's Doc Holliday, who was with us on the venture," said Creek, slapping me on the back. I allowed a bit more hot wind to blow around before telling them that Wyatt wished to gather us together. They followed me out, and when we reached Bat's house, he and Wyatt were there. Bat was gracious enough to leave us alone but not before passing me a look that said his town would be well rid of me.

"Boys, we are not going to stay on here," Wyatt said. "I want to try Gunnison, as it is known to be a hospitable and enterprising town. Are you up for that?"

Jack looked at Creek and then to Wyatt. "We are not, I am sorry to say. We like it here and are tired of moving around. Masterson seems agreeable to our staying."

"Fair enough," Wyatt said. "In that case, we'll split the Wells Fargo money four ways so every man has a stake." Here he pulled out a wad of bills and divided them equally. "We are leaving today," he said. "Won't be the same without you fellows."

"Likewise, Wyatt," Creek said, extending his hand. "I am proud to have ridden with you."

Jack said much the same and both shook my hand as well. "I'll miss you, Jack," I said, "but I will be happy to be away from that God-awful snore. And, Creek, try not to get up to too much trouble."

"Look who is talking." Creek laughed.

We got our horses from the livery, packed our saddlebags, and set out. Masterson stood out front to see us off. I was happy to leave him behind but more so to be embarking on the next leg with just Wyatt. Trinidad was soon but thin memory, while ahead lay promise. I was most enthused and Wyatt rode along seeming relaxed. We reached our destination late that afternoon.

Gunnison sat in a wide river valley that was covered in thick grass abundant with wildflowers. I noted lupine, columbine, and mules ear, which I found a most welcoming sight, as if nature had prettied up and opened her arms. Cattle grazed in the valley and a fine river wound along. Up above were pine forests below high peaks. Being a higher elevation, it was cooler than Arizona and not nearly as dry. The change was welcome on my outside but a concern for the inside.

Main Street was busy, as with any town. It boasted the usual stores and saloons plus two fine hotels. We stopped and tied our horses, then sought a meal at a little restaurant, and it was there that Wyatt said he intended to camp outside of town. This surprised me, seeing how we had the Wells Fargo money.

"It has to last," he said when I questioned him. I did not argue, as the last thing I wanted was to cross him again. I would put up wherever he chose so long as we had privacy.

After we ate, we scouted around town some, then rode out to find a spot to camp. It was coming on dusk so we needed to settle in, and soon Wyatt declared he had found perfection. Not far from the river there lay a cluster of trees surrounding a grassy spot. He hopped down with his bedroll. I looked around. "Home," I said.

"For now," he assured me.

As darkness fell, we stripped and got underneath a blanket, solving our differences with a good fuck. It is amazing how a come can fix everything. Once satisfied, I lay in Wyatt's embrace thinking how beautiful the night and how happy I was. Hotels and their beds mattered little in the greater scheme. Comfort was truly at hand. I also suspected Wyatt forgave me my Trinidad mishap, for he wrapped his arm tightly about me. We said nothing, which likely helped.

Next morning I woke to a dick entering me and I did not object even as I hacked throughout a most pleasurable assault. Wyatt took little note as he rode out his come, then flipped me over to suck my cream. Once he was done, he declared himself hungry and suggested breakfast in town to which I agreed, once I could right myself.

"I thought you had that tamed," he said as I tried to drown the cough with whiskey.

"Lying around two weeks was required. If I continue doing that I can keep it down, but I prefer to enjoy my days, so you'll have to put up with my noise and spitting."

"It's not a problem, Doc, just a concern."

"I appreciate that and will treat myself accordingly."

We ate flapjacks and bacon in town, hearty stacks that fueled us for the day. We then walked about to note various businesses as possible ventures for Wyatt. When he said he wanted to let the marshal know, as a courtesy, that we were present, I deferred. "I'll be over there," I said, pointing to the Gold Dust Saloon across the street.

Wyatt passed me a stay-out-of-trouble look to which I replied, "I know, I know. I will make every effort to do no harm."

At the saloon's door, I looked back to see Wyatt watching me. I tipped my hat to him and went inside where I found a place much to my liking. It was done up nicely and filled with many eager to lose their money. I was welcomed into a poker game by men who saw me not as a threat or opportunity but as a person of interest, like playing cards with me might make them shine. Wyatt would have been proud of my effort, but of course it was easy when nobody accused me of cheating or sought to make a name for himself by doing me in.

I did not know the time when Wyatt came in. He joined the game, won some, lost some, then cashed out and left. I paid little mind as I was on a winning streak such as I had not known in some time. Later on, Wyatt appeared again, and when I kept gaming, he came over, leaned down, and said, "You going to go all night?"

"I am winning, Wyatt. You do not turn away Lady Luck when she comes calling."

"You'll make yourself sick."

"I appreciate your concern, but I can see to myself."

He stood up. "Then you'd best do that," he said and he strode away. I glanced at the back of him, which was a view I much admired, but I was not about to have him dictate my sporting life. Thus I continued play through the night and into the morning, taking whiskey to control my malady while skinning several men. By the time Wyatt returned, the sun was well up and though I persisted with the game, I was not in the best of shape.

"I am not going to carry you out of here," Wyatt said as I attempted to drown my cough. I had taken more whiskey than usual as my circumstances were more than usual. Unfortunately, while I gained money, the malady gained me; thus I was somewhat shaky as I cashed out and thanked the men for a fine game.

Once out front, however, I balked at returning to Wyatt's camp. "I prefer a hotel," I said.

"You're drunk, Doc," he countered.

"I may be drunk, but that does not affect my desire to collapse onto a bed rather than hard ground." Here I started to a nearby hotel. I was at the desk registering when Wyatt came up behind me.

"All right," he said.

"Oh, do you also wish a room?" I asked.

He did not appreciate the humor and stepped back to leave me to securing accommodations. When I faltered on the stairs, he kept me upright and went ahead to unlock my door. He then pushed me onto the bed.

"Will you stay?" I asked.

He did not answer. He pulled my flask from my coat and tossed it beside me. "Here, have a nightcap," he said and he left. Two days later, I ran into him at a restaurant.

"Doc," he said as I joined him at his table. "Where you been?"

"Indisposed, as you well know."

"You're a sorry sight," he said, to which I coughed a reply. "Why in hell do you do it to yourself?"

"I am earning a living," I said, as if I hadn't said it a dozen times before, though the term "living" might be a reach.

"You are going to do yourself in."

"You mean before my illness does it on its own?"

This was unfair and I was immediately ashamed of trotting out my malady as a defense. Wyatt's expression slipped to a sort of puzzlement, like he'd been suddenly set adrift in a leaky boat.

"I am sorry," I said. "I don't want my malady to get between us."

"It's a little late for that."

Now I was at a loss. "What would you have me do? Take to a bed and have you sit holding my hand while I gain health and nothing more? Or better, lie out there in your camp and attempt the same? I will not become an invalid."

"Even if it kills you?"

"I am already well along that road, Wyatt, and I am willing to shorten the journey to make it a more pleasant one."

To this he had no reply, so we left it alone. But that night I went out to his camp because I felt better, mostly due to his presence.

Chapter Twenty-five

As he had done in Tombstone, Wyatt bought up several mining claims in Gunnison. He also took a job dealing faro at the Evergreen Hotel, which had the finest saloon and card room in town. I kept to my usual sporting life, and the two of us passed several months that were further improved when Wyatt gave up his camp life and moved to the hotel.

The day of his move, I knew no end of excitement. He insisted on residing at the Evergreen as they knocked down the rate for employees, and I had to admit the room was bigger and finer than what I had managed at the smaller Franklin Hotel. Thus I took up in my man's room, which we celebrated with an entire afternoon in bed.

"I never want to know hard ground again," I said after he'd about worn me out. I nuzzled a fat pillow, then lay my head on it to look upon Wyatt, who reclined in satisfaction.

"We've done pretty well out there," he replied.

"I do not dispute that. We do pretty well wherever we are, but you must admit, a bed is most welcoming."

That I fought my way through my words was not remarked upon. The malady was now ever present, thus I drank more and at times got into scrapes by way of drunkenness. Wyatt was most patient, as I did not shoot anyone. He had also made friends with the law, so heads were turned at minor incidents. We thus went along batching it as I had envisioned, my heart, unlike my lungs, thriving.

When I would enter the Evergreen card room, I would always stop to watch Wyatt at work, the stir he brought on running from dick to heart and back. Among the talk and smoke and piano music, I would allow that we belonged to each other now, and this would color my mood to the point of rendering me near impervious to slights that might once have sparked gunplay.

"I am becoming downright mellow," I told Wyatt one morning.

We had both come in around two a.m., him at the end of his shift, me cashing out to join him. "I have not fired my pistol in months."

"I'm proud of you, Doc."

"We do well for each other."

"That we do."

He then started talking of the future, and that was when the fly fell into the soup. "One day a claim is going to pay off big and we'll have enough to build a Holliday Saloon," he said. "How would you like that?"

"I would like it fine," I replied as the idea crashed around in my mind like a wild bronc.

"If pardons come through, we could even go back to Arizona. I have not given up on Tombstone, as there is still promise there," he went on while my bucking bronc worked to unseat me. Wyatt had kept in touch with Dan Tipton, who gave him progress, or lack thereof, regarding pardons requested from Governor Tritle. As if this was not enough to put upon me, he then spoke of going to California.

"You'd like it there," he said. "Dry, but not like Arizona, more hospitable. And it is wide-open in both land and opportunity." Here I fell to coughing and busied myself with whiskey to calm both the hacking and my mind. "We could even visit San Francisco," he went on. "I've never seen it."

He exhibited such good spirits that I could do nothing but play along, even as an awful awakening pressed down upon me. For the first time in ten years, I was being made to look ahead—because Wyatt looked ahead. A future had never been in the cards for me, and I had always played that hand, even though it was a bad one. I lived the here and now and did not consider what could not be mine. But now, I had to look ahead, however difficult the prospect, because Wyatt, in his practical determination, failed to consider that a future was not something I could attain.

I had no idea what had set him on such a path at this particular time, but he was so enthusiastic that I could not point out the fly in the soup. I could only watch it thrash about and sink to ultimately spoil the meal. He was more animated than usual, talking up a storm, but as he rambled on, my thoughts were elsewhere.

My mother always remained in my heart, but she now came forward to address my predicament, Alice Jane Holliday, a most loving woman who died at thirty-seven of the same malady I carried. Her last weeks remained vivid, not only for her suffering but as a window on what lay ahead for me. Would I survive more years than she, or would my having embraced a less genteel life rob me of even thirty-seven? Ironic that I, in my thirty-second year, was now playing odds against myself and finding them less than promising.

Undressed, Wyatt and I climbed into bed, and the only way I got him to stop his planning was to crawl down and suck his dick. Once the soft morsel was on my tongue, he issued nothing more than a welcoming moan, thus getting us past this unfortunate turn.

From then on, however, I could not chase off what he had brought between us, and I was most torn as his plans were meant to honor and enhance our bond. He wanted more for us and he was such a determined man that he would likely manage to get it, but what then? Open the Holliday Saloon and hold a wake? Receive pardons from the governor and thank him but say only one was needed? Go to California with me hobbling along, which would surely be my state by the time we undertook the journey? The cough that I had lived with for ten years became a mockery of life, a harbinger of a future not to be enjoyed.

Things continued well between Wyatt and me so long as I kept him in the here and now, and I made every effort toward that end. Fortunately, he seemed content at having laid out his plans and went along in the present with his enterprising and faro dealing. I continued my gaming and enjoyed him to the fullest, though at times I still courted Lady Luck to the point of exhaustion. I was powerless to resist her seductive call, and poker games often went on for a day or two, after which I was sometimes carried to our room by the very men I'd cleaned out. Wyatt continued to frown upon what he considered indulgence, but under that frown he saw to my needs when I was indisposed. At times, however, I woke to find him sitting at the bedside looking grave, and it was in my reassuring him of a speedy recovery that I came to see I did not wish to die in his company.

I said nothing on this, as it was my future, not his, but I mulled over the prospect as I spent a couple of days recuperating from the latest thirty-six hour poker game. Wyatt had survived his brother's death and would survive mine, that I did not doubt, but it was not the after that struck me. It was the before. I could not bear the thought of him enduring my final months, as it was a slow and painful death, pneumonia further weakening badly compromised lungs until they could no longer support life. I would not have him watch me die as I had watched my mother.

For a while, I tucked away this awful conclusion just as I had for ten years tucked away the certainty of an early death. We continued to batch and Wyatt began to prosper while I won more than lost. Still, I found myself too often drinking more than my malady required in an effort to subdue the dilemma that now haunted me. Though Wyatt had often said he admired my capacity for liquor, he became angry when he had to carry me up the stairs and put me to bed not because my lungs had failed but because I was too sozzled to walk.

Fucking remained our constant. Wyatt, undemonstrative otherwise, gave his all with his dick, and I contented myself with the knowledge that feelings did rise inside him, just as his rod rose up to spear me. I received him with joy, then later endured near sorrow, for to leave him, as I knew I must do, would break my heart. At times, I became voracious upon his body, sometimes to the point of his comment. "Christ, Doc, I'm spent. Let it alone."

I made a joke and got him to laugh, coveting even this as I now coveted everything about him. Curling up against him, I pushed the future from mind, but it no longer went far. The more we gained from each other, the more Wyatt looked ahead, and I played along so as not to ruin the moment, even as such talk was now most painful.

One night, as Wyatt worked his faro game, I cashed out and went walking about town. I had limited my drinking and thus remained sound of my mind, which was maybe not the best thing in my situation. But I needed to think upon things and so, on a warm late summer evening, I ambled along Main Street, lost in thought as to how to leave the man who had become my life. Parting considerations drew me back to Georgia where, in 1873, at age twenty-two, I was told to leave for warmer climes or die. I thus bid my family good-bye and boarded a train west, and I now called up those moments to feel what had been my first failure of a future. A promising life as an Atlanta dentist was already under way when I left. I recalled closing the dental practice. I saw my father's reserve as he wished me well upon my way, my stepmother chiming in with some nonsense I scarcely heard. My uncle John, my greatest supporter, shook my hand and offered encouragement. "You will do well, John. You will do well." My cousin Robert, my best friend who was just going off to dental school, promised yet again that we would open a joint practice when I returned. Even Sophie, the slave who had taught me cards, bid me a tearful farewell. I could see them all on the platform as the train pulled away, as I left everything I had known, everyone I loved. Once out of their sight, I had cried like a baby.

But I had set aside this failure and gone on to build a new life. Unconventional, yes, but it gave me Wyatt, and I would not have missed him for the world. He alone had filled the emptiness. He alone cared to such extent that my heart opened as never before. I adored his stern manner, his power, the rare laugh, the hard sex, the nursemaid, the caring and thoughtful man. We partnered better than any two men I knew. Yet I had to move on.

To what? I wondered. The leaving at twenty-two had been to save my life. This time it would be to shield the end, to go off somewhere and expire in private. There was nothing the least positive in the move, yet I saw no way around it. I had a choice. Stay and subject Wyatt to the prolonged end or spare him. I cared enough to spare him.

There was not enough fucking to satisfy me anymore. I knew it not only desire but a need so deep it could never be filled. Still, I gave it one hell of a try. I would get Wyatt so worked up he'd go at me something fierce, and when he fell back, sweaty and spent, I'd still be at him, tugging his dick, licking his every inch. In the night I would wake and get a hand on him, bring him along as he lay half-asleep, and when I had him erect I'd climb on and ride him until I got what I wanted, working my dick to shoot along with him. It would about do me in, but I did not care. I wanted him to fill me. I wanted to stay filled.

Then the day would arrive, and with it our occupations and daily living, the little things that make up two men sharing a room. I treasured the smallest incidents, something misplaced then found, some chore needing attention. I took pleasure in doing for him, such as I could. I saw his clothes to the laundry, chose restaurants for meals, and now and then I suggested a ride out of town where we would lay bedrolls and have a fuck under blue skies as it was late summer and conducive to being naked in the open. Once spent, we would call up old times on the posse and how we managed to satisfy ourselves, no matter where. I would bask in such moments, but always there lurked the fact that I was going to leave.

I chose to begin on a day when my cough was under as much control as could be managed. "Buck Newby says there is a new saloon over in Leadville and they are looking for somebody to deal faro," I said. "I am thinking it might be a good opportunity."

We were at supper and Wyatt's fork paused, then went on to his mouth. He chewed at length before issuing a reply. "Do I have to remind you we are still wanted men? We are keeping a low profile here. Moving to Leadville would bring us out into the open, which remains a danger. It is not a good idea, Doc, I don't care about the opportunity. You can find a faro game here."

"I am feeling confined by Gunnison, if you want the truth," I said, my gut churning with the lie. "Yes, there are faro games, but this place is too settled while Leadville and Denver are booming. Don't you miss that excitement? Tombstone was the best of it, if you don't count the Cowboy menace. It crackled with opportunity and excitement and there were more people coming in every day. I'm told Leadville is enjoying the same prosperity, and I think it would be good to try it."

He set down his fork and looked at me hard.

"I won't be held back, Wyatt," I said.

"If you think that is what I am doing, then go on. Go to Leadville. Get yourself extradited to Arizona, where they will kill you before you reach jail."

"I will have to take my chances."

That was it. He stood, tossed money onto the table, and walked out. I sought a saloon and got very drunk, waking in jail next morning. When somebody nudged my leg, I batted him away, refusing to open my eyes. "Come on, Doc," Wyatt said. "Time to go."

"How did I get in here?" I asked as I attempted to stand. My cough took hold so hard it bent me over and I was allowed to hack and spit some before being pushed out of the cell.

"You made a scene on Main Street," Wyatt said as we walked along. He attempted to hold me by the arm, but I shook him off.

"I can manage," I snapped, to which he said, "Not very well."

He took me to our room, where I refused to lie down. The cough was upon me, but Wyatt was not helpful regarding remedy. "You need to get sober for a while, Doc. You are pickling yourself."

"I am pickling my illness," I argued. "My body just goes along for the ride."

"Don't get smart with me. I am trying to help you."

"Then pour me a drink." I coughed. "I am in goddamn pain."

He got the bottle, poured me a drink, and stood while I tossed it down. He then refilled the glass. "Damned if you do, damned if you don't," he observed.

"Such is my life."

He strode to the window and looked out for a bit, then went to the dresser and fussed a minute. A chair then occupied him for about three seconds, after which he got up and came over to sit beside me on the bed. "There are places we could go that are hospitable to your condition," he said. "I asked Doc Sawyer about it and he says there are fine establishments that are most comfortable and do consumptives a wonder of good."

"Sanitariums," I said, blowing out a huff, which made me cough. "You would put me into a bed in some ward and have me treated like an invalid."

"You make it sound awful."

"Because it is. I am going to live my own goddamn life. I decided that when I was assigned this curse and I will not do otherwise. I am going to Leadville and deal faro until I drop."

He backed off. "I'm sorry. I have no right to tell you what to do. It was just a suggestion because you seem the worse for wear."

"I have been the worse for wear for years, Wyatt. I will manage."

He put his arm around me. "That you will. I sometimes forget you are as stubborn as I am. What a pair."

"What a pair, indeed. I'll drink to that." And I finished my drink which, on top of the first, assisted me into the day. "I need to wash up," I said and I rose and began to strip off my upper garments.

Wyatt sat watching me, saying nothing. I don't think he considered me serious about Leadville, and that was fine as it would spare him the truth until it was upon him. For now, we could be ourselves, and so I washed up, shaved, and felt better for the improvements. When I went to the wardrobe to find a fresh suit, he said not to bother and I turned to face him.

"You up for it?" he asked, throwing off his jacket.

"I am always up for it," I said, at which I began to undo my pants. We were soon naked and on the bed, Wyatt pleased at this positive turn, me knowing it might be our last.

He treated me so gently I had to get after him about it. "I won't break, Wyatt. Never have before and not going to start now." I reached down to his hard cock and gave it a tug. "I need you something awful."

He applied spit to his cock, eased me onto my back, put my legs up onto his shoulders, and shoved into me, at which I attempted to issue an exclamation but got only a cough. "Quiet down," he said, which I managed as he began to thrust. He still took it easy and I was treated to that fine body in the exquisite motion of fucking me. He moved like a big cat, smooth and steady with fire in his eyes as desire set upon him. I enjoyed watching his rise, for it became very plain on his face as his jaw tightened, his breathing labored, his chest heaved. Finally, he could not hold back and began to pound my bottom, pushing me further back so he could drive his prick deep into my bowels. It was there that he spurted his load, crying out as he did. Sweat flew as he rammed it home, and I lay imprinting the look of him onto a memory that would have to serve me until my demise.

At last, he withdrew and sat back. My cock was up and after he'd gained a few breaths, he took hold, began to work me. I thrust into his grip, which got us working together, me fucking his hand and him looking at the connection until I bucked and shot my cream. My cough jumped in, but nobody cared. It was mere annoyance at such a time. Wyatt pumped me until I ran dry, then let go, leaned over, and began to lick the come from my belly. That was a sight to behold, that masterful tongue lapping spunk until I'd been thoroughly cleaned. He then sat back and wiped his mouth. "Never get enough," he said. "May have to have another taste later on."

He then eased down on top of me, nuzzling my neck, nibbling and kissing. I thrilled to the feel of his lips so near my mouth. He lingered some time and I basked in the attention until he finally rolled off and lay on his side, looking at me. I could see in an instant he thought he had erased Leadville, and I did nothing to counter the notion, as the moment was most sublime. Nothing was said of leaving. Nothing much was said at all. We lay quiet, his hands playing over me, mine likewise on him. We moved around on the bed to get at each other in a long and blissful exploration, attending familiar places, poking and prodding, licking and nipping until the day was well along. Finally, Wyatt got me onto my side, got in behind, and slipped it in. As he give me a near-languid fuck, he reached around to pump my cock and we worked ourselves slowly and steadily toward another climb.

He truly did manage to push Leadville from my mind, but only so long as we were entwined. When he shot his load into me and worked another few spurts from my dick, things were over. He lay back, as did I, him content in dissuading me from leaving, me looking at when to go. I ran a hand up his arm and held on for a bit, then tore myself away. There was no other avenue toward what I had to do. I washed up, sought a fresh suit, and began to dress.

"Where are you going?" he asked.

"Leadville."

He sat up and I looked at him. "It is not easy," I said, "but it is what I want."

I watched as he took in the finality. He clamped his mouth shut as his chest heaved, but he held back any plea. He was a proud man and I counted on that. I knew he would not demean himself by trying to stop me. He would respect my wishes. After a minute or two, he got up, washed, and dressed. "You're sure?" he asked at the door.

"I am sure."

He nodded, paused as if he had something to say, didn't say it, and left. When the door slammed, I let the tears roll but kept on with gathering my things.

He was out front when I came out of the hotel. I went over to him and put out my hand. "If you get to Leadville, look me up," I said.

His expression was stricken, and it all but killed me that I was doing this, but I would rather him stricken with me standing before him in reasonably good form than lying wasted in some bed. "Doc" was all he said as he shook my hand.

I then sought my horse and rode away.

CHAPTER TWENTY-SIX

Much to my surprise, my lungs still held breath three years later when I heard Wyatt and his wife were in Denver. Though my body was much compromised by the unrelenting progress of my illness, I could not deny myself a chance to have a better parting than what I had allowed before. Thus I spiffed up and sought the Windsor Hotel where they were stopping, it was said, on their journey from Aspen to California.

The years without Wyatt had been divided between Leadville and Denver, both of which were most hospitable, as many found it a novelty to be in company of such a notorious fellow. Wyatt had been right about the need to lie low, as the very first year I had suffered arrest and attempted extradition to Arizona. It was Bat Masterson, of all people, who came to my aid by way of filing false charges that required my remaining in Colorado. Arizona finally conceded and Colorado granted me permanent parole, although this was jeopardized for a while when I shot a man. A fair fight it was, but there still came jails and courts, which ultimately saw me freed. These events were well behind me when Wyatt arrived.

Speaking without coughing was now nearly impossible, and my weight had dropped as pounds I could little spare slipped away. A pharmacist who doted on my notoriety provided laudanum at no cost, as I was now in reduced circumstances since my illness robbed me not only of breath but of nimble fingers and quick mind. I eked out a living that had once been bountiful, but I did manage and so, on the big day, entered the Windsor Hotel looking and feeling my best.

They sat in the lobby talking to each other and I spent a few moments watching before going over. Wyatt looked much the same although his mustache was longer and his hair slicked down. He still wore that stern expression. I knew he had married Sadie Marcus the year after we parted, as people always, when they heard news of him, hurried to tell me. I was happy he had sought the actress he'd met when she played Tombstone. They had flirted at the time, but Wyatt never went beyond that. Now they made a fine couple.

I made my way to them and Wyatt saw me partway. He rose to his feet and stood in wonder as I approached. "Doc," he said, extending a hand.

"Wyatt," I replied, gripping him. "When I heard you were in Denver, I wanted to see you once more, for I can't last much longer. You can see that."

"What I see is a whole history and a fine friend," he said. "You remember Sadie? Sadie, Doc?"

I shook her hand as she offered warm greetings and then, good wife that she was, she excused herself. "I'll leave you two awhile, as I have things to tend to upstairs. It is a pleasure to see you again, Doc."

I had forgone laudanum this day as I wished my head clear, my senses sharp, but as a result was in some distress in my chest. Still, I refused to let it intrude on this special time. Wyatt and I sat in the lobby side by side on a plush red sofa, catching up.

"I heard you did some law enforcement in Aspen recently," I said, at which he scoffed.

"I may have pinned on a badge for a short time, but I think I was only wanted for my ability to intimidate a man, and it turned out that was all I needed. I tapped the robber on the shoulder and said, 'I want you,' and he gave up without a whimper. Such was my final duty as marshal. I turned in the badge and we are now headed to California and a town called San Diego, which is south of Los Angeles. It is said to have a fine climate and much opportunity. I mean to open a saloon there. But how about you, Doc. What have you been up to?"

"I divide my time between Denver and Leadville, manage to earn my way at gaming as always. I also attempt to stay out of trouble."

"I heard Arizona almost got you."

"That they did. Masterson set a plan and saved the day. A good man."

When silence fell, I sat feasting on Wyatt's presence, as it still did not fail to rouse me. My forlorn body awakened to one man only and here he was, strong as ever, grim-looking yet speaking most gently and allowing time for my cough to subside. He graciously did not ask about my prospects.

"Did you hear they brought charges against Johnny Behan?" he asked.

"I did not."

"Malfeasance, but those courts can't make anything stick, so he was released. But he is now out of politics and law enforcement. Turns out he was submitting excess bills for services rendered and not paying posse men, but then we knew that all along."

"A sort of justice, then."

"And Ike Clanton was killed by a detective hired by Graham County to rid the area of outlaws."

"Even better."

We sat talking for quite some time, and I learned Wyatt had gone back to Dodge City for a short while, then to Idaho where he part owned a saloon in Eagle City. Then he got into mining claims again but did not prosper as disputes arose and the gold played out.

"Was sheriff of Kootenai County a while," he went on. "That is in Idaho. Mostly property rights cases, but some gunplay. No killing, though. We were in El Paso after that, then to Aspen, where I partnered in another saloon."

"A restless man," I noted.

"I suppose. I am trying to prosper, and it is not easy."

This led us to talk of Tombstone, which we did at length, reliving good times with his brothers and some posse days, all without the killing. I then asked after the family. "Virgil is sheriff of Colton, California, where the folks live," he said most proudly. "One good arm is enough for a determined man, and he is well respected. The others all do well. Louisa remarried. Ma and Pa survive."

There rose a temptation to call up our personal exploits, as it would have done me well to speak of fucking, to say the word to him once more and maybe get his dick stiff, but I fought this down out of respect for his married state. It did not bother me that he had turned to a woman, as I knew it acknowledgment that no man but me would do for him.

When I saw Sadie descend the stairs, I knew the visit was at an end. I stood. Wyatt stood. "Isn't it strange," he said, "that if it were not for you, I wouldn't be alive today, yet you must go first. I am most grateful, Doc, and always will be."

I threw my arm around his shoulder. "Good-bye, old friend," I said. "It will be a long time before we meet again."

I released him but neither of us could yet part. Tears were in his eyes when he finally said, "There are no words."

It all rose up in the next instant, a thousand words never uttered, a thousand emotions never expressed. My last chance stood before me, but out of deference to this man who was my all, I said only, "I know. Me too."

He nodded, then turned to Sadie, who had come up beside him. Before they could leave me, I hurried away. Down the street, I sought a saloon and a whiskey, which I threw back in celebration of the fact that my demise would go easier knowing Wyatt Earp would long continue.

EPILOGUE

Doc Holliday died in Glenwood Springs, Colorado, on November 8, 1887, two years after he last saw Wyatt Earp. He was thirty-six years old.

Wyatt Earp died in Los Angeles, California, on January 13, 1929. He was eighty.

About the Author

Dale Chase has written male erotica for fifteen years with 150 stories in magazines and anthologies, including translation into Italian and German. She has two story collections in print: *The Company He Keeps: Victorian Gentlemen's Erotica*, which won an IPPY silver medal award from the Independent Publishers Association, and *If The Spirit Moves You: Ghostly Gay Erotica.* Her stories have most recently appeared in anthologies *History's Passions*, *Riding the Rails*, *Erotica Exotica*, *Wings*, *Hot Daddies*, *Hot Jocks*, *Tented: Gay Erotic Tales from under the Big Top*, *Beautiful Boys*, *I Like to Watch*, *Bears in the Wild*, *Time Well Bent*, *Biker Boys*, *Rough Trade*, and *Bi Guys*. Chase lives near San Francisco and is at work on an erotic novel about John Wesley Hardin.

Books Available From Bold Strokes Books

Ladyfish by Andrea Bramhall. Finn's escape to the Florida Keys leads her straight into the arms of scuba diving instructor Oz as she fights for her freedom, their blossoming love…and her life! (978-1-60282-747-9)

Spanish Heart by Rachel Spangler. While on a mission to find herself in Spain, Ren Molson runs the risk of losing her heart to her tour guide, Lina Montero. (978-1-60282-748-6)

Love Match by Ali Vali. When Parker "Kong" King, the number one tennis player in the world, meets commercial pilot Captain Sydney Parish, sparks fly—but not from attraction. They have the summer to see if they have a love match. (978-1-60282-749-3)

One Touch by L.T. Marie. A romance writer and a travel agent come together at their high school reunion, only to find out that the memory of that one touch never fades. (978-1-60282-750-9)

Night Shadows: Queer Horror edited by Greg Herren and J.M. Redmann. Night Shadows features delightfully wicked stories by some of the biggest names in queer publishing. (978-1-60282-751-6)

Secret Societies by William Holden. An outcast hustler, his unlikely "mother," his faithless lovers, and his religious persecutors—all in 1726. (978-1-60282-752-3)

The Raid by Lee Lynch. Before Stonewall, having a drink with friends or your girl could mean jail. Would these women and men still have family, a job, a place to live after…The Raid. (978-1-60282-753-0)

The You Know Who Girls by Annameekee Hesik. As they begin freshman year, Abbey Brooks and her best friend, Kate, pinkie swear they'll keep away from the lesbians in Gila High, but Abbey already suspects she's one of those you-know-who girls herself and slowly learns who her true friends really are. (978-1-60282-754-7)

Wyatt: Doc Holliday's Account of an Intimate Friendship by Dale Chase. Erotica writer Dale Chase takes the remarkable friendship between Wyatt Earp, upright lawman, and Doc Holliday, Southern gentlemen turned gambler and killer, to an entirely new level: hot! (978-1-60282-755-4)

Month of Sundays by Yolanda Wallace. Love doesn't always happen overnight; sometimes it takes a month of Sundays. (978-1-60282-739-4)

Jacob's War by C.P. Rowlands. ATF Special Agent Allison Jacob's task force is in the middle of an all-out war, from the streets to the boardrooms of America. Small business owner Katie Blackburn is the latest victim who accidentally breaks it wide open, but she may break AJ's heart at the same time. (978-1-60282-740-0)

The Secret of Othello by Sam Cameron. Florida teen detectives Steven and Denny risk their lives to search for a sunken NASA satellite-but under the waves, no one can hear you scream… (978-1-60282-742-4)

Andy Squared by Jennifer Lavoie. Andrew never thought anyone could come between him and his twin sister, Andrea…until Ryder rode into town. (978-1-60282-743-1)

Finding Bluefield by Elan Barnehama. Set in the backdrop of Virginia and New York and spanning the years 1960–1982, *Finding Bluefield* chronicles the lives of Nicky Stewart, Barbara Philips, and their son, Paul, as they struggle to define themselves as a family. (978-1-60282-744-8)

The Jetsetters by David-Matthew Barnes. As rock band the Jetsetters skyrocket from obscurity to superstardom, Justin Holt, a lonely barista, and Diego Delgado, the band's guitarist, fight with everything they have to stay together, despite the chaos and fame. (978-1-60282-745-5)

Strange Bedfellows by Rob Byrnes. Partners in life and crime, Grant Lambert and Chase LaMarca are hired to make a politician's compromising photo disappear, but what should be an easy job quickly spins out of control. (978-1-60282-746-2)

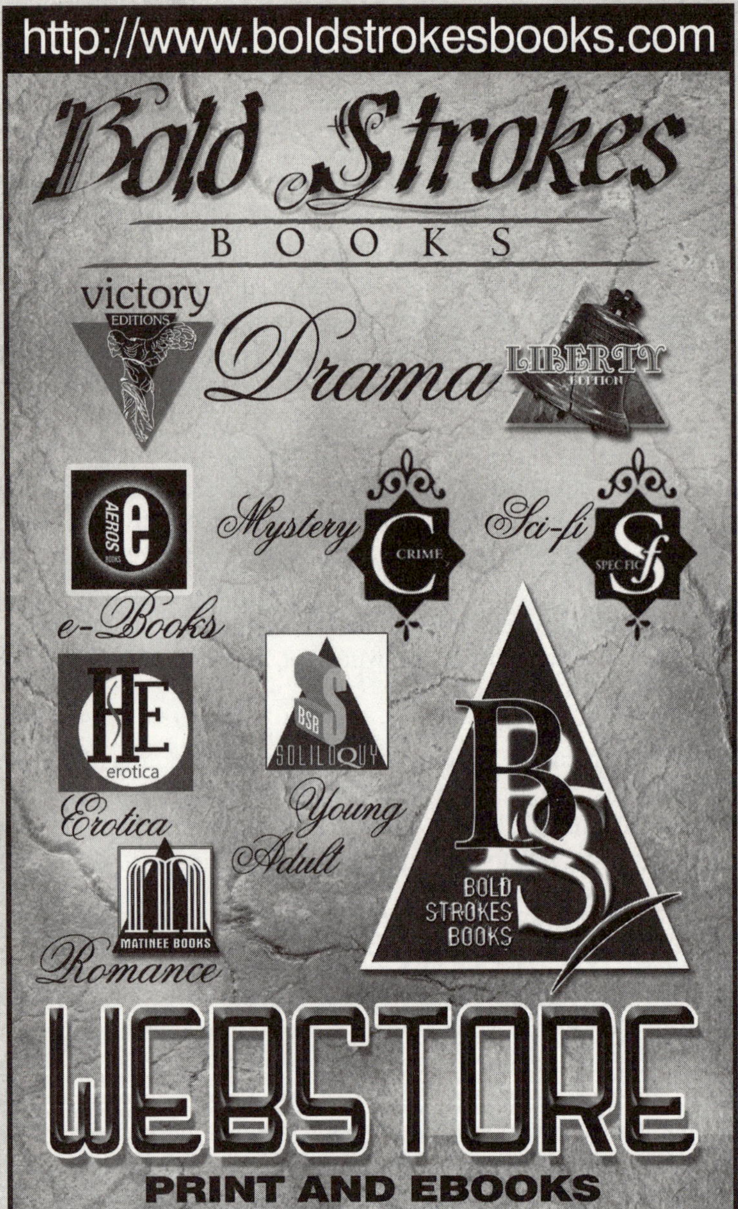
http://www.boldstrokesbooks.com
Bold Strokes
BOOKS
victory
EDITIONS
Drama
LIBERTY
EDITION
AEROS
e
e-Books
Mystery
CRIME
Sci-fi
SPEC FIC
Erotica
HE
erotica
BSB
SOLILOQUY
Young
Adult
BOLD
STROKES
BOOKS
MATINEE BOOKS
Romance
WEBSTORE
PRINT AND EBOOKS